Academy

of

Assassins

AN ACADEMY OF ASSASSINS NOVEL

STACEY BRUTGER

Copyright © 2017 **Stacey Brutger**

Cover artist: Amanda Kelsey of Razzle Dazzle Design (www.razzdazzdesign.com)

Editor: Faith Freewoman (www.demonfordetails.com)
Proofreader: Jan A.

All rights reserved.

ISBN-10: 1979060568
ISBN-13: 978-1979060561

To my readers—

Thank you for all your encouragements.

This book is for you.

Enjoy!

And to my husband, as always.

Other books by this author:

BloodSworn
Coveted

A Druid Quest Novel

Druid Surrender (Book 1)
Druid Temptation (Book 2)

An Academy of Assassins Novel

Academy of Assassins (Book 1)
Heart of the Assassins (Book 2)
Claimed by the Assassins (Book 3)
Queen of the Assassins (Book 4)

A Raven Investigations Novel

Electric Storm (Book 1)
Electric Moon (Book 2)
Electric Heat (Book 3)
Electric Legend (Book 4)
Electric Night (Book 5)
Electric Curse (Book 6)

Clash of the Demigods

Daemon Grudge (Book 1)

A PeaceKeeper Novel

The Demon Within (Book 1)

A Phantom Touched Novel

Tethered to the World (Book 1)
Shackled to the World (Book 2)
Ransomed to the World (Book 3)

Coming Soon:

Daemon Scourge (Clash of the Demigods – Book 2)

Visit Stacey online to find out more at www.StaceyBrutger.com
And www.facebook.com/StaceyBrutgerAuthor/

Chapter One

*M*organ cursed her luck as she dangled over the edge of the rooftop.

Tiny bits of gravel dug into her fingertips, weakening her hold, and her weight did the rest, resolutely dragging her over the edge a centimeter at a time. While her body was conditioned to withstand the strain, she could do nothing about gravity.

Morgan glanced down—all three stories—and saw the guard taking his own sweet time buttoning up his trousers after taking a whiz.

The mansion was headquarters to one of the oldest covens in the country and patrolled regularly by enhanced soldiers, their paranormal bloodlines making them the perfect hunters. If she tried to pull herself over the ledge, even breathed too hard, she would be discovered.

When she twisted to peer over her shoulder, grit under her fingers shifted dangerously, dragging her closer to the edge, and dropping her another inch.

In the distance, Morgan spied the group of twenty or so elite soldiers she'd been watching the past week enter the thicket, none of them more than a few years older than herself.

Her attention locked on the soldier bringing up the rear, something about the sheer animal grace in the way he moved drawing her attention. She took a deep breath, then gritted her teeth, hating the distance between them that prevented her from catching even a whiff of his scent. While she might have enhanced vision, strength, and speed, smell completely failed her, her nose barely better than a human's.

As his black-clad form disappeared into the woods, her heart seized painfully, instinct warning her if she stayed behind they wouldn't return from their mission in one piece.

Morgan twisted until she located the guard at the edge of the building, and huffed a sigh of impatience when he continued to linger.

She couldn't risk being discovered and stopped.

The need to protect the soldiers was a compulsion she couldn't ignore.

A light mist began to fall, dampening her clothes, making her failing grip on the stone parapet—the only thing keeping her from plummeting to the ground—even more precarious. Being a few miles from the coast of Maine ensured a lot of rainfall, but it usually blew over relatively quickly.

When the guard finally turned the corner, Morgan released a heavy breath and rested her forehead against the cold stone. She tightened her grip, lifted her knees to her chest, planted her feet against the wall, then shoved off, propelling her body away from the mansion, sending herself soaring through the air.

She plummeted three stories, twisting mid-fall to land lightly in a crouch, and surveyed her surroundings in a quick sweep, but the guards were more concerned about keeping the enemy out than anyone sneaking away in the middle of the night, their lax patrol allowing her to sprint undetected into the woods after her quarry...the group of soldiers.

She scrunched up her nose, not sure why everyone considered them so special.

They invaded the coven a week ago, disappearing each night to hunt paranormal creatures—or what humans call *monsters*.

Mucking around in her territory.

Doing *her* job.

She'd avoided them up until now, their last night at the coven. She couldn't wait for them to be gone and no longer poking their noses where they didn't belong. She wanted to have nothing to do with them, but trouble was brewing, the runes etched along her spine tingling in warning that something dangerous was near.

Despite the seriousness of the situation, it felt good to be doing something after being cooped up in the mansion for the last few days.

Since she was female, she was not invited on the hunts, the males believing she'd be too much of a distraction.

She snorted in derision.

She was the best hunter in the coven.

If danger was near, she couldn't sit back and do nothing.

Since she wasn't human, she wasn't someone the coven wasted resources on to protect, nor did she possess enough magic to be deemed *valuable*.

When paranormal purebloods hit puberty, they came into their powers. Many bloodlines had become diluted after centuries of breeding with humans, and those with too much human blood often never ascended and were labeled a mutt—people like her. So, while they could still have enhanced senses, speed, and strength, they never fully developed to their full potential.

Though she'd been told over and over that no female was capable or strong enough to become a protector, it didn't stop her from training.

It meant she needed to be better, faster than everyone else, just to prove her worth.

The MacGregor, leader of the coven, found her wandering in the woods with no memory of her past when she was a child. When he discovered she wasn't human, he raised her the only way he knew how...training her to be an assassin.

That didn't mean he protected her.

The opposite, in fact.

He pushed her harder, demanded more from her.

Some days she wondered if he wasn't actually trying to kill her.

On the up side, he turned a blind eye when she slipped away at night to hunt. She took precautions to make sure she wasn't caught, but she had no doubt the old man knew. He was too shrewd not to know every single thing going on under his roof. If the witches had any inkling of her escapades, they would demand to have her memories wiped and shipped off to live as a human.

Only she wasn't human.

She was created to hunt.

She knew nothing else.

She refused to lose everything again...she wouldn't survive starting over a second time.

Morgan pushed herself harder, her muscles beginning to burn, the world around her blurring as she tried to outrun her chaotic thoughts.

Even when the elite soldiers assigned to protect the coven did their best to beat her to a pulp and called it training, they couldn't argue with her natural talent. She had an uncanny ability to track creatures who'd escaped the Primordial World, a magical realm that existed alongside Earth. The Primordial World was where all supernatural creatures originated. The coven's primary mission was to protect the human world from supernaturals at all costs by capturing and returning the creatures to their own realm, or killing them outright if they were deemed too dangerous.

While most creatures who gained their freedom wanted nothing more than to live in peace, there were a number who preferred murder and mayhem more.

No rules.

No one to stop them from wreaking total destruction...except trained assassins like her.

As she hurried after the soldiers, a familiar shadow detached from the trees and streaked toward her. She skidded to a stop, and he flashed her a cheerful grin, the monster gleefully revealing a mouth full of wickedly dangerous teeth.

"Ascher."

The hellhound was her only companion. They had bonded when she rescued him from a witch's trap a few years ago. In return for his friendship, she protected him from the coven, keeping him hidden when the witches went on their hunts.

She knew he wasn't completely from the human world, that he was dangerous, but he was loyal to her, protecting her while she hunted. He listened to her without judgment, though that might have more to do with the fact that he couldn't speak. He was her best friend—her only friend to be perfectly honest—and she couldn't resist reaching out to touch him, taking comfort from the near-burning heat of his rough, velvety fur. Small wisps of smoke rose from where his paws touched the forest floor, giving away his contentment, and the warm scent of coal tinged the air.

He stilled at her touch, his eyelids sliding half-closed, a rumble of pleasure vibrating in his chest. At the sound, he broke away, almost embarrassed, and shook himself. Then he looked at her as if nothing had happened, his tongue lolled out, waiting for her orders.

She didn't know where he went when she wasn't around. The one time she tried to follow him, he easily caught her and gave her a reproachful look.

She hadn't tried again.

Knowing wasn't worth risking their friendship.

She signaled him for silence, pointing to the barely-visible trail the soldiers left behind. As if understanding, he peered into the darkness, then took off in a mad dash after the men with a speed she had no hope of matching.

"Wait up!" Morgan darted after him, her mind only half on her surroundings.

Despite all her training, she'd never come across anything higher than a category three monster while hunting. Category one was for those who escaped the void because they wanted a better life. They were no threat, the creatures often given sanctuary, and left to live in peace.

Category two were the mischief-makers. As long as they didn't endanger humans or put them in harm's way, they were left to their own devices.

Category three were the monsters who had no intention of blending in with humans. They saw people as chattel to be used as a slave workforce. Though it might be accidental, it was only a matter of time before the mistreatment of their slaves ultimately ended in death.

The coven's job was to return them to the void.

Categories four and five were reserved for the ones assassins hunted down and exterminated.

They saw humans as prey.

They took pleasure in dominating and torturing, and had no intention of living tamely among what they perceived as lesser beings.

Which was why they were in the woods tonight—something was terrorizing the nearby town of Apple Valley.

At first it was small pranks.

Missing garbage cans.

Cars parked in the wrong driveways.

Trees snatched bare of any leaves.

She was guessing an imp.

Once an imp locked onto a target, their mischievous pranks would eventually turn deadly.

Animals began to go missing recently.

Once an imp selected a new home, it was only a matter of time before the town was infected with an entire nest. She'd been chasing this imp for a week.

Last night, she arrived in town to the sound of children screaming, terrified of the boogeyman that was trying to drag them underneath their bed.

The parents chalked it up to nightmares, but a thread of doubt lingered when they couldn't explain the bruises covering their children's little bodies.

It was time to put a stop to the mischief before things went too far and the supernatural world was exposed.

Morgan sped through the woods, the half-moon the only source of light. She tied her waist-length black hair into a sloppy knot, then increased her speed to catch up with the hellhound only a few yards ahead of her.

When the hound darted sharply to the right at the last second, she nearly plowed into the clearing where the soldiers were waiting. She threw herself sideways, barely keeping her presence secret, then glared reproachfully at the hound.

Ascher huffed out a breath at her antics, snickering as she pushed through the thicket to reach his side. "You did that on purpose."

He shrugged his shoulders in a human-like way, not denying the accusation, then turned his attention toward the men.

Morgan followed his example, immediately noting the group had split in half, the other team already gone. Two men stood out, both slightly older than the rest.

One was blatantly studying the younger soldiers as if they were recruits, his slight sneer screaming boredom. He was tall and lean, his beauty almost alien, but what drew her attention were the two swords peeking over his shoulders. Even from this distance, she could sense there was nothing human about him. If she concentrated hard enough, the faint taste of cinnamon peppered her tongue.

Elf.

She crinkled her nose, already disliking him. Elves were known for their snobbery, and usually preferred to remain in the Primordial World, not caring that the constant struggle between the two realms would ultimately destroy both races.

Once the humans were hunted to extinction, it was only a matter of time before the elves suffered the same fate.

The other man had his back to her, alert for any threats, but even from the distance she recognized him as the one who caught her attention earlier. He was now close enough to answer the question that had been plaguing her.

He smelled of warm earth and hot stone on a blistering summer day.

He had dark brown, shoulder-length hair, but it was his broad shoulders that made her eyes linger longer than they should. He was lanky, but every inch of him was packed with muscle. She wanted him to turn around so she could see his face, but some instinct warned her if she saw him, her fate would be sealed. The future suddenly felt shaky and uncertain, and it had everything to do with him.

He appeared to be the leader. The younger recruits looked to him for guidance, more than a few gazing at him with an obvious case of hero worship, and Morgan realized this must be a training session of some type.

The territorial drive to protect her hunting ground eased off.

She was about to pull away and leave them to their skirmish when the leader gave a silent signal, and the small team melted into the trees.

Curiosity got the better of her, and she trailed after them.

After they traveled another mile deeper into the forest, her skin began to tingle in warning, and her whole body came alive.

A rift had opened.

Her curiosity about the men vanished at the possibility of a hunt, the need to protect overriding everything else, and she quickly overtook the group, Ascher hard on her heels. When the hellhound slowed, she followed his lead, spotting the second set of soldiers a few yards ahead.

As soon as she saw them, she took cover in the brush, and Ascher joined her.

One of the guys, no more than a year older than herself, stood well over six and a half feet tall, like a giant of old. When he lifted his head, sniffing the air, she realized he was some kind of shifter—most likely a wolf. His sandy brown hair was shaggy, reaching well past his shoulders, and her fingers twitched to touch. If she concentrated, she could pick up his wild, earthy, fresh green scent.

She didn't worry about being discovered, her natural scent so faint it was practically nonexistent thanks to her unknown heritage. She almost wished the shifter would spot her just so she could see the color of his eyes—she bet they were a deep brown a girl could get lost in.

The big man froze, picking up on something she'd missed while she was distracted, and she shook her head, not sure why her usual focus was so scattered around this group of men.

When the shifter's hand shot up in the air, her ruminations halted, and everyone came to attention, the men standing back-to-back, searching the trees intently. Most of the kids seemed excited at the prospect of a fight, while a couple were practically quaking in their boots.

Instead of searching the area, Morgan closed her eyes and concentrated. The markings on her back began to burn as the danger increased. She ignored the near-debilitating pain and focused her senses on the world around her.

Every creature with even a drop of paranormal blood had at one time emerged from the void, the space between the two realms where pure magic originated. Without a natural barrier to protect it, magic gradually spilled into the Primordial World many millennia ago. It soon became home to the supernatural. Proud of their heritage, paranormals began using the term void as slang for the primordial realm, and the name stuck.

While the magic in their blood faded over time for some, she was able to trace even the smallest contamination. She sensed the creature immediately, and it was closer than she'd thought.

Just as her eyes snapped open, the monster launched itself through the trees, crashing directly into the werewolf, and throwing them both to the ground.

Chapter Two

*T*he creature was massive, and completely in beast form, his head and shoulders that of an enormous bull. It took her brain precious seconds to process that he was an ancient minotaur, something that hadn't been Earthside for over two millennia, their species nearly extinct.

The beast roared at the wolf, clouds of steam billowing out his nostrils and into the chilly night air. He lifted his hooved hands, determined to stomp the wolf to a pulp.

The shifter managed to twist to the side at the last second, and the earth vibrated with the impact as the hoof thumped into the ground so hard it sank into the earth.

The wolf threw a punch, but the enormous minotaur didn't even flinch.

Not willing to admit defeat, the wolf threw a right hook, smashing his fist into the creature's snout.

That got a reaction—the minotaur's bellow of pain trumpeted through the night, but instead of retreating, it only served to make the beast more determined to pound the wolf to paste.

The recruits were so shocked they remained frozen, the tips of their weapons lowered while they watched the fight. A second later, one of the men gathered his wits enough to lift his crossbow and took aim. Unfortunately, the arrow bounced harmlessly off the minotaur's rough fur and pinged off into the trees. The beast's mantle came halfway down his arms and stopped mid-chest, protecting his vital organs.

Infuriated at the attack, the minotaur twisted his head, aiming his horns to eviscerate the wolf.

In an awe-inspiring display of strength, the wolf grabbed the bull's horns, stopping the forward momentum, the muscles of his arms bulging as he prevented the minotaur from disemboweling him.

But slowly, inch by inch, the horns descended, drawing dangerously closer to the wolf.

The archer was smart, aiming the next set of arrows at the lower portion of the minotaur's human body, shooting one after another, almost faster than she could track, advancing with no sign of fear. Something about him drew her gaze and held it. Unfortunately, instead of creating a distraction, his efforts only enraged the beast more.

The horn settled against the wolf's chest, and a grimace of pain twisted the wolf's face.

Morgan couldn't stand by and do nothing.

Without conscious thought, she palmed her knife and sent it spinning through the air at the only vulnerable spot she could find.

The blade landed true, sinking deep into the minotaur's left eye.

The beast lurched backward with a roar, then wrenched the knife out and flung it away.

Unfortunately, his head was so enormous, the six-inch blade had failed to reach his brain.

But the distraction was all the wolf needed. He unsheathed his claws and slashed the minotaur's human torso and legs until both men were liberally coated with the beast's blood.

She gripped the tree next to her until her fingers ached, wishing she had her own set of claws to join the fray.

Only pureblood can choose between their human shape or their natural monster form.

Regrettably, she couldn't change at all, but she refused to allow that to deter her. She just needed to be a faster, better fighter.

Unable to resist the lure to join the battle, she edged forward, only to pull up short when Ascher's teeth sank into her pant leg, hauling her back to reality and away from the bloodlust taking over all rational thought.

It was one of the reasons she hunted alone.

When bloodlust consumed her, she was worse than any monster.

Then joining the battle became moot when the leader of the other team burst into view. He took in the scene at a glance, then picked up speed, and plowed into the minotaur.

To her surprise, instead of bouncing off the minotaur like she expected, the bull went flying.

The soldier reached out a hand and helped the wolf to his feet, then they both pulled out matching blades and advanced. A quick glance over her shoulder showed the elf had taken the kids to the side, then proceeded to lazily watch the battle, his weapons held casually in his hands.

Morgan turned to see both soldiers dance around the minotaur, their blades flashing in the dim light. Then the leader gave a nod, and the wolf launched himself forward, wrapping his arms around the beast from behind and tackling him to the ground.

The beast snorted at the surprise attack, then began to push up, his arms bulging with the strain under the additional weight. The leader darted forward to make the kill. Unfortunately, he didn't approach from the bull's blind side. The beast bucked, sending the wolf smacking into the tree hard enough it left the guy dazed, and he crumpled to the ground.

The leader persisted, deftly dodging the wickedly long horns. He attacked the minotaur with no wasted movements, his body sleek and magnificent, his speed incredible as he hacked away at the beast, avoiding the thick, nearly impenetrable hide. Watching the leader's muscles flex and release became hypnotic, a complicated, lethal dance, and she leaned forward, fascinated by him despite knowing better.

The wolf finallypushed himself upright, shaking his head as if to clear it, and staggered to his feet.

He turned toward the elf and lifted an arm. The elf sighed, then flung one of his swords through the clearing, the blade spinning end over end.

The wolf deftly plucked it out of the air, then strode determinedly toward the battle.

The leader saw the movement, ducked under the minotaur's wild swing, and rolled out of range.

The wolf leapt forward, jumping nearly ten feet through the air, and brought up his sword.

The blade hit true, sinking deep into the beast's back, punching clear through the minotaur's chest.

Passing right through the heart.

The beast swung around madly, but the wolf had already sprung free.

The creature clawed at his back, frantically trying to reach the pommel of the sword, then flung his head back in defeat and bellowed in rage and pain. As he lumbered forward, his eyes latched on the leader. He pawed the ground, leaned forward, and charged.

The leader stood calmly while five hundred pounds of raging bull barreled down on him.

Waiting until the last possible second, he flung himself out of the way, his feet skidding across the dirt, then spun to face the threat, his blades ready…only they weren't needed.

The beast had plowed into a tree, impaling his horn through the trunk. No matter how hard the creature pulled and jerked, the minotaur was stuck.

The leader got to his feet, grasped the pommel of the sword sticking out of the minotaur's back, and pulled it free.

Blood and gore dripped from the tip, and the mighty beast fell to his knees, his shoulders heaving as he desperately struggled to breathe. Covered with sweat and blood, the minotaur gave one last bellow before the leader lifted the sword and beheaded him.

The body thudded heavily to the ground, and the corpse immediately began to decay, black goo oozing up through the skin until nothing but an inky puddle remained.

The process took only minutes.

The recruits began to cheer, and she allowed herself a small smile at their victory. When the two warriors shook hands, the smiled faded, and she couldn't help feel a bit envious of their smooth teamwork.

When the leader turned, she sucked in a harsh breath as she got her first good look at him.

He was a little over six feet, lanky and lean, his frame covered in deliciously toned muscles, but it was his handsome face that hit her so hard her chest hurt—like a long-forgotten memory of something she'd dreamed, something beautiful that evaporated when she awoke, and left a nagging ache behind that wouldn't be banished. His pale green eyes scanned the group, not missing a detail. They were hard and ruthless and spoke of danger, and a hunger she couldn't identify swamped her.

She took a step toward him, craving just a touch, when Ascher wedged himself in front of her, nearly tripping her when he didn't budge, and she glared at the hellhound.

The distraction broke the spell. She shook her head at her folly, not certain what came over her, disconcerted by her lack of control. Self-preservation took over, and she was eager to put as much distance between them as possible.

"Stay here. Watch."

Ascher curled his muzzle in a silent snarl, his blue eyes disturbingly human as he studied her, his gaze knowing.

Morgan blushed even as her attention was involuntarily drawn back toward the clearing.

As if he sensed her regard, the leader glanced over at her location, pinning her to the spot.

Despite knowing he couldn't see her, she was caught by his piercing eyes, and her heart fluttered madly against her ribs. She took an involuntary step forward, drawn to the barely restrained wildness in him, when Ascher placed a possessive paw on her foot.

The hellhound was clearly disgruntled, his eyes narrowing on the soldier, ready to attack.

More unnerved than ever, Morgan backed away, trembling from the physical ache to join him. "Just keep watch," she whispered to the hellhound.

She darted away before she gave in to the nearly overwhelming compulsion to throw herself at a complete stranger. Needing to burn off her troubling emotions, Morgan ran hard, pushing her body to its limit, but it did little to outrun her unexpected reaction to the group's leader.

A pained yip from a dog echoed through the trees, yanking her out of her musings, the sound so unexpected, she nearly crashed into a tree. After she regained her footing, she altered course, her feet barely touching the ground as she dodged trees and fallen logs, eager for a fight.

She slowed as she neared where the sound originated, waiting for some sign.

Two minutes later, a snuffling noise, similar to a pig, came from her left.

The imp.

Her forgotten prey.

Instead of following the sound, Morgan veered right, and deliberately stepped on a twig.

The snap was like a crack of a shotgun in the silence.

A few seconds later, she heard the sound of pursuit.

Morgan reached into her pocket and took out the gaudy jewelry she picked up at a pawn shop, tossing a few pieces randomly in her wake. The brighter and shinier the trinkets, the more impossible it would be for the imp to resist.

A squeal of outrage nearly ruptured her eardrums.

Nothing maddened an imp more than to disrespect what he considered treasure.

Morgan slowed, then reversed her course, slipping silently between the trees...and caught sight of a small, barely two-feet-tall imp. The creature was rummaging through the underbrush. Large, bat-like leathery wings were tucked along his back, allowing it to jump to great heights, while its hands and feet were tipped with deadly claws. The tail lashed back and forth as he collected his bounty, the speared tip easily capable of slicing or piercing flesh. When it lifted its head, she spotted black, beady eyes, and a tiny, upturned nose so disfigured it appeared almost skeletal.

Its skin was as thick as a tire and just as hard to puncture. They were lightning fast, and could turn deadly when cornered. The small creature had yet to kill, so it was her duty to capture and return it to the void.

Morgan unwound the thin metal rope from her waist, creating a loop, preparing to drop it over the imp when the little devil's head snapped up.

It spotted her instantly.

Some of the trinkets slid through its fingers as it stood immobile, then it squealed and darted off into the woods.

Morgan froze for a second in shock—an imp would never abandon his treasure.

Only when the little beastie disappeared into the trees did she snap back to herself. "Shit."

Morgan surged after it in pursuit, nearly tripping over her own feet in her rush.

She couldn't let him escape.

He wouldn't fall for her trap a second time.

Unfortunately, no matter how hard she pushed herself, the imp remained elusive. Every time she thought she lost him, she spotted the flicker of his tail or heard his distinctive, telltale snort.

The thrill of the hunt heated her blood, and she knew, even though she couldn't remember her past, that she'd been created for this—the hunt, the chase. She was so focused on her task, Morgan lost track of her surroundings, until she was drawn farther into the woods than she normally wandered.

Her unease grew.

Something was off.

It took her a few seconds to realize what bothered her—the absolute lack of any animal chatter or buzz of insects.

Memories of mutilated animals and half-eaten pets flashed in her mind.

She'd assumed the imp was responsible.

Now she wasn't so sure.

Morgan came to a halt, cursing herself for the rookie mistake of making assumptions.

The only warning she got was a slight burn of the runes carved into her back and shoulders.

She whirled, lifting her arm, then staggered under the numbing blow that was meant to incapacitate her. A bright lash of pain streaked down her arm, tearing open a ragged gash, and warm blood trickled down her arm.

Instead of facing off against a mischievous imp, she was confronted by a seven-foot monster.

The beast lifted inch-long claws clearly meant to slice his prey's flesh from bone with one swipe, the tips darkened by her blood. He smiled wickedly, revealing three rows of serrated teeth, then slowly licked off her blood with a lizard-like tongue.

Hunger sharpened his features, his blood-red eyes shimmering in the darkness, devouring her with his gaze. The creature's bulky form was pitch-black, making him almost disappear into shadows from one blink to the next.

Wraith.

Her mind immediately went through dozens of escape scenarios.

Unfortunately, none of them left her alive.

The problem with wraiths was they were made of shadows, and only took form when they attacked. Even as she watched, the shadowy creature began to dissolve.

She wrapped the thin metal rope around her fist, but knew it was a long shot. Her fists or weapons would pass right through him. If she had her sword, she might be able to take off his head with a lucky blow. The only sure way to get rid of a wraith was to send them back through the rift from which they emerged.

Too bad she had no magic to compel the wraith to obey.

That left her with only one option…negotiation.

"What do you want?" She relaxed her stance, her muscles liquid and ready to leap out of the way.

The wraith chuckled, his form floating a few inches off the ground as he circled her. "You."

His voice should have sounded insubstantial, but it vibrated in her chest, the threat tugging at the runes along her shoulders. The wraith was at least three times her size, but thanks to her unusual inheritance, she was stronger and faster than most hunters.

The blood flowing from the gash on her arm became sluggish, the edges of the wound slowly closing.

Instead of killing her outright, the wraith studied her curiously, and the runes stamped along her spine chilled until her skin felt like ice, the magic sinking deeper into her body.

The urge to attack and rend him to pieces with her bare hands nearly overwhelmed her.

But she refused to descend into bloodlust, not certain she would be able to stop killing once she started, hyperaware of the soldiers still in the woods. She curled her fingers into fists, her nails biting into her palms, the sting of pain almost pleasure as she wrestled her body and emotions back under her control. She couldn't allow anyone to discover she was different, or her dream of being a full-fledged assassin would never become reality.

She would not turn feral.

She cocked her head, studying her opponent as her heartbeat fell back to its normal rhythm. "The imp was a decoy."

The wraith vanished and almost immediately shimmered back into view a few feet to her right, his teeth flashing in a gruesome smile, his obsidian skin glittering when he took shape. "I must say, I'm disappointed. Luring you into my trap was almost too easy. The whispers from the primordial realm promised a challenging hunt." His heavy brows lowered as he hovered closer. "Though I am surprised you managed to eliminate the minotaur."

Shock swept over her at the possibility of two warring creatures working together—to capture her. The cultured, exotic accent of his voice was completely at odds with his grotesque form. He made her want to forget the danger, made her want to lower her weapons and go to him. She rubbed her pounding temples, the pain helping block some of the effects of his voice. Like a soulless monster, he used his compelling voice ruthlessly, hypnotizing his prey and luring his victims into the shadows and the arms of certain death.

Morgan ignored the tug in her gut, the craving to surrender, and instead concentrated on the magic flowing in her blood as it rapidly spread through her veins. A tug similar to the pull of a magnet came from directly in front of her.

Magic was attracted to magic.

The stronger the magic, the more intense the pull.

She might not be able to cast magic, but she wasn't a complete null.

The rift was directly behind the wraith.

All she had to do was go through him to send the wraith back where he belonged.

Morgan narrowed her eyes, a deceptively simple plan forming, and she shrugged. "Well, I would hate to disappoint you."

Instead of waiting for an answer, she charged him, bracing herself for impact.

At the last second, just as she hoped, the wraith shimmered and dissolved.

Morgan burst through his insubstantial form, her runes burning painfully at the contact. When she emerged from the other side, she struggled against the need to gag, reeling as the pain from the runes shot down her spine. A fine, acidic coating of clear slime drenched her from head to foot, little of her body spared the dunking.

A small blessing was it evaporated quickly.

The wraith spewed a series of curses in a garbled tongue that sounded vaguely familiar. Instead of slowing down, Morgan picked up speed, breathing through the already-fading pain, heading straight toward the rift. The closer she got to the void, the more her skin tingled.

The wraith shimmered through the trees in pursuit, his howl of rage reverberating through the woods, sending a shiver of dread down to her soul. The haunting wail was a war cry, the sound triggering a primal imperative to flee, and she fought the urge to run in a blind panic.

As long as the wraith didn't take form, he couldn't hurt her.

The wraith was a category four monster—strong, but not all-powerful.

Her skin tingled painfully, and Morgan knew she was closing in on the rift.

"There is nowhere you can run, little mouse. You'll wear yourself out, making yourself an even easier target."

She swallowed hard at the taunt and veered left, altering course, the hairs on the nape of her neck rising, and she imagined she could feel his chilly breath against her skin. Though she knew the fear was the side-effect of his voice, it didn't lessen her body's involuntary response. She had no doubt that if she listened to him for long, her brain would shut down, and she would surrender just to make it stop.

When she emerged from the forest into a small clearing, the tingling of the runes escalated until she felt as if someone was trying to carve them out of her flesh. In the middle of the area, a section of displaced air shimmered, the temperature dropping until she could see her breath frost the air.

The rift.

Morgan skidded to a stop and whirled to face the threat.

"You're almost making this too easy." The wraith floated out into the clearing, not even winded, studying her again, seemingly disappointed with her lack of fight.

Something about his tone caused bile to burn the back of her throat.

He wasn't trying to kill her.

In truth, he probably could have killed her at any time.

For some reason, he wanted her alive, and that scared her even more.

Chapter Three

$\mathcal{M}$organ loosened her grip around the metal rope, allowing it to uncoil at her feet, determined not to give the wraith what he wanted without a fight.

All she had to do was get him close to the rift, and she could send him into the void.

Much to her annoyance, the imp crept into the clearing, its beady eyes locked on her.

"What do you want with me?"

"Me? Nothing." The wraith solidified, seemingly amused by her question. "But someone has put a price on your head." The creature wandered closer, completely unconcerned by the threat she posed. "What baffles me is why no one would pick up your contract."

Her lips thinned. "You're a mercenary."

Morgan was an orphan.

Of no value whatsoever.

Who would put a bounty on her head?

Or more importantly, why?

The wraith sighed heavily, displeased when she ignored his question. When he floated toward her, Morgan could stall no longer. She used her speed to dodge his hands, then slammed her fist into his ribs. She met resistance for a second, then his form dissolved.

Using his abilities against him, Morgan began to swing the rope.

If the wraith wanted to grab her, it would need to take shape.

He hovered outside the spinning metal as he studied the problem.

"Foolish girl." Without hesitation, he walked boldly into the whirl of metal, allowing it to pass through his body.

Less than a foot away, he ducked under the swirling metal and reached for her.

Without hesitation, Morgan jerked down the metal rope, grabbed the opposite end and quickly slipping it over the wraith's head, locking the links around his neck. Using all her strength, she wrenched back, hearing the bones of his spine creak in protest.

The wraith hissed in pain, dissolving in an instant, only to re-take shape a few feet away, gingerly touching his neck. He appeared startled that she'd nearly taken off his head. In a few more seconds, she would've had him.

His face hardened, his blood-red eyes darkening with rage. "You're going to pay for that."

Morgan snorted. "Did you honestly expect me to simply turn myself over to you?"

She angled slightly to the left until the rift was directly behind him.

Then she once again began to wind the thin rope.

A growl of fury emerged from the wraith.

Inch-long claws clicked in the silence, as if he was envisioning what he would do once he got ahold of her. His pupils seemed to grow while she watched. She couldn't turn away.

Pain pierced her skull, and she could feel his darkness crawl inside her head. The rope drooped and lost speed as she fell under the wraith's sway, and her imagination took over. Claws dug into her flesh until her body jolted with agony. It took all her control to blink away the image of herself, sans skin, her body a pulpy mess, completely disgusted with herself for allowing him inside her head for even a second.

"Impressive. Very few can break away from me once I get inside their minds."

Her head snapped up at his disgruntled tone. Her moment of inattention had allowed the wraith to get within arm's reach.

She whipped her arm back, the metal rope chiming in the silence, but when she tensed to fling it toward the wraith, the metal caught on something behind her and wouldn't budge.

Then she had no more time to think when the wraith streaked forward.

A blow hammered into her solar plexus, launching her backwards. She stumbled, then dropped into a crouch, unable to catch her breath. Only her training allowed her to function past the panic of her lungs not working.

The clink of metal caught her attention, and she watched the rope she'd dropped slink across the clearing. She fisted her hands, cursing her carelessness. Following the rope, she saw the imp, his beady eyes gleaming with avarice. He gave her a sinister smile, drool dripping from his teeth as he slowly and inexorably looped the weapon loosely around its small, clawed hand.

Morgan had suspected the imp and wraith were working together, but actually seeing it boggled her mind.

It was a well-known fact that different paranormal species were not friendly with each other, often territorial and willing to fight to the death over their prey.

Unease churned in her gut at the aberration in their behavior.

No way would she be able to take them both out on her own.

If she wanted to survive, she needed to get rid of the imp first, since he was the weaker of the two and easier prey.

From the corner of her eye, she saw shadows shifting. Morgan swiveled, spotting the wraith's insubstantial form skim over the forest floor, and instinct took over.

She threw a punch, aiming for the wraith's throat, only to have her whole fist pass through his body. A thin film of cold slime coated her hand up to her wrist, and pain streaked down her arm.

He had no such problem attacking her, dancing around her almost lazily as he landed blows. With each searing flick of his claws, gashes opened up all over her body, digging deeper and deeper with each cut.

It was all she could do to get out of his way.

When he aimed at her face, she lifted her hand, stopping his fist just short of slamming into her jaw. Her fingers slowly sank into his cloudy form, but didn't pass through, and she gazed at her hand in speculation.

The goo.

It allowed her to touch him back, if only for a few seconds.

Morgan gave him a cocky grin. Every creature had a weakness, and she'd found the wraith's. "How about we make this fight a little more even?"

Not giving herself time to change her mind, she dove toward the insubstantial creature. Passing through him was like taking a cold dunking in a stagnant swamp, but the wraith screeched, as if she was peeling off his skin.

She only had a few seconds before the slime evaporated, so she had to make it count. She slammed her foot back, wanting to cheer when her boot connected with his back and sent him flying.

Unfortunately, he passed completely through the tree without the satisfying crunch of bone, and she scowled.

She took a step after him to finish the fight when the faint sounds of leaves crackled behind her.

Without hesitation, Morgan leapt sideways, bruising her ribs when she slammed to the ground. She watched the bat-like creature, his wings spread wide, sail through the air where she'd been standing only seconds before.

The imp.

Morgan lunged forward, and grabbed the rope that trailed after the creature. The heavy, flexible metal smacked her hand hard, tearing into her palm when she tightened her hold.

The imp was pulled up short when the rope drew tight, and she yanked as hard as she could.

The creature squealed in fright, unable to shake loose from the metal tangle, and slammed to the ground with a heavy thump that vibrated up her legs.

Its small body lay unmoving, but she knew better than to think she'd killed him.

Scrambling to her feet, she braced her legs, then used her considerable strength to haul back on the links.

Still stunned, the imp hadn't let go of the weapon, and she watched as the creature flew up once more with a pig-like squeal, flopping around for purchase like a fish out of water.

It finally shook loose of the prison of metal and spread its leathery wings, but far too late.

The imp crashed into the rift.

The barrier rippled even as the imp shrieked in denial. With a flare of bright light, the imp disappeared into the void, where it would remain trapped. Without the help of a powerful witch or another rift, it would not be able to pass into the human realm again.

A blow to the back of her skull sent her to her knees. Her ears rang sharply, and she cursed her carelessness.

Never lose track of where your enemies are at all times was one of the simplest, most important rules of battle, and she foolishly allowed herself to be distracted.

As Morgan leaned down to grab for the rope, her movements sluggish, the wraith took shape in front of her, and calmly stepped on the metal. "I think not."

He swung out, his foot connecting with her jaw, sending her flying backwards. She landed on her back, the world around her spinning as she struggled to stay conscious.

She waited for the wraith to use his claws on her, bracing for pain.

Instead, he clamped his hand around her ankle and dragged her toward the rift. Rocks and twigs gouged into her shoulders and back, but she barely felt the scrapes as a bone-deep terror rocked through her.

She would not go back.

Darkness rose from inside her, a deep, black nothingness that threatened to swallow her whole, her mind struggling against turning feral. If she tipped over that edge, she knew she would never emerge completely sane.

The torque she wore burned unexpectedly, clamping around her neck like a vise, halting her downward spiral and allowing her to function.

The knowledge that she'd been in the primordial realm before shocked her, and she tried to grab for the missing memories of her childhood—only to smack into a solid wall, her past still firmly locked away.

The runes marking her shoulders flared in warning, making one thing clear…whatever tragedy occurred when she was a child took place in the Primordial World. Instinct warned her that if she crossed the barrier now, she would never return…possibly not even survive at all.

Morgan twisted, grabbing for anything to stop her forward momentum, her fingers leaving deep furrows in the earth, but her efforts didn't slow the wraith in the least.

She rolled onto her back, repeatedly kicking at his shady form until her foot was coated with slime. With each strike, the wraith grunted, but refused to release her.

She was only going to get one shot at this.

When she was sure her foot was sufficiently covered, she bent her legs, pulling herself closer to the wraith, and kicked out for all she was worth.

Her blow caught him in the back of the knee.

He automatically released her to catch himself as he toppled forward or risk falling flat on his face.

"You bitch." The wraith glared at her, slowly pushing himself to his feet, his face twisting with hatred, his eyes malevolent. "You're becoming a pain in my ass."

He took a menacing step toward her, and Morgan scooted backwards.

She needed a plan.

If she didn't come up with something soon, she had no doubt he would win this battle.

A vicious snarl tore through the silence, and Morgan laughed in delight. "You are so screwed."

The wraith hesitated, scanning their surroundings. He had only seconds before her reinforcements arrived, and he knew it.

Morgan barely gained her footing when the wraith streaked toward her, yanking her around until she was facing away from him, then wrapped his arms around her from behind, pinning her own arms at her side. Morgan kicked back, then cursed when her foot passed through him, the slime having long since evaporated.

A frustrated growl escaped her throat. "This is getting old."

She knew with certainty that if she didn't do *something*, Ascher would arrive too late.

As fear churned in her gut, the runes activated and sizzled against her skin, and she welcomed the pain. To her shock, the wraith shrieked in agony, the magic searing him at every point of contact between them, and the smell of charred flesh filled the air. She buried her squeamishness and ignored the instinctual need to pull away. If she showed any hint of weakness, she was a dead woman.

The large, black hellhound burst into the clearing, his chest heaving from his mad dash through the trees. Wicked, three-inch fangs flashed when he snarled, hatred making his blue eyes glow. Nearly two hundred pounds and three feet tall, his appearance was enough to scare the shit out of any quarry.

The wraith used her body as a shield, his arms banded around her tightening until her ribs creaked in protest, stealing her breath.

"Ascher." His name was no more than a whisper, her lungs unable to draw enough air.

It didn't matter.

He heard her plea.

He immediately crouched low and launched himself through the air.

Morgan braced herself seconds before Ascher plowed into them.

The impact knocked her free of the wraith's clutches, and she smacked the ground so hard her vision dimmed. The sound of vicious snarling rang in her ears, and she woozily pushed herself up on her hands and knees.

To her surprise, the wraith appeared injured, his normally black, cloudy form pierced by a number of large, transparent holes. Ascher was crouched low to the ground to her right, protecting her while she recovered, his eyes tracking his prey.

The wraith floated right in front of the rift.

Instead of escaping, the wraith cursed, then lunged for her.

Acting on instinct, Morgan flung herself backwards…in time to see Ascher sail over her head, and slam into the wraith.

The momentum sent them both flying through the air…directly into the rift.

"Nooooo!"

A flash of light blinded her, and the barrier rippled then began to fade as the magic powering it dissipated. Morgan sprang to her feet and rushed forward, already knowing it would be too late.

The rift was gone.

And so was Ascher.

Chapter Four

Morgan stomped back and forth across the clearing, cursing when she called upon the dormant magic in her blood and nothing happened. The runes on her back remained frustratingly unresponsive. The torque was preventing her from accessing the power.

She focused on the embers of her anger, wanting to trigger her rage and rip the torque off her neck, but even with her extra strength, no matter how hard she tried, the metal wouldn't budge. While she understood the torque was protecting her, right then, she felt nothing but hatred for it.

Without magic, she couldn't open the rift.

She couldn't go after Ascher.

The loss devastated her, the hollow feeling expanding, crushing her chest, until breathing became difficult.

They were after her, and Ascher sacrificed his life for hers. If the hellhound had been born with too much human blood in his system, he would be dead within days. The magical atmosphere of the primordial realm would weaken him until he slowly and painfully wasted away.

He was at least part hellhound. He also accidentally ingested some of her blood when he bit her when he was injured, linking them together, but she couldn't stop fretting…what if their connection wasn't enough to save him?

Morgan wanted to stay, wait for the rift to open again, but it could take days or even weeks.

And even then it didn't guarantee Ascher would be waiting for her.

What if the wraith returned?

Or something worse?

His sacrifice would be for nothing.

With a heavy heart, she turned away, feeling as if she was leaving part of her soul behind as she headed back to the mansion.

All she could do was wait and hope for his return.

She refused to believe he was dead.

Refused to believe he wouldn't return to her.

She first met the hellhound when she found him caught in one of the cruel traps the witches placed throughout the woods to catch creatures from the void. The beast was clearly starving, his leg severely injured from the serrated jaws of the bear trap. Despite knowing it would be dangerous, she couldn't allow him to suffer. If the witches discovered him, they would conduct painful experiments on him with their magic.

When they learned what they needed, they would drain him of his essence, taking the primordial magic that gave him life, until he expired, riddled with agony. The "experiments" would go on for weeks, and Morgan had no stomach for torture.

She had pulled her weapon from its sheath to put him out of his misery when their eyes met.

The intelligence there caused her to hesitate, and she reluctantly lowered the blade, instinct urging her to help him instead.

When she edged closer, the beast snarled ferociously, jerking back, causing his leg to bleed freely.

He saw her as the enemy.

Knowing she would be in serious trouble if anyone learned what she was about to do, Morgan sheathed her blade, then reached for the torque around her neck. The necklace contained a spell to trap her magic in her body, blocking others from discovering her darkest secret.

When she was a child, the torque was immovable. No matter how hard she tried, she wasn't able to take it off.

Until a few years ago.

By accident, she learned that when she was around certain creatures, she was able to remove the necklace so she could help them.

She also learned that she was able to break any spells or curses when the torque was off…such as the one preventing the hellhound from escaping the trap.

The first time the necklace detached, the surprisingly heavy metal came away in her hands, and her neck felt naked without it. The relief at being free almost made her giddy…until the magic carved into her back began to build.

The power would gain strength and continue to grow, until it seemed it would consume her from the inside out. Only when she couldn't take the pain anymore did she replace the torque. The metal would click into place, warming in welcome, as if glad to be home.

The witches didn't know she carried magic, and she had no intention of telling them. They were ruthless, many of them believing their powers made them special and above the law. After being treated worse than a slave by the witches for the past ten years, she wanted nothing further to do with them.

The torque helped keep her secret, often changing its shape, as if trying to amuse her. It was protecting her, not the prison shackles as she originally feared.

In order to rescue Ascher, she needed magic to release his foot from the contraption. Different sigils were etched into the metal, the spell glowing slightly to her enhanced senses. Only a witch would know the combination to open the trap.

But if she had enough power, Morgan could destroy the spell altogether.

Much to her surprise, the torque came away easily, curling itself around her wrist like a snake. Almost immediately, the runes along her back shimmered to life. The hellhound sensed the change, and crouched down, his head lowered, never removing his gaze from hers.

She moved slowly, not wanting to startle the hound, and gripped the edges of the trap. Magic surged down her arms and slammed into the metal. The light from the spell dimmed, bowed under her magic, until she heard a crack. The sigils grew tarnished, the glow of the spell floating in the air like a cloud of sparkling red dust before dissipating.

The rusty metal screeched in protest when she used her enhanced strength to wrench it open.

The hellhound whimpered in pain, his leg clearly broken.

Morgan carefully lifted his limb out of the trap, unprepared when the hound lunged forward and clamped his jaws painfully around her wrist. Teeth sank deep, drawing blood, and she sucked in a startled breath.

Almost as fast as it happened, the hound whimpered low in his throat and retreated, staring at her remorsefully. Morgan knew she should run, knew he couldn't follow, but the pain in his eyes tempted her to linger.

She ripped off the bottom of her shirt, and carefully approached the hound, gingerly wrapping his injury.

Then she noticed the collar clamped painfully around his neck, so brutally tight, his hair had been rubbed away, his skin chafed and so abraded that nothing remained but a motley collection of scabs.

When she touched her fingertips to the collar, magic jolted into her so hard she was knocked off her feet, landing flat on her back.

The spell shattered, and red, sparkling dust floated in the air, leaving her feeling like she'd wrenched something deep inside.

The runes on her back burned like hellfire, wiggling under her skin like worms burrowing through her flesh, and nausea rolled through her. The markings were changing shapes—which should have been impossible. The torque tightened painfully on her arm, and she obediently unwound it, replacing the metal around her neck.

As soon as the torque clicked into place, the pain eased, and she shivered in relief, grateful the disturbing feel of her flesh rippling had stopped.

She was startled when Ascher licked her face, and she peered up into his clear blue eyes. She reached out, tentatively brushing her fingers against the rough, velvety fur-like hide covering him, noting the collar was gone. Seconds later, he turned and bounded into the woods.

For the next few weeks, Ascher stalked her every time she ventured out, careful to keep his distance.

Both of them pretended not to notice.

When she hunted at night, he joined her, and they quickly became inseparable.

The perfect team.

When the witches discovered the pairing a year later, they demanded she turn the creature over to them.

Morgan refused, accepting the inevitable beatings as punishment for her defiance. MacGregor finally overruled them, declaring it was more important to catch the creatures harming humans than capture and experiment on a simple hellhound. Though he wouldn't admit it out loud, she sensed he was pleased to know she was no longer hunting alone, that she had a protector, no matter how unlikely.

That didn't stop the witches from setting their traps for him in secret.

As she neared the mansion, she saw it was ablaze with lights, shining like a beacon in the night, and her stride slowed.

That couldn't be good.

For a half a second, she debated heading back into the forest, but she wouldn't shirk her duty.

What if there was a problem with one of the soldiers?

A tiny clutch of worry tightened her gut.

What if there had been more creatures hunting her?

While the soldiers seemed more than capable of protecting themselves, that didn't mean they were indestructible.

She pulled her shoulders back, ignoring the sting of her injuries, and reluctantly trudged toward the place she called home…coven headquarters, and her own personal hell.

Chapter Five

$\mathcal{M}$organ approached the mansion cautiously and decided she could learn more by using an indirect approach. She swerved off the path to detour around back, planning to scale the wall when a guard emerged from the shadows by the majestic stairs.

"You might as well use the front door. They're waiting for you." Harold was tall but lean, his blond hair cut brutally short, so the strands only held a hint of curl. But, tough as he looked, he also was one of the few guards who actually made an effort to be polite to her. His main charge, the lead witch at the mansion, was the same woman who relentlessly pursued her favorite pastime—that of making Morgan's life a living hell.

Catalina.

Her shoulders slumped at the coming confrontation, but she nodded. "Thanks."

His blue eyes softened slightly, but the bonding marks on his shoulders tying him to Catalina prevented him from offering any friendship.

If Catalina ordered him to beat the crap out of her, he wouldn't hesitate to obey, though he wouldn't enjoy it like the other guards.

Harold was part of the legendary death squad. One of the few elite assassins. Most of the warriors considered Morgan beneath their notice, and trained her with daily beatings to force her to quit. After a few months, she began to fight back, and they no longer found it amusing when they were the ones lying on the ground broken and bleeding at the hands of an eighteen-year-old girl.

It was their job to protect the coven, and they saw her as a liability who would get them killed.

Morgan refused to allow their prejudice to deter her, and relentlessly persisted with her training.

She trudged up the marble stairs, stopping before the large, ornate double doors, admiring the snarling lion-head knocker. The whole mansion was made of stone and so much magic it radiated from the building.

It had been created to withstand a siege against the deadly creatures they hunted. The building was stationed next to the largest rift in the world, and the coven was the first line of defense.

When she touched the knocker, magic shimmered up her arm. Once it confirmed she wasn't the enemy, the latch clicked and the door opened soundlessly.

She stepped into the opulent mansion, shivering at the way the doors closed on their own and sealed her inside. Everything was a pristine white—the walls, the floors, even the ceiling and the grand staircase. It was supposed to be prestigious, but managed to look sterile instead. She felt more at home in the forest.

The ornate, gilded frames on the twenty-foot wall to the right displayed every MacGregor who'd been in charge of the coven over the past five centuries, leaving the mansion looking pompous, rather than what it was…a functional fortress and last bastion against paranormals.

Morgan strode forward, her feet barely a whisper on the marble floors as she headed for the stairs.

"Morgan, please enter." The gritty male voice emerged from the large office to the left, and she barely resisted the urge to cringe. She trudged toward the doorway, wondering how MacGregor always knew where she was when he didn't have even a lick of magic in his blood.

Part of her wondered if the young soldiers had spotted her in the woods despite all her precautions, and tattled on her.

When she surveyed her appearance, she sighed. Her pants were dirty, stained with blood, and ripped in multiple places. Her shirt was in even worse condition. At least most of her wounds had stopped bleeding, though a few of them were so deep that even with her advanced healing abilities they had yet to close completely.

Taking a fortifying breath, Morgan pushed open the door, her heart beating a little faster at the possibility of seeing the young soldiers again, up close and personal, and she grimaced at the betraying thought.

But when she scanned the room, they weren't there.

Disappointment pinged through her, and she couldn't help being annoyed with herself. Then she shrugged it off and strode forward to stand in front of the MacGregor's desk.

She loved this room, the dark oak paneling reminding her of a Scottish hunting lodge. A large fire always burned in welcome, but what she loved more were the two whole walls covered with ancient tomes containing myths and legends from around the world. She'd spent hours in this room, taking refuge in the books, but it was the man behind the desk who drew her gaze.

The MacGregor was a burly warrior well past his prime, who reminded her of a gnarled old grizzly. Though he might have retired from active duty over twenty years ago, he kept himself in great physical shape. A knotted, twisted scar climbed out of the collar of his shirt, wrapping around his neck, where he had nearly been beheaded. His hair was silver and wild, reminding her of a shaggy sheepdog. Wrinkles creased his face, giving him a severe expression, and she couldn't help wondering if it would crack if he ever smiled.

Sharp, faded blue eyes raked her from head to toe without giving away a hint of what he was thinking, the intelligence in them intimidating, even after all the years she'd trained with him.

He sat ensconced behind a desk at least eight feet wide and three feet across, the surface covered in equal measure with weapons and paperwork, plus an ancient computer that failed to start half the time.

She came to attention in front of him, holding still under his perusal, ignoring the trickle of blood that ran down her back. Only when he gave her a nod did she relax her stance and study the other occupants of the room.

Five witches were currently in residence, while two more were out on missions with their squads. Each of them exuded the tremendous power that had earned them their prestigious spot in the Maine coven.

Three of the witches were sprawled in chairs, their magic tightly contained, sparing her only a glance, then proceeding to ignore her. Each had black hair, dark eyes and skin so deathly pale they reminded her of corpses—and showed as much emotion as one. Morgan dubbed them The Triplets, since she never spotted one without the others.

Of the remaining two witches, one had flaming red hair and pale skin, her dainty form surprisingly voluptuous—the quintessential image of a witch. When her green eyes latched onto Morgan, she scrunched up her nose, disdain oozing from her pores, before lazily going back to paging through the book in her lap.

The last witch was Catalina. The woman could be considered gorgeous, with light brown hair cut in a wavy bob, a dainty figure, and refined features normally reserved for supermodels...until you looked into her eyes and saw only insatiable ambition staring back.

She made no bones about wanting to be the next—and youngest—MacGregor, and she was ruthless enough to do whatever it took to make it happen.

She stood to the right of the desk, her hands on her hips, and glared at Morgan with hatred burning in her eyes. To Catalina, Morgan was nothing more than a mongrel who should have been drowned at birth. Because Morgan wasn't a witch, she was considered subhuman, and a nuisance.

A sneer curled Catalina's lips, and she snorted in derision at Morgan's disheveled appearance. The Maine coven was very old, and many considered it an honor to be appointed to serve. She clearly thought Morgan wasn't good enough to even lick the floors. "Look at what the cat finally dragged in. I don't know why you indulge her like you do. She's nothing but trouble, pretending to be something she's not."

MacGregor waved his hand, and Catalina subsided with a scowl.

Morgan forced herself to remain relaxed and not react to the taunt.

Only males were eligible to become warriors—the ultimate assassins.

Despite knowing Morgan had to work twice as hard to earn her spot in the coven, Catalina saw her as a distraction and roadblock to achieving everything she wanted. When Morgan first arrived, the witch had decided to experiment on her, and received a rude surprise when Morgan managed to break every curse and spell she cast.

Which only pissed Catalina off more, and Morgan shivered, remembering the pain when the witch tried to rip Morgan's useless magic out of her body, only to fail when her unknown magic sank deeper and deeper into her bones, hiding until it became untouchable…even to her.

When MacGregor discovered what Catalina had been doing, he took Morgan under his wing, making her untouchable. While she doubted MacGregor had any great affection for her, his gruff kindness cemented her loyalty to him. His brutal training didn't matter. He was helping her achieve what she wanted, and she was determined to prove to everyone that she wouldn't break.

She would become a warrior, even if it killed her.

MacGregor's protection and favoritism only served to infuriate the witches more.

It galled Catalina to be forced to obey an old warrior, but she dutifully followed his orders.

For now.

Each coven was tied to an area, but it was the building itself that selected the most eligible and capable person to rule it…the MacGregor. Morgan suspected the house and the MacGregor were tied together somehow, but she didn't understand the mechanics.

If the witch ever took over control of the Maine coven, Morgan didn't doubt for a second that Catalina would hunt her down like a criminal and imprison her so they could resume their testing.

"Come here, lass."

Morgan broke her stance, carefully easing closer to the MacGregor while taking care not to leave her back exposed to the others.

When she neared the desk, he held out a gilded envelope of heavy cream vellum with her name embossed grandly in gold foil across the front. "Do you know what this is?"

"No." She shook her head, reluctant to take the envelope, her gut churning, warning her that accepting it would irrevocably change her life forever.

Catalina snorted, only subsiding when MacGregor cast her a warning glare. Then she crossed her arms defiantly, unable to hold her tongue. "There must be some mistake. There is no way the Academy of Assassins would allow a mutt like her in their ranks."

A vein began to throb on MacGregor's forehead as his anger spilled over. "Then it's a good thing it's not your decision to make."

His disdain for her opinion was obvious. Before anyone else could protest, he waved a hand at them. "Your objections have been noted. You're dismissed."

The old man was unpredictable, which made him dangerous. It was one of the reasons Catalina didn't challenge him for his position. She wouldn't win, and she knew it.

Morgan was conscious of the witch's hate-filled eyes on her, but didn't give the witch the satisfaction of acknowledging her. As they filed out the door, Catalina flung a spell at Morgan, her magic a living, breathing thing as it battered at Morgan's already-abused body.

Pain nearly buckled her knees as liquid fire poured into her many wounds. She breathed through the agony, the runes on her back heating as they quickly countered the magic before dispelling it completely.

The witches' laughter reached her seconds before the door clicked shut, and the wards on the room slammed back into place, granting them privacy, and protecting her from further retaliation. Ignoring their spiteful antics, Morgan never once took her gaze from MacGregor or reached for the card he held.

"You're kicking me out."

It wasn't a question.

She kept her face blank, but acid burned the back of her throat at the betrayal.

First Ascher disappeared, and now her safe, somewhat predictable life was being torn from her.

Slowly but surely, she was losing everything that meant anything to her.

His eyes flickered with sorrow, not denying it. "They have summoned you regularly for the past five years, but I selfishly fought to keep you here. Unfortunately, what I want no longer matters."

He pushed back his chair, withdrew a key from his pocket and unlocked the bottom drawer of his desk. He removed a shoebox and pulled off the lid. Nestled inside were at least two dozen envelopes similar to the one he'd placed in the center of his blotter.

Morgan was stunned, uncertain what to feel.

"You've been selected to train at the Academy of Assassins. We've received an invitation once a year since I took you in my care, but this year we've been receiving one a week." He set the lid aside, and pushed the box forward. "They are no longer accepting *no* for an answer."

"I'm not a true witch." She blurted out the automatic protest. "I don't belong there."

She hunched her shoulders, conscious of the runes carved into her back belying her claim, and absently brushed her fingertips across the torque around her neck, comforted when the metal warmed at her touch.

To be truthful, she didn't belong anywhere.

She only felt at home hunting.

It was what she was born to do.

"While most students are sponsored by previous members who have survived its training, the Academy itself issues invitations to those whom it needs—including warriors. I've taught you everything I can. I'm an old man, and I don't take students on lightly, but there is a fierceness in you, a determination to achieve the impossible that can't be matched. You don't relent until you get what you hunt. It's a rare quality."

Morgan knew they shared the thrill of the hunt, a sense of kinship and comradery, if not affection.

As if reading her thoughts, he sighed, his shoulders drooping, and she was shocked to see a crack in the wall the old man erected around himself. He rubbed a hand down his tired face, giving her a frank look. "I hate to see you go, but you can't hide here forever. You're too good. You're destined for more."

Morgan flinched at his gruff words—for no matter how much she didn't want to hear them, they were true. She was merely biding her time here.

He pushed the invitation closer to her. "Maybe I did you a

disservice not sending you to the school sooner, but I couldn't resist training you myself."

A rare smile briefly touched his lips, and she felt hollow at the finality of his words.

He picked up the envelope and handed it to her, giving her no choice but accept her new future.

"The Academy is the most prestigious school for our kind. Only the best of the best are ever invited."

A niggling suspicion danced at the back of her mind, too ridiculous to contemplate, but she couldn't dismiss it. "The soldiers tonight, the ones who've been here all week—they're from the school, aren't they?"

A crafty grin came and went from his face. "They are the elite. Each year, students apply to be trained as warriors, and must pass the trials to be allowed into the program. The training is tough, rigorous even for warriors with our enhanced skills. Only a fraction are mentally and physically equipped to fight, and even fewer graduate.

"For the first time, I allowed them to have their trials here to prove to you that you will fit into the school." He used one finger to touch the edge of the shoebox still on his desk, straightening it. "You have questions."

Morgan took his comment as permission to speak. "You said the school invites people. How did they even get my name?"

He gave a deep chuckle, the lines of his face creasing. "While this mansion is full of wards, the school itself is imbued with so much magic it's become sentient. The building itself does the selection. It knows who needs to be trained."

Morgan scowled, not liking the idea of being surrounded by a bunch of kids in training, and got down to the one question that mattered. "Do I have a choice?"

"No, you should've been sent off long before now. You need to train with people your age, and make contacts who could be invaluable later in life." He shook his head and chided her. "Hunting isn't meant to be a solitary occupation. Not only is it dangerous to hunt alone, it will get you killed. You need to find people you trust to fight at your side."

As if anticipating her protest, he shook his head, scowling when she opened her mouth. "Your hellhound isn't enough. You're good enough to be leading a team. We need you."

She unbent a little at his gruff tone, her thoughts flashing to Ascher, and her heart ached anew.

She doubted she could find anyone better and wondered if she would ever see him again.

Once anyone went through a rift, they needed magic to send them back Earthside—usually a once-in-a-lifetime opportunity.

Though she struggled to accept the truth, she had to face facts. It was doubtful he would ever return.

Maybe it was best to leave. The mansion was steeped with too many memories, very few of them good. Without Ascher, she wasn't sure it was worth staying any longer.

Her nerve endings tingled with excitement at finally being allowed to hunt with a real team, refusing to believe her anticipation had anything to do with seeing the soldiers again, then immediately hated herself. Her happiness at finally escaping the coven felt too much like a betrayal to Ascher.

A second away from accepting his decree, she stopped when she noticed the slight tension around his eyes, and her suspicions sharpened. "What are you not telling me?"

He leaned back in his chair, wove his fingers together and rested his hands on his chest, his eyes crafty as he gazed at her, reminding her there was a reason they called MacGregor Madman Moran. "What makes you think I'm hiding anything?"

His skill as a hunter was legendary, hundreds of students petitioning every year to train under him. In the beginning, he selected a few pupils, but they always failed his stringent training. After a while, he stopped trying.

Until her.

He was hard on her, but she understood why—he was training her to be the best, and was determined to do whatever it took to achieve it.

Though he was rough around the edges, tough beyond measure in his training methods, he'd softened when he realized she refused to accept defeat.

"I know you, old man. You know something you're not telling

me."

Humor danced in his eyes before he grew serious. "You're being called to the Academy now, not only to be trained, but to investigate who has been killing students. Three witches have died so far."

Morgan shoved away her roiling emotions like the soldier he trained her to be and focused on what would be her first assignment. "What do you know?"

He picked up a file from his desk and handed it over. "Not much. The headmistress sent over everything they've discovered, but the file is painfully thin. You will be on your own. I don't need to emphasize how important it is for you to find the killer quickly."

"Yes, sir." Her fingers itched to crack open the folder and get started. As if understanding her need, MacGregor nodded permission, and she flipped it open, then froze.

A graphic picture of a girl lying facedown was splashed across the page. Her shirt had been torn away, leaving her back exposed and looking incredibly vulnerable with the nobs of her spine standing out in stark relief.

That was not what captured her attention.

No, it was the markings brutally carved into her flesh.

Markings so similar to her own it was like looking in a mirror.

She flipped through the rest of the pictures.

Her brain pushed past her stunned shock to finally notice the differences. Half of the runes were incomplete. The girls must have perished before the killer had finished. Runes were a way for a witch to boost her power, but it was taboo to permanently mark themselves with them.

Human bodies weren't meant to hold so much magic. Eventually, their blood would become infected by the magic, and it would ultimately kill them. Only those with strong ties to the void could contain such power, but only one or two runes at most.

More would be pure suicide.

Magic had burned through the bodies of the girls in the photos, leaving the marks a black, charred mess. Streaks of blood had dried on the bodies, the girl's faces twisted in screams of terror and pain, evidence that they had suffered through the unbearable, excruciating torture.

She quickly flipped through all the pictures again, avoiding the lifeless eyes staring accusingly at her.

It should've been her.

She heard those words as clearly as if they shouted them.

When she lifted her head, it was to see MacGregor studying her with sharp eyes.

"Do we know how they were taken?" Her voice was hoarse as she waited for him to demand answers. Her mind flashed back to the wraith who tried to pull her through the rift, and couldn't help wondering if the two might be connected somehow.

It was too coincidental.

MacGregor shook his head. "We have no idea. It's something you need to figure out and stop."

"What are they trying to achieve?" The question was directed more at herself than him, but he answered anyway.

"That's what we want you to discover. We believe the attacks will increase. The school is under siege. With your age and training, you're the perfect agent to find out what's happening without alerting the kids…or the killer."

Morgan had two choices—leave and head out on her own, or go to the Academy.

Either way, she could no longer stay at the coven.

Life as a rogue hunter was rough, and not for the faint of heart. Most didn't live past their prime, but everything inside her rebelled at the thought of attending the Academy. One thing kept her from rejecting the invitation out of hand…if she went rogue, she had no doubt more girls would be brutally tortured, and it would be her fault.

"When do I leave?" Bands tightened around her chest as she reluctantly accepted her fate.

"Tomorrow." Sensing her need to get started, MacGregor waved her away and opened a file on his desk, his head bent as he went back to work. "Pack and be ready to leave by six."

She studied the clock. She had three hours to wash off the stink of the hunt, pack, and catch an hour of sleep. She studied his burly features one last time, then turned away, wondering if she would ever see him again.

It felt like good-bye.

When she reached the door, MacGregor spoke again. "Was your hunt successful tonight?"

She turned to see he had a pair of reading glasses perched at the tip of his nose, peering up at her over the rims with avid curiosity and a hint of envy, since he was rarely able to hunt anymore, being too inundated with running the coven.

Morgan hesitated, not sure how much to share. If he knew a demon had tried to kidnap her instead of kill her, he would assign her a contingent of guards, which was unacceptable. They would just get in her way. "The imp proved to be a challenge, but the mission was successful. He was dispatched back through the rift."

"Well done." MacGregor nodded, not expecting any other answer, but his gaze flickered down to her wounds, and his eyes narrowed, clearly not fooled. Her injuries were too vicious to have been inflicted by one small imp. But instead of confronting her, he returned to his task, silently dismissing her.

Morgan relaxed as she headed out the door, not bothered that he hadn't shown any concern over her injuries.

They were soldiers.

As long as she was standing, not missing a limb or bleeding to death, she was fine.

MacGregor taught her that.

She headed up three flights of stairs, mentally sorting through which weapons she should take with her.

Chapter Six

$\mathcal{M}$organ rolled out of bed the next morning, grimacing when she saw the sparkling, rust-colored dust covering every surface of her room. The runes crawled across her back, stilling the instant she woke, the weight of them pressing heavily against her skin.

A daily reminder of their presence.

The first time she woke to something wiggling under her skin, she freaked out, and refused to go back to sleep, reading book after book about runes.

Every mention said they were only used in two ways, either to boost power or for protection.

Since she had no access to magic, she gradually accepted the alternative.

During the third night without sleep, her body simply shut down, and she had no doubt it was the runes compelling her to rest.

Apparently they would protect her…even from herself, if needed.

Now, five years later, she'd grown used to it.

Almost.

She suspected her primordial side was emerging, trying to take over when she was at her weakest—when she fell into the unconsciousness of sleep. So far, the runes had blocked the change. At one time, Morgan prayed for this very thing, longing to fit in at the coven, but now she feared what kind of monster she might become. What could be so terrible that the protective runes were preventing the change? And would any of her remain if the markings lost the battle?

The sounds of the household waking jolted her away from her morbid thoughts.

The staff was preparing breakfast and maintaining the grounds, while the soldiers were changing shifts and preparing for another day of training.

And she would no longer be joining them.

Buoyant at the thought, Morgan shuffled sleepily toward the bathroom, suddenly excited to leave. As it did every morning, the torque around her neck warmed, stretched and twisted, spinning into a delicate chain with a silver charm…of a sparkling shoe.

She narrowed her eyes for a few seconds, then snorted at the foolishness. "Cinderella. Except I'm not exactly going to a ball, and I don't need any prince to save me. I can do that all on my own."

She turned away from the mirror, stripping out of her clothes and unwrapping the bandages she'd placed over the worst of her injuries. The wounds were healed, leaving behind deep bruises that ached when she moved. Before nightfall, they will have faded as well.

She tossed the bloodied bandages into the garbage next to last night's outfit and plucked a shirt and pair of pants out of her dresser, not bothering to look at what she grabbed. No need, when the only clothes she owned were T-shirts and black leather pants.

With an eye on the clock, Morgan pulled an old, worn duffel bag out from under the bed and set it on top of the mattress. In minutes, she had all her clothes packed, but it took longer to decide which weapons to take. She couldn't bring them all, because only a fraction of them would fit in the bag. After a few seconds of indecision, she removed half the clothes, leaving her with four outfits and enough room to add another set of knifes, a group of throwing stars, half a dozen daggers, and a second rope of pliable metal.

After a short battle, she managed to pull the straining zipper shut and hefted the bag over her shoulder, staggering slightly under the weight, staring regretfully down at the double broadswords, the worn staff she trained with when she first arrived, two dozen smaller blades of different types and styles, and the three different types of bows left on the bed. There simply wasn't a way for her to sneak them inside the Academy without being spotted.

With one last sweep of the room that had been home for the past ten years of her life, she quietly closed the door and headed down the stairs. Knowing she only had a few more minutes, Morgan hurried outside, managing to dodge the patrols with ease as she slipped into the forest.

She raced through the trees, the duffel heavy against her back, until she reached a small clearing by an outcropping of stones. She rounded a large rock and spotted the small opening of the cave. Even before she entered, she knew Ascher wasn't at their normal meeting place.

Devastation stole her breath, and it was hard to swallow around the knot in her throat. For some reason, she expected to find him waiting for her like any other day. On unsteady legs, she turned away, almost unable to leave the cave, but she knew no amount of waiting would bring him back.

As she trudged toward the mansion, she was suddenly fiercely glad to be leaving. She couldn't bear to stay now that he was gone. When the mansion came into view, she could barely control the need to tear into anyone stupid enough to mess with her. As if sensing her volatile mood, none of the soldiers approached as she headed up the stairs of the mansion—much to her disappointment.

She came to a stop outside MacGregor's study and closed her eyes, feeling defeated. If she accepted this assignment and walked out the door, she could never return.

Then she stiffened her spine.

If she learned what was killing those girls, she might be able to trace back what happened to her, and maybe recall her missing years.

The temptation was too great to resist.

Inhaling deeply, she lifted her chin, pushed back her shoulders and knocked on the door.

"Enter."

Recognizing a command when she heard one, Morgan twisted the knob and did as instructed. MacGregor stood in front of the fire, his hands behind his back as he gazed down at the flames. "I wasn't sure you were going to come in or not."

Morgan decided to be truthful. "I wasn't sure myself."

MacGregor turned toward her with a heavy sigh, his bushy brows lowered. "I almost wished you'd changed your mind."

"Sir—"

"Bah," he waved a hand and headed toward his desk. "Forgive a sentimental old fool." When he turned to face her again, a hardened warrior stood before her. He scanned her from head to foot and nodded. "You'll do. Ready?"

It wasn't a question, but Morgan snapped to attention.

He beckoned her forward. "Stand here."

Curious, she followed him to the corner of the room, stopping before a clouded mirror. It looked centuries old, and she'd never given it a second thought. The golden frame was tarnished and flaked, the glass itself warped.

MacGregor reached out and tapped the glass twice.

The image wavered with a silvery ripple. Once it hit the frame, seven sigils etched into the wood began to shimmer, the markings so faded and worn she hadn't even noticed them. As the sigils began to glow, the images in the mirror solidified, revealing a whole new world.

"A transportation spell?" She shot a questioning look at MacGregor. She never heard of such a thing.

He smirked and shook his head. "Good guess, but this is something even rarer."

She glanced back at the mirror, and her mouth fell open. "Mirror magic."

MacGregor's chest puffed up, and he smiled proudly, tickled at sharing one of the secrets of the coven with her. "The older covens had these mirrors installed when the buildings were constructed. Very few people can activate them. It takes a special gift few possess and a lot of magic to create, so this mode of transportation has fallen out of practice, not to mention not everyone can pass through them without suffering side effects. The school occasionally uses them for emergencies."

She eyed the mirror with trepidation. "How does it work?"

"Pure primordial magic. You must focus on the location you want when you activate the spell. People can become lost inside the void if they aren't careful."

Not a comforting thought. This type of travel also meant the human side of her would be briefly poisoned when the otherworldly magic came into contact with her skin. "Good to know."

He waved a hand at her. "No worries, lass. A…" Color filled his cheeks, his tone a bit gruff as he tugged at his shirt collar. "…friend from long ago crafted this mirror. It leads directly to the Academy."

Morgan could only nod. Taking a deep breath, she hesitated, not sure how to say goodbye to the old man who meant so much to her. Before she could turn, a rough hand settled on her back, helping her along by shoving her through the portal.

"Goodbye, lassie, and good luck."

Stifling her sudden scream, she instinctively brought up her arms and braced for impact. And fell right through the mirror instead. The world around her shifted and spun, shadows darkened her vision, and she realized she was standing inside the void. Clouds drifted in the distance like a school of fish, resembling tiny flecks of shimmering metal. As the shadows began to thicken, she could almost swear something shifted inside the gloom. Before she could investigate further, the runes on her back dug into her skin, the necklace warmed around her throat, and she felt herself tugged toward a bright light.

She expected her skin to burn as the light engulfed her.

Instead, she was unceremoniously spit out on the other end of the portal. She tripped, then caught herself, her heavy bag nearly overbalancing her. When she whirled, the giant wall mirror was already fading, giving her one last image of MacGregor standing alone in his study before he vanished. The sigils on the frame went cold as the magic powering the spell drained away, leaving behind nothing more than a giant mirror, her image reflected back at her, her small body almost lost in the gigantic room.

Turning slowly, she saw a series of steps leading up three stories, the stairs stretching nearly as wide as the room. Ten-foot-wide arched openings were on either side of the room on each level. She couldn't see the top floor.

The place was a weird combination of a castle and a school. Despite being deserted, the Academy smelled of teenagers, sweat and hope, hormones and anxiety, and a healthy dose of unrepentant lust. The humidity made her feel like she was breathing in more than air.

Even simply standing in the entryway made her skin tingle with the magic imbued into the very stones.

A light breeze swept through the room, wrapping around her in welcome. She bowed her head as a sense of belonging settled into her bones. The runes relaxed their hold, and tension eased out of her shoulders.

The peace was shattered when the massive door to her left creaked open. Morgan reflexively stepped into the shadows, hefting her bag higher on her shoulders, not sure what to expect when a group of people entered.

The kids were obviously students, chatting and laughing animatedly. They walked past her, none of them even acknowledging her existence, allowing her to study them freely.

Four girls stood out, obviously the leaders of the pack, their pink pastel outfits custom designed. Unable to help herself, her lips curled in disgust. How were they supposed to fight and defend themselves in skirts so short their girly parts were almost showing? Not to mention the material was so thin, it offered no protection from claws and teeth.

Behind them, the only two guys in the group were hauling at least ten bags of luggage each, struggling to juggle everything and still keep up with the group. One girl noticed the commotion and waved her hand. The two guys carefully set everything down by the door before hurrying to catch up with the others.

As they began to climb the stairs, a lanky young kid hurried into the room after them, tripping over the luggage left by the door, and sending the baggage flying like bowling pins. The loud clatter caused everyone to turn, and the four girls in the group scowled.

The kid was beyond skinny, about Morgan's height, but all arms and legs. As he straightened and looked around the room, his eyes landed on her and he blushed a deep red. "Sorry. Sorry."

He jumped and lurched around the scattered bags, nearly tripping again in the process.

One of the witches whirled to face him. "Why don't you watch where you're going, wizard? Or can't you manage even that much control?"

The kid went white, turning his skin splotchy, his eyes dropping to the floor. "I don't want trouble."

"Of course you don't. You know you won't win." The snide comment was full of malice, spite sparkling in her eyes as the lead girl began to advance on him.

Morgan waited for the others to protest, someone to stand up for the kid, but they all appeared to be enjoying the show. The two guys stood behind the girls, their attention locked on the floor, and Morgan surmised they were often subjected to the same treatment.

Morgan waited for the kid to grow a pair, but he shrunk into himself when the four main girls began to circle him like birds of prey.

"Why do you persist in coming to a school where you don't belong?"

Magic built in the air, static dancing along her skin, and the runes began to warm.

Even as she watched, a red glow engulfed the tips of their fingers.

When the girls reached out, a spark leapt from their hands.

The guy flinched, a whimper escaping him. He squirmed, trying to get away, but another girl reached out, shocking him again.

"Why don't you defend yourself?" The lead girl smirked. "Oh, that's right. You don't have magic. You're nothing but a wizard. You can only play with spells."

Rage burned in Morgan's gut, her lips curling in dislike, the girls reminding her too much like the witches at the coven.

She'd put up with it for years before learning to fight back.

No more.

"Leave the kid alone."

The lead girl paused, her eyes sweeping the room, then locked on her. The rest followed her example. She scowled, tossing her blonde hair over her shoulders, a sneer twisting her face. "Or what?"

Morgan shrugged out from under the strap of her bag, letting it thunk to the floor, and placed her hands on her hips. "Or I'll make you."

She scanned the group of students to gauge the threat.

None of them were pure, so it gave her a slight advantage.

The majority of the females were witches with minor powers. The exceptions were the main four. The rest appeared content to watch.

She could work with that.

The blonde snorted, her annoyance clear. "You're only a soldier, nothing special. You should watch yourself. Your kind are a dime a dozen here, and easy to make disappear."

Exactly like the witches at the coven, they saw soldiers as beneath them. And they disliked her even more for confronting them about their bad behavior and ruining their fun.

It wasn't her place.

The blonde lifted a brow in challenge, then shoved the guy so hard he landed on his ass on the floor.

Something inside Morgan snapped.

Before she even registered what she was doing, she was moving. She pulled her blades and leapt the distance between them, standing protectively in front of the poor kid.

The girl stumbled back, her eyes bulging in fear, before quickly regaining her composure. Then her pale blue eyes narrowed dangerously. "You're going to pay for that, bitch."

Magic bloomed in the air.

Morgan dodged the first blow, tightening her grip on her weapons and slowly advancing.

The group mumbled uneasily and fell back.

The next spell slammed into her so hard, it stole her breath. Frost skated across her skin, and the runes burned and stretched in reaction. Instead of shattering the spell as they had in the past, the symbols swirled, changed shapes and consumed the magic nipping along her skin.

When she didn't freeze solid, the blonde gave a squeak, tripping over her own feet as she scrambled backwards. "Impossible."

Morgan was a foot away when the witch screeched one word. "Protect!"

One of the guys leapt down a flight of stairs, coming to a stop between them.

A shifter.

Aggression filled the air, his vicious growl echoing against the stone. His eyes turned a feral shade of yellow, the human in him completely submerged. Claws tipped his fingers, his fangs were bared, while his predatory eyes tracked her every move.

"Break her legs." The blonde straightened, her chin lifted high so she could glare down at Morgan. "Let's see how well you can hunt when you can't walk."

Morgan automatically dropped into a fighting stance, refusing to retreat, knowing running would only make her look like prey. She met his gaze, refusing to back down, and braced herself for attack, but the small wolf didn't move.

To her shock, he lowered his head in submission.

"What the hell is going on?" the blonde snipped in fury at having her command denied.

The young guy at her back inched forward, nervously clearing his throat. "The school hires shifters to patrol the grounds. For those who can afford them, they can be contracted as personal bodyguards. Unfortunately, while shifters are dangerous, they can easily lose control. To protect themselves from retaliation, the witches collar them. They have no choice but to obey their masters...unless they meet someone more dominant." He gazed at her in awe. "Like you. He can't touch you."

Unnerved by his awed reaction, Morgan glanced at the emotionless kid before her, appalled to see his personality completely wiped away, and her lips flattened at the barbaric practice. "They're nothing more than slaves."

She put away her blades and approached the wolf. "I can remove the collar and offer you freedom."

Something flickered in his eyes, and the wolf melted down to a young guy once more. Instead of answering, she was completely mystified when he returned to his mistress's side.

"I don't understand."

"Of course you don't." The blonde glared at the wolf, who ducked his head and scurried up the stairs. If he had a tail, it would be tucked between his legs. "What the hell kind of freak are you?"

Morgan barely resisted flinching. "A mutt."

Everyone fell silent and gawked at her.

"I very much doubt that. No mutt can control a shifter the way you just did." The guy Morgan rescued stepped to her side, and lifted his chin to indicate the wolves. "The collars are a mark of ownership. It offers protection to the less dominant shifters. They see it as a mark of pride."

Morgan was appalled. "You're joking."

He shook his head, quickly stepping back when the blonde strutted forward like a ruffled hen, tugging at the bottom of her skirt. "You're going to regret this. When the headmistress learns you've attacked us, you will be kicked out faster than you can draw your weapons."

Morgan raised a brow, not intimidated in the least. "She'll know you're lying."

She appeared generally confused. "It will be my word, along with my friends', against yours."

"She'll know you're lying, because if I had attacked, you would be dead."

That seemed to take the school's princess aback, but she quickly recovered and raised her perfectly penciled brow. "You'll be kicked out of school even before it starts. I'll make sure of it."

"You can try."

Blondie scowled, clearly displeased that Morgan wasn't quaking in her boots. "What do you mean?"

Morgan pulled out her invitation.

The girl's shock made being sent to the Academy almost worth it.

"You've got to be shitting me. They must be desperate if they are dredging the bottom of the barrel for your kind. You're just another wannabe hunter." The witch scanned her from head to foot, dismissing her as a persona non grata.

Morgan nearly laughed at the insult. Her faded and scarred leathers saved her life more than once, and would again. They were stupid if they thought their opinion mattered.

After spending years trapped at the coven, these girls were minnows compared to the piranha who had tormented her throughout her teenage years.

She was there for a job, not to make friends.

She wasn't a hopeful youth, wishing to be assigned to the best covens. She'd been there, done that, and had the scars to prove it.

She wasn't a newbie to be swayed by the fear of being shunned.

Life outside these walls was not glorious.

It was blood and guts and death.

If they wanted to survive, they needed both strength and skills earned through hard work and sacrifice. It wasn't something they could acquire by bowing and scraping at the feet of snobs.

To taunt them, Morgan smiled and raised a brow.

The blonde growled under her breath. She whirled, tossing her hair over her shoulder. "Come. She's not worth the effort. Leave her to the hunters. They will eat her alive soon enough."

They sauntered off, clearly thinking they won the round.

Morgan only smiled mockingly at the dismissal, watching the witches scurry after the lead bitch. Morgan wasn't bothered by the threat. Hunters always thought she was easy prey…until they learned she wasn't so easy to beat into submission.

"You've made a powerful enemy. She's going to make your life hell."

The kid was painfully lean, and a touch of burnt anger rose from him, along with the sour stench of fear. "It was bound to happen sooner or later. No sense waiting for it."

The kid blinked repeatedly as he stared at her. Concerned, Morgan snapped her fingers in front of his face. "You all right? Should I get someone for you?"

He came back to himself, a blush darkening his cheeks. "No, I'm fine. I'm waiting for someone."

"Oh?" Not really curious, Morgan turned away and picked up her bag, intending to get settled in her room and begin her investigation. The sooner she found the killer, the sooner she could get out of there and on with her life.

"Yes, I'm waiting for a new student." He pulled a crumpled sheet out of his pants. "Morgan."

She stifled a sigh and turned to face him. "You found her."

"What?" The word was a squeak, and the girls who reached the top level turned to peer down at them. "That's not possible. You're supposed to be a guy. My new roommate."

The girls burst out laughing. "Maybe you'll get lucky having her as a roommate and lose your virginity, Neil."

Clearly pleased about getting in one last taunt, they turned away, once again chattering and tittering like a witless flock of birds, their good mood restored as they disappeared down the hall.

The kid blushed furiously, glancing at his feet, clearly miserable.

"Why don't you show me where to store my things, then give me a tour?"

His head snapped up. "But there's clearly been a mistake."

Morgan wanted to be gone, already missing her solitude at the coven, but stifled her feelings. "From what I heard, the Academy assigns rooms."

Neil nodded miserably. "I'll let the headmistress know about the mistake, and—"

"But the Academy doesn't make mistakes."

The guy blinked owlishly, his glasses crooked on his face, a lopsided smile quirked his lips. "You'll stay."

She reluctantly gave a nod and watched him race up the stairs, glancing repeatedly over his shoulder to see if she was following, nearly tripping over his feet in the process. "When the others find out that you stood up to Harper, you'll be a legend. You're going to love it here."

"Great." Her sarcasm bounced right off him, and Morgan sighed heavily.

She very much doubted it.

Chapter Seven

$\mathcal{A}$s they traveled down one hallway after another, Morgan's curiosity got the better of her. "Where is everyone?"

Despite herself, she was curious to encounter other hunters. Memories of the soldiers who fought so well at the coven flashed in her mind, and she quickly squashed the spark of excitement. After the confrontation with the witches, she was no longer eager to meet them.

They would be no different from every other hunter she'd met over the years, very much a product of their upbringing.

She would always be considered an outsider.

The students at the school had been training together for years, the bonds of friendship and loyalty cemented between them, and would not be extended to someone like her.

Neil peeked at her over his shoulder, possibly sensing her foul mood, then quickly turned around when he found her looking at him. "It's Sunday, but school doesn't officially begin for most students until next week. New students and hunters are the exception. You'll probably need to meet with advisors all week so they can gauge your level of skill." He smiled brightly. "Students will go through orientation and assessments this week, while hunters start their trials, so the teachers can decide who will be cut and who they will train. The majority of the students will arrive in stages during the week, so it's not all chaos. A few of the older students will show up early…those who want to get a head start, those who don't have anywhere else to be, while others come early so no one can usurp their rule."

The way his shoulders hunched, she didn't have to guess the category in which he fell.

"Are you really here to train as a hunter?"

Morgan pretended she didn't see him studying her out of the corner of his eye. She was used to the disbelief. "Yes."

He skidded to a stop outside a plain wood door, similar to dozens of others all down the hall. "Then you should know, even if you're a girl, it's not acceptable to harm a witch…it doesn't matter the provocation."

Morgan grinned, not caring if her smile wasn't friendly. "Oh, I'm well aware of the rules. Whatever punishment they want to hand down will be worth it."

He shook his head, his voice softening in warning. "No witch will ever hunt with you if you don't obey them."

Realizing he was trying to be helpful, she gentled her smile. "I have no intention of hunting with witches. I don't trust them to have my back, since they see us as cannon fodder."

He gaped like a fish, and she pointed to the door. "Is this my room?"

He nodded mutely.

Ignoring him, she pushed open the door. The room was utilitarian—a bed, a wardrobe and a matching desk and chair. An assortment of books was stacked at the edge. Everything was bland, no decorations of any kind. A doorway to the right led to a bathroom, connecting her room to the one next door. "Yours?"

"Yes." His voice was a squeak, and he cleared his throat. "It's not much. We should tell the headmistress. I'm sure we can find you a better room. Something away from the guys' dorms." He wrung his hands nervously, his feet shifting as he glanced at the doorway connecting their rooms.

"Where do the rest of the hunters stay?"

He blinked at her. "Here, of course."

Morgan dropped her bag on the mattress, yanking open the zipper. "Then it's decided."

She pulled out her weapons, organizing them on the bed, ignoring

Neil hovering in the doorway. She put her meager clothing in the wardrobe, the four outfits leaving it glaringly empty.

"Oh, wow."

Morgan whirled at his comment, lunging forward to quickly grab his wrists, stopping him before he could touch the weapons. Bones ground under her grip.

"Sorry. Sorry." The kid winced, watching her with wide eyes, and she quickly dropped his arm.

"Never touch another hunter's blades. Unless you know how to use the weapons, they are dangerous." She waved a hand at the bed. "You see these as our weapons, but you must never forget that the hunter themselves are the greatest threat. These are just tools, and they take years of practice to master. One slip and you can lose a hand...or your head."

When Neil looked ready to keel over, she kicked out the desk chair. "Maybe you should sit. You don't look well."

He groped for the inhaler in his pocket, fumbling to bring it up to his mouth. After two deep breaths, he recovered slightly, a little color returning to his face. He nervously pushed his glasses up his nose.

His body was thin, all angles, elbows and knees, his clothes too large for his frame, as if he'd recently lost weight. His skin was pale, a sheen of sweat clinging to his skin. His brown eyes sparkled feverishly, the whites slightly jaundiced. If she listened hard, she could hear his heart pounding irregularly in his chest.

"You're dying."

Neil gave a bitter laugh, struggling to stand, but ended up falling back on his ass in the chair. "All wizards are dying. It's the nature of our existence. While we're able to use magic better than any witch, it burns through us faster, because our bodies are unable to process it. The more we work spells, the more we become infected. Sicken. Die."

"Then stop using magic."

It seemed the logical choice.

"And what? Pretend we're human? Is it what you would do? You're female. You aren't a hunter, but you're here to train as one, even though you know it will eventually kill you. Would you quit?"

"No." Morgan blew out a breath, then studied him carefully. "So what are you doing to stop it from happening?"

Anger melted away from him, and he gave her a tentative smile. "Research."

"Which is why you put up with the abuse." And why he wouldn't stand up for himself and risk retaliation.

"The Academy was originally from the void, torn from the rift so long ago, no one remembers when or how it happened. There are nooks and crannies all over the castle. If there are answers, they will be here. Unfortunately, there are hundreds of rooms to search and thousands of relics. Plus, when the hunters aren't out saving the world, they're collecting artifacts which have been smuggled out of the Primordial World. They contain too much magic that could prove dangerous to both sides of the realm if they fell into the wrong hands. Sooner or later I'll run across the answer. Hopefully, it won't be too late."

Morgan wished she could offer him some hope, but she didn't know of anything to reverse the effects of magical poisoning.

"This is your first day. I should let you settle in." Neil rose and shuffled toward the door.

"You must know this place like the back of your hand. Do you have a map? Everyone else has been here for years and probably knows their way around this place blindfolded. I could use any advantage I can get." She needed to find a way to move around without being noticed.

Her first priority had to be finding the killer. The marks on her back were too similar to those in the pictures of the murdered girls. Whoever was doing this was searching for her, and wouldn't stop until they found her.

She had to make sure she found them first.

"Sure, there should be one in with your schedule."

Morgan followed where he pointed and spotted the embossed folder on her desk. "Thanks."

Neil smiled, and stopped by the door. "Just stay away from the basement. They don't want us down there. It's mostly full of relics and weapons from the other realm, and they patrol it regularly."

His warning piqued her curiosity, the mention of weapons a lure she couldn't resist. She opened the folder and pulled out her list of classes. Defense magic. Battle fighting. Creature hunting. Weapons training. Primordial knowledge. She breathed out a sigh of relief, glad she wasn't stuck with too many irrelevant classes.

"What's wrong?"

Morgan's head snapped up to see Neil staring at her in concern. "Nothing. I just expected to have field training—to actually go out on hunts."

"It's not allowed for First-Years. It's too dangerous. Field training is only allowed after your instructors pass you."

Disappointment sank its claws in her, but maybe it was for the best.

She needed to focus on her mission.

Training and hunting with other hunters was not important.

She couldn't allow the temptation to distract her.

Neil tapped his hand on the wall. "I'll leave you to it. Best read those books. You'll be needing the information for your classes."

Morgan turned, spied seven thick tomes and sighed again.

"Thanks…" But by the time she turned around, Neil was gone.

Dismissing him from her mind, she shut the door and quickly stashed her weapons about her person and the room, leaving behind a dozen or so weapons in her bag. She shoved it under her bed and picked up the crime folder. This time she flipped past the images and focused on the file.

The information was sparse, mostly stats pertaining to the victims—breed, years at the Academy, family.

Nothing stuck out as relevant to the case.

Reluctantly, she pulled out the pictures again, setting them side by side.

Besides the markings carved into their flesh, none of the girls were similar in any way.

Except they were all witches.

The glyphs carved along their spines were disturbingly similar to the markings scorched along her own back and shoulders.

The magic was burned right out of them, charring the bodies in the process.

Morgan didn't have a clue why she survived and they didn't, but whatever the reason, it couldn't be good.

It left her as a target for anyone else who made the same connections.

When nothing else leapt out at her, she closed the file with a sigh.

Not trusting her room to be private, Morgan stood and surveyed the small domain. Hiding places were few and far between. After a moment of debate, she carefully tilted the four-hundred-pound wardrobe up three inches and slid the folder underneath. She straightened, dusting off her hands and grinned at her own cleverness.

It was midday, too early to venture out and snoop around without attracting more attention. She grabbed one of the tomes and the map and made herself comfortable on the bed. After charting where the bodies were found, Morgan studied the floor plan...and couldn't make sense of anything. Doorways led into walls. Stairs vanished into ceilings. Hallways led into dead ends.

She scowled and tossed the map aside.

Someone must have sabotaged her copy.

It was the only explanation.

With a few hours left before nightfall, Morgan cracked open the dictionary-sized book and began to read. She wasn't far off in her guess. Thousands of creatures were listed in the books, some she'd never even heard or seen before. Underneath were listed their strengths and weaknesses, enemies and allies.

The writing was ancient. Though she didn't recognize the language, her brain translated it easily, another perk of her mysterious heritage, and she was soon fascinated by the categories of primordial creatures and their origins.

Only when she began squinting did she realize the sun had finally set. Rolling off the bed, she grabbed the map, scanning it one more time, then headed out. She took a left out the door, striding in the opposite direction from the main Academy. As she worked her way down the hall, traveling through one after another, the castle started to feel eerily familiar.

She studied the stone walls and archways, but she couldn't place where she'd seen them.

It was like a dream she couldn't quite remember.

She was so distracted, Morgan turned a corner and almost

smacked into a wall.

She stopped, completely confused. According to the map, there should have been a hall in front of her. When she turned to recount her steps and locate where she took a wrong turn, she gasped and flung herself backwards, barely saving herself from a nasty trip down a set of stairs that hadn't been there moments before.

Goosebumps spread down her arms as she turned full circle.

She was in an alcove, where the only direction she could go was down.

Pulling a blade from the sheath tucked into the back of her pants, she carefully crept down the stairs.

The staircase was narrow, while the steps were so shallow they were almost like a decline instead of actual stairs. The smell of dirt filled the cramped space, so she knew she was underground, the lights practically nonexistent.

MacGregor said the Academy was sentient, but she hadn't believed him until now, and she silently wondered where she was being led.

Then she ran into a black fog of complete and absolute darkness. Even with her keen eyesight she couldn't penetrate the sea of black. The darkness seemed to invade her senses, leaving her twisting and turning about in the underground maze, and a tightness clutched her chest at the thought of being permanently lost.

A second later a familiar stench reached her nose…a combination of charcoal and sulfur she associated with creatures from the void. She was no longer alone. Morgan put her back to the wall, not wanting to accidently stumble through a rift.

If a rift could be opened inside the school, it would make sense how something could slip inside the Academy walls and kill the girls.

Sounds became muted. Shadows shifted and swirled, distorting her vision further, and she knew whatever was downstairs with her was using some sort of trick to fool her mind.

It wanted her to run, wanted to chase her down like she was prey.

Not going to happen.

Morgan straightened, holding the blade close to her side. Inhaling deeply for courage, she resolutely closed her eyes, relying on her heightened senses to keep her alive. MacGregor blindfolded her for three weeks until she learned to defend herself blind.

To her surprise, the training came back to her like second nature.

She filtered the sounds, focusing on the threat. She pushed away from the wall, giving herself room to move. If she listened closely enough, the magic imbued in the stones of the Academy gave off a slight, almost imperceptible hum, allowing her to gauge the size of the room.

Something cackled behind her, and Morgan whirled, quickly giving chase, her only clue to the creature's location was a trailing scent of burned marshmallows.

Anger twisted in her gut as she imagined the other girls being lured downstairs, terrified and alone in the dark, knowing they were going to die horribly.

But something didn't make sense. The locations of the bodies were wrong. They were killed in their own rooms, behind locked doors, no signs of a forced entry.

No, whatever she was chasing, it wasn't her killer.

It enjoyed the thrill of the chase too much.

Which didn't mean she could allow his mischievous ways free rein at the school.

With her eyes closed, Morgan wasn't able to move fast enough to catch the bastard.

Which left her only one way to trap him.

Bait.

Morgan slowed, then stopped completely.

Only then did she hear it.

A faint tapping.

Above her.

Morgan lashed out, the tip of her blade striking true.

A loud squeal nearly ruptured her eardrums.

Or that was the excuse she used for not hearing the footsteps pounding toward her. Before she could turn, she was tackled to the ground, her blade spinning out of her hands. Cursing silently, Morgan brought up her knee, slamming it into something solid.

She expected her assailant to go flying from the strength of the blow, but he only grunted.

The shadows around the room began to lighten, barely giving her enough time to see the fist aimed to remove her head. She twisted to the side and watched his hand slam into stone. Instead of shattering bone, a swirl of dust and shards of rock shot into the air, peppering her face.

The tiny nicks stung.

She brought up her elbow, slamming it into her attacker's face.

He rocked backwards, and she brought up her feet, kicking him in the chest, giving herself precious room to move.

The darkness had almost retreated completely. Morgan flipped to her feet, whirled and snatched up her blade, twisting to face her attacker—and froze.

She recognized him immediately as the soldier from the forest who had so fascinated her.

Up close, he was even taller, more muscular than she imagined.

And more intimidating, his pale green eyes so intense she had a hard time looking away.

His face was rough, full of angles, almost too lean, the stubble along his jaw giving him a bad boy edge, his lips full and firm, and she imagined what it would feel like to have them caress her own.

"You." His voice was deep, a rough whisper that sent a shiver down her spine. He stared, lifting a hand as if to touch her and see if she was real, when the creature shot between them with a cackling laugh, diving for the only exit.

Her legs nearly went out from underneath her. The soldier reached for her, but Morgan ducked under his arm and scrambled after the black shadow, inexplicably afraid to have him touch her.

"Wait."

Morgan heard the soldier shout, but ignored his order. She increased her speed, not sure if she was running after the creature or away from the hunter. "He's getting away."

His curses echoed against the stones, and he quickly followed her almost soundlessly.

"How did he get in here?" Morgan darted around a corner, nearly clipping her shoulder on the tight turn.

"Nothing can get into the Academy. The place a veritable fortress, the wards too thick to allow anyone entry without being granted permission." The words were a growl of frustration, then he muttered, "He escaped from his cell."

For a wild moment, her mind flashed to the wraith who tried to kidnap her, and Morgan wondered if she had been sent to the Academy for her own protection.

No one could get in or out.

She would be safe.

Which made no sense.

No one else knew about her close escape.

That left her with an important question…if demons couldn't get inside the Academy, who was killing the students?

Chapter Eight

$\mathcal{M}$organ might be fast, but the soldier was faster, gradually edging closer. When the hall split into opposite directions, he reached forward and grabbed her elbow, nearly jerking her off her feet as he dragged her to a stop. His touch sent a wave of static up her arm, making her whole body feel alive. Instead of jerking away, she stared up at him mutely, barely resisting the urge to shuffle closer.

"Go left. At the end of the hall is a set of stairs that will lead you out of the basement."

It was an order.

Morgan scowled and jerked away, feeling foolish for allowing herself to be distracted, conscious of their captive getting away. "I can help."

"Now."

His roar was so fierce, Morgan was halfway down the passageway before she came to herself. He acted so much like MacGregor, every inch of him demanding and imperious, she'd automatically obeyed.

By the time she whirled to confront him, he was gone.

She debated for all of a second whether to follow, then shrugged. The morpheus creature, one of many different varieties, had the ability to muddle and confuse the senses, but they weren't considered dangerous, more of a nuisance. He could handle the beast on his own.

Resentful of being sent to her room like a child, Morgan rubbed her arm, where she still felt his touch, wishing she could erase it so easily.

Once on the ground floor, she saw only more and more gray stone.

Leaving her with no idea where in hell she was.

Curiosity got the better of her, and she gingerly touched the wall. A small, welcoming vibration from the stones greeted her. She jerked her hand away, rubbing her fingertips together, the nerve endings still tingling from the brief touch.

Too restless to return to her room, Morgan decided to try a quick experiment. Closing her eyes, she reached out until her fingers barely brushed the wall and blindly followed the path the castle chose.

Ten minutes later the vibration faded.

Her eyes popped open to see a long galley-style kitchen before her. Stovetops lined one wall, while dishwasher racks and a pantry that rivaled a grocery store stood opposite. Stainless steel islands marched down the center. At the far end of the room stood a walk-in freezer and three side-by-side refrigerators.

When no one rushed out to shoo her away, Morgan made a quick sandwich. As she put the supplies away, she caught a reflection of light from the corner of her eye. Grabbing her sandwich, she followed, and soon was standing in front of a small door, the upper portion covered with panes of glass that allowed her to see outside. It must be where they delivered supplies.

When she touched the knob, she expected to be blasted by wards. Instead, the door creaked open. Giving in to temptation, she walked outside into the night, the weight of her blades sitting comfortably within reach if anyone thought to mess with her.

Moonlight illuminated a small garden off in the distance, the slight mist giving the area a haunting feeling…like she had fallen through time. Lured forward, she entered the small hedge maze. Mythical statues of creatures were placed throughout, some so fierce she gave them wide birth, disturbed to feel as if their eyes were following her.

At the center of the maze was a nicely maintained clearing. A number of benches and tables were scattered about the space in clusters, and Morgan took a seat with her back against the hedges. A large gargoyle statue stood sentinel next to the bench.

Crouched, the gargoyle was massive. Standing, he would be close to seven feet tall. Giant wings arched well above his head and wrapped protectively around his back. Claws tipped his hands and feet, while a tail almost as long as he was tall lay coiled around his feet, and his pointed ears were almost covered by his long mane of hair. Carved from stone, the chiseled body was as impressive as it was intimidating—he was all muscle. Only a small loincloth granted him any privacy. One word came to mind as she stared at him—powerful. He had a big forehead, a prominent brow, his face perfectly proportioned, handsome even. His expression was both fierce and intense as he surveyed his domain.

Morgan felt surprisingly comforted, even protected in his shadow. The cool air felt refreshing after such a stuffy day...until she thought about the confrontation in the basement.

Despite her secret hope, the hunters in the school were no different from those at the coven, refusing to allow her to do her job because she was a girl.

To her disgust, they weren't even going to give her a chance.

Losing her appetite, she set her sandwich aside, and eyed the fearsome gargoyle. She could have sworn the statue had shifted, crouched closer to her, as if hearing her thoughts and offering comfort. After studying him for a full minute and nothing changed, she blamed her overactive imagination on the questionable light.

The statue was so lifelike, his expression so hungry, she reached out and ran a finger over the arched tip of his wings. "You're welcome to finish the sandwich."

At the sound of crunching gravel, she whirled, her mind flashing to the escaped prisoner. She grabbed for her blades but didn't pull them as she scanned the garden. The mist had thickened, the statues keeping her hyper-aware of her surroundings and what could be hiding in the shadows. When she saw nothing alarming, she reluctantly released her hold on her blades.

When Morgan turned, the sandwich was gone.

She stared in disbelief at the spot a moment longer, then glanced at the gargoyle and the slight curve to his lips and reluctantly shook her head. "It must have been an animal."

Her mind flashed to the textbook she'd just read. It told of a gorgon who turned paranormal creatures to stone, using them to stand guard. When danger threatened, they would come to life and protect the Academy. After they served their time, they were given their freedom. Many creatures would gladly agree to serve if it meant they didn't have to return to the primordial realm.

Morgan thought it was nonsense, but as she studied the statues, she wasn't so sure anymore.

Goosebumps raced along her skin as she imagined being trapped as a statue, frozen for years or even decades, forever watching life pass them by.

Too unnerved to go back to her dorm room and sleep, Morgan decided to search the outside of the school for weaknesses, and investigate how an intruder might enter.

As she rounded the front of the castle, the pristine, lush lawn changed to stone.

After a few more steps, she stopped short.

The Academy was a frickin' honest-to-goodness castle on a mountain.

The fortress was carved into the mountaintop, the three different levels spread out before her. The wall surrounding the castle was nearly a mile away. The main building where she stood was four stories high, the space massive, while the other levels of the sprawled Academy were only one or two floors. The ground floor appeared to be a garage, and a narrow, single-car, immaculately paved road emerged from the building to wind down the mountain, the trail quickly swallowed by trees. Beyond the wall was a vista of nothing but trees, stretching as far as she could see, and she couldn't help but be grateful she was sent by a more direct route.

She jogged toward the edge of the first ridge, noting the only thing preventing her from falling twenty feet to the next level was a stone guard rail.

The castle itself was pristine, the brown stones of the outer walls blending almost seamlessly into the surrounding trees. There were no stairs. The only way to reach the lower levels was to jump or head back inside and search for a way down. Morgan took the more direct path, and vaulted over the railing, landing lightly on her feet.

As she circled the school, searching for weaknesses, she discovered the grounds were swathed in wards. The back side of the castle had a large but narrow terrace, the edge slightly overhanging a sheer drop some several hundred feet down the mountainside. The jagged ravine was intimidating as hell, the steep incline strewn with tons of rock and a scraggily tree here or there. She took in the view of the world beyond, the vista breathtaking despite the danger. As the wind whipped and tugged at her clothing and hair, she could almost imagine she was flying.

The school was impregnable.

Either someone had to let the murderer inside...or someone inside was the culprit.

After spending most of her nights hunting, Morgan wasn't ready to succumb to sleep. It wasn't even midnight. She wandered around to the front again, searching for stairs, but found nothing. Gauging the distance to the lowest level, she grabbed the stone railing, swung her legs over the side, and dropped thirty feet to the ground, touching grass for the first time since the garden.

As she roamed the grounds, heading toward the wall surrounding the castle, a howl sounded in the distance.

Inside the walls.

Morgan looked behind her, back to the wall she'd just dropped from, but even with her enhanced strength, she couldn't jump thirty feet to safety. The walls were sanded smooth, leaving her with no hand or footholds to scale.

The lack of stairs now made sense.

The perfect trap.

Narrowing her eyes, she whirled and drew the two blades strapped to her thighs, then waited for the creatures to round the corner.

A massive black shadow sped toward her, low to the ground.

Then another.

And another.

Wolves.

Shit.

The mass of undulating fur and muscle charged toward her, their shapes growing impossibly larger, their hunger for the chase swelling in the air, causing her legs to twitch with the need to run.

Morgan crouched low as a tingle of magic danced over the lawn, the hairs on her arms lifting, and she changed her initial opinion.

Not wolves…werewolves.

They began to circle, their fur ruffled, their eyes glowing and fangs flashing, but instead of bloodlust as she expected, she only sensed their curiosity. Very carefully, Morgan sheathed her weapons and lifted her hands. To her surprise, the largest of the wolves detached from the shadows, pushing his way forward, urging the others away with a nip and growl.

It was only then that she understood…they were patrolling the grounds.

She studied them, but didn't see any collars.

Which meant hired guards.

As the large wolf neared, his fur appeared to be a sandy brown with white undertones, but his brown eyes were what startled her the most…human intelligence and wolf cunning stared boldly back at her.

The wolf's eyes reminded her of Ascher, and pain rippled through her so strongly, she had trouble swallowing, the loss of him too fresh not to feel as if she was being stabbed in the chest.

She cleared her throat and shrugged. "I mean you no harm. I was just taking a look around."

To her surprise, the wolf jerked his head, mock-nipping at her. Morgan stumbled back, thinking he was reprimanding her, but hesitated when he did it again. When he gave her a play bow, butt in the air, his tail waggling, understanding dawned, and she smiled when she realized she was being invited to run with the pack.

"Thank you." Tears sprang to her eyes, and she lowered her gaze, unable to explain how much the tiny gesture meant to her. Morgan took off, putting on a burst of speed, quickly catching up with the rest of the pack. She could tell which of the werewolves were more human and which were almost completely animal by the strength of the magic wafting off them. After five minutes of proving she could keep up with them, they stopped casting her suspicious looks and simply ran.

Every time she veered too far away from the pack to investigate something, the lead wolf would nip at her leg, going as far as to catch the fabric of her pants to pull her along when she ignored him. She was both exasperated and charmed by his antics.

Accepting that she wouldn't be allowed to roam on her own, she stayed with the group.

The run was rigorous, grueling to her human body, but she couldn't remember when she had so much fun.

After an hour, the head wolf led her away from the others. He guided her toward the garage, then pawed at the door. When she reached forward to open it, the wards on the building prickled against her skin, becoming almost painful. To her surprise, the door unlatched, granting them access. The first thing she saw was more than two dozen different types of vehicles, from vans to sports cars.

She expected the area to be pitch black, but the castle appeared to have an ambient glow, giving her enough light to see, but no matter how she searched, she couldn't find the source of the lights. When the wolf yipped, Morgan reluctantly turned and followed him through the twists and turns of the castle. They passed two more doors when she realized she was in the exact spot where she started…near the entrance to the garden.

When she stopped, the wolf used its shoulder against her leg to nudge her along.

The extra two hundred pounds made her stagger.

To keep upright, she sank her fingers into his fur, and they both froze.

She expected his fur to be wiry, but underneath was warm, silky fluff. When he didn't protest, her curiosity got the best of her, and she ran her fingers over his shoulders.

Very slowly, as if afraid to scare her, the wolf leaned against her more, tipping his head in silent invitation.

Morgan couldn't refuse.

She gently traced the tip of her finger over his ear, surprised by the thick, fuzzy fur. When she touched his head, she used her nails to reach his scalp, and the big doofus practically melted into a puddle at her feet.

Morgan was utterly charmed.

Magic tickled along her skin, enticing her closer, tempting her to linger.

After another five minutes, she sighed. "I'd better get inside before I'm missed."

The wolf grumbled, reluctantly gaining his feet.

When his eyes turned on her, she froze, completely forgetting he wasn't Ascher, that he was also part human…and she had been rubbing him like some domesticated dog.

He gave her a goofy grin, as if understanding her mortification, silently laughing at her. When he nudged her forward again, she obeyed, wishing she could outrun her chagrin so easily.

By the time she reached her room, her cheeks still burned with embarrassment, but she was pleasantly exhausted.

* * *

Morning came all too early, the sun a splash of mauve across the horizon. Training would begin in an hour, giving her time to warm up and get familiar with the school before the rest of the students arrived. Knowing she wouldn't be able to sleep any more, Morgan threw on some clothes, debated over which weapons to bring, and ultimately settled on less was more. After a quick study of the map, she went in search of the gym.

She entered the lit gymnasium cautiously, but found the room empty. A little more at ease, she scanned the area, immediately drawn to the wall full of weapons. While some of the lower weapons were clearly practice pieces, those higher on the wall, while well cared for, had been used for battle.

Though she would have love to study them more, none called to her. After another search of the room, Morgan set herself up in a corner near a radio. Turning it to a rock station, she stripped herself of weapons, closed her eyes and began her morning routine of stretching and warming her muscles. The blasting music helped her focus and organize her thoughts.

Forty minutes into her workout, students began to filter into the room. She studied them for a few minutes, then closed her eyes again, blocking out the stares, and began to pick up her pace. Only when she heard them begin practice did she forget about them. An hour later, two words broke her concentration.

"Holy shit."

Morgan's eyes popped open, and her gaze immediately locked on the same hunter she confronted last night, the same hunter who took out the minotaur with such ease.

Also the same hunter who banished her from the hunt.

He stood twenty feet away, facing her, mimicking her so effortlessly they were mirror images of each other, the flex and release of his muscles so smooth, it was almost mesmerizing. He was studying her face so intently, her skin began to prickle under the attention, and she faltered.

He stared at her as if he knew her and had waited a lifetime to find her.

The speaker stepped forward until he stood between them, his eyes flicking back and forth. "He's been unbeatable for years, developing moves I've never seen before...until now."

Morgan recognized the guy from the forest hunt—the archer.

He had longish black hair, wavy enough for her to imagine running her fingers through the strands, his blue eyes mischievous as he began to circle her. He came to a stop in front of her, a playful smirk on his face. "I'm Draven."

"Knock it off."

The leader scowled at his friend, looking seconds away from decking him, when he thought better of it and veered away, marching to the middle of the room. "Fall in."

Morgan jumped at the bark.

The students immediately snapped into line like soldiers, and she toweled away the light sweat gleaming on her skin.

"Best hurry, or he'll single you out." Draven rubbed his thumb over his mouth, as if to hide that he was speaking, and strolled away.

That's when she saw the other two hunters she recognized from the woods standing by the door, their relaxed poses belying their alert eyes.

And they were all watching her in varying degrees of fascination.

She could always tell a hunter by the way they carried themselves—all relaxed and ready for action at the least hint of trouble.

Deciding to play along, Morgan spared a remorseful glance at her weapons, but fell into line as ordered, distancing herself slightly from the others, not fully trusting them so close. She preferred to have room to move in case she needed to defend herself. Out of the thirty people in the room, there was only one other girl.

"I am your instructor. You will call me Kincade."

Morgan snapped her head around in shock and studied the guy who was not much older than her own age.

"You're here because you want to become hunters. You have all passed the first trials, which means we have already cut a third of you from the ranks. If you pass this class, you will get your wish. You will be here at dawn. Training will be held for three hours."

Kincade walked down the line, gazing and assessing each kid as he passed. Some students stood straighter, while others almost cowered. "You will fit your other classes around your hunting schedule. After lunch, you will report back and practice until supper. Those who are deemed worthy, who excel, will then be allowed out on assignment with us."

As he neared her end of the line, Morgan stiffened, unable to tear her eyes away from the way he prowled toward her.

"You will be judged on your skill. If, by the end of the next week, you are found worthy, you will be assigned to an elite team, where you will then train until you are one cohesive group." He came to stop in front of her, and slowly lifted his gaze, dragging his eyes up from her feet, over her legs, along her torso, not missing a detail, stopping to stare into her eyes.

The pale green of his gaze struck her like a blow.

They were hard.

Judgmental.

It was clear he didn't want her there.

And her spirits plummeted, her chest aching, as if she'd lost something important, which only served to piss her off.

Morgan stiffened, and lifted her chin. She would not allow the likes of him to drum her out. Catalina hadn't been able to destroy her, and she wouldn't give him the satisfaction either.

He scowled when she didn't cower, then turned sharply on his heel. "You will learn how to fight, as well as practice offensive driving, and rotate guard duty. You will be graded on your every move. When you are not here, I expect to see you in the library researching how to capture and kill the many different species who come through the rifts. This knowledge is what will ultimately save your life and that of your team."

Kincade strode away from the group, stopping in the center of the room and crossing his arms. "Everything you've learned over the last few years at the Academy will be put to use, but it's your wits that will keep you and your team alive. All your hard work, everything you worked for since you entered the Academy, will either pay off, or you will start over next year…if you think you can hack it."

Draven stepped forward, the other two guys following suit, lining up side by side with Kincade.

They were obviously a team.

The elite.

Perfect assassins.

They were all in their early twenties and battle-hardened, evident by the scars littering their bodies.

Any warmth in Draven's blue eyes turned frosty as he surveyed the students, assessing them with a practiced look. "Each elite team will sponsor anywhere from one to three trainees, which means that even if you pass the class, you might not be selected. We want the best of the best. We need to be able to trust you with our lives. Not everyone will fit into the dynamics of existing teams. You might have to wait for the right group to have an opening."

Since few hunters ever retired, an opening occurred only when one of them was killed.

"I want to see what everyone can do." Kincade dropped his arms and turned to walk off the mats, his men following. "Each one of you will face off with one of us."

When they reached the end of the mat, the men turned and waited.

"Shit. I hope I don't get Kincade."

Morgan glanced at the kid next to her, the guy maybe twenty and packed with solid muscles. He was speaking to a younger kid on the other side of him who, though smaller, was more tightly wound. She wouldn't write him off.

"Why?" Both guys turned toward her, eyeing her suspiciously. Then the larger one shrugged.

"Kincade's the best, but also the toughest on recruits. Everyone wants to be on his team, but fears it as well. They are assigned the most interesting and brutal cases. They pull off the impossible." A fervor to be one of them burned in his eyes. "You have your work cut out for you. There haven't been any huntresses in hundreds of years."

Morgan nodded soundlessly, uncomfortable being next to him, finding his tone somewhat snide.

They were supposed to be working toward becoming a team, but she suspected he would do whatever it took to earn a spot on a team, even if it meant cheating and taking out the competition.

Chapter Nine

"*A*ny volunteers?"

Morgan's head snapped forward to find Kincade's eyes locked on her...challenging her. She wondered if it was payback for interfering with his capture last night.

Taking a deep breath, she stepped onto the mat.

Ignoring his men, not even sparing them a glance, Kincade stalked toward her. He bent his head from side to side, flexed his shoulders, never once looking away from her, as if she was a dangerous animal.

Without hesitation, he launched himself at her. Morgan slid out of the way, lashing out with her foot, landing a blow to his thigh. She spun, barely dodging away from the fist aimed at her face, then leapt away from the hand aimed at her solar plexus.

She didn't spar with others very often, and had trouble gauging how much to pull her punches. He scowled at her, accurately guessing she was holding back, and threw himself into the battle, pushing her for more.

She played defensive for the first few minutes, familiarizing herself with his movements, taking a glancing blow to her jaw and shoulder in the process. When he swung to cuff her ear, she caught his arm and twisted, wrenching his shoulder, nearly taking him to the mat. She only let go when his foot lashed out and she flung herself out of the way.

He wasn't pulling his punches, instead doing his best to beat the crap out of her, like every other soldier she'd ever run across.

He didn't think she was worthy.

To hell with that.

She was done playing.

She picked up her speed, ran forward and dropped to the mat, sweeping his legs out from under him. He hit the mat hard, grunting when he smacked the floor. She kicked out, aiming for his face, only to have him bring both arms up to block her foot.

Her muscles warmed up while they moved back and forth, exchanging blows. The more they fought, the more liquid their movements became, until they were a blur, their dodging and thrusting a complicated dance.

While the students remained quiet, his teammates cheered at every blow she landed, heckling Kincade every time she blocked him.

As if sensing her distraction, he growled at her. "You're holding back."

Without giving her a chance to counter, he doubled his attack, until she could barely keep up with him. It was only then that she realized he had been going easy on her.

Like all of them, he was a creature of the primordial realm.

The next blow he landed was on her shoulder blade, right over the wound she took fighting the wraith. Her already protesting muscles screamed for mercy, and she struggled to remain upright.

While his hits were hard enough to crack bone, whatever he was doing also made his movements slightly sluggish. "No fair to use your powers in a fight."

Up until now he'd been mostly silent, and he scowled at her. "Fighting isn't fair. If you want fair, I suggest you go home."

His words stung, but he was right.

Morgan used her advantage of speed against him, which gave her a slight edge. Unfortunately, he was so good he still managed to land one blow for every two of hers. Her knuckles hurt like she was punching stone, the impact of her blows reverberating up her arms.

She danced away, circling him, searching for an opening.

She wouldn't win fighting him in a fair match. Since she couldn't guess his breed, she had no way of knowing his weaknesses. She was guessing something stone, but not an ogre or troll. She needed to restrict his movements, limit the force of his hits.

Not giving herself a second to hesitate, she ducked under the fist that had the power to crack her jaw, grabbed his wrist, then twisted and tossed him over her shoulder.

Only he reversed the grip, dragging her down with him.

They landed with an audible thud, the floor actually bouncing underneath them.

The men in his group cheered. Then he rolled until she was under him, every inch of him pressed against her, the warmth and weight of him threatening to distract her.

Their eyes locked, and he hesitated for a second, looking almost as confused as she felt.

Not willing to be distracted from the fight, she quickly jerked her arm up, slamming her elbow against his jaw.

"Son of a bitch." It felt like she cracked her bone instead of his face, her arm going numb.

Kincade grunted, but acted like she'd given him a love tap. Wanting to get away from him and her conflicting emotions, she heaved up, flinging him off her. Morgan didn't waste time and flipped to her feet.

To her chagrin, he spun effortlessly midair, landing on one knee, his foot planted, and then glared at her. "Stop holding back."

The growl made her flinch.

Like he knew something.

The threat of discovery had bloodlust thickening in her veins, and she curled her fingers into fists as she battled the need to rip him apart. To keep him safe, she backed away, putting distance between them. If he touched her again, she was afraid she would snap.

"What breed are you?"

Morgan gritted her teeth, wanting to refuse to answer, but knew they would find out eventually. "I'm a mutt."

She didn't know her heritage, and without proof, they would not categorize her as anything other than a mongrel.

For the first time, genuine emotions showed when he snorted. "You're the least mutt-like person I've ever met."

His comment was almost complimentary, his eyes warming as he slid them over her body, and she nearly tripped over her own feet.

She narrowed her eyes, her fury building at the blatant lie.

The runes on her back heated in warning, but Morgan paid them no attention. Moving almost faster than the eye could see, she darted forward, and used him as a punching bag. Though he was fast, he wasn't able to block all her blows. She ignored the pain, fed off it, gratified when he began to retreat.

"She could take him." The shifter spoke for the first time, the one who barely escaped being gouged by the minotaur, his voice sounding awed.

Morgan wasn't impressed.

She should already have won.

She studied her opponent, narrowing her eyes when he seemed to almost know her moves before she made them.

No one was that good.

While she was distracted, Kincade did something she wasn't expecting. He wrapped her in a bear hug, pinning her arms at her side, squeezing the breath out of her.

Only after a minute of struggling, when black dots began to dance in her vision, did she realize he was talking to her. "Stop."

She gave one last wrench, trying to fight free, but to no avail.

He picked her up off her feet and flung her to the ground, knocking what little remaining breath she had out of her. Her back arched off the mat, the pain nearly shutting down her brain. Not willing to give in to it, she slowly rolled to her side and pushed up on her feet, swaying as she tried to remain upright.

"Shit." Draven rubbed his jaw, and they all gaped at her in disbelief.

Kincade shook his head. "You're vicious and fearless. You don't know when to back down."

This time, his words didn't sound like a compliment.

"Those traits will get people around you killed."

For some reason, she felt like she'd let him down.

"You're used to the luxury of fighting with a team," she replied, "but you don't allow for those who are forced to fight alone. If I give up, it means I'm dead." Her legs became steadier as they began to circle again. "If I give up, it means I'm not doing my job, and humans will pay for my failure."

"It's suicidal." His disdain hurt more than the bruises on her already-aching body. "We can't risk you fighting on another team. I won't be responsible for you getting other people killed."

Morgan stood in stunned silence, unable to believe he was dismissing her on the first day. The back of her throat ached at being rejected once again.

"That's why you will be assigned to my team. If you can't learn to work with others, you will be dismissed." Her head snapped up to stare at him, uncertain she'd heard him correctly. "Understood?"

Morgan was poleaxed, and it took her another few seconds for it to sink in—that it had been a test—before she gathered her wits enough to give him a curt nod.

Morgan limped toward the edge of the mat and took a seat on the unforgiving, fold-out gym seats, watching Kincade and his team systematically beat the rest of the kids black and blue. The other students kept glancing at her, some with awe, some with pity, while a few were downright jealous.

She ignored them and watched her new team, her stomach fluttering at the prospect of working with Kincade and his men.

Not wanting to mess up this opportunity, she used the time to study how each one fought, cataloging their strengths and weaknesses.

The giant shifter took the next competitor. She expected him to use his strength and size to win, but he was more cunning and ruthless, landing two easy blows that dropped his opponent.

The elf strode out next, appearing bored with the whole process. After a quick perusal of his opponent, he didn't even wait for his student to attack, viciously taking him out with one blow, never once revealing any emotions.

The last member strode out for his match, the one who called himself Draven. Instead of a direct approach, he danced and played with his opponent. At first she thought he was giving the student a chance to fight back, but in the next second, he rendered his adversary unconscious, and the kid had to be dragged off the field.

They were all brutal and efficient and deadly.

Then it was Kincade's turn again. After a few minutes, she began to realize what bothered her about him—he wasn't mimicking her unique fighting style—they fought the same way. While her movements emphasized speed and agility, he changed them slightly to make the best use of his enhanced strength.

She couldn't help wondering who had taught him.

By the end of the second hour, everyone was groaning, sweating and cradling their bruised body parts, while the bastards had barely broken a sweat.

In the end, she was the only one assigned to Kincade's team.

Only two others were assigned a team at all.

While it was gratifying to be chosen, it would also make sneaking around all the more difficult.

After everyone had their asses handed to them, the hunters strode toward the center of the mat, not even winded. "Those assigned to a team—your first assignment will be tonight. Think of this as an internship, where you will get one chance to prove to us you really belong here. Study up and be ready to go. We will be leaving the compound at dusk. The remainder of you will remain behind on guard duty."

With that, they turned and headed toward the door.

The students began to file out...well, limp out.

Morgan detoured, quickly grabbing her weapons, ignoring the rest of the class. When she was the last one remaining, she headed toward the door.

Only to stop short when she saw all four of her new team members waiting for her.

When no one spoke, she shrugged. "When should I be ready to go?"

Draven's lips quirked in a smile, and he lazily pushed away from the wall. "We head out at dusk to clear a gaggle of gremlins out of an abandoned warehouse."

Morgan grimaced, and he laughed. "So I take it you've dealt with them before?"

She turned and began walking down the hall. "They stink, and if you touch them, that stench will follow you around for weeks. Not to mention they're a bitch to clear out. Miss just one, and they will infest the whole building again in a matter of days."

He winced when she mentioned their number one defense

mechanism, as if remembering his own experience of being doused in urine, and she couldn't help but chuckle when he fidgeted with his clothes.

As she turned the corner, strong fingers grabbed at her elbow, sending a bolt of static up her arm. She jerked away, instantly knowing who had touched her, disturbed by her instinctive urge to lean into him and seek more.

It was him.

Kincade.

"Don't." She wasn't used to people touching her.

After so many years of nothing but painful pinches or slaps or fists, any touch now made her uncomfortable.

Made her want things she couldn't have.

Like friends.

Or lovers.

While he obeyed, he wasn't deterred, keeping pace with her step for step, so close he was practically frog-marching her. "What were you doing in the basement last night?"

"Why were you there?" She countered. She didn't think he could be the killer, but she had to know.

"I was searching for missing artifacts. Weapons." He raised a challenging eyebrow at her. "Your turn."

The rest of the men fell silent, glancing between the two of them, none of them looking inclined to interfere, all seemingly fascinated by the exchange.

Except for the big man in the back. He kept his attention locked on her, the warmth in his eyes bringing heat to her cheeks. Uncomfortable under his regard, she quickly began walking again as she debated her answer. After a short, internal debate, she saw no reason to lie. "It's a new location. I went out to explore. Don't tell me the first thing you do when you're unfamiliar with your surroundings isn't to get the lay of the land."

He ignored her retort, his eyes narrowing as he stared at her. "Why the basement?"

She rolled her eyes at the interrogation, but decided to play along. "The school has a mind of its own, and I was curious enough to follow where it led."

Her answer only made him glower more.

Draven whistled, lifting his brows. "I can't say I expected that."

It was her turn to gawk at him. "What do you mean?"

"While the Academy is sentient at times, it hasn't been active in decades. It only obeys certain people."

"I wouldn't call leading me into a dark, dank dungeon obeying me exactly, especially when I didn't give it any orders." Although she protested, part of her mind hesitated. She had wanted to find out more about the school. Maybe it picked up on her intentions. Or maybe it wanted her down there to help capture the morpheus creature.

Her curiosity got the best of her, and she hesitantly asked the question she wasn't sure she wanted to know the answer to. "What kind of people?"

"A champion." The elf spoke for the first time, the spark of interest in his eyes sending a chill down her spine. There was nothing human in his look…more like a scientist examining a specimen, wanting to take her apart to see what made her tick.

She quickly turned away. "And what exactly is a champion?"

"A warrior who can control anything that originates in the void." He paused, his deep, forest green eyes softening slightly, his voice emerging as a soft whisper. "Royalty."

Morgan stared at the elf blankly, then she shook her head and picked up her steps. "That's a myth. Everyone with the royal bloodline died out more than a decade ago."

"Not everyone agrees." He spoke so softly, she almost missed it.

She wished she had.

As she turned the corner, the door to her room came into view, and she picked up her pace, practically jogging to get away. She grabbed the doorknob like a lifeline, blocking their entrance by standing in front of it. When no one seemed inclined to leave, she leaned against the doorjamb. "You're all awfully young to be training new recruits. Where are all the adults?"

"They are all assigned to covens and protecting the gates. While they're doing their duty, the kids are sent to the Academy to be trained and protected."

Morgan was appalled. "You take away their children?"

Kincade scowled down at her, and she winced, clearly having offending him.

"It is considered a privilege to be accepted into the Academy. They will receive the best training, and training is what will keep them alive out in the real world. Every year there are more and more humans, but fewer of us to protect them. Every creature who wants to remain Earthside has to serve their time. Those with training are ninety percent more likely to survive any confrontation with the creatures from the primordial realm. Lone hunters don't survive long. If given a choice for your child, what would you decide?"

Morgan lowered her eyes at his intensity.

He was right.

"Sorry." Needing time to gather her wits, wanting to escape their attention and rebuild the walls between them, she open the door and sidled through the small crack. They were muddying her thoughts, and she couldn't have them distracting her.

But before she could shut the door firmly, a hand slapped against the wood. She jerked her head up, her senses crackling to life, her hand automatically dropping to her knife, when she saw Kincade's maddening face peering through the narrow opening. "What do you want?"

"You live here?"

Morgan rolled her eyes. "What gave it away?"

His eyes narrowed dangerously.

"Open the door."

The rough voice was an order, and before she could check herself, she obeyed. By the time her brain caught up with her actions, Kincade shoved his foot in the crack of the door, and then it was too late.

All four men barged into her room.

"What the hell!" It was all she could do not to drop into a crouch, her hands itching for her blades to draw blood.

The men kept a careful eye on her as they systematically took apart her room, one even slipping into the bathroom to search.

"What are you doing?"

In seconds, they began to pull out the weapons she'd so carefully hidden and set them across the mattress.

"Again. What the hell?!?" Morgan straightened, turning to keep them all in sight.

None of them answered her or even acknowledged her existence. Very carefully, she crossed her arms and leaned against the wall to watch, knowing there was nothing she could do to stop them if she wanted to stay at the Academy.

It was proof of why others couldn't be trusted.

Why she preferred her own company.

She would say they were thorough, though. They found the blades under the bed, the dresser, and the one behind the door—even the one under her chair. They found the blade above the dresser, the one hidden in the curtains, the one she'd stashed under her pillow. Another guy slipped under the bed, locating the second weapon, and pulled out her bag of backups. The big guy cast her a startled look but quickly dropped his gaze, a slight blush on his cheeks as he slipped his hand between her mattresses and pulled out another. He studied the weapon in his hand, brushing his fingers reverently over the pummel. She shivered, easily imagining how he would be with a woman. Almost reluctantly, he gently placed the blade next to all the others.

The bed was covered when they were done.

"Jesus." Draven ran a hand over his head in awe, gazing at her small arsenal. "Were you expecting to go to war?"

All the guys looked at her and she could only shrug, feeling slightly embarrassed and a tad defensive. "What? A girl's got to protect herself."

"Against what?" the elf asked, watching her appraisingly, more curious than ever.

Kincade didn't join in the teasing. "Is this all of them?"

"Shouldn't I at least know the names of the guys who've had their hands in my underwear drawer?"

Draven gave her a wicked grin, sauntering forward to whisper in her ear. "Any time you want to return the favor and search my drawers, I'm game."

Morgan couldn't help it, she grinned and pulled out the ten-inch blade she kept at her lower back, holding it under his chin, then trailed it down his chest suggestively. His laughter faded, his eyes turning cold as he backed away and raised his arms in surrender. "I would, but I doubt your blade would be able to compete with mine."

He blinked once, then burst out laughing. "Oh, I like you. I truly do."

Without taking his eyes away from hers, he pointed around the room. "I'm Draven. The asshole is Kincade. The big, strong silent type there is Ryder. The fairy is Atlas."

"Tuatha Dé Danann." The elf scowled at Draven before giving her a short bow.

"Is. This. All. Of. Them?"

Much to her consternation, Kincade was not to be sidetracked. Conceding to the inevitable, she shrugged. "Mostly."

One of the guys snorted, then cleared his throat when Kincade glared at the lot of them.

"What else?"

Morgan gave one last ditch attempt to distract him. "I'm going to miss my orientation."

"Then I suggest you stop stalling."

She slumped against the wall in defeat. "You missed the one taped to the top of the inside of the closet, the one in the light fixture and the one in the bookshelf."

Instead of being appeased, Kincade crossed his arms. "What else? Or did you want me to do a more thorough search myself?"

Hating the thought of him touching her things, she mimicked his stance and looked down, admiring the tip of her boots. "You missed the one in my left boot, and one in my jacket on the back of the door."

"Jesus." Draven shook his head in awe, while the other three retrieved the remainder of her weapons.

"And the bathroom?"

Bastard.

"Since when is it illegal for hunters to bring their own weapons?"

When he made to enter her bathroom, she sighed in defeat. "One in the toilet tank, one under it, another under the sink, taped behind the pipes."

"She's even worse than you, Kincade." Draven sang from the bathroom, quickly returning with her small stash.

When he finally turned away from her, he studied her small armory.

He touched a few of them—she wanted to say admired them, but he didn't say it in so many words. When he straightened, he gave her a hard look. "You are responsible for your weapons. You're here as a hunter. Don't let me catch you fighting another hunter using your weapons without supervision, or you will be penalized."

Surprise shot through her, along with a curl of pleasure that she would be allowed to keep her blades—then she realized why he'd searched her room in the first place. Her good mood vanished, and her fascination with him cooled, offended by his implications. "I'm not your thief."

His eyes softened, but before he could speak, Neil stopped in the doorway of their shared bathroom. His face brightened when he saw her, then he scowled when he spotted the others. His crooked glasses gave him a harmless, hapless expression, but he appeared willing to help her if she needed it, a small spark of energy snapping between his fingertips, but the frightened, glazed look in his eyes said he was praying she didn't. "You okay?"

"Of course. In fact, they were just leaving." She grabbed the door and held it open, giving them a pointed look. "Right?"

They obediently dragged their feet to the door…all but Kincade.

He continued to stare at Neil, his eyes a frosty, hard green.

It made all his critical glances at her look like he was a lovesick fool.

When his eyes swept over her, she quickly lowered her gaze, uncomfortable with her train of thought.

She heard his boot scuffle over the floor as he neared, and cursed when he stopped in front of her, resting his hand on the edge of the door above her head, leaning into her, silently demanding she acknowledge him.

Morgan wanted to resist the temptation of him, resist the heat radiating off him that invited her closer, the fresh earth smell of warm stone making her want to linger and stretch against him to bask in his warmth.

When the silence stretched awkwardly, she reluctantly raked her eyes up, skimming over his impressive chest, those broad shoulders begging her hands to explore, the stubble on his jaw making her fingers itch to touch, past those luscious lips so temptingly close, and landed on green eyes so warm she found her staunch resolve to maintain her distance softening. "Huh?"

His lips quirked at her reaction, and she stiffened her spine, wincing at her obvious response to his nearness. "We will meet out front at dusk. Be prepared to move."

He walked out the door, passing much closer than necessary before disappearing down the hall.

Leaving her completely flustered and confused at the mixed signals he was throwing at her.

"I thought I would walk you to orientation, maybe give you a few pointers."

When she peered at Neil, he was politely staring at the bed, sparing her embarrassment.

She could've kissed him. "Sure, that would be great. Why don't I take a quick shower and meet you in the hall in five minutes? I'll knock on the door when I'm done."

"Sure." His pale skin flushed at the mention of their shared shower, and he hastily backed away, tripping over his own feet in the process. "Sure. I'll…uh…just…um…get ready."

Chapter Ten

$\mathcal{M}$organ took the fastest shower on record, but still ended up being five minutes late when she and Neil stopped outside the orientation hall. She grabbed the long hanks of her hair, wringing out the excess water before dragging the strands back in a sloppy ponytail.

"You'll do fine. Mistress McKay is tough, but fair, if you give her a chance. Everyone in the school has been in at least one of her classes. I'll be there if you need me."

She glanced at Neil in surprise. "You're coming in?"

He blushed at her blunt question, self-consciously running a hand over his choppy hair, which looked like he'd hacked off the ends himself. "While hunters join teams, witches have covens. Often, older students watch orientation, both to keep an eye on the competition and suss out potential members as well."

Her spirits plummeted. "Great."

Exactly what she needed—more attention.

"It's really painless." Neil appeared so earnest, sweetly trying to ease her apprehension, that she gave him a strained smile.

But he was wrong.

In her experience, magic always hurt.

"Let's get this over with." She pushed open the door, and immediately became the center of attention of the whole assembly. There had to be over a hundred people in the hall.

She located Harper and her entourage almost instantly, and barely stifled her sigh at the coming humiliation. While a few adults were in attendance—possibly other teachers—the rest of the room was filled with teenagers of all ages. In the front of the stadium-like classroom sat those barely out of grade school.

"Miss Moran, it's good of you to join us." An older woman, her light brown hair scraped back from her face and secured at the base of her neck, wore a dour expression at odds with her youthful complexion, barely spared her a glance before returning her attention to her desk. "Please take a seat."

Neil gave her a friendly nudge with his shoulder, then took up position near the door, leaning awkwardly against the wall.

Ignoring the snickers from the balcony, Morgan surveyed the room, sighing when she saw the only seat available was front and center. Nervous energy swirled in the auditorium, the younger students shifting away from her as she walked past them, giving her a moue of distaste, as if they smelled something foul.

Little snots.

When she refused to look away, a few of them shifted uncomfortably and quickly dropped their gazes. When she sat, everyone scooted their chairs away from her. Morgan simply smiled, relaxed in her chair, and stretched out her legs, crossing her feet at her ankles.

The kids were a mixture of guys and girls. What didn't surprise her was neither side, hunters or witches, wanted anything to do with her.

Prejudice was indoctrinated into them young.

"Tonya."

A cute little girl in a pretty white dress and a shimmering blue sash around her waist bounced to her feet when her name was called. She practically skipped to the front of the room, her ponytail bobbing with confidence as she stopped in the center of a circle of ancient sigils chiseled into the stone floor. Never once had she doubted her place in the world.

Mistress McKay gave an elegant wave of her arm, and light flashed up from the sigils as magic swelled throughout the room. The air around the circle shimmered into view, sparkling a faint red where it rose up from the floor. "What is your craft?"

"Earth, Mistress."

"Very well." McKay wrote something down, then straightened. "Begin."

The kid scattered something across the floor, then held out her hands, her fingers splayed wide. She narrowed her eyes, mashing her lips together as she concentrated. Very lightly, a trickle of magic danced against Morgan's skin. After a good five minutes, three sunflower plants began to sprout. Without soil. Without water. Without sun. In ten minutes, a foot-tall plant stood before them. The girl gave a pleased nod and dropped her hands, but the use of magic had exhausted her, leaving her skin pale and coated with a light sheen of sweat.

Two more kids were picked. One made a book fly in a small circle, while another soaked the floor when he made it rain. Inside the room. With nothing but his thoughts.

Then the first hunter was selected.

"Chase."

Instead of heading toward the circle, a slim guy strutted toward the desk and placed his hand on a rock.

Nothing happened.

McKay studied her watch. After five minutes, she gave a nod. "Step back."

Curious, Morgan leaned forward, but still saw nothing but a rock.

Everyone else appeared satisfied.

"Morgan Moran."

Though she expected to be called, hearing her name made her jump. Snide chuckles rose from the gallery, but she ignored them.

"Send her home where she belongs."

McKay scanned the crowd, her expression so severe, it was enough to silence the hecklers.

"Moran. I used to hunt with a Jack Moran."

"He must have liked you, since you survived." Morgan spoke without thinking. She had to be one tough broad to still be alive, strong in her own right, after hunting with Madman Moran. She wasn't what Morgan would have expected, especially since the woman barely reached her shoulders, an itty-bitty thing who looked like she belonged in an ivory tower protected by dragons.

McKay turned toward her with an inscrutable expression. She

could almost be pretty if she let down her hair and smiled. "I see you know him well."

Wishing she'd kept her mouth shut, Morgan shrugged. "He raised me."

Now she got a reaction.

McKay's eyebrows rose in surprise, and the first spark of interest lightened her almost silver eyes. Sharp. Intelligent. "He must have liked you…since you survived."

Morgan couldn't help it, she grinned at McKay's identical reply. "It was a close thing."

McKay's lips kicked up at the corners before she glanced down. Morgan could understand why the MacGregor would hunt with her. She was no-nonsense like him, and hated the bullshit.

"You're listed as a hunter?" She frowned, looking at Morgan in question, as if expecting her to protest.

"Correct." Morgan lifted her chin, waiting for the snub.

Witches treated hunters as second-class citizens.

She shouldn't expect anything else, even from the teachers.

McKay merely hummed, leaning forward to take notes. The front of her shirt parted slightly, enough for Morgan to see four wicked slashes marring the front of her chest, trailing over her collarbone to disappear into the shirt.

They were deep.

Brutal.

It was a miracle she'd survived.

"Impressive." Without looking up, McKay's whisper was hardly more than a breath of air. "Jack doesn't suffer fools gladly, and he wouldn't have sent you here if you didn't have what it takes."

McKay straightened as if nothing happened, and pointed her pen at the rock. "Place your hand on the stone."

Morgan snapped to attention, unconsciously clenching her fingers into a fist. "Why?"

Instead of impatience, McKay gave her a slight smile. "We're here to test your level of magic. This rock is from the primordial realm and reacts to magic."

"I don't practice." Morgan barely resisted shoving her hands behind her back.

"Not a problem. If you place your hand down, we can confirm

that you have no magic and adjust accordingly."

That was the problem.

She had magic, but she refused to use it—unheard of for a witch.

Morgan reached up, gripping the torque tightly and sent up a silent prayer.

Her fingers hovered over the stone, half expecting it to reach out and bite her. Instead, she sensed nothing from the rock. It could have been any one of the million used to build the Academy. Taking a deep breath, she pushed her hand down.

The rock warmed, and she tried to jerk her hand back, but it stubbornly remained stuck.

Primordial magic swarmed up her arm, spreading heat in its wake, and began to burn mercilessly when it hit the runes engraved into her flesh, the magic battling for possession of her soul. The world around her wavered and darkened, her insides twisting until she feared she was going to be sucked down into the rock.

The torque tightened, diverting the worst of the magic.

It wasn't enough.

Her back felt as if it was being fileted from her body, the runes twisting and worming under her skin, fighting against the pull, the forces trying to tear her apart.

Rage tore through her, a primal scream of pain and fury crawled up her throat. "No!"

The stone under her hand cracked. The world around her rippled, swirled and dipped before slowly righting itself. It took all her concentration to hold back the feral urge to give into the dark side she'd always denied.

She would not turn into a primordial monster.

After three controlled breaths, the wild impulse gradually faded, and she felt like herself once again. When the world came back into focus, the rock under her hand was nothing more than dust. Mortification burned through her, and Morgan dusted off her hands.

"Sorry." Her throat was scratchy when she spoke, her stomach still churning as she pried her other hand away from her torque.

The room was deathly quiet.

McKay studied what remained of her rock, then glanced up at her curiously. "You have magic."

"Not active." Morgan frantically shook her head. "Dormant

magic I can't access."

McKay didn't look convinced. "What was your craft?"

Morgan had never chosen a focus of study—no point when she wasn't able to do anything about it but writhe in pain whenever she tried to access it. MacGregor insisted she learn the basics, and she humored him, but she had no interest in learning more.

"I'm a null. The only talent I have is the ability to break any spell or curse." Morgan refused to have the future she had mapped out before her altered. She was too good a hunter to be sidetracked. She couldn't bear to be trapped in a future she detested. "I can't cast."

An inability to cast was tantamount to a terminal illness for witches.

Some of the teachers who had crowded closer to get a better look now turned away in pity, not wanting to get too near, as if her inability to cast was catching.

McKay didn't appear convinced, but after studying Morgan for another few minutes, she reluctantly conceded. "Very well. You won't be expected to attend classes, but I do expect you to read the books I assign you, and give me detailed reports on what you've learned. You will stop by my office after your evening practice, and we will go over your assignments."

Her relief was so intense her legs nearly dropped out from under her.

"Thank you." Morgan wasn't sure if she'd spoken out loud or not, but McKay gave a slight tip of her head in acknowledgment.

That's when Morgan knew McKay was covering for her.

She knew the truth.

Or she suspected.

Morgan had more than just basic magic.

And the runes on her back were growing in power, enhancing her abilities.

Sooner or later, she would no longer be able to hide it from everyone else.

Even though the runes were covered, the thin shirt she wore felt like a flimsy barrier. She turned on her heel and darted from the room, ignoring Neil's shout to wait.

Chapter Eleven

*T*he walls of the Academy began to close in on her, and Morgan desperately needed to escape the suffocating primordial magic.

She didn't trust it.

Worse…she didn't trust herself near it.

She clutched the metal around her neck for reassurance. As if her touch activated it, the torque began to stretch and twirl, reshaping into a chandelier necklace with little daggers hanging from each twisted metal strand—a silent vow to keep her safe—and she hiccupped on a laugh at the inevitability of her future.

Her shameful secret burned and twisted through her gut. The marks along her spine felt heavy, threatening to crush her. Instead, the runes heated, wrapping around her ribs like a hug.

She wasn't reassured.

Sooner or later the torque would fail to protect her, and the magic would escape.

The necklace was already weakening.

Morgan picked up her pace, instinctively turning right at the four-way hall, and spotted two large double doors some distance ahead. She leapt off the top step and dropped down a whole flight of stairs, rolling onto her shoulder to absorb some of the impact. Seconds later she was up and running again. Even as she neared, the great doors creaked open, giving her a wide-open view of the mountain vista.

People milling about outside turned to gawk at her when the doors banged open.

The large terrace out back was startlingly narrow.

Instead of fetching up against the stone railing, strong arms wrapped around her from behind. She was spun around, dragged away from the precipice, until her back was smashed against the stone wall of the Academy.

The move was so swift, Morgan didn't react as she struggled to catch her breath.

A large body was pressed intimately against her, every inch of him hard and packed with muscles. He smelled wild and green and of freedom, a combination that made her want to bury her nose against his chest.

She was so distracted, it took her a second to notice the weapon at his hip.

"You found it." She reached out, touching the blade she'd lost in the forest the night before she left for the Academy. When she looked up, she wasn't surprised to find Ryder gazing down at her. He had his hand braced against the wall above their heads, the other resting on her hip, holding her close.

She watched him swallow, his grip tightening, and she could have sworn he leaned closer to sniff her hair.

She should have shoved him away, but something about the way he ducked away from her look, almost bashful at being caught, stayed her hand. His shoulder-length hair was windblown, different shades of blond streaks lightening the brown in what should have been a shaggy mess, but she liked it. It suited him. Stubble lined his face, giving him a gruff appearance she found appealing. He was almost too pretty to look at without blatantly ogling at him like some love-starved dork.

He nodded, reluctantly straightening, putting a whole two inches between them, and withdrew the blade. "You saved my life."

Morgan shivered at the growly tone of his voice. It was so deep she wanted him to say something else just so she could feel it rumble through her again. She waved away his praise for her small part in the fight. "You give me too much credit. You had the minotaur well in hand. I've never seen a team fight together so smoothly."

His eyes flickered toward hers, pleasure brightening them before he quickly looked down again. He flipped the blade, caught the tip, and thrust it out to her.

The expression on his face made it look like she was stealing his favorite toy, and she didn't have the heart to take it from him. Though he was big and bold, there was something very gentle, almost fragile, about him when he gazed at her.

"Why don't you keep it?"

His head snapped up, hope shining in his soft, whisky-colored eyes. He searched her face and, at the moment it appeared he would return the weapon anyway, he reverently re-sheathed it at his side.

Before either of them could react, a large wolf edged its nose between them, wiggling his entire body for attention.

Morgan grinned at his enthusiasm, but when she reached out to brush his fur, Ryder's large hand clamped around her wrist, engulfing her arm in his grip. Though she was tall, his size almost made her feel dainty. She peered up at him in question, and she nearly quailed at his hard expression, his wolf hunkered close to the surface.

"He's a werewolf."

Morgan blinked up at him, not at all surprised, since the beast was the size of a small pony. "Yes."

Ryder blinked in surprise, studying her closer before he spoke. "You're not afraid."

It wasn't a question.

"Of course not."

But instead of being pleased, he scowled down at her. "Wolves are not dogs. A person should never touch a werewolf. They are more likely to take off your hand and eat it, all the while smiling at you."

It wasn't that Morgan didn't believe him, but Ascher and the wolf last night never showed any inclination to attack. Her markings didn't react to them at all. Instead, she'd swear that the beasts enjoyed her company. She was sure of it. The wolf sitting docile a few feet away from them didn't show any reaction to their discussion.

She concentrated on the markings along her back, but didn't pick up anything other than eagerness and joy. "I don't see it. All I can sense from him is his willingness to play, as if he's inviting me to join his game or something."

Ryder's eyebrows shot up, and even the wolf seemed to be staring at her oddly, until she grew uncomfortable.

"You can sense animals?"

Morgan wished she had simply nodded and avoided all these awkward questions. "No, not really. It's more that I am sensitive to anything from the primordial realm. Although werewolves no longer live there, they still use magic when they transform. It allows me to get a sense of danger. If he posed a threat, I would've sensed it."

"Have you told anyone else about this ability?" He took a step toward her, then checked himself.

There was an urgency in his voice she wasn't sure she liked. "No. Not really."

At her answer, tension melted out of his shoulders. "Good. Don't."

Morgan wouldn't have been more surprised if he'd reached out and goosed her.

Before she could ask for more information, he glanced around them suspiciously, his sharp eyes missing nothing. "There are a lot of creatures who won't be happy if they learn about your ability to sense them. They survive on anonymity. Most would view your skill as a threat. While it might be a useful trait for a hunter, it would also paint a target on you."

Morgan deflated a bit. Why wasn't she surprised?

The more clues she unearthed about her mysterious past, the more the danger stalking her intensified.

"Thank you for the warning."

When she didn't scoff at him, Ryder seemed to find the ground fascinating, scuffing his feet against the stone a little restlessly. The wolf inched closer, nudging his head under Ryder's hand, and he scratched at the beast almost absently. "This is Kaleb. He turned last month and is getting his wolf legs under him. Right now, he's pure wolf until he can remember his human side."

"You mean he's stuck?" Morgan gaped at the wolf in dismay, the same wolf who had his eyes closed in ecstasy. It was almost too easy to forget they were human underneath the fur.

Ryder seemed to regret bringing up the conversation at her gauche question, glancing at her out of the corners of his eyes. "Some transitions are traumatic. Kaleb was bitten, not born, so it's hard to know if he will ever return to his human form."

Sadness darkened his eyes for a moment. "It will make his life harder. If he doesn't earn a place in the pack, or find a witch to take him under her protection, his chances for survival are slim."

The prospects sounded so grim, Morgan glanced down at the wolf, noting for the first time the hollowness of his stomach, the slight outline of his ribs. She had assumed he was a growing pup. Now she wasn't so sure.

"What will happen to him?" She spoke in a hush, not wanting to disturb their peace. She suspected they didn't get much of it.

"For now, he'll run with the others and guard the Academy. Hopefully, he'll be noticed and gain a sponsor."

And she had no doubt Ryder was doing everything in his power to make it happen, even walking him on school grounds during the day. Despite her resolve to keep her distance from the rest of the students, she was softening toward the big man.

The wolf lifted his head and gave a bark, then charged off down the pathway.

"*Shite.*" Ryder took two long strides after the beast, when he seemed to remember her.

He stumbled to a stop, half turned toward her, clearly torn, but she waved him off. "Go."

He gave her a blinding smile, and she was blindsided by her sudden shortness of breath for a completely different reason. While he was gorgeous, when he smiled he was absolutely stunning. It completely rocked her that he didn't have a posse of women chasing after him.

To her surprise, talking with him calmed the panic that had been clawing up her insides like a deranged leprechaun digging for gold.

He reminded her everyone had their own troubles.

She might be sinking, but she knew how to swim.

She would find her way out of this mess, as she always had in the past.

As she passed the double doors and headed back inside, she nearly plowed over a breathless Neil.

"Where have you been? I've been searching for you everywhere!" He bent over, his hands on his knees, panting to catch his breath. "I even tried to cast a spell to find you, but it was like you didn't exist."

Morgan reached out, straightening the glasses on his face, but no matter how she adjusted them, they remained askew, and finally she dropped her hands in defeat. "Remember, magic doesn't work well on me. I believe I've developed a sort of immunity to it."

She should have, considering how many torture sessions the witches put her through.

Neil straightened, pressing his hand against his side to lessen the pain. "What you did in class was amazing. I don't think they've seen anyone with so much power in decades."

Morgan turned on her heel, wanting to get away from his excitement. She made a fool of herself in class. "Its power I can't access. Touching magic is painful. I was lucky the rock exploded and not my head."

"Oh, yeah." He had the grace to blanch, his interest fading a bit.

"Why does it matter so much?"

His mouth dropped open in astonishment. "You're kidding, right? Not only can witches open and close portals, but the more power they can master, the more respect they get." At her confused expression, he continued. "The less power a witch controls, the more they're turned into a lackey, nothing more than brood mares in the hope that they can produce stronger offspring. It's why witches are allowed so many mates. The stronger the witch, the more hunters she is allowed to select as her protectors."

Morgan grimaced, remembering the deplorable way Catalina treated the hunters at the coven. "Hunters deserve more respect."

Neil shrugged his bony shoulders, not agreeing or disagreeing. "There is one witch for every fifty hunters. It's no wonder they see them as disposable. While hunters might fight the creatures who pass through the rift, only a witch can close a portal and stop the spread."

A babble of voices came from down the hall. When they turned the corner, the doors to the cafeteria stood open, the place more of a food court. "Hope you don't mind. I'm starved."

"Sure." Morgan's stomach growled at the delicious smells. Instead of the cafeteria and benches of a normal school, there were a number of what appeared to be little food stations, each offering delicacies from different nationalities.

She followed Neil to a little deli offering burgers and fries. The line was short, the food hot and surprisingly tasty. And plentiful, which was good, since a good portion of a hunter's day was spent keeping sharp and fit, which burned a lot of calories.

Watching Neil eat almost made her lose her appetite. Though he dug in with gusto, he missed his mouth half the time, ketchup smearing his face, talking with his mouth full, regaling her with stories from his first year. A snort escaped him when he laughed, and she smiled reflexively, the sound kind of charming in a dorky way.

Teachers circled the room, a few of them staring at her a little longer than normal before glancing away when she caught them gawking at her.

"They're monitors." His lips curled in a snarl with all the ferocity of a puppy. "Don't worry about them. They only interfere when someone's on the verge of death. Otherwise, you're on your own. They consider it part of our training to keep our own selves alive."

As if fate was determined to make her day a miserable failure, Harper and her entourage entered the cafeteria, and all eyes in the room were automatically drawn toward them.

And with reason.

Their outfits had to cost a fortune, their froufrou clothing so tight, it could have been painted on them. It wasn't conducive to fighting or running or even walking…or breathing, for that matter.

When their eyes connected, a spark of malice gleamed in Harper's blue eyes. "I do have to say, you fail your exams spectacularly. We'll have to hope you do better as a hunter. It would be a shame for you to be sent home the week you arrived."

The three girls of her entourage twittered like magpies.

"No need for your concern." Morgan pushed away her almost empty tray, and rose to her feet. "I've already been assigned to a team. In fact, we go out on our first mission tonight."

Her pink lips puckered in displeasure, a scowl darkening her face. "Who?"

Morgan wished she'd kept her mouth shut.

Too late now.

Harper would discover the truth eventually.

"Kincade."

Harper stalked closer on the stilts she called shoes, and Morgan was surprised to see they were the same height, though she had a good twenty pounds of muscle on Harper. "You leave him alone. He's mine."

The hissed words were meant as a threat, but Morgan laughed. "Kincade doesn't strike me as your type."

"He's the best, and so am I." She poked her finger at Morgan, waving it around like a weapon, but stopped short of touching her. "It's only a matter of time before we're paired, so don't get any ideas."

Morgan was surprised steam didn't rise from Harper's dainty ears. She wanted to taunt the twit more, but the mention of pairing and mating disgusted her, and she wanted nothing to do with it. "You go ahead and stick with your assigned mates like good little robots. If I ever decide to take a lover, it will be my choice."

For some reason, Harper burst out laughing. "Oh, how quaint. Let me know how that works for you."

Chapter Twelve

*N*eeding to work off some steam, Morgan headed toward the gym.

The sight of Draven and Atlas sparring brought her up short.

Or maybe sparring wasn't quite accurate—beating the crap out of each other might actually fit better. She scooted around the edge of the room, then leaned against the wall to watch them work, so fascinated she didn't notice the mats' old, sweaty smell.

The men's every move was elegant and beautifully controlled, their muscles like well-oiled machines. The rest of the world didn't exist while they each focused solely on annihilating the other. It was hypnotizing to watch.

While both men were phenomenal fighters, each fought with a completely different style.

Atlas was smooth, almost elegant, every blow and step placed with precision. Draven was no less captivating as he bounced on his feet, studying his opponent and waiting for an opening, every inch of him raw power and passion.

Water versus fire.

Neither was willing to give an inch.

Morgan wasn't aware of edging closer, until Draven spotted her and grinned—which meant he didn't see the blow that knocked him clear off his feet and flat on his ass.

"Sorry." She winced in sympathy, feeling foolish her thoughtless actions had distracted him and cost him his match.

Both men were panting, so sweaty their clothes stuck to their bodies, leaving nothing to the imagination. Draven rolled over with a groan and sat, staring up at her. "No worries. If you think you can do better, you're welcome to try."

Excitement tingled over her skin at the chance to train with them. It had been so long, she hesitated, suddenly uncertain.

Atlas studied her for a moment, then heaved a sigh. "Very well."

She practically skipped onto the mat, while Atlas walked over toward the pile of weapons and picked up two staffs.

The elf was lithe, a quiet observer, ever watchful, and also so breathtakingly beautiful, it made her shy away from looking directly at him. His skin was pale, and so smooth it resembled polished stone, his brown hair was long enough to cover his pointy ears, the strands a little wild, the only thing that seemed to defy his control.

When he turned, he threw one of the staffs at her, and she deftly plucked it from the air. She hefted the weight of it, moving her feet step over step. The staff was about six and a half feet long, the wood worn smooth after years of use. It was about an inch around and fit well in her hands. She guessed it was a bit under ten pounds.

She spun it experimentally, the muscle memory from sparring with MacGregor coming back to her. It had taken her a week of bruised knuckles to learn how to hold the staff and another few weeks of battered arms and shins to learn she needed to know where her body was at all times. After six months, he deemed her adequate.

Atlas whirled the staff so quickly, a soft, musical hum sang through the air.

Then, without warning, he was moving. The end of his staff swung toward her head in a streak. Her training came back in a rush, and she thrust up her own staff in the nick of time, the impact reverberated up her arms. She jumped, whirled, spun and dodged as she struggled to stay ahead of his blows.

Every time she ventured out on the offensive, she got a whack for her troubles.

A tap against her thigh.

A smack on her arm.

A thwack against her ribs that made her falter.

Twice she landed on her ass, once when he swept her feet out from under her in a surprise attack, and a second time when she'd planted her staff and used it as a vaulting pole and he swatted her out of the air like a pesky fly.

After an hour, her muscles felt raw and achy.

Morgan lifted her staff, swiping the sweat away from her face with the back of her arm, refusing to give up, refusing to relent.

Then Atlas did something unexpected. He stepped back, planted his staff at his side and bowed, never once taking his eyes off her. "You did well. With a few lessons, you could become unstoppable."

Draven gave a wild whoop, shooting her a broad smile. At some point, Ryder had joined him. He stood with his hands tucked under his arms, as if to keep himself from coming to her rescue, but even he looked impressed.

Morgan nearly wilted against her staff to catch her breath, completely flummoxed by their responses. "What do you mean? I was awful. I barely made contact a dozen times."

"That's more than any of them have ever managed." Atlas tipped his head toward her cheering squad, his lips twitching so slightly she almost missed it.

She scowled, not sure she believed him.

"Believe it or not, the first time we sparred, every one of them spent more time on the mat than their feet." Atlas collected her staff, but paused before turning away. "Your speed is incredible. You were in motion the instant I lifted my staff, almost anticipating my strategies. And you were getting better. You're almost as good as a Tuatha Dé Danann."

His green eyes reminded her of the hills of Ireland, so intense she could imagine being there just by gazing into them. Cinnamon wafted up from his skin, the sweet smell completely at odds with his unbending posture. "Thank you?"

Morgan wasn't sure it was a complement or not, but he nodded and strode away to replace the weapons. "We will train again tomorrow."

It wasn't a question.

When Morgan hobbled off the mats, Draven and Ryder were waiting. "You were amazing."

"Hardly." She grabbed a towel and wiped her face, stifling a groan from her protesting body.

Draven's smile fell so quickly, she shivered at the quicksilver change. "You don't understand. We're barely good enough for him to bother to train with us. Only because we're team members does he grudgingly beat us to a pulp. To have an elf offer to train you is an honor. It means he sees you as a worthy opponent."

Morgan peered at Atlas over the edge of her towel, not sure it was a good thing, even less sure what to make of him.

"He's on his sabbatical. The Elven people come to Earth to serve their time and learn how humans function. They almost never return Earthside after they've finished their sabbatical. They're stiff, strict, and unbending sods, but they are the absolute best fighters. So when he says he will train you, believe me, it is an honor."

Morgan was humbled.

"I didn't even think he liked me."

Draven snorted. "He doesn't like anyone, but he finds you interesting enough to deem worthy of his attention. So soak it up. Don't waste this chance."

She wasn't sure of his assessment, but she accepted his advice at face value. Ryder glanced at the clock, then at her. "We'll be leaving shortly. If you hurry, you should be able to grab a quick shower."

She bolted upright at the reminder, took a few steps, then turned and looked at him over her shoulder. "Thanks."

Without waiting for a response, she dashed out of the gym, and charged toward her room. She was showered, changed and buckling her last weapons on her person when a knock sounded on the door.

Draven waited on the other side, dressed in full battle gear.

She couldn't help but stare.

Leather had been made for a man such as him, her own scuffed pants looking shabby by comparison.

"Ready?" There was a hint of flirtation in the way his mouth curled up at her reaction, but his eyes and voice were all business. Again, she wondered about the man underneath his playboy exterior. Every once in a while, she caught the hint of deep loneliness, a black pit of despair when she looked in his eyes.

"Yes." She snapped the door shut behind her, following him down the stairs.

And couldn't help but notice the view from the back was almost as captivating as the front. With conscious effort, she tore her eyes away, her cheeks heating at her wicked thoughts, uncomfortable with her uncharacteristic emotions.

She needed to get back to what was important—the hunt. It was time to set aside this other nonsense.

As they traveled through a warren of passageways, she discovered she was a little nervous about her first mission with them, worried she wouldn't live up to their expectations.

It shouldn't matter.

She didn't come here to make friends.

She should be more worried about finding the witch-killer, but somehow she was being sucked into their high-octane lifestyle.

They made her feel less like a freak.

Like she belonged.

A dangerous feeling, one she refused to let worm its way in her head and distract her.

When they entered a familiar tunnel, she knew they were heading toward the garage.

What she didn't expect was to find Harper and Kincade standing so close the witch was practically wrapped around him.

Every ounce of good cheer vanished. "What's she doing here?"

Draven glanced at her, then at Harper, barely covering his own grimace. "Once we herd the gaggle of gremlins, she'll be able to open and close the portal. This should be a quick in-and-out mission."

Kincade deftly extracted himself from the queen bitch's clutches, not seeing her scowl when he walked away. "Our target is a warehouse infected with gremlins. We are only to exterminate them as a last resort. Any questions?"

No one said a word.

"Then load up."

Everyone headed toward the van. Kincade slipped behind the wheel. Ryder opened the passenger door, ready to heave his bulk inside when Harper sauntered forward and commandeered the front seat right out from under him.

Like he was some damned servant to cater to her every whim.

It didn't even dawn on Harper that he wasn't opening the door for her.

A muscle jumped in his jaw as he closed the door with a soft click and climbed in back. Morgan was appalled to realize this was his life.

He deserved better.

Atlas soon joined him in the back seat. She piled in next, Draven right on her heels. They were barely seated when Kincade stomped on the gas. Draven pulled out the blade tucked into his boot, calmly running a whetstone along the edge over and over. Instead of being calmed by the repetitive motion, darkness oozed from his pores, obliterating any hint of the flirty, carefree guy she first met.

Ryder continued to stare out the window, refusing to meet her gaze. While everyone else was armed to the gills, he only had one blade…the one she gifted to him.

She blinked, startled by the notion that he couldn't bear to be parted from her gift.

Her stomach dipped wildly, and she shoved away such a foolish notion.

It was a fine blade.

That had to be the reason.

Right?

And yet, Morgan wasn't convinced.

Tearing her eyes away from Ryder, her attention landed on Atlas as he calmly ran a cloth over a pair of short, double-edged swords that looked wickedly sharp and totally deadly.

Of all the men, he appeared the most relaxed…as if excited at the prospect of a good fight.

Instead of the joking and comradery she'd become used to hearing from the team, the van was ominously silent, each man lost in his own world. Morgan wondered if Harper had upset the balance among the men…or worse, if her own presence was the one to ruin the cohesiveness of the team.

Bile rose in her throat at the thought, and she turned to stare out the window.

They drove down the twisty mountain road for what felt like hours. When Harper set her talons on Kincade's arm, Morgan's annoyance turned to disgust while she watched the witch try to work her wiles on him. She only felt marginally better when he immediately extracted himself under the guise of adjusting the thermostat. The blonde chatted away incessantly, until Morgan wanted to lean forward and stab the bitch. Something of her thoughts must have telegraphed itself to Draven. He leaned over into her seat with wide eyes, blocking her view. He uncurled his fingers to reveal a pair of headphones.

She nearly sagged in relief and gave him a grateful smile, plugging them in her ears.

And couldn't have been more surprised at the choice of music.

Instead of heavy rock, the song was an old Irish ballad of lost love.

She was immediately entranced by the tragic love story, the soaring notes touching her soul, and her heart grew heavy in her chest over the loss of something she would never be able to feel.

The sun had long since been banished from the sky, the moon nothing but a sliver hanging above them, when they pulled up on the outskirts of town and parked in front of what appeared to be an abandoned building. Darkness drenched the warehouse, giving the steel structure a Gothic vibe. A small lake shimmered in the distance, wisps of fog rising from the calm waters like ghosts, warning away unwary visitors.

While the guys threw open the van doors, she reluctantly removed the headphones.

From the corner of her eye, she saw Atlas and Ryder doing the same, and felt a sort of kinship with them. Then it hit her...everyone else was used to riding with Harper, and brought along their own protection. Mirth bubbled up in her chest, and she barely resisted the urge to laugh at them...and made a mental note to pick up a pair of her own ASAP.

She almost felt bad Kincade had to suffer the whole ride.

Almost.

When Kincade cut the engine, sounds returned in a rush...or the lack of sounds.

Not even insects dared buzz.

The total lack of life was so eerie, the hair on her arms lifted in warning.

Whatever was here had either scared away even the smallest of life forms or—knowing gremlins—had eaten them. They must have moved on to bigger prey, since Kincade and his squad had been called in to deal with them…like a stray human or two. As if picking up on her thoughts, Draven studied their surroundings as well, the intensity of his expression making him look ready to burst into action at any moment.

The rest of the group carefully exited the vehicle, stretching their muscles, their eagle eyes missing nothing despite the darkness.

As everyone gathered around in a group, she ended up across from Kincade. He gave her a hard look, clearly wanting to say something, but tightened his mouth and turned away instead. "We'll split up into two teams. Harper, Atlas and Ryder are with me. Draven, you will be in charge of Morgan. We will enter the warehouse, then split up. We'll head right, while you go the opposite way, and sweep the warehouse. When you find the nest, signal us, and we'll get the portal open and corral them together."

Ryder's and Atlas's expressions hardened, ready to protest, but Kincade's glower silenced whatever they were going to say.

Draven, if possible, looked even grimmer.

They all turned toward Harper, and Morgan understood.

She was just a hunter.

Expendable.

They needed to protect their asset.

"Agreed."

Kincade's head snapped toward her, and the tightness in his shoulders eased when he saw she understood.

Without another word, everyone scattered. The men merged into the darkness like they belonged there, easily disappearing from view.

Harper might as well have glowed for all the effort she put into blending.

The warehouse turned out to be built of steel and concrete, a veritable fortress.

The gremlins had chosen well.

The door gave a screech of protest when Atlas wrenched it open, the elf wincing at the racket, before slipping into the warehouse.

Instead of an empty warehouse, the racks were full of boxed merchandise, blocking their view and making the mission more of an obstacle course. Harper lifted up her hand, and a small orb began to glow, bobbing gently in the air. When she touched the small light, it sounded like she ran her finger along the edges of a wine glass. But whatever she did, the orb seemed to understand and attached itself to her. It rose ten feet in the air, and hovered above her, illuminating enough of the area so she wouldn't trip.

Even Morgan had to admit it was a neat trick, although she wondered about the light pinning a target on them.

Then she understood.

It was a compromise.

Harper couldn't see in the dark. She would only end up stumbling around, attracting attention. At least this way she would be able to see what was coming at them and hopefully defend them. As the team split up, Morgan reluctantly followed Draven, worried that Harper would get the others killed if it meant keeping herself alive.

They passed three racks of goods, the shelving thirty feet in the air, when she heard rustling, like an army of rats were moving above them.

Morgan instinctively armed herself with one blade in each hand, but knew they would be useless for defense if the gremlins were organized and decided to attack all at one time.

"The queen is in charge. They won't do anything without her permission." Draven's comment didn't reassure her, since the queen was usually the most vicious of the bunch.

A stack of boxes began to teeter, giving her only seconds of warning before they began to rain down on them. Morgan charged forward, grabbed Draven about the waist and tackled him to the ground. They skidded on the cement a good few feet, and a couple of boxes heavy enough to be full of rocks struck her legs. A sharp stench stung her nostrils, and Morgan covered her nose with the back of her hand. The boxes were doused in urine. When she pushed upright, she looked back through watery eyes and saw the pathway behind them was completely blocked.

They had no choice but to go forward.

"Thanks." Draven stood, offering her a hand, the other he used to pinch his nose shut. She accepted his help, stooping long enough to retrieve her knife.

Above them, about a dozen creatures began to cackle, hoot, and screech as if they were watching an event.

They were being toyed with.

"They were expecting us."

"Not us." Draven's voice was grim. "They were expecting humans. Based on their level of organization, the group has obviously done this often."

Meaning the gremlins had caught and consumed more than one human.

Packages stacked on the floor began to rustle on both sides of the shelving, the boxes jolting as the little bastards zipped down the racks.

She spun to keep them in sight, awed at how incredibly fast they moved.

A shadow flew overhead. When she tipped her head back, she saw a dozen creatures no more than two feet high leap the fifteen feet across the aisle. She threw a blade, managed to hit one, but her weapon bounced harmlessly off its hard, reptilian hide. They scampered up the shelving and disappeared into the boxes as her blade clanked harmlessly to the ground.

There appeared to be three different varieties. The majority of them were varying shades of green, covered with warts and black, oily spots. Those were the males. The younger ones were a light tan, slightly smaller, but no less deadly. A couple had bright yellow bellies, but no less hideous. They were the females. Their eyes were pure red, their black pupils narrow slits. Some had distinctive stripes, while others were marked with scars, whether from battle or decoration, she wasn't sure.

One evil little critter, slightly bigger than the rest, glared down at her from his crouched position, his scars prominent on his body, a bold slash gouging deep ruts across his face. He was the commander, battle-hardened and vindictive about having his space invaded. His large ears were thin and leathery, swiveling to catch even the slightest sound, the left one kinked where it had nearly been torn off. His claw-tipped hands were wrapped around the metal grates of the shelving, his arms almost as long as his entire body, which made climbing and running on all fours easier.

This one appeared to be covered with some kind of goo that dripped down the shelves. The ammonia smell was nearly enough to knock her out. Tufts of scraggly hair stuck up from the top of his head. He sneered, revealing dozens and dozens of bloody, razor-sharp teeth.

He lifted his hand and gave her the finger, then quickly ducked behind the boxes with his mates.

Both sides of the shelving erupted in giggles.

"We're sitting ducks down here. We need to head up." She peered at Draven, and he backed up a step, as if reading something in her expression. Morgan smiled grimly. "How do you feel about being bait?"

He grimaced, then glanced up at the top of the shelving thirty feet in the air. "Better than I feel about being an acrobat. You're faster than I am, more flexible."

Morgan sheathed her weapon. When she went to retrieve the one that had fallen, he grabbed her arm. "No undue risks. Don't let them draw you away. Yell if you get into trouble."

"Understood. Go. I'll let them follow you, then climb."

Draven hesitated a moment longer, clearly not wanting to leave her alone, then huffed out a resigned sigh. "Kincade is going to kill me."

With that cryptic remark, he turned on his heel and ran down the aisle, whistling a jaunty tune. While a few remained behind to watch her, the majority clearly saw her as no threat, and clambered across the boxes in pursuit.

Not wasting a second, Morgan leapt up, grabbed the edge of the third shelf and began to climb. Angry chittering erupted above her, and she spotted four gremlins arguing, appearing distressed when she didn't collapse on the floor, weeping in terror at the sight of them.

When they fell silent, the hair on the back of her neck stood on end. She leaned back to get a good look at them, unnerved to find the four of them staring down at her with yellowish eyes and malicious smiles that didn't bode well.

Two clambered down, one lashing out at Morgan's hands and arms, aiming his claws for her face, while the other one dove for her legs. She swung at the one trying to gouge out her eyeballs, but it scampered out of arm's reach. The second one latched onto her legs like a deranged monkey, using his teeth and claws to gnaw at her leathers like she was his own personal chew toy.

"Son of a bitch." Pain shot up her leg as he began to shake his head, his teeth sawing back and forth, and she wondered if the little beast was trying to tear out a hunk of her flesh or rip her leg off altogether.

Not to be outdone, the first gremlin lunged for her face. Morgan swatted the claws away, and nearly lost her balance in the process.

All the while, the two remaining on top ripped open the boxes and began lobbing metal spoons at her, one going so far as to bean her on the head when she didn't dodge fast enough.

"Enough."

She never realized something so small could bedevil her so much.

She reached out, ignoring the claws digging into the fleshy part of her hand, snagged the toothpick-like leg of the nearest gremlin and flung the creature as far as she could. The gremlin gave a scream of anger as he flew through the air before splatting across the floor, leaving a black smear behind him, his little body ending up a twisted mess.

Then, to her consternation, he lumbered to his feet and limped off, dragging his damaged leg behind him, leaving a trail of dark ooze.

The monster on her leg gave a scream of rage and renewed his attack.

"Get." She brought up her leg and slammed the creature into one of the metal posts. "Off."

Slam.

"Me!"

The critter clanged against the metal like a gong, then dropped like a rock to the ground, landing with a surprisingly solid thud for something so small. He turned and hissed at her with evil eyes, quickly dragging himself under the shelving, and Morgan couldn't help but shiver at the malice.

And received another bash across the back of her head, reminding her she still wasn't alone. As she reached the top, one leaned over and screamed, the high-pitched sound threatening to make her ears bleed.

Not to be outdone, Morgan screamed back at him in frustration.

The gremlin was so startled, his mouth snapped shut, and he staggered back, hastily covering his ears.

Of course.

Their large ears meant they were sensitive to even the slightest noise.

Morgan snatched at the next spoon aimed for her head and beat it against the metal. The creatures cowered, grabbed their ears, twisting away to escape. In seconds, they turned tail and ran.

Morgan breathed a sigh of relief and dropped the spoon.

If there had been more of them, they would've overwhelmed her, using their sharp teeth and claws to whittle her flesh down to bones in a matter of minutes.

A deep foreboding tore through her chest, until she thought her heart was being ripped out. "Draven."

Chapter Thirteen

Morgan scrambled to the top of the shelves, uncaring of the noise and raced to the spot where she last saw Draven disappear.

And found nothing.

Panic tightened the back of her throat.

She couldn't be too late.

Taking a couple steps back, she ran and leapt the fifteen feet between the aisles. The boxes collapsed under her weight, nearly dragging her over the edge. Morgan struggled upright and raced over the tops until she found her target.

"Draven." She nearly sagged in relief, her heart beating so hard her ribs ached.

He was alive.

He'd been running up and down the aisles, attracting such a crowd, they were now stalking him.

He stood in a small clearing at the center of the warehouse, every direction seething with gremlins.

He had nowhere else to go.

If they reached him before she did, he wouldn't stand a chance.

With a burst of speed, Morgan drew her weapons and let them fly. She managed to pick off a few, their bodies flying backwards under the weight of the blows, but it didn't kill them.

Half of them turned toward her with a shriek of rage and charged.

The other half began to pour out of the shelving like a waterfall of creatures, dropping down to corner Draven. The ones in the aisle stalked forward, their beady little eyes hard, practically salivating at the meal in front of them.

Morgan kicked two of the gremlins out of the way, clearing a path, and stepped over the edge.

Gravity took hold, and she dropped thirty feet to the ground, landing only a few paces away from Draven. She grinned up at him, noting drops of blood on his clothes, his haggard appearance, but he was thankfully still in one piece. "You started without me. Not fair."

He shook his head, but a slight smile lifted his lips. "I could say the same for you."

"A girl's got to have *some* fun." Morgan shrugged, not even feeling the tiny puncture wounds littering her body as she swiped away the black goo crusting her leather pants. It wasn't anything she hadn't dealt with on numerous other hunts.

The gremlins halted their advance at her appearance, milling about until the big one smacked the smaller ones next to him, his chatter sounding like scolding.

"Any ideas?" Draven gripped his weapons, going back to back with her, facing off against the small horde.

When one ventured near, he lashed out with his boot and launched the creature in the air.

"Maybe." Morgan grimaced, when a totally foolish idea came to her. "You're going to think it silly."

He huffed out a laugh. "I'll take silly over sharp claws and teeth ripping me to shreds."

Morgan kicked away a nasty gremlin leaping for her face, the creature going in for a quick kill by ripping out her throat. "Sing."

"What?"

He sounded so appalled, Morgan turned to see he had paled and backed away from her as if she'd threatened to cut off his man parts.

Then they had no more time.

There were more than forty gremlins surrounding them, and even more skulking closer. Morgan recalled the last song she'd heard, the one in the van, and began to sing.

Her voice was clear, if slightly off tune, and she fought a blush when Draven gaped at her like she was a freak.

Then the nearest gremlins paused and crept forward, quietly

chirping. A few of them sat, their gravelly voices humming along in harmony, although horribly off-tune, making her wince. They began to bob their heads, their eyes sliding shut.

More and more began to join them.

But it wasn't enough, her voice didn't carry far enough to ensnare them all.

She gestured toward Draven, willing him to join her.

He glanced around the warehouse, noted the same thing, and his face completely shut down. He stared at her with shattered eyes, and she'd felt like she asked him to slit his throat.

Then he began to sing softly.

Holy shit, he could *sing*.

Angelic came to mind.

She faltered for a second so she could simply enjoy the beauty of the sound. The notes were light, almost like he was playing an instrument, and totally enthralling.

She had thought the song beautiful and heartbreaking in the van, but now it nearly devastated her.

The click of nails on granite jerked her back to the present and away from the snare of his voice, and she shook her head to clear it before joining him.

He gave her a baffled look, completely ignoring the danger around them, his voice floating effortlessly as he wove it over and around her own.

A commotion in the group of now-docile gremlins caught her attention, and she spotted the big, scarred gremlin pushing and shoving at the others, trying to wake them as he worked his way through the crowd. His damaged ear must be protecting him from falling under the musical spell completely.

Morgan grabbed her knife, drew back her arm and let it sail.

It hit true, the hilt smacking the gremlin between the eyes as she intended, knocking him on his ass and out cold.

The rest of the team emerged from the shadows, almost herding a couple of zombie-like gremlins toward the sound.

Kincade wasn't pleased, openly glaring at Draven.

Harper looked just as pissed when she saw Morgan was alive and well, and Morgan took pleasure in noting that her perfect clothes were rumpled, her long hair a little shorn and snarled in spots.

Atlas had a few rips in his clothes, but appeared unharmed. He scanned her from head to toe, then gave her a nod. Kincade had a few bruises, his left side was covered with black goo, but it was Ryder who caught her attention. He was covered with blood, his clothes nearly black with slime. Ragged wounds littered his arms and torso, and even his legs were marked by deep gouges in his leathers.

The gremlin in his grip was clearly the queen.

If Morgan thought the males were ugly, this creature was even worse. Not only were her features warped with scales and warts, it looked like her teeth were longer and sharper than the rest.

Thankfully, she seemed just as enthralled as her subjects.

Kincade gestured toward Harper, and magic immediately pooled in the room. Power tugged at the runes on Morgan's back, and she struggled to keep the magic from pulling toward her. Hearing her plea, the metal of the torque thinned, wrapping around her neck over and over, snuffing out the almost irresistible draw of magic.

The magic rebounded in the room as it released its hold on her. Within seconds, a portal tore open between the worlds. One by one, they began to systematically gather the gremlins and toss them into the void. Morgan stood, wincing when her wounds stung, then grabbed the nearest enthralled gremlins and went to work.

It took thirty minutes before she was sure they had them all.

The rift snapped shut with an audible pop, and the air sounded hushed as the song faded.

"What the hell did you think you were doing?" Kincade strode toward Draven, and Morgan stepped between them.

"It's my fault." Morgan hastily hopped backwards when he nearly plowed over her. "I noticed they were sensitive to sounds and made a calculated guess."

Kincade removed plugs from his ears, tossing them violently to the floor. "Of that I have no doubt, you reckless little fool. You not only risked your life, but his as well—on a stupid guess. What if you had been wrong?"

Each word staggered her, hitting harder than any blow, and any closeness she felt to the team vanished under his harsh regard.

What was worse?

He was right.

It was her idea to split up, her idea to send Draven off as bait.

Worse, it would have been her fault if he had been torn apart in front of her eyes.

"And it worked. Ease off." Draven pushed his way between them, shoving Kincade away. "And for your information, it might have been her idea, but it saved our lives. In case you hadn't noticed, we were surrounded. Do you think you would've been able to fight your way through all of them to save us?"

Kincade ran his fingers through his hair. "It's late. Head back to the van. We'll discuss what happened when we reach the Academy. For now, get your injuries checked out. Harper, Atlas, you're both with me. We'll do one last sweep and dispose of the remaining bodies."

Tension stretched among the team, people taking sides, and Morgan hated that she was at the focus of the dissension.

"Morgan?" Draven's voice was so soft and understanding that tears burned her eyes.

"I'm fine." She quickly stooped so they wouldn't see her face, gathering up her missing weapons and heading toward the door.

As they neared the van, Draven and Ryder hovered over her like nervous hens. "Really, guys, I'm fine. See?" She held out her battered hands. "My wounds are already beginning to heal."

Both dutifully glanced down, but neither appeared convinced.

"But the two of you look the worse for wear. You," she pointed at Ryder, nearly gagging at his stench. "Take yourself down to the lake for a good dousing."

When he opened his mouth to protest, she waved him away and wrinkled her nose. "We'll be trapped inside a vehicle with you for hours. Believe me, you'll be doing us all a favor."

Heaving a sigh, he lumbered away on silent feet. He seemed so defeated, she took a step after him, but forced herself to stop.

He didn't halt at the water's edge, but kept walking until he was submerged.

Morgan waited for him to resurface, refusing to look at Draven, swallowing past the lump in her throat to speak. "He was right. I'm sorry. If it wasn't for me, you wouldn't have been in danger."

"Bullshite." He scowled, wrenching the rear door open almost violently. "Every mission is dangerous. He's really pissed because he didn't expect us to be overwhelmed. Our weapons were worthless. The only thing we could use to kill them was sheer brute force. He blames himself for things going wrong and took it out on you. Kincade's old school. He doesn't believe women should fight—he was raised to believe they should be protected. Something about you triggers his asshole side."

He rummaged around inside the van, pulling out a bag of supplies. "My guess is it's tearing him up inside that he wasn't there to protect you."

Morgan snorted at the absurdity of it. "You're wrong. He doesn't even like me."

"You don't understand." Draven handed her a towel and a bottle of water, and she dutifully cleaned the worst of her injuries, swiping away at the last of the goo on her pants. "Kincade trained his whole life to be a member of the elite. He chose this life, pushed himself to be the best for the sole purpose of one day being able to protect the woman who would bear his mark. I think it bothers him that despite being the best, he hasn't been marked or claimed."

Morgan was baffled. "What does that have to do with me?"

She dabbed at the claw marks across her knuckles, barely feeling the sting, curious about his answer.

"You committed the worst sin in his eyes." Draven accepted the empty bottle from her, shoving it in the bag with the rest of the trash. "By fighting, he sees you are not only risking your life, but denying a warrior his chance at a mate if something happens to you."

"There is a slight flaw in your theory." She stood back as he slammed the door shut, turning to watch Ryder ruthlessly scrub his hair. "Witches go out hunting all the time."

"You're right, but they also have at least five hunters with them wherever they go. Witches are not only protected by hunters, they can also use their magic to defend themselves. You actually throw yourself at danger." Draven dabbed at a nasty wound on his arm and winced. "Two very different things."

"Mutts are never chosen as mates, so your theory is not exactly without fault."

Draven's hand stopped, a confused expression on his face. "You might not know your breed, but you are no mutt."

Yearning churned in her gut at his certainty. "I'm a null, almost the exact opposite of a witch. I've trained all my life as a hunter. Everyone put their lives at risk tonight, and I was no different."

He shook his head, his bangs falling into his eyes as he glanced up from bandaging his wounds. "But we're expendable. With or without magic, you're more valuable than you believe."

"No hunter is expendable." She shifted her feet, uncomfortable at the genuine warmth in his eyes.

The sight of Ryder jogging back toward them, his shirt sticking to him like a second skin, stole the rest of her thoughts. Draven edged closer, nudging her shoulder. "You might want to mop up the drool."

Her cheeks burned at being caught, and she shoved him back. "Jerk."

But she was grateful for the distraction and the ability to pull her eyes away.

"Better?" Ryder's voice was gruff, the uncertainty on his face melting her heart.

Giving into temptation, she leaned forward, ignoring the way he stiffened, and inhaled, relieved to smell the wild, fresh green scent she associated with him. "Yup."

When she stepped away, his whisky brown eyes seemed to glow.

He looked at her like the rest of the world had vanished.

"Okay, big guy." Draven chuckled and steered him away, shooting her a reproving look as he opened the van door. "Into the back."

When Ryder was seated, Draven gestured for her to wait, waving her away from entering the van. "I hope you know what you're doing."

Morgan was baffled about his change in behavior. "What do you mean?"

He studied her face, searching for something.

If anything, his expression turned grimmer, and her stomach sank in dread.

"Do you know I'm a siren?"

Morgan blinked at him at the sudden switch in conversation and shook her head.

"Not even when you asked me to sing?"

Again, she shook her head. "I don't think it mattered to the gremlins. All I knew was my voice didn't carry far enough to capture them."

Draven rubbed his jaw as he continued to stare at her. "I really can't tell if you're playing dumb or if you really don't know."

Morgan was becoming offended. "Just spit it out."

"He's a werewolf." He jerked his thumb over his shoulder, pointing at Ryder in the back seat.

"Okay." She knew that, then her mind flashed to the wolf she ran with the first night, and the light dawned. It had been Ryder. Then blushed wildly as she recalled the way she ran her hands all over him. "Oh."

"And the light dawns." Draven grumbled under his breath as he leaned against the van.

She snapped her attention to him. "Don't be an ass. It's not like people go around wearing signs."

But she should've known he was the wolf out on the front lawn.

Instead, she let his pretty face distract her.

Draven pointed to himself. "I'm a siren."

"Yeah, you said that before." She scowled, not sure she liked this side of him. It smarted that he would rub salt in her wounds. "Not everyone is lucky enough to know their past."

His eyebrows disappeared in his hair, his mouth dropped open, then he began to sputter. After a few seconds, he burst out laughing.

Fed up, Morgan shoved him so hard he thudded into the van hard enough to leave a dent.

"Oh, I like you. I really do." He raised his hands in surrender, grinning like a loon, and Morgan threw up her hands, completely baffled at the swing in his emotions.

"Gah." She stalked away from him, shaking her head. "You're insane. It's the only thing that makes sense. You hide it so well, I didn't even suspect."

The snorted laugh behind her only served to annoy her more.

She whirled to find Ryder had opened the window, leaning his forearms against it, the two men talking in hushed whispers until they saw her staring at them. She kept her distance at their innocent looks. "Do I even want to know?"

"How much time have you spent around other primordial creatures?"

Morgan crossed her arms defensively and scowled at them. "Very little if I can help it."

"You were raised in the Maine coven." It wasn't a question, but clearly a probe for more information.

"You could say the witches and I didn't get along. Torture has a way of doing that."

Their expressions darkened, but it was Ryder who spoke. "What?"

When neither seemed willing to let the matter drop, Morgan heaved a sigh, wishing she'd kept her trap shut. "MacGregor found me living in the forest when I was ten. I had no memory of anything before then, still don't. I had been surviving on my own for a few months when he took pity on me and convinced me to go back to the mansion with him. Duty done, he handed me over to the witches.

"It quickly became apparent that I didn't have any magical talent, but when they noticed I seemed to be immune to their spells, they took it upon themselves to run a few invasive tests. When they pushed me too far, I fought back." Morgan studied her short nails, picking at them as remembered pain rippled down her spine. "That's when MacGregor took interest in me and decided to train me himself."

"I became off-limits. Mostly. They took their revenge by having their hunters join in my 'training' in guise of weekly beatings." She gave them a fierce grin, not caring that it wasn't friendly. "So no, I wasn't raised with any other primordial creatures."

The door to the warehouse banged open, breaking the awkward silence, and the rest of the team emerged from the infested warehouse unharmed.

"Finally." She shoved Draven aside, opened the door and climbed in her seat, refusing to acknowledge either of them. To sour her mood more, she spotted Kincade and Harper walking side by side like a lovey-dovey couple.

Another reminder that she wasn't good enough.

Well, fuck them.

She was raised as a hunter by one of the best.

She had a mission to accomplish.

There was no sense in making friends when she would be leaving as soon as she found the killer.

To discourage conversation, she grabbed the earbuds and cranked up the music as loud as it would go.

Chapter Fourteen

*T*hey arrived back at the school well after midnight. Everyone piled out of the vehicle and scattered, relieved to be free of the oppressive silence. As soon as Atlas stepped out of the van, he headed toward the exit and escaped. Morgan was hard on his heels when Kincade spoke.

"Report to the infirmary and get checked out."

Ryder strode not-so-casually on one side of her, Draven on the other, and both nodded.

Morgan easily slipped away from them and headed toward her room. She had a murder to solve. "Morgan?"

"Hmmm." She glanced up to find everyone's eyes on her. "What?"

"The infirmary." Ryder peered at her, his brows furrowed in concern.

"No need. I'm fine." No one moved. "See?"

She held out her hands.

Draven snatched at her wrists and inspected her injuries with a frown.

The worst of the wounds had healed over, the nasty claw marks now resembled nothing more than cat scratches.

"How?" He ran his thumb over her skin in a light caress that send her stomach soaring. Uncomfortable at his closeness, feeling her resolve to keep her distance weaken, she wiggled her fingers free and retrieved her hand.

"We're primordial creatures." She clenched and unclenched her fingers, still remembering his touch, and shrugged. "We heal fast."

"Not that fast." Draven kept his eyes locked on her, trapping her, then jabbed a thumb over his shoulder. "Only Ryder can heal so quickly."

When she glanced over his shoulder, she saw Kincade bearing down on her, full speed. Morgan unconsciously backed up until she smacked into the wall behind her. He placed his hands on either side of her head, effectively trapping her, and ducked until he was right in her face.

Her stupid heart fluttered at his nearness.

The smell of fresh earth and warm stone curled around her, inviting her to stretch against him and linger.

Then he went ahead and ruined her fantasy by speaking. "You will either follow my orders, or you will remain behind when we're called out on our next mission."

Morgan jerked back, whacking her head against the wall in the process—too bad it didn't seem to knock any sense into her. She glared up at him while she rubbed the spot, baring her teeth in a snarl, and finally muttered the answer he wanted. "Fine."

"Come." Draven struck his hand between them, snagged her shirt in his fist, then dragged her free. "I'll show you the way. A trip to the infirmary is mandatory for anyone with an injury after a mission. They check us over and clear us for our next mission."

He gently nudged her toward Ryder, and both of them hustled her off down the hall. When she glanced over her shoulder, Kincade had not moved, his head dropped forward to rest on his chest.

Her skin crawled when Harper placed a hand between his shoulders and leaned forward to whisper in his ear.

"Those two deserve each other." Morgan resolutely turned away.

"No one deserves that," Draven countered, then shrugged when he caught her staring at him.

They reached the infirmary in ten minutes.

A woman stood from behind her desk, setting aside her book. "Who's first?"

Ryder whipped off his shirt, and Morgan nearly swallowed her tongue, fascinated by the way the muscles of his back flexed when he moved.

"Down, girl."

Without taking her eyes off Ryder, Morgan shot her elbow back, hitting Draven in the gut so hard he grunted.

Ryder sat on an exam table, giving her an even better view of his chest and mouthwatering abs. Then she noticed the dozen or so bruises and scratches littering his body. None appeared too deep, but they had to sting, yet he didn't complain when the nurse began to dab iodine on them.

Morgan tore her eyes away, glancing around the room. They appeared to be in a front office. There were two exam tables, one desk, and three cabinets full of different types of medicine and bandages. At the far end of the room was a wall with one large observation window, granting them a clear view into the next room, and a single door leading into it. Beyond the window stood a row of twelve beds, none of them currently occupied.

"You're next."

Morgan whipped her head around at the soft voice and grimaced to find the nurse staring expectantly at her. She ungraciously thrusted out her hands. "I'm fine."

The nurse merely lifted a brow, and gestured toward the table.

Morgan snorted. "Not happening."

"Then you don't hunt." The nurse smiled politely, but there was a bite to her tone. "Next."

Draven promptly removed his shirt, smiling charmingly at the nurse like the ideal patient.

Bastard.

The nurse's touch lingered on his skin well after she placed the last bandage. Draven kept smiling, but his blue eyes had cooled considerably.

"Done?"

The nurse startled at her voice. Draven jumped off the table and slipped his shirt over his head before the girl had a chance to turn around again.

For her trouble, Morgan received a scowl from the nurse.

Once more she lifted her hands. "You're not getting my shirt off."

The runes on her back rested heavily against her skin.

No one could ever know about them.

She would not become some lab rat.

"Er…" Ryder looked suddenly uncomfortable. "We'll wait in the hall."

Without waiting for an affirmative, he grabbed Draven and dragged him out the door.

"Fine." The nurse glowered, slapping iodine not so gently on her scratches, not even bothering to splash any on her legs. "Not my problem if you want to get yourself killed. Females don't last long fighting. Just don't get the others killed while you're out there trying to prove something."

Morgan jerked her hands away from the viper, sick to her stomach to realize everyone else must think the same thing.

Even Kincade.

The nurse resumed her seat, picked up her book, and began reading.

Ryder and Draven were waiting in the hall for her, both snapping to attention at her appearance. "She's wrong."

Of course they heard.

She mentally heaved a sigh.

"Is she?" Morgan discovered she felt protective of them, especially since she knew she would be leaving. "You can't dispute that I'm disrupting your team. It puts everyone in danger."

"That's one way to look at it. How others might see it." Draven turned serious. "Let us walk you to your room."

Something about his tone made her feel vulnerable. "Sure."

One man stood on either side of her. Instead of feeling uncomfortable and crowded, Morgan actually relaxed a bit. They were on the second level, only one more floor to go to her room, when she inhaled deeply and braced herself. "Okay, spit it out."

"I'm a siren. When people find out, they shy away from me. Since we can manipulate other people's emotions with nothing more than our voice or touch, they automatically don't trust me." He hunched his shoulders a little bit, and her throat ached at his dull tone. "Sooner or later, everyone I meet questions themselves."

"Not everyone," she protested. "Your team members trust you

implicitly."

"Over time." He reached for the pommel of his dagger, gripping it unconsciously. "Both men and women seek me out, wanting to forget, or seeking a thrill, and I give them what they want."

"You crave touch." Morgan felt queasy at what he was forced to do.

"It's the siren. Giving in to cravings keeps the demons at bay."

Meaning, if he didn't keep the siren fed, he could accidently kill someone with no more than a brush of his fingertips. "I understand."

He swallowed hard at her words, his breathing harsh.

They were only a few doors down from her room when Ryder heaved a sigh. "I'm a werewolf. We don't make friends. If we're lucky, we're either born into a pack or join one. The rest of us are either hired guards or servants. I chose this team. They are my pack now."

Morgan stopped outside her door, not wanting them to leave. "I don't get it. Why are you telling me this?"

Ryder snorted, and pinched the bridge of his nose. "That's why."

Morgan just blinked, completely baffled.

"Because you don't care." Ryder gave her a broken grin. "I sang in front of you. While the others had to plug their ears so they wouldn't be affected, you just paused, then went about your business."

Ryder reached over and opened her door. "Not to mention that on your first night at the Academy, you were confronted by a pack of werewolves…and you didn't attack. Instead, you ran with them."

Draven gently nudged her into her room. "Whether you know it or not, you're one of us."

She gaped at them in stunned surprise, feeling her heart wrench open at their words, offering her something she'd never known she wanted…acceptance…family…unfailing friendship. While she was staring at them mutely, they both smiled and closed the door in her face before she could formulate a reply.

* * *

Morgan tossed and turned for most of the night, unable to forget what they said, obsessing over it. At the first touch of dawn on the horizon, she hopped out of bed, unable to stand being alone with her revolving thoughts for another second.

Although she arrived at the gym over an hour early, every member of her team was already going through maneuvers. Atlas stood on the small mat in the corner, holding two staffs, clearly expecting her.

He caught sight of her hovering in the doorway, gave her a brisk nod, then tossed her a staff. "Ready?"

The smack of the wood against her palm felt good, and Morgan removed the half dozen weapons on her body, then met him on the mat. As other students arrived, they paired off and began sparring. A few of them would stop every now and then, watching her get her ass kicked, before they were waved away to start their own match.

The team wove their way through the groups, offering suggestions, giving tips.

Thankfully, Kincade kept to the other side of the room, only sparing her a glance when she took a particularly nasty hit. He would scowl, as if disappointed in her performance, before returning to his own training.

After three hours, Morgan was drenched in sweat and groaning when she tried to force her back straight. Atlas, the prick, barely looked rumpled as he collected the staff from her. "You did well. In a week, you might even be able to take me."

He strode off, and Morgan was tempted to slit his throat to stop the torture, stifling a groan at the thought of another full week of training at his hands.

"Fall in."

Morgan jumped, startled when Kincade barked out his command. She hobbled across the room, taking her spot at the end of the line. The only thing that made her feel any better was none of the other students were in much better condition.

"Three of you have already dropped out of training or were dismissed after the first day." Morgan stood up straighter in surprise, uncertain why Kincade allowed her to remain on the team after last night. "There is no shame admitting you can't cut it." Everyone glanced back and forth down the line, trying to gauge who hadn't made it. To her disappointment, the loudmouth and his friend were still there. Unfortunately, the only other girl was not.

"Today's test involves tracking and evading." Kincade rocked back and forth on his feet, his hands still clasped behind his back.

Morgan's heartbeat sped up at the chance of spending time outside by herself, doing what she did best…hunting.

Then he went and ruined it.

"You are the target." Kincade gave her a devilish smile, practically rubbing his hands together. "My team and I will be stalking you throughout the school. Your job is to evade us. You will be graded on how long it takes us to locate you, and whether you have the ability to slip away before we catch you."

Groans sounded up and down the line. Morgan nearly joined them, her good mood splatting on the floor at her feet.

Kincade had now made her job hunting the killer nearly impossible.

When she glanced up, it was to find herself pinned under his gaze, and she immediately knew he created this test specifically for her.

He wanted to keep an eye on her, and would use every method at his disposal to spy on her.

The bastard.

She narrowed her eyes, determined to turn his ploy against him. He must have caught something in her expression, and his smugness dropped away. He only looked more determined. "Dismissed."

The game was on.

Chapter Fifteen

*F*or the next hour, Morgan decided to use her time to search each of the victims' rooms. As she expected, they had been cleaned. Unfortunately, they had also been magically wiped. Primordial magic saturated the rooms, leaving behind no traces of the girls or their murderer. She touched the furniture at random, hoping to pick up on the horror that had taken place, but everything seemed so normal it gave her the heebie-jeebies.

The next two rooms were the same.

All personal effects were gone.

The students very existences were wiped clean.

Leaving her exactly nowhere.

For the first time, she began to doubt she would find the killer on her own before he struck again.

The bastard was good.

It galled her to ask Kincade and his team for help, but her pride wasn't worth the cost of another life. She would just have to approach him the right way. From what she'd seen of him and his team, they wouldn't refuse her plea if it meant catching a killer.

Thinking about them reminded her of today's test.

So far, she'd managed to elude her team members as they systematically eliminated the other fighters one by one, but she knew it was only a matter of time before the entire team began hunting her in earnest.

The same way the primordial magic saturated every nook and

cranny of the Academy, the runes on her back had spread and infected every cell of her body, the change somehow allowing her to tap into the magic of the Academy.

To test her theory, she decided to cheat and find the guys before they found her. She closed her eyes and concentrated on their distinct scents. Much to her surprise, Morgan was led down the twists and turns of the hallways, then up a set of stairs…directly toward a suite of rooms.

Instead of being lead toward the guys as she expected, she ended up in their dorm—or more aptly, their barracks. A number of rooms were spread out around her like spokes on a wheel, and the main area, which was more of a gathering place, was decorated with the bare minimum of a table and chairs and a couch. Natural lighting from the large bay windows filled the large space. No knickknacks, no pictures, nothing to give it any kind of personality.

Morgan hesitated in the doorway, her heart fluttering madly as she surveyed their domain. Everything up to this point could be explained away, but if she dared to step over the threshold, she would be knowingly violating their privacy.

Then she remembered the way they ruthlessly tore apart her own room.

Turnabout was fair play.

She boldly crossed into their domain, promising herself just a quick peek to satisfy her curiosity. If she didn't touch anything, it wasn't really snooping, right?

There were ten doors leading off from the main living area. The first room was neat as a pin, the bed made with tight corners, and nothing but weapon after weapon on display. The room had Atlas's name all over it. The next two rooms were empty. The last room was a bit more cluttered, weapons and a surprising number of books scattered throughout. Even without his scent everywhere, she would have known it was Kincade's room. The bedspread was haphazardly thrown on the bed, as if he left in a rush. A large, cloudy mirror stood against the wall, near the foot of his bed.

The room directly across from his was bare as well. She almost moved on when she recognized Ryder's clean, fresh scent, and she half expected to find an open window. There were no pictures, no books, the room so stripped of personality, her throat ached at the lack of possessions.

This was supposed to be his home.

As she moved to the room next door, she began to question the wisdom of invading their privacy. Draven's room was exactly as she imagined. His covers were thrown on the floor, piles of clothes everywhere, not one surface clean.

Each room was much like the men.

But there were so few personal artifacts, it was like they didn't exist outside their life as a hunter, and she was suddenly incredibly sad.

They deserved more.

They *all* deserved more.

Morgan couldn't bring herself to finish snooping and hurried out of the room, struggling with an unexpected dilemma. Not only did she feel bad for sneaking around behind their backs, but what she found only made them more human.

Drat them.

Over the next hour, Morgan spotted each of the four guys spying on her at one time or another, but she didn't linger long enough for them to catch up. With each new spotting, the men grew progressively more serious about their hunt.

Atlas frowned every time he searched a room and didn't find her, more perplexed than upset. She caught him almost smiling at one point, then he really put his whole attention into the hunt. The intensity in his eyes, a glint of something predatory, sent a shiver of dread down her spine, and she knew she didn't want him to be the one who caught her.

It didn't feel like a game anymore.

And Morgan was more determined than ever to evade them.

She could see Draven found the experience amusing, but after the first hour, boredom took over. Thanks to his heritage, she wondered if hunting people hit a little too close to home.

Kincade, of course, became progressively more pissed, narrowing his eyes at her when he caught a glimpse from across a room, clearly suspecting she was cheating somehow, but couldn't figure out how…yet.

It was Ryder whom, no matter how hard she tried, she couldn't elude. He left her alone, observing her as she traveled from room to room, but every time she looked up, he was slightly closer.

He wasn't stalking her…not exactly.

It was more like he couldn't help himself.

Morgan didn't feel a qualm of remorse for using the Academy's sentience to maintain her distance. Half the day was gone, but she didn't dare stop for food. The men had teamed up, systematically clearing floors and rooms, trying to corner her.

As she darted around the corner, seconds ahead of Atlas, she nearly tripped over a large brown wolf. As soon as she spotted him, she planted her hands on her hips and scowled. "No fair. No one can outrun a shifter."

He huffed out a snort, much like a laugh, then turned tail and disappeared down the hall. He returned less than a minute, pulling on a shirt.

Her eyes dropped to his exposed chest, helpless to resist all that tantalizing skin.

They both froze.

"Where'd you get the clothes?" Her face heated at the way it almost sounded like an accusation. Her brain short-circuited at the sight of such delectable skin and muscle, and she sure as hell didn't know why. She'd seen dozens of men naked during her training. Then why did the men on the team affect her so deeply?

She didn't like it.

"There are dressers and cabinets throughout the Academy, placed there especially for shifters in case of emergencies." Ryder was calm as he very slowly dragged down the rest of his shirt. "You should be careful the way you look at us. Wolves will see your attention as a sign of interest, and they will show off in hopes that you might be receptive to them."

Morgan jerked her eyes up to meet his gaze. "What?"

"They will think you're interested in their services."

Morgan didn't think he was talking about being a guard, and it appalled her. "Have you…" She broke off at the inappropriateness of her question. "Never mind. Not my business."

Mortification burned in her chest.

"No." He flung his tangled hair back, scratching his scalp as he ran his fingers through the shaggy, streaked strands, and she curled her fingers into fists to curb the irresistible impulse to help him, almost missing what he said next. "I always knew I wanted to be a hunter."

She fell silent and hurried down the hall, scooting around him, afraid to open her mouth.

She didn't do small talk.

She didn't have friends.

Who knew carrying on a conversation would be so hard?

Ryder easily kept pace. "You have good instincts. You kept ahead of us for hours by placing your scent all over the school and clouding your trail. You seemed to know the moment we were closing in on you."

It wasn't exactly a question, but curiosity was alive in his eyes.

Morgan snorted. "Kinda hard to miss a big wolf following you."

His expression turned serious. "Most never see me."

Her face heated at the intensity of his statement, sensing a larger meaning behind it, then she tightened her lips, annoyed she'd given so much away.

"You haven't run across many shifters."

She shook her head, grateful for the change of subject. "There were no shifters at the coven."

"You've never heard of us?"

At his persistence, Morgan looked at him curiously. "I wasn't exactly included in…well, anything…at the coven." She grimaced in distaste and turned away. "Their idea of fun and games wasn't something I wanted any part of. And there was very little about shifters in the books I was given to study. They were listed as the ultimate guards, and described as being vicious to hunt down if they needed to be eliminated."

"Never hunt one." She flinched at his harsh tone, and he rubbed a tired hand down his face, softening his voice. "They are too dangerous. Even the best hunters are no match for them. We hunt our own when they go feral. It's too dangerous for others. One bite, and the hunter could die or, even worse, turn."

"What do you mean—feral?" More than curiosity made her ask.

Maybe if he knew of a way to stop from going feral, she might be able to stop her own darkness from taking over.

"It's when our animal takes complete control and refuses to turn back into a human." There was such sorrow in his tone, her throat closed, her own problems forgotten.

"Who?"

"My father." His voice was hoarse, his head bowed low.

Based on what she remembered from her readings, werewolves were raised by their fathers. Morgan got the feeling that Ryder was the one who put his father out of his misery. His honor wouldn't allow him to leave the job for anyone else. "I'm sorry."

"He didn't mean to bite me, but he was too far gone by then. Those of us who don't have packs don't survive long on our own. Which is why we pledge ourselves to the school and go out on some of the more difficult hunts." A touch of pride brightened his eyes.

"I would love to go out with your group sometime." He stiffened, and it didn't take a genius to figure out she'd said something wrong.

"Hunting with a shifter is a skill. A strong bond must exist between hunter and shifter." He nervously ran his palms along his pants. "Never run from a shifter. They enjoy the hunt, and might mistake you for prey."

Morgan laughed, then choked when she realized he was serious. "You would never hurt me."

She knew it with quiet certainty.

Warmth shone from his eyes, but before he could speak, a group of witches entered the hallway. The change in him was instantaneous. He bowed his head and stepped out of the way—like some kind of damn servant.

Static filled the air, waking the markings on her back, a clear sign that the witches were using magic, which never boded well.

She recognized one of them as Harper's friend. They sauntered past Morgan like she didn't exist, and headed straight for Ryder. They circled him, touching him, and he flinched away from their stroking hands.

Something was wrong.

Bile rose in her throat when she realized Ryder was unable to move away, and her mood changed from bitchy to downright black.

Morgan reached through them, grabbed his wrist, and pulled him away, protectively shoving him behind her. "I think we're late for training."

The witch scowled at having her fun ruined, shooting Ryder a covetous look. Then a smirk curled her lips, the static in the air crackling. "Why don't you let him decide?"

They were trying to influence him, and Morgan's hand unconsciously tightened around his wrist.

Not going to happen.

Ryder gently placed a hand on her shoulder, and she half expected him to shove her out of the way. "You're right. We should go."

The witch's mouth dropped open in shock. Morgan took advantage of their distraction, pushing Ryder ahead of her. He twisted around in her grip until he was hauling her along behind him.

When they were clear, Morgan jerked away. "Why didn't you stand up for yourself?"

A snarl twisted his mouth, either because of what she asked, or possibly the loss of her touch, she wasn't sure. He fisted his hands, as if to stop himself from reaching for her. "You don't think we try? She can control animals. I have enough wolf blood flowing in my veins that I must obey."

"That's barbaric." Horror took the starch out of her spine. "What can you do to fight it?"

"Only a collar showing ownership, or a mate, can protect any of us." Ryder deflated, unconsciously inching closer until his arm brushed against her with each step. While the touch made her uncomfortable, it eased the urge she had to go back and use her fists on the witch who took such cruel advantage of him.

The thought of him being owned like some dog snatched the breath from her lungs. "Why haven't you chosen a mate? I mean, your life would be easier, wouldn't it?"

Ryder nearly tripped over his own feet at her blunt question. "Despite what you saw, it's usually not so bad. Most wolves would welcome the attention."

"But not you."

"I'm a hunter to my core. I know myself. I would go feral if I was trapped under someone else's control."

Morgan shifted a little uncomfortably at his intense expression, nodding at his not-so-subtle warning to not get attached. A burning sensation spread through her chest at his answer, but she couldn't blame him.

"I should go." He took two steps away from her, then paused, keeping his back to her, those incredibly broad shoulders like a wall. "Witches don't mate with wolves."

Morgan stepped back, the words hurting more than if he'd shoved her away. "I understand."

He glanced at her over his shoulder, his brows lowered, his eyes incredibly sad. "Our wolves choose who we mate. Much like witches, we have little choice in who is selected."

Before she could process his cryptic reply, he was gone.

That was the second time someone mentioned not having a choice about who they mated, and Morgan couldn't make heads or tails of it.

Lost in thought, Morgan wasn't watching where she was going. The sensation of ants crawling over her skin stopped her on the spot. Her head snapped up, her hand falling to her blade as she scanned the area.

Kincade met her gaze boldly from across the room.

He made no pretense of spying on her, slicing through the crowd toward her like a predator on the hunt.

And she was his target.

Morgan spun, intent on heading back the way she came, only to see Atlas striding down the hall, his intense gaze locked on her in grim determination.

Yikes!

Morgan bolted toward the nearest door, cursing her luck when it turned out to be a women's bathroom. While Atlas might hesitate to enter, Kincade would not. If anything, it would grant her no more than a few seconds before he stormed into the room.

The door barely shut when she dashed across the room and dragged the metal garbage can behind her. She tipped it over and wedged it between the door and the wall.

Hopefully that would buy her a few precious seconds.

As she rounded the corner to survey her surroundings, she nearly cheered when she spotted a window.

Without a second's hesitation, she hiked her foot up and hauled her ass up on the sink to peer outside. She was on the opposite side of the school from the garden, two stories aboveground.

Doable.

Popping the latch, she wrenched the window open, then jumped and hauled her torso through the small opening as the first bang clanged against the upended trash can behind her.

Time to move.

She wiggled until half of her body was free of the window, when her hips became wedged in the narrow frame.

"You got to be kidding me." Morgan placed her hands against the stone, pushing and twisting until her hips finally slid free, earning her a series of bruises and scratches for her troubles.

Then she was falling head-first toward the ground.

She lashed out, kicking the wall, using the momentum to spin around.

And just in time.

The ground rushed up toward her.

She landed heavily on her feet, then rolled a couple times to slow her speed.

When she finally stopped and turned, she saw Kincade trying to wedge his body through the small opening, but his shoulders were too broad. He slammed his hand against the stone, glaring down at her in frustration.

She gave him a cheeky grin and waved.

His mouth twisted in a reluctant smile of appreciation for a second before he disappeared from view.

His smile held her immobile, and she blinked stupidly up at the now-empty window, craving another look.

From the first, she found his tough exterior attractive, if not downright mouthwatering, but when he smiled, her heart fluttered like a stupid pixie was caught in her chest.

While he wasn't traditionally gorgeous—he was too lethal for that—his smile had the power to wreck the image she had of him of being untouchable.

And for the first time in her life, she wanted to touch back.

Which was a bad idea.

Really bad.

Morgan popped to her feet, knowing she only had a few minutes before he continued his pursuit. A thrill shot through her at having him so openly chasing her, but the thought of him actually catching her was both tempting and terrifying.

It reminded her that she wasn't there to have fun.

She was supposed to be catching a killer.

The rooms gave her no clues, but she wondered about the bodies.

With that in mind, Morgan sneaked back into the Academy and whispered her request to the walls. Like a magnet, she was pulled deeper into the bowels of the building. Twenty minutes of twisting, winding passageways deposited her outside a door labeled 'Morgue'.

Not thrilled at the idea of looking at a weeks-old decomposing body, she headed toward the file cabinets first. The reports gave the bare minimum of facts, the same reports she had been given. She was about to close the folder when she spotted handwritten notes.

Kincade was the one who found all three bodies.

That in and of itself did not alarm her. Of course he was the one who would be called to investigate. No, what confused her was he seemed more concerned about missing artifacts than the death of three witches.

Unless he knew something she didn't.

Something that wasn't in the reports.

As she slowly closed the folder, memorizing the drawer numbers, she replaced the files and slammed the cabinet shut with a bang. Something nagged at the back of her mind, and she knew she was missing an important clue.

Walking down the cool room, she counted out the numbers, a little freaked to see the morgue was so huge. Thankfully, the three girls rested side by side. She inhaled deeply for courage, then pulled open the drawers.

Instead of decomposing corpses, the girls were perfectly preserved by magic, thank the heavens. But it wasn't the sight of the dead girls that froze her blood. It was the sight of the runes. Unlike her clean marks, these were crude, carved into the vulnerable flesh of their backs. Even after weeks, the scent of scorched flesh lingered over their bodies, the sour stench of magic gone bad tarnishing the runes and making them unusable.

Whatever the murderer was trying to accomplish, he hadn't succeeded.

Yet.

Then she saw something that wasn't in the photos—there were additional runes on the bodies.

As the markings on her back crawled across her skin, Morgan realized it was her ability to null magic that allowed her to see what someone wanted hidden.

The newly revealed marks weren't different from hers as she'd believed.

They were *exactly* the same.

The chill in her body spread to her soul.

The killer cast a spell to hide the real intent behind the ritual.

She needed to find out what the runes meant before someone discovered she had the same markings…and lived to tell the tale.

She had a sinking feeling she wouldn't enjoy the outcome if it was discovered.

Chapter Sixteen

$\mathcal{M}$organ managed to filch a quick sandwich from the kitchen before she hurried to the only place that could offer her answers…the library.

She spent two hours going through book after book, leaving towering stacks surrounding her, but found nothing. A few times she thought she was being stalked through the shelves, but girlish giggles let her know she wasn't the intended prey.

After selecting another five books, she resumed her seat and cracked open the first tome.

"You're not even trying to hide." Draven grabbed the chair across from her, then spun it around to straddle it. He carefully pushed aside a stack of books, which wobbled precariously at being disturbed, so he could have a clear view of her.

Morgan didn't even lift her head from the page she was scanning. "You stopped hunting hours ago."

"I left the hunt to those better suited to the job." Draven crossed his arms over the back of his chair, resting his chin on his forearms. "You're hard to track. I'd swear your scent was everywhere…even in our rooms."

Her hand faltered as she turned the page, a slight tell, but enough that he noticed if the narrowing of his eyes was any indication. No way in hell could she pull off innocent, so she kept her face blank and her head down. "Yeah, very odd."

He pouted playfully, but curiosity sharpened his eyes. "You're not the type to quit on a test. So what is so important that you would risk your future?"

Very reluctantly, Morgan slouched in her chair, debating how much she should say. She couldn't keep beating around the bush, or the killer would strike again, and that death would be her fault.

His clothes were practically falling off him, and she realized he had most likely been the cause of the giggling she heard earlier. A twinge went through her at the thought of him with another girl, but knew by the look in his eyes that he'd already forgotten the other girl's name.

From the first, he always played straight with her.

She refused to believe her instinct about him was wrong.

Mind made up, Morgan flipped the dusty book around so it faced him, and pointed to what she'd found.

Symbols.

Some of the same symbols on her body.

"Pages have recently been ripped out." She ruffled what remained of a few sheets of paper that had been hacked out of the book. "They took a ritual."

The charm she found so riveting drained away as the hunter in him rose. He grabbed the book, pulling it forward to scan the pages. "What do you know about this?"

There was no accusation in his tone, but he sounded decidedly less friendly.

Morgan rubbed a finger across her bottom lip, arguing with herself about how much to share. While the killer might target them, holding back information relevant to an active hunt would almost guarantee it.

She reluctantly stood, releasing a heavy sigh, nerves jittering at actually sharing her secret with anyone. She turned her back to him, then began to lift up her shirt and cami.

"Morgan…" Draven's strangled voice faded as her shirt rose higher. "Shite."

"Do these look familiar to you?" She glanced at him over her shoulder.

"*Shite!*" Draven stood, staring at the runes as if he'd seen a ghost. "Where did you get those?"

Morgan dropped her shirt, tugging at the hem until she was sure she was covered. "I have no idea. I suspect it's why I can't remember anything before the age of ten."

Draven swallowed painfully, his gaze haunting. "Everyone found with those markings is now dead."

"No, they died during the process." She grabbed the book with the symbols and slapped it shut. "I was sent here to investigate their deaths. I think the Academy has summoned me to stop the killer...one way or another."

"You're going to use yourself as bait," he snarled, then grasped her arm above the elbow and began dragging her after him. "Come."

Morgan could have broken his hold, but didn't.

He was right.

She couldn't do this alone.

"Can you actually read that book?" He stared at the ancient volume clutched to her chest as if it would sprout legs and walk away.

"Some. Enough to know it's a ritual. But I need those missing pages to figure out more." Draven practically frog-marched her through the Academy and up an endless flight of stairs, until they reached the rooftop. Unwilling to give up his grip on her, he kicked open the door, not even slowing his momentum.

The whole team was in attendance, jerking to their feet at their abrupt appearance. At the sight of them, her resolve wavered, and she began to doubt the wisdom of involving them. Despite her determination to keep her distance, she'd already committed a grave sin...she'd grown to care for them.

Before anyone had a chance to speak, a loud horn from Viking times drowned out everything else.

An emergency.

Adrenaline jolted through her as the men snatched up their weapons.

They were ready to move in moments.

Kincade halted in front of them despite the urgency, his concerned gaze tracing her face, sending her heart flapping like the wings of a witless wyvern against her ribs. "Can this wait?"

Morgan spoke before Draven had a chance. "Yes."

"Good." He sheathed the blade he held, then walked past her.

"Go to your room and stay there."

Her mouth fell open at his command. He walked away before she could argue. The rest of the team trailed after him, each casting her a wary look. Some were sympathetic, others relieved, but none protested the order.

Fuck that.

She waited for the door to latch behind them, then followed, stashing the book in the stairwell, wedging it into the small ledge above the door, then hurried after them.

She saw the men split up, Kincade entering the headmistress's office while the rest stood at attention in the hall. Just when she stepped back to retreat, the headmistress looked up and pinned her to the spot.

"Come, Miss Moran." She held open the door to her office. "Since this involves you, you might as well join us."

That couldn't be good.

The woman was tall but impossibly thin. Not sickly, but dainty. Then it clicked…faerie. Her bones were small to enable her to fly.

Morgan swallowed hard and joined them with some trepidation. Faeries weren't the wish-giving, sparkling fairy dust sort from fairy tales. They were carnivorous, with needle-like sharp teeth and a powerful venom strong enough to kill with one bite. When the headmistress smiled, even though her teeth were normal, Morgan flinched.

"I'll be in to join you both shortly." She firmly shut the door behind Morgan, leaving her alone with a furious Kincade. But even faced with the looming threat of being shut in a room with an angry trained assassin, she couldn't help wondering where the faerie kept her wings.

* * *

Morgan hovered in the doorway, trepidation slithering down her spine, then she grabbed the same daring she used to hunt monsters, ignored Kincade, and plopped into the seat across from the headmistress's desk.

Kincade slowly rose to his feet from where he was leaning against the window ledge, his expression thunderous. "I gave you a direct order. What are you doing here?"

"My job. You?" Morgan knew she shouldn't be flippant, but his continual animosity was like a sore tooth. His dislike reminded her that she was an outsider and would never be one of them. At the thought, all the fight leached out of her, and she couldn't stand to look at him. His repeated rejections hurt something deep inside her. "Listen, I was summoned here to find a killer...or maybe I'm the bait...I'm not sure anymore. But once I've solve the murders, I'll either be sent back to the coven or dead, so you won't have to worry about me anymore one way or another. How about we call a truce until then?"

Morgan didn't even hear him move.

One second she was sitting in her chair, the next she was spun around, the metal feet of the chair screeching across the stone floor. Kincade bent close, placing his hands on either side of her chair, preventing her escape. "No."

"No?" She stared at him in disbelief, her anger flaring like a struck match at having her truce thrown back in her face. "To hell with you."

Morgan lifted her feet, planting them on his chest and shoving hard.

Instead of flying across the room as she expected, the stubborn bastard barely budged. She dropped her feet, getting right up into his face, unable to keep the snarl out of her voice. "What are you? Made of stone or something? Back off."

At the sound of metal shrieking in protest, she glanced down to see the arms of her chair being twisted into a tangled mess in his grip. Instead of feeling threatened, his strength sent a whirlwind of tiny furies shooting from her gut up to her throat. Very slowly, Morgan tipped her head back, bracing for a blow.

What she didn't expect was for his lips to crash down on hers.

Both froze in shock.

It was a toss-up which of them was more stunned.

Morgan had been kissed before. Since she wasn't a witch, some hunters didn't think she was due the same respect, and they were usually rewarded with a kick in the balls.

This was different.

Kincade tasted different, his lust awakening something inside her that wanted more. The hunger was irresistible…and she couldn't help wanting something for herself just once.

Knowing this was a once-in-a-lifetime opportunity, Morgan was determined to make it worth it…even if she knew she would regret it later. She sank her fingers into his hair, her hands tingling from the soft strands, and took control of the kiss, biting and nibbling at his lips until he opened his mouth.

Instead of shoving her away, he hesitated for two seconds, then his mouth grew demanding, taking more, his hands coming up to cup her face, tipping her head back, so he could plunder her mouth. The instant he touched her face, she was sucked under his spell, and left craving more.

The rest of the world disappeared when he reached down and hauled her out of the chair. Somehow, her legs found their way around his waist, his hands under her ass, and she shivered from the heat of him as it soaked into her skin until the only thing that mattered was *more.*

He slammed her up against the wall, seeking more, waking a ravenous hunger in her she hadn't known was possible. She dragged him closer, arching against him, shivering at the feel of heat and hard muscle. The tingling in her hands turned into a burn that spread under her skin, dragging her reluctantly out of the haze of pleasure. She tore her lips from his, struggling to catch her breath, resting her forehead against his shoulder to curb the impulse to lick her way up his neck. "What the hell was that?"

"You will not place yourself in danger." At the growled words, she jerked her head up. His fingers tightened possessively on her hips, hard enough to leave bruises, the heat in his eyes burning brighter, and she shivered at his complete loss of control.

While part of her loved it, the other part of her rebelled at his demand.

Self-preservation won, and her lust cooled. She jerked her hands from where she'd been absently brushing the back of his neck and shoved away from his chest. When it looked as if he wasn't going to let her go, she grabbed his ear, gave it a vicious twist, and wrenched it backward. A growl rumbled in his chest, and she gulped when it looked like he would devour her.

Much to her surprise, he obeyed and released her.

Slowly.

Almost…reluctantly.

She slid down his chest, conscious of his hands running up her sides, and she nearly changed her mind and climbed back up.

It took all her concentration to remember what they were even arguing about. Right. He wanted to swaddle her in bubble wrap, treat her like she didn't know which end of the knife to use, and she hated it. "That's not your decision to make."

"Like hell." He grabbed her arm, swinging her around to face him. He looked torn, both confused and furious, as he stared down at her. "What do you mean you were summoned here?"

Morgan raised a brow at his tone. "The Academy sent for me. Didn't you find it odd that I joined the Academy at my age? With my skills?"

He released her like she'd burned him, then stood stock-still. Instead of feeling good about pushing him away, she felt sick to her stomach.

"Why don't you stick to your investigation of missing artifacts while I search for the killer? Then I will get out of your hair, and you won't have to worry about protecting me anymore." The hoarse, scratchy words shredded her throat. And her heart. "You stay out of my way, and I'll stay out of yours. Deal?"

She held out her hand, craving his touch one more time before she had to give him up.

He looked like she'd offered him a dead rat to eat, his hands fisted at his side as if he wanted to strangle her or yank her over his knee and spank her.

"I could hear you two bickering all the way out in the hall." The headmistress entered the room, briskly circling the desk and bracing her hands on top, giving them both a disapproving look.

Kincade flushed at the rebuke, but Morgan just crossed her arms, going cold as she wondered what else the woman might have heard.

"Please have a seat." Without waiting for them, she settled behind her desk.

Kincade held out her chair, and Morgan gingerly sat, very aware of his hulking presence lingering where she couldn't see her. She didn't like having him there, uncomfortable not knowing what he was doing. As he circled her, his fingertips brushed across the nape of her neck, before commandeering the seat next to hers as if nothing happened.

Goose bumps marched across her shoulders and down her arms at the unexpected touch. One by one, the markings warmed in the wake of his fingertips, reacting to his touch much the way she did…they wanted more.

The thought of the runes, with their deadly magic, anywhere near Kincade turned her skin cold and clammy.

Death followed everyone with those marks.

She wouldn't have him be one of them.

"Kincade already came to me with his concerns that the two cases might possibly be connected. Our duty is to keep the students safe." The headmistress pinned them both under her stare. "Bearing that in mind, you will work together."

"But—"

When the headmistress focused on her, Morgan saw her pupils swell until her eyes went completely black. No whites at all. Morgan nearly swallowed her tongue and quickly bit back what she was going to say. The strength of the woman's magic filled the room until every breath was a struggle.

In reaction to the magic, the runes along her spine burned like acid as her own magic struggled to escape her. It wanted to destroy the threat. The torque on her neck warmed, twisted, and bent, the metal crawling up her collarbone, until it encircled her throat like a choker. She almost snorted when she looked down and saw tiny metal faeries dangling around her neck.

Morgan took them as a symbol of faith, and tried to swallow the festering rage living in the magic. It hurt. Hurt like her bones were melting inside her body. What she wasn't able to smother, the metal managed to absorb. As the ringing in her ears faded, voices rushed back.

"You've been given a lot of latitude because of MacGregor's belief in you. He's never thought anyone good enough to sponsor before." Her musings might be contemplative, but the look in her eyes was more assessing. While she might trust MacGregor, she was reserving her judgment on Morgan.

That, Morgan could understand. "What do you mean—sponsor?"

The headmistress's brows furrowed, then smoothed out, quickly hiding her surprise. Her irises returned to normal as an eerie, blue-green color swirled back into the center. "The Academy only allows a select few within its walls. Students must be sponsored by previous graduates. They stake their reputation on the candidates they nominate."

The blood drained from her head, shock knocking the breath out of her. She had no clue MacGregor believed in her so completely.

"I hope you live up to his praise, or you won't last long."

Those ominous words tingled along her spine, and Morgan knew if she failed she wouldn't be kicked out of the Academy—she would be dead.

Kincade stiffened, ready to defend her, but Morgan didn't bat an eyelash. Tougher people than the headmistress had tried to kill her and failed. "Yes, ma'am."

Understanding passed between the women.

They would both do what was necessary to keep the Academy safe.

The headmistress flipped open a folder on her desk, getting back down to business. "Kincade is our best. You will work together to clear this case."

Kincade's lips flattened, his dislike of working with Morgan clear, and his rejection cut deep.

Morgan wasn't any happier.

While she knew the runes would eventually kill her, she had no intention of taking him down with her. "Pairing us wouldn't be wise. It will put him at risk."

"You have no access to magic, so you decided to train as a huntress. The only way you will achieve your goal is by training with the elites." The headmistress tipped her head toward Kincade. "That means working with him and his men. This school creates only the best graduates...for a reason. If you can't work with others, how do you expect to be a success? Your job is about more than killing. It's also about protecting the innocents...even if that means you have to work with contentious people. The choice is yours."

She threaded her fingers together and set them on the blotter in front of her. "Unless you no longer want to hunt. No one would blame you. Women are more suited to working magic. There is a reason there are so few huntresses in history. It's harder on women, because we're called to give more, sacrifice more. Are you up for it? Or is MacGregor's faith in you misplaced?"

Morgan couldn't stop hunting.

It was in her blood.

The headmistress was right, failure was not an option. This wasn't about her. It was about stopping the greater evil, and they had a murderer to catch. "With or without magic, I am a hunter first. I know nothing else."

"Good. Now that we have that settled," the headmistress released a heavy breath, still focused on Morgan. "I have some bad news. Your coven has been attacked."

Morgan couldn't speak for a moment, not sure she heard her correctly. More and more nasty creatures were entering through the rifts, but attacking a coven directly took balls.

Unless they were desperate and searching for something.

Or someone.

Her.

Guilt was like a meaty hand tightening around her throat, threatening to strangle her.

"Were there any survivors?" Sounds intensified, drowning out her surroundings, her world narrowing down to a pinpoint. Her guts twisted into a Gordian knot as she waited for the answer.

The headmistress's face softened. "It is unknown. We've had no contact since they reported the initial attack. Kincade and his team will secure the mansion and the rift. We'll keep you informed as soon as we learn anything."

"What? No!" Morgan held out her hands beseechingly. "You need me there. I know the coven. I know the forest. More, I know where the rifts open. You need me."

She couldn't let them leave without her.

They would be in more danger than they even knew.

"Her emotional attachment to the coven will make her a liability. My team will be more effective without her." Kincade's betrayal gutted her, souring the kiss they shared earlier.

She had been foolish to believe, even for one second—she shook away the thought before it fully formed. She hated knowing her hands still tingled from touching him, and she itched to reach for her blades, wanting to cut him as deeply.

Everything she held dear was falling apart. She refused to abandon her coven, too. "The headmistress just told us to work as a team, but at the first opportunity, you're cutting me out. I've proven my abilities to MacGregor, and I won't sit here on my hands like a helpless female. I'm going—with or without you."

Kincade rose to his feet and stomped toward her, his mouth opening to tear into her.

Morgan was braced for a fight when the headmistress held up her hand. "She's right. We can't afford to turn down help. She has the skills to keep herself alive. She goes with you."

"Fine." Kincade's scowled, but something in his eyes raised her hackles. "But on one condition—she must obey me."

Chapter Seventeen

$\mathcal{M}$organ prowled her corner of the basement room, not trusting herself near the others. She glared at the wall-size mirror, wishing she had the ability to activate the spell without them so she didn't have to wait.

Kincade and his group stood around a table at the center of the room, looking serious and deadly while they studied aerial maps and grid placements, going over strategies. She wanted to march over there and demand they hurry, but Kincade made it clear he didn't welcome her help.

Not that it would do any good to speed them along.

They were waiting for the support team to finish their preparations.

Once Kincade and his team cleared the mansion, a second team would travel through the mirror, bring the wards back up, and prepare a triage. While she understood they needed to be prepared, they were also stopping her from helping MacGregor.

It had been twenty minutes since she'd learned of the attack, and every second counted in battle.

"How are you holding up?" Mistress McKay magically appeared at her side...although it could be that Morgan was so busy glaring at the others she hadn't noticed her approach.

"Impatient." Morgan welcomed the distraction, absently noting the tightness around McKay's eyes, the strain thinning her lips.

McKay was worried, too.

Not good.

Morgan bounced on her feet, trying to rid herself of nervous energy.

She wanted to move now.

Every second they delayed could cost lives.

When she scanned the room for any signs of progress, she saw Kincade glare at her, rubbing his arm like she'd given him cooties or an STD or something. Pain ricocheted in her chest, and she wanted to march over there and smack him.

"He's a good man. He's just not used to anyone like you. It leaves him off-balance."

"He's an ass who doesn't even bother to hide his dislike. It was there the first time he set eyes on me. He didn't even try to give me a chance." Morgan turned away when she remembered the rest of what McKay had said, and grabbed the distraction with both hands. "What do you mean, *like me?*"

"I would say, since you're still here, he *is* giving you a chance." The small rebuke from McKay smarted, cooling off her ire a tad. "Kincade has been trained from birth to be the best hunter, but his time is limited. Sooner or later, he will be paired with a witch, and his duty will be to protect her."

Morgan scowled. "What do you mean paired?"

"I see MacGregor failed to teach you everything." Mistress McKay rolled her eyes, then sighed. "The magic inherent in a witch's blood can cause a chemical reaction in a hunter. This reaction will bind the witch and hunter together."

"Like slavery." Morgan shuddered at the thought of being trapped in such a way after years of watching the witches at the coven treat their guards worse than dirt. "A hunter has no choice but to protect his female. I can't understand why so many here look forward to it."

"They don't get a choice of who they're pair with. They must trust fate." She nodded to Kincade. "He knows his time is growing short."

Morgan could understand his dread. The thought of him being tied to some female against his will made her physically sick. "How awful."

"No." Mistress McKay stepped in front of her. "Not at all. In the old ways, it was considered an honor. Some witches have perverted the pairing, but most take it seriously. When he's selected, his DNA will alter, and he will *want* to protect her. Everything he's been through is considered training for his true mission—to protect his mate."

A deep yearning to be loved that fiercely tore through her, but Morgan didn't trust it. She'd seen it go bad too many times to believe in fairy tales.

Though she didn't actively practice magic, she was keenly aware that she had the potential to cast magic if it ever woke up. The thought scared the crap out of her. It was why she vowed never to choose a mate and risk it going so horribly wrong. As if picking up on her volatile emotions, the markings on her back rippled and stretched, wanting to hunt. Morgan bit back a groan of pain, not sure how much longer she could contain the magic.

"This is taking too long." She glared at the mirror impatiently.

"MacGregor is tough. He won't go down without a fight." Despite her bracing words, worry shadowed McKay's eyes. "He'll hold them off."

Morgan nodded, but she knew the old man wasn't invincible. He hadn't been actively hunting for years. She was also afraid that given an opportunity, Catalina would stab him in the back to clear the way for her to become the new head of the coven.

As her aggression swelled, the runes sank more heavily into her body, the magic seeping into her flesh and bones…spreading. The necklace she wore absorbed most of the magic, and the metal twisted and turned, spiraling up her neck until her throat was protected by a layer of chain mail.

"Oh, my."

At McKay's reverent whisper, Morgan reached up, covering her necklace self-consciously, cursing that she'd forgotten the woman's presence. The torque almost never changed in front of anyone, and if it did, most didn't notice when it happened. "The metal is imbued with magic, and reacts to my emotions to protect me."

McKay tore her attention away from the torque, reluctantly looking up to meet Morgan's gaze, her eyes shimmering with knowledge. "Yes, it is protecting you, but—"

"Time to go."

Her blood turned molten at Kincade's words, her curiosity regarding the necklace's origin forgotten. The men headed toward the mirror, and Morgan prodded them to hurry.

"Bring him back to us." McKay spoke to her alone, a fierceness in her eyes that matched MacGregor's indomitable will. For the first time, Morgan saw how the two of them worked together...they would have been unstoppable.

Morgan nodded once. "I'll do my best."

McKay stepped between the towering men. Though she might be small in stature, the sheer power she gathered around her caused everyone to turn, parting for her as she strode toward the mirror.

As the magic built, it felt like the runes on her back were being peeled off her skin, fighting against being called forward. A flash of heat splashed into the room when the magic was released, the blast catching the mirror dead center, causing the silver surface to ripple. The sigils surrounding the frame glowed a bright gold as the spell sprang to life.

"Traveling through a mirror can cause motion sickness if you're not used to it. Most people can't handle the impact of pure primordial magic. It's a hundred times more potent than the magic witches use, so you must be careful and not linger. The longer you're in contact with the void, the more seriously it will affect you. Consequently, the purer your heritage, the fewer adverse effects it will have on you."

Not caring about what price she had to pay, Morgan grabbed her weapons and charged forward.

"Morgan, wait!"

She dodged the arms reaching for her, raised her fists to shield her face, and leapt through the portal.

"Son of a bitch."

The last echoes of Kincade's voice faded as the mirror sucked her into the void. The darkness wrapped around her in welcome, the runes on her back growing heavy...but the expected pain never came. The markings became fluid, seeping under her skin, spreading, slipping into her bloodstream, lighting her on fire as it sped through her system.

Nothing she did halted the warm burn.

It felt…comforting.

And Morgan knew that was a bad sign.

She raised her hands, feeling like she was almost floating in a warm liquid, cocooned and protected.

Oddly enough, it felt like the home she'd never known.

Then a bright light blazed in the distance, jerking her forward, and she was spit out on the other side. Being kicked out of the void wrenched the warmth from her bones, shoving her back into the brutal world. Pain slammed into the marks along her spine like thousands of needles piercing her body as the runes rose toward the surface of her skin once more. The torque took longer to respond than normal, and she feared it was because the markings were growing in strength. Soon, the necklace wouldn't be able to help regulate the pain at all.

She allowed herself a few seconds to mourn the loss of the peacefulness in the void, then shrugged it off and focused on the mission.

Finding and saving MacGregor.

Morgan was surprised to see the guys had arrived first.

Atlas was staring at the mirror, steadily flipping his knife, when his gaze caught hers. He fumbled the blade, slicing his finger. His perfect hair was ruffled for the first time, revealing his pointed ears.

They were…cute.

When she opened her mouth, Atlas tipped his head toward the center of the room.

Kincade prowled back and forth, everyone standing some distance away, dangerous energy snapping around him. His broad shoulders and impressive chest stretched his black shirt with his every move. His brows were lowered, his jaw clenched, everything about him lethal. He wasn't handsome, more like striking, even more so with the pissed-off expression on his face.

Morgan stepped toward him, then stumbled when the world twisted away from under her feet.

After the void, this reality no longer felt familiar.

As soon as she stumbled, Kincade's head snapped up. In seconds, he was at her side, catching her arm and yanking her up against him, knocking the breath out of her—no way would she admit she'd lost her breath for any other reason. Her palms tingled at the contact, the yummy static of him spreading up her arm. Her fingers craved to explore more, wanting to touch every inch of him.

This feeling was different from when she sensed magic.

Something more.

The scent of warm earth and hot stone eased the churn of nausea trying to twist her inside out. His pale green eyes scanned her face once, then again, as if to reassure himself. His arms tightened around her, and her heart skipped a betraying beat.

Then his brows slammed down, and he released her, dismissing the incident as if nothing had happened. As if he didn't feel the connection. "You should feel better soon. Vertigo is not an uncommon side effect of the void."

Mortification burned her cheeks at the abrupt change, and she wondered if she'd imagined their connection. She jerked her eyes away from him to see Draven standing sentry by the door, the devil-may-care look gone. His blue eyes softened when they met hers, the dead look in them fading, and he gave her a quick nod of greeting. The black leathers he wore were slim, revealing his deceptively muscular body. Normally covered from head to toe, tonight he had his sleeves rolled up.

She gasped.

Every inch of his forearms was covered with scars.

Questions burned the tip of her tongue, but she bit them back. It wasn't her place to ask. Everyone had secrets. She had no right to pry, not unless she was willing to reveal her own.

Ryder stood by the windows, the big man nearly two heads taller than herself. His size should be impossible to miss, but he stood so still, it was unsettling. His skin was tinged a bit green, one hand gripping the window frame, and she wasn't sure if it was to keep him upright or to keep him from ripping something apart. Instead of staring outside, his gaze was on her. His sandy brown hair was knotted, his whisky eyes practically glowing as he pinned her to the spot. Held tight in his right hand was her blade.

"Ryder?"

He blinked, his human side returning, and he dropped his gaze, turning away from her.

Instead of being relieved, his withdrawal only troubled her more.

Morgan turned away, surveying the room, and froze.

They had landed in MacGregor's study, only the destruction was so complete, she hadn't recognized it.

The total devastation gutted her as efficiently as a knife.

The once peaceful room was decimated. Books were yanked off the shelves, bindings ripped, pages shredded, the shelving snapped in half. The desk wasn't in much better shape, the wood smashed into slivers no bigger than toothpicks. Even the bricks of the fireplace were broken and cracked. Everything that made the room her haven had been destroyed.

This went beyond rage.

This was complete annihilation.

As if, when they didn't find what they wanted, they couldn't contain their fury.

Her.

This was all because of her.

The room spun and twisted, breathing becoming a struggle.

She had to know. "MacGregor?" She winced at the hope in her voice. She knew exactly how unlikely it was for anyone to have survived.

Ryder eased closer to her, gently gathering her to his chest when she thought her knees would give out. She grabbed his shirt, barely managing to remain upright.

He ran his hands up and down her back soothingly, over and over, as if she was on the verge of shattering. She wasn't sure he was wrong. He radiated heat, but it scarcely warmed the chill ghosting along her skin.

It took her a few moments to realize the rumbling in his chest was him speaking. "He's not here. He must have gotten the witches out. He's not here."

Kincade's sharp eyes scanned her face. "Ryder, stay here with her. The rest of us will scout the mansion and report back in five." The men were already in motion when she shook her head.

Instead of abandoning her or cursing at her, Kincade offered her compassion.

"Wait." She pushed away from Ryder, embarrassed by her meltdown. The wolf reluctantly released his hold, but remained within touching distance, and she wasn't sure if she was annoyed or relieved. "I'll be fine. We need to move fast. The longer we wait, the less likely the chance of finding survivors."

Kincade strode toward her, his movements sleek and deadly. He grabbed her jaw, tipping up her face, his touch surprisingly gentle. He studied her, clearly undecided, and she knew he was going to leave her behind by the way his mouth tightened.

"If you leave, I'll find a way to slip out of the mansion without you." She jerked her chin away from his touch, her voice hardening. "I won't wait for you to clear it. I've lived here for years, I've been ruthlessly hunted by the witches here, so I know every nook and cranny. From one step to the next, you won't even notice I'm gone."

A muscle ticked in his jaw, but, much to her surprise, his lips curved slightly, and he nodded. "Lead the way."

Without hesitation, Morgan headed toward the exit, her blades in her hands before she was aware of drawing them.

The door hung drunkenly from its hinges. She touched the wood, but the once-friendly magic had been completely drained. "Whoever attacked was organized and strong enough to take down a mansion imbued with magic, their sheer numbers overrunning the hunters."

Kincade nodded in acknowledgment.

Taking his nod as approval, she shoved against the door, her blood whooshing in her ears as she slipped out of the study, terrified of what she would find.

As she crept into the foyer, the first thing she noticed was the powerful double doors had been ripped clear off the mansion, red dust exploding into the room, as if whatever managed the feat had torn the magic right out of it. The granite should have been indestructible, but cracks ran up to the ceiling, while sections of the floor were shattered. Scorch marks marred the once-pristine walls, evidence that the witches hadn't given up without a fight.

The guys spread out behind her, Ryder and Kincade remaining close, the silence deafening as she processed what she was seeing.

Blood and guts stained the walls and ceilings, bits of human body parts strewn across the entryway. Following the trail, she saw the twisted bodies of the hunters littering the lawn like discarded toys, with their limbs missing and heads lopped clear off.

Then it clicked what she was seeing.

Only hunters.

"The witches are gone."

The men glanced at each other, and she waved away their concern. "No, I mean all the bodies are men."

Kincade cast a swift look at the remains, then swung around sharply. "Ryder?"

Without further prompting, Ryder closed his eyes and lifted his face to the air and inhaled, his large chest expanding, his muscles stretching impressively. "Whatever was here is gone. I smell blood and death, but nothing else in the immediate vicinity." When he opened his eyes, the whisky color glowed as his wolf stared out at them. "I don't sense any magic."

Meaning the witches had escaped.

Possibly MacGregor as well.

"Spread out. Pair off. Keep each other in sight at all times."

Morgan hurried toward the stairs, pausing at the bottom step when she saw Atlas disregard the order and head toward the basement alone. "Be careful. They have a lab down there where they run their experiments. If the creatures were set free from their cells, they may attack." Morgan unconsciously rubbed her wrists. "Not all of them are exactly sane anymore."

Kincade gave a jerk of his head, and Ryder quickly accompanied the elf.

With another hand signal, she watched Draven peel away and stand guard at the main door.

Then Kincade turned toward her and waited.

She took it as permission and leapt up the stairs two at a time. The damage upstairs wasn't as thorough. At the top of the stairs, she headed straight toward the double doors. "This room was originally intended as a ballroom. The coven mimicked the original designs, but converted it to a gym and armory." She gestured down the hallway. "There are two entrances, and this corridor wraps around the entire second floor. There are only about a dozen rooms along the way. The third floor has more."

Kincade grimaced and reluctantly nodded. "I'll take the third floor."

She watched in amazement as he left, surprised that he actually accepted her assessment.

While Ryder might have confirmed no one inside remained alive, that didn't mean there were no nasty surprises left behind.

Morgan opened the first door and began her own search.

Room after room, she found the same…nothing.

No bodies. No surprises. After she searched the last room on her floor, Morgan headed down the stairs, and walked toward Draven. "Nothing."

She went to peer out the door, and Draven blocked her with his shoulder. "Don't."

Morgan swallowed hard, the brief glimpse she had of outside flashing in her mind. "That bad?"

He nodded, his face grim, his pale blue eyes dead.

Footsteps thundered up the stairs, and Atlas and Ryder charged into the room. Both men were breathing heavily. Ryder's eyes were a little wild, while Atlas's usually hard eyes were soulless.

As Atlas came toward her, she gripped her weapons harder. "What the hell were they doing down there?"

Ryder's attention snapped toward Atlas, and he took a step forward, ready to intervene, when she waved him off. The wolf studied her from head to toe, leaving her feeling exposed.

He saw too much.

He knew what it was like to be targeted by witches, how far they would go, and what little protection people like them had. She turned away from the promise of retribution in his eyes, refusing to allow herself to feel anything. It was a weakness she couldn't afford.

Morgan narrowed her eyes at Atlas's accusation, her heart going dead in her chest. "I don't know. My guess, based on the time I spent chained down there as one of their experiments, is they were trying to find a way to harvest the magic from the creatures who escaped from the rifts—me included."

He flinched, a telling sign when he normally revealed nothing.

Harvesting magic from a creature was a death sentence, a slow, agonizing way to die, much like having one's soul ripped out.

"When I proved troublesome to them, resistant to their torture, MacGregor became curious and investigated." Morgan's smile was all teeth. "They lied and explained they were studying the creatures, cataloging their strengths and weaknesses. He, of course, didn't believe their shit, and took me into his custody. Not everyone was so lucky."

Morgan sheathed her blades, pulling her thick black hair off her back and trying it into a messy knot. "When a rift would open, I helped as many as I could escape, sending them back through the void. It only served to annoy the witches more." She smiled up at Atlas. "You might say I was a pain in their asses. It was only a matter of time before they collected more. Rescuing them became trickier. More dangerous."

"Jesus." Draven's voice was hoarse. "They could've killed you."

Morgan shrugged. "Believe me, the witches tried. Good thing I proved to be hard to kill."

Atlas blinked at her, then pinched the bridge of his nose. "He meant the creatures."

Morgan paused, then placed her hands on her hips. "So, let me get this straight. Are you mad because I allowed the creatures to be held captive, or because I helped them escape? I'm confused."

Draven edged between them, pushing a loose piece of her hair behind her ear. "Morgan..."

She sighed the way his husky voice drew out her name, his affection melting her anger better than any siren magic. "I wasn't in much danger. I had help. He wouldn't have let anything happen to me."

Her eyes burned as she remembered how Ascher had protected her, and how he ultimately suffered the consequences for it. She couldn't allow these men to suffer the same fate. "MacGregor offered me what protection he could, but I'm a hunter. Your stupid rules make the witches untouchable. Don't you think the others knew what was happening?" She pulled away and paced. "No one cares, not if it means they can access magic from the void. It's pure. Undiluted."

"That makes no sense." Atlas frowned at her. "The magic in the void is too powerful. It would rip them apart."

"Unless they can extract it from others—think of the subjects of the experiments like a filter. They take the abuse while the witches get the byproduct."

Atlas glanced around the room, then peered out the door. "If what you say is true, it would be war. No one from the primordial realm would allow what the witches were doing to stand. This is retaliation."

Morgan wanted to agree with him, but couldn't speak the lie. "That's one possibility."

"What do you know?" Kincade's deadly voice cut through the room, and the men parted to let him through.

It took conscious thought not to shift nervously under his hard stare. "I think they came for me."

Kincade stopped only a foot from her, gripping his hair as if he would rip it out, his eyes on his feet. "You came here—insisted on coming—knowing they were hunting you?"

A tremor jolted through her at his ominous, rough voice. "I had no choice."

His head snapped up as if he'd been jabbed with a cattle prod, a vein throbbing in his neck. "You put us all in danger with your selfish behavior."

Her insides crumbled at his accusation, the words shattering her fragile hope for a future with them. The back of her throat aching that he would believe her capable of doing such a thing.

She thought they'd accepted her as one of them.

Ryder edged forward to come to her aid, but halted when Kincade snarled at him. "Don't you fucking dare."

"I came to keep you safe. I couldn't let you walk into a trap."

He snorted dismissively. "All you had to do was tell us."

He spun away, as if unable to stand the sight of her, and her chest hollowed out at his rejection. "I was on my way to tell you when we were summoned. Then it was too late. I couldn't tell you, because you would've left me behind."

"Damned straight. You will stay here." Kincade then proceeded to act like she didn't exist. "Atlas, give the others the all-clear to bring the second team through. Ryder and Draven, scout the yard. We'll move out in five."

When he made to follow the others, Morgan stepped into his path, unable to escape the conviction that if she allowed him to leave without her, she would never see them again. "You need me to show you where the rift is located. If anyone survived, they would be there, trying to close the gate, and stemming the flow of creatures entering this realm."

Morgan flinched when he lifted his head and looked at her.

His eyes were dead, devoid of all emotions. "No."

"The longer you search for the rift, the more creatures will escape to wreak havoc." She shoved away her foolish emotions, locking them down so she could do what she must, even if everyone on the team came to hate her. "If anyone survived, they are out there, waiting for help."

"She's right. Anyway, if we leave her, she will only figure out a way to follow us. She'll be safer with us." Atlas came to her rescue as he emerged from the office. "The others are on their way. We need to move."

Kincade didn't curse, didn't react in any way as he studied her.

His skin rippled as something shifted beneath the surface, reminding her that he was something *other* as well. "You will remain at my side at all times. If you disobey, I won't hesitate to knock you out, drag you back here, and shove you through the mirror back to the Academy myself. Understood?"

Morgan would have cheered if it didn't feel like her heart was breaking. "Yes."

She watched him walk out the door, but the distance between them was much greater.

"Give him time."

Morgan gave a start when Atlas spoke from right in her ear. "What?"

"He's worried about you and doesn't know how to handle his protective instincts. Bringing you along goes against everything he holds dear, against how he was raised. He lost someone close to him, and it nearly destroyed him. You terrify him."

Morgan snorted. "You're wrong. I'm nothing more than a hunter, not one of his precious witches to be worshipped. It's better he accept that now."

Chapter Eighteen

Morgan took off into the forest, hyper-aware of the men spread out in her wake. Each moved silently through the trees, the moonlight illuminating their path. Instead of shutting out the runes on her back, she concentrated on the connection and welcomed the magic. As if aware of her attention, the runes stretched and settled more heavily under her skin, and she felt the pull deep in her gut, guiding her toward the rift.

They had covered half the distance when a furious growl split the air.

She would recognize that snarl anywhere.

"Ascher!"

Without hesitation, Morgan altered course, yelling at the others over her shoulders. "Keep straight. The rift is only a little farther ahead."

Cursing erupted behind her. To her surprise, the whole team followed her trail. It almost made her stop. Duty fought loyalty for a long second, but Morgan didn't hesitate, didn't slow.

Ascher was in trouble.

A few meters ahead was the small cave system she had used to store supplies.

It would make sense for Ascher to take shelter there.

Then thinking was over when shadows on her right shifted. Something solid slammed into her and send her catapulting into the trees. Ryder's roar of rage filled her ears. Her shoulder glanced off a tree, instantly numbing her arm and sending her spinning through the air. Before she could halt her momentum, her back smacked into a large oak. She thumped heavily to the ground, the breath knocked out of her, a jarring pain shooting down her spine.

Only training kept her moving. She straightened in time to lift her arm, blocking the blow meant to cave in her skull. It wouldn't kill her, but it would hurt like a bitch and incapacitate her. That's when she got her first look at what had attacked her.

A ghoul.

Wearing only a loincloth.

She blinked, thinking the blow must have scrambled her wits.

Ghouls never crossed Earthside. Once they did, their death was guaranteed. Whatever animated and kept them alive in the void rapidly deteriorated on Earth. Until then, they were vicious and unrelenting killers, only stopping when they eventually rotted and fell apart, but not without first wreaking havoc and destruction everywhere they went.

Morgan lashed out with her foot, but the ghoul easily caught her ankle in hands that hung well past his knees, and wrenched her forward.

"Come." He grunted the command, his tongue so black and swollen, it made speaking difficult. His lips had rotted off, leaving his teeth exposed in a macabre smile, revealing upper and lower inch-long fangs. His jaw came forward a few inches, reminding her of a crocodile waiting to snap shut on its unsuspecting prey.

All that remained of his hair were a few straggly scraps, his scalp looking like patches had fallen out in clumps. The body was a walking skeleton, no extra fat, only bones and skin so thin she could see the cords of muscles underneath, each of his ribs clearly defined. Even from the distance, she could see the ghoul's skin was slick and slimy with decay, a rotten, grayish-green color.

Everything about him was primitive.

Primordial.

Something dragged out of nightmares before humans even crawled out of the ooze.

As she was hauled behind him, the stench of rot was so strong, breathing became difficult. The smell crept into her mouth until she could taste it, leaving her with the urge to scrape her tongue.

He walked on his toes, his feet similar to dinosaurs of old, his heels more of a joint than part of his foot. His hands and feet were tipped with claws, the limbs stretched out, almost skeletal, barely covered with skin. When he went to take another step, she rolled, kicking the back of his leg out from under him. As he began to fall, she used her momentum and rolled, breaking his grip.

They ended up crouched, facing each other.

His eyes were a milky white and green, and she could have sworn she saw little maggots swimming inside his eyeballs, and her stomach lurched alarmingly. The ears were stretched, sprouting hair so thick little critters were crawling in them. It brought a whole new meaning to brain-rot.

Then she noticed there were three other ghouls in the clearing, keeping the team busy.

She was on her own.

When the ghoul sprang forward, Morgan flung herself backwards, grabbing her blades and gutting him as he flew over her head. Bile sprayed her, and he gave a bellow of rage.

While the creature frantically shoved his blackened intestines back inside, Morgan sprang to her feet. She shot forward to finish him, until she noticed one of the creatures had Kincade pinned, and he was barely blocking the slashing claws trying to whittle him down.

They wanted her alive, but the men weren't so lucky.

Morgan ran forward, leapt toward a tree, stepping up the trunk to gain the height she needed, then kicked off. She pulled her knives, allowing her momentum to carry her, and planted the blades deep into the creature's neck, then crossed her arms, using brute strength to decapitate the ghoul.

Gunk covered the front of her as the body crumbled and began to decay, turning into a pile of slimy ooze, leaving her facing a bleeding Kincade. A nasty cut ran across his temple and a dozen or so more marred his arms and torso.

"You okay?"

Instead of answering, Kincade grabbed her shoulders, and threw them both sideways. They hit the ground with a thump that vibrated heavily through her, Kincade's bigger form completely covering her, landing on her like a pile of bricks. Over his shoulder, Morgan saw a ghoul reach down for them, his claws aimed for Kincade's unprotected back.

"Roll."

He didn't hesitate.

Morgan jackknifed into sitting position while thrusting up, her weapon catching the ghoul under the jaw, the blade piercing through the top of the skull. The same movement impaled her on the tips of the ghoul's claws. They speared her shoulder, the nails so sharp they sank in without resistance and scarcely a burst of pain.

The skeletal, greenish face began to dissolve around the blade, part of his flesh falling in glops on her hand. She barely pulled her legs out of the way when the ghoul collapsed in on itself, the decaying stench so strong, her eyes watered.

The claws in her shoulder oozed out of her injuries, and the wounds sealed themselves, leaving only a few drops of blood dribbling down her front. She shook out her hand much like a large dog shaking his head, and thick strings of slime went flying. If possible, the gunk smelled even worse. "I'll never be able to get the stink out."

Kincade was crouched, frozen, only a foot away from her, unable to tear his gaze away from the blood smeared down her clothes.

He didn't even blink, lost in some nightmare inside his head.

"Most of it isn't my blood." Morgan gently ran her fingertips along his jaw, finding his skin frigid under her touch, and she wrapped her hand around the back of his neck, trying to warm him. "It's your blood."

Morgan was conscious of the sounds of fighting behind her, but she couldn't leave him frozen and vulnerable. She leaned closer, her lips just a breath away from touching his, and whispered to him, hoping to reach him wherever he'd gone. "Come back to me."

He grabbed her wrist like a lifeline, his personality slowly entering his eyes again. Then he stood, drawing her up along with him. "What the hell were you thinking?"

His low, gruff tone uncurled the knots of dread in her stomach—his usual grouchy self was back. "They weren't going to kill me. They need me alive. You're a different matter."

"That wouldn't have stopped them from hurting you." A muscle jumped in his jaw, as if he was holding back from saying more. He poked and prodded her shoulder, refusing to look up at her, and she sucked in a sharp breath when he hit a sensitive spot.

"Hey, careful. I said *most* of it wasn't my blood." In truth, his probing hurt like a bitch, much more than the initial wound.

Up close, she noted his injuries were shallow, surface cuts at most—as if something under his skin had blocked the ghoul's claws from cutting deeper.

"Stop it." She slapped away his hands, backing away. "What do you say we finish off the last two ghouls?"

Morgan grabbed one of the blades she'd dropped, wiping off the other one on her thigh.

Atlas and Draven were systematically hacking away at a ghoul twice as big as the others, standing well over ten feet tall. It was misshapen, as if two ghouls had been smooshed and cobbled together—or one had eaten the other—his back humped, the ridges of his spine nearly piercing his flesh, one arm bigger, more muscular than the other, and nearly twice as long.

Neither hunter was able to reach the creature's head and separate the brain from his body for a true kill before being swatted away like a pesky fly. It had warts or tumorous lumps all over, almost like pustules that looked ready to burst. Draven finally threw himself at the ghoul's leg, picking up the limb and forcing the creature to stagger to keep its balance.

Atlas ran forward, ramming into the ghoul's side, tipping the monster over. A roar of outrage escaped as the creature toppled, his weight shaking the ground as he landed, even tree branches swaying in reaction.

Morgan had no doubt this was this beast who made short work of the mansion.

Without hesitation, Atlas ran forward, dodging fists with three-inch-long claws, and leapt into the air. One after another, he tossed throwing knives, each weapon striking true. The first two blades took out the creature's eyes, and they popped like grapes, white puss and maggots spilling down his face. Spittle flew as he bellowed in pain and grabbed his face.

Atlas landed and rolled, pulling out another blade, then lunged forward again.

The weapon disappeared into the giant's ear, the muscles of Atlas's arms straining as the knife slid deep.

Right into the brain.

The body rippled, then stilled, slowly melting into a pile of greenish gelatin.

Both Draven and Atlas stood panting, every part of their bodies covered with goop, their hair and clothes plastered to them.

When Morgan scanned the clearing, she didn't find any sign of Ryder or the last ghoul. Fear poured through her, and she took off running.

"Wait!"

Morgan ignored the shouting behind her, following the path of destruction.

She didn't have to go far.

Ryder stood with his back toward her, systematically carving the ghoul he had pinned to the tree into itty-bitty pieces, the creature's spine clearly visible through his torn neck, and half his body, what was left of it, appeared melted, slowly dribbling to the ground in great chunks.

Though ghouls were huge, they were no match for Ryder, his large frame practically dwarfing what remained of the creature.

"Ryder?"

Draven grabbed her arm to prevent her from getting any closer.

The muscles of Ryder's back stiffened, his movements slowing, his head cocked at the sound of her voice.

Even from the distance, energy crackled, biting painfully along her skin, and fear burned along the back of her throat.

Something was wrong.

"He's dead."

Ryder swung one more time, completely severing the head from the body, then dropped his arms to his side, his shoulders heaving. She pulled away from Draven and approached cautiously. "You did it."

She took one more step, then noticed what was bothering her.

Ryder was gone.

Before her stood his wolf in human form.

His eyes glowed a whisky brown, claws tipped the ends of his fingers. The shape of his jaw was wrong, and she realized it was because he had way more teeth in his mouth than should be possible. Morgan reached out, slipping her hand into his, carefully avoiding the hard claws, ignoring the way Kincade cursed under his breath behind her.

Slowly, his grip tightened, and he lifted his face toward her. "There you are." Morgan smiled, giving his hand a little squeeze. "Unfortunately, the fighting isn't done yet. I need to have Ryder back. Do you think you can give him control?"

A rumbly little growl resonated in his chest, and she clucked her tongue. "I know you want to help, but Ryder is who we need right now. How about when we're done, you and I will go for a run at the Academy?"

The wolf cocked his head, studying her closely, then the bright glow in his eyes dimmed. The magic around him was sucked inward as his wolf retreated, until only a trace of it remained. Ryder's jaw popped back into place, his teeth slipping beneath his gums, the claws at the tips of his fingers disappearing back under his skin.

Ryder reeled under the change, clinging to her hand while his consciousness rose to the surface. He glanced around the clearing, quickly processing what he saw. It didn't take long for him to realize he'd lost control. His head snapped toward her, his eyes glued to their joined hands. He jerked away from her hold, then grabbed her shoulders and shook her. "Never do that again. I could've killed you."

Morgan reached up and grabbed his forearms, waiting for him to calm down. "I don't believe a word of it."

His fingers bit painfully into her arms. "He's a beast. When I'm in my other form—when he takes control from me—I can't protect you."

"No, but your wolf can." She reached up and pulled his face down to hers. "I trust you and your wolf. You're one and the same to me."

He inhaled deeply once, then again. "I won't risk you."

Morgan slid her arms around his neck and hugged him, offering him what little comfort she could. Although she wasn't used to physical contact, she knew his wolf craved it. "We'll deal with this later. Right now, we need to move. Can you do that?"

She didn't think he was even breathing, his arms hanging awkwardly around her shoulders. Then he inhaled deeply, her scent seeming to comfort him, and he nodded. She lowered her arms, dragging her hands over his shoulders, surprisingly reluctant to step away.

But Ascher was waiting for her.

She needed to go.

When she dropped her arms, she curled her hands into fists, already missing his warmth. "Ready?"

Ryder studied her eyes, then nodded, as if he'd found what he wanted.

Morgan looked behind her, finding Kincade.

"Go."

She didn't need to be told twice. Morgan took off at a run, heading straight for the cave. Every step she took sent pain reverberating through her, her wounds protesting the jarring pace. Blood began to trickle down her shoulder in earnest. She'd taken so many injuries recently, it was slowing down her normal speedy healing process.

Her shoulder had crunched ominously from when she hit the tree, the bones shattered at the very least. She could feel them knitting together. Slowly. Painfully.

She charged into the small clearing, hope surging in her chest at the possibility of seeing Ascher again.

Only to find the area empty.

Her spirits plummeted, and she spun in a circle, wondering if she imagined the howl.

The men emerged behind her, weapons drawn, looking a little wild, only easing back when they spotted her.

Kincade strode toward her when a shadow separated itself from the trees and leapt between her and the hunters, its vicious snarl launching her heart into her throat.

"Ascher!" Joy exploded in her chest, and Morgan took a step forward, ready to throw herself at him, when everything happened at once.

"Stay back." Kincade crouched, his weapons at the ready, his eyes locked on the hellhound, waiting for an opening. "Hellhounds are vicious and won't hesitate to attack."

Ascher growled and hunkered lower, moving to keep himself between her and the others.

"Stop." Pleasure at seeing him again evaporated at their asinine behavior. "He's a friend."

Treading carefully now, Morgan edged closer. "Peace."

"Hellhounds don't have friends, they have masters. They are too wild, too unpredictable to be allowed to run free. They are solitary creatures, nearly extinct, but when captured, they have no choice but obey their master in all things. They can be fierce protectors and highly valuable to certain parties—and will turn on them at the first opportunity."

The description was chilling.

Morgan didn't believe him.

Ascher was different.

Ignoring the men, she focused on Ascher, then went lightheaded as she noticed the many wounds scattered all over his huge frame. She didn't see the blood until she got closer, his black, rough velvet-like fur disguising it. Small wisps of smoke rose from where his paws touched the forest floor, giving away his agitation.

The strength drained out of her legs, and she dropped to her knees. "What happened?"

With one last growl, Ascher turned his blue eyes toward her. He exhaled heavily, puffing out smoke, giving one last menacing snarl at the team, then limped slowly toward her. Morgan reached out for him, not sure where to touch him, afraid she would hurt him more. Then he took the options away from her by collapsing in her arms, almost flattening her under his weight.

She eased him down onto her lap, then ripped off her shirt and pressed it against the nasty claw marks raked across his ribs. The tank top she wore wasn't in much better shape, coated in blood and practically shredded, leaving her skin exposed.

Especially the runes on her back.

If anyone looked closely enough, they would see the markings peeking through the blood and grime beneath the strands of her hair.

She didn't care who saw them, too concerned about saving Ascher to worry about it.

"He saved our lives." Morgan twisted in surprise and saw MacGregor leaning heavily against the opening of the narrow cave. He was deathly pale and shaky, but alive—and looked like he had the crap beat out of him.

Unsurprisingly, Catalina emerged from behind him, looking disheveled but whole.

A shame.

Howard and three other hunters also emerged, each more banged up than the last. He gave Morgan a nod of greeting, cradling his arm to his chest, his left eye nearly swollen shut. The only other witch was one of the triplets. Blood covered her face from a nasty gash on her forehead, her skin incredibly pale. She slapped at one of the hunters who reached out to help her, glaring at him in disdain.

The ungrateful bitch.

Morgan turned away before she did something she would regret.

A painful tingle swept up her right hand, as if an army of fire ants had been let loose under her skin. Magic simmered in the air, spiraling downward, settling over Ascher before sinking into his rough, velvety fur. Even as she watched, wisps of smoke rose from his body, his black form quickly turning charcoal.

Her hands heated where she was touching him.

She watched, completely dumfounded as sparks, then flames, engulfed his form. Arms grabbed to pull her away, but she hadn't taken two steps when a hand reached out of the smoke and latched onto her wrist.

She waited for her skin to blister and crack from the heat, but the expected pain never came.

Instead, the air cleared, and she was staring down at a guy she recognized from her few visits into town. "You."

The last time she saw him, she'd been trying to hunt him down and ask why he was following her. But every time she got close, he vanished.

It took her brain a few seconds to process what she was seeing. "Ascher?"

Morgan jerked away from the arm around her waist, ignoring Kincade's curses, and dropped to her knees next to the now-naked man. He was tall and lean, not a spare inch of fat on him. His light, sandy blond hair was wild, with a hint of curl, his cheekbones high, his lips firm…everything about him oh, so touchable. His pale, drawn expression hinted at pain, but those piercing blue eyes…she recognized them anywhere.

The center of her palm stung, the pain wrapping around her hand and up her wrists, but she ignored the discomfort and grabbed her shirt, pressing it once more against the ragged wounds along his ribs.

His legs were thickly muscled, and fresh blood bubbled up from the nasty puncture wounds on his thigh. Claw marks and scrapes covered nearly every inch of him, too numerous to count. "Dear God. How are you still alive?"

MacGregor came to her side, resting a heavy hand on her shoulder. "If not for him, we would've all died. He got us out of the mansion, drawing the attack away from us. He—"

A deep, wet, hacking cough took MacGregor by surprise, nearly doubling him over, and her gut tightened in concern. He looked even worse up close.

"We need to get them back to the mansion."

Catalina sighed, but reluctantly agreed. "Take MacGregor. Your men and mine will head toward the rift. We need to close it before more ghouls come through."

Morgan was already shaking her head, annoyed to see Catalina already trying to act as the MacGregor. "I can't carry them both."

Catalina lifted a perfectly sculptured brow. "Leave the hellhound."

"Fuck you." Morgan pressed down harder on the wound. Only when Ascher flinched and groaned did she wince, cursing herself for a clumsy fool. "Sorry."

Morgan glanced around at their small, motley group. "None of your people are up for another confrontation. We need to head back, seek treatment, and gather reinforcements."

"She's right." MacGregor halted the argument before it had a chance to begin.

Then he collapsed.

Kincade barely caught him before he hit the ground.

* * *

The trip back to the mansion was long and torturous, her body protesting the abuse. Her shattered arm had healed, but it had taken most of her energy, leaving her drained. They paused only long enough to dress Ascher, and hastily bandage the worst of their wounds. By the time the mansion came into view, the puncture marks in her shoulder had begun to bleed again.

Kincade carried MacGregor, while Ascher hung between her and Ryder. The rest of the team acted as guards, protecting their retreat.

The relief team was waiting for them in the study.

Both MacGregor and Ascher were eased into their waiting hands, and Morgan watched anxiously while they cleaned away the blood and checked the makeshift bandages they applied.

"The headmistress needs to be informed of what's happening." Though Kincade didn't look at her, she knew he was going to send her back.

"No, I can help you locate the rift. I—"

"No need. I'll show them." Catalina took another sip of water from the bottle in her hand, all the while staring at her over the top. "You have no magic. Going along would be useless. Only a real witch is able to close the rift. See to MacGregor. The ornery old bastard won't listen to anyone else."

Morgan was torn between duty and concern for her friends.

She didn't trust them to be safe unless she was there to protect them.

"You can't stay here." MacGregor swam in and out of consciousness, his hand latching onto hers with a surprisingly strong grip. "You can't let them find you. You'll only be safe at the school."

Morgan stilled.

He knew something about her past.

Something he'd never shared with her.

Her stomach churned at the betrayal, like she was being devoured from the inside out, but before she could demand answers, he passed out cold.

"They need you more." Atlas was staring down at the hellhound with a look in his eyes that made her want to step in front of Ascher.

"If you stay, you'll only be a distraction. Go."

It was an order.

Even if she disagreed with the team, they gave her no choice.

She either went under her own steam, or they would make her.

Bastards.

When she turned away, Atlas lifted a hand out to her, but halted before grabbing her arm. "Be careful."

If she didn't know better, she would say he was concerned—which made no sense, since he was the one going into battle.

The last triplet stood in front of the mirror, already casting her spell.

Magic filled the air, stronger than the last two times she'd traveled.

Primordial magic.

"Something's wrong." Morgan pulled her blades and edged closer to the mirror, taking up a protective stance.

The witch halted, but the magic didn't. The mirror rippled, the sigils turning from a dusky gold to a sickly green. The image of the room twisted, then vanished as a portal whooshed open. Instead of the Academy, a stranger was reflected back at her.

"I don't have much time, princess. You're in danger." The man shot a terrified glance over his shoulder, his movements jerky. "I'm using the last of my power to contact you. I can't protect you Earthside any longer. You must come home."

Something about his soft voice made her skin crawl, sending her heart slamming against her ribs at the mere sight of him. "Home?"

She was looking at a male version of herself.

His hair and coloring were the same as hers, but that was where the similarities ended. He was downright gorgeous, but something about him made her want to puke.

"Don't you recognize me?" A small, charming smile tipped the corners of his lips, and the compulsion to run nearly overwhelmed her.

Morgan shook her head, unable to speak past the lump in her throat.

"I'm your cousin…Ethan. I've come to save you."

Chapter Nineteen

"Save me?" Morgan parroted, fighting the urge to vomit. No matter how hard she tried to move, she couldn't step away from the mirror. Something was pulling her forward, and it was all she could do to resist the compulsion.

Ascher stumbled to her side, barely conscious, and grabbed her hand.

Ethan scowled at the beast, something dark moving in his eyes. "They are killing young girls in their search for you. They won't stop until they find you." He held out his hand to her. "We must hurry, we don't have much time."

Morgan's stomach dipped dangerously at the truth of his words.

"I say we turn her over." Catalina's voice was cold.

Ascher snarled, and Morgan grabbed for him before he could lunge at Catalina. The witch was completely unfazed. "We're talking about witches losing their lives. She's not worth their loss."

It was her job to protect others, and if going with him would stop the killings, what choice did she have?

The mirror rippled, the portal fading, and he scowled, clearly frustrated. "They are not your friends. They're trying to keep you from your birthright. This is your home. They're keeping your powers imprisoned. I can help set you free. All you have to do is step through the portal."

Kincade completely ignored Ethan and stepped in front of her, his distrust of the other man clear in his eyes. "Someone is going to a lot of trouble to get their hands on you. We need to find out why first."

Magic shimmered in the room as the portal began to shut down.

"We have to go." Ethan held out his hand toward her, and she felt another tug of magic urging her to go with him. "Now."

"No." Kincade and Ascher spoke in unison, both of them blocking her path.

Her heart did a funny flip at seeing the two of them working together.

MacGregor shoved aside the young woman wrapping up his head. "If you go through that gate, you will not be going alone. Ascher is too weak to protect you, and he'll end up killing himself when he follows." The effort of speaking winded him, and he gave a loud, hacking cough that left his lips bloody. "Kincade will follow, too. Possibly the others. What do you think will happen to them in the void?"

They would die.

For her.

It was too much.

As if sensing she was weakening, MacGregor struck. "He can't force you to go with him. The torque is keeping you hidden. He knows more about the murders than he's saying. Don't sacrifice yourself now, not when you might be the only one who can stop the killings."

Overwhelming relief slammed into her.

The last thing she wanted was to be anywhere near her cousin.

"Don't be foolish." Annoyance flickered across Ethan's face. When she made no move to go to him, he dropped his hand, and every expression on his face vanished. "Remember this. What happens next is your doing. You *will* submit to me…eventually"

The surface of the mirror shimmered, and his image disappeared.

The magic from the Primordial World flashed into the room and seeped into her skin. The runes on her back flexed, pressing deeper into her body, dragging the magic into her very bones and absorbing it.

Ascher sagged against her, and she shoved away her troubling thoughts, wrapping her arms around his waist to keep him upright.

"We need to get you and MacGregor back to the Academy."

"And you." MacGregor wilted. "They now know what you look like. They're going to come after you hard and fast. We need to speak with the headmistress and let her know trouble is coming."

The mirror rippled as the witch opened the portal, and the sigils flickered, turning back to gold. Her image shimmered and faded, replaced by the reflection of the Academy. Morgan took a step forward, dragging Ascher with her, until Catalina stepped in her way.

"The hellhound stays. He's a danger, his identity unknown. He could be the one who led the attack. We can't risk it."

Fury bubbled up from Morgan's gut. Her hands curled into fist, fighting against the urge to deck Catalina.

"He was injured saving your life, you ungrateful bitch." She refused to leave Ascher behind. Never again.

Catalina smirked. "Too bad you don't have any power to run the mirrors. It's not your decision."

The fuck it wasn't.

Morgan strode forward, pulling a barely conscious Ascher with her. Catalina's smug smile faded. Without a second's hesitation, Morgan twisted and brought up her elbow, slamming it into the witch's face. Bones gave a satisfying crunch, and the bitch dropped to the floor, clutching her nose, blood gushing between her fingers.

Ignoring the shocked gasps, Morgan stepped over her legs, then shoved Ascher through the mirror. She turned, and saw Draven hauling MacGregor to his feet, a grimace of pain crossing the old man's face.

Knowing he was in good hands, Morgan stepped through the mirror.

The darkness wasn't so deep this time. She could almost see shadowy shapes moving, and the air wasn't as cold. The markings along her back burrowed deeper, until they felt stamped into her bones, her spine arching as liquid heat rushed through her blood.

The pleasure lasted only a few seconds, when pain slashed deep into her body, the worst of her wounds searing shut in one vomit-inducing second. Her vision dimmed, the world spun, and she was yanked forward, then spit out through the other side of the mirror.

MacGregor had arrived first, but only by a few seconds.

Their abrupt arrival startled the waiting team.

Not wanting people to look too closely at Ascher, needing to get him away from the others, Morgan snapped out orders. "Get MacGregor to the infirmary. And someone get the headmistress. She needs to know about the latest developments."

Three people hoisted up the old man, while more were assessing and working on his wounds. In under a minute, he was on a gurney and on the way out the door.

One person ran for the headmistress.

Which left Morgan to deal with the remaining two.

"We're the first wave. The rest remained behind to close the rift. There are more wounded. Replenish the supplies and get more people in here."

The snotty girl from the infirmary glanced suspiciously at the mirror. "How many?"

Survivors.

Morgan swallowed hard at the pitiful number. "Six."

The girl blanched, then squared her shoulders. "Bring me your friend, and I—"

"You're in charge here. You need to be prepared for more injuries. I'll take him." No way in hell was she leaving Ascher again.

She needed to find a place to stash him, somewhere no one would look for him.

If they found out he was a hellhound, they would—at best—remove him from the school grounds. At worse, they would have him killed.

Not happening.

Grabbing Ascher's arm, she hauled it over her shoulder, taking most of his weight, and dragged him out of the room. Even with her extra strength, he was dead weight.

The first place they would look would be her room.

She knew of only one place where people wouldn't think to search for them…the guys' barracks.

She reached the first landing and half propped, half pinned Ascher against the stone as a group of people hurried down the hall. She thought she managed to elude everyone, until the last person she wanted to see stumbled into view and spotted her.

"What happened?" Neil rushed forward, sounding alarmed as he helped lift Ascher when he began to slide down the wall. "Let me help."

"No."

Neil stopped, his face losing all expression, and she felt like she just kicked a puppy. "We can't take him to the infirmary."

Then he did something she never expected. He sniffed Ascher. Instantly, curiosity brightened his eyes. "What is he?"

She didn't want to tell him, but she couldn't risk that he would try to stop her. They needed to get moving. "Hellhound."

"Holy shit. Really?"

Something about the way he studied Ascher reminded her of Catalina—like he wanted to take Ascher apart to see what made him tick. Bile churned in her stomach, and she cursed herself for foolishly trusting the boy.

She needed to get Ascher away.

Now.

"I can hide him in my room."

Morgan took more of Ascher's weight and began to move them faster through the halls. "No, I won't risk him being discovered."

"I can disguise his smell. No one would ever know." The urge to shove Neil away and protect Ascher was nearly overwhelming. The darkness inside her stirred, and she breathed deeply to push away the need to eliminate the threat.

"No. Using magic hurts you. I won't help you kill yourself." Morgan steered them toward a set of stairs, then took all of Ascher's weight against her. "Anyway, the hunters are too good. I just need time to stitch up his wounds and get him out of here alive. I can take it from here. The less you know about us, the less trouble you will be in."

Neil shot her a confused look, but obediently backed away, his glasses knocked askew. "Okay."

Dejection slumped his shoulders.

The curiosity in his eyes didn't vanish.

It sharpened.

Wanting to ensure he didn't follow, she quickly smiled at him. "But you can do something...if you're willing."

He immediately nodded. "Whatever you need."

"Can you make sure no one follows us?"

Neil chewed on his bottom lip in indecision, studying Ascher harder, and Morgan tried to shield him with her body the best she could. "You sure? If he gets loose and hurts—"

"I'm sure." Morgan could feel Ascher's blood trickle down her back where they were touching. "He's in no condition to hunt. I can handle him. Please?"

Very reluctantly, Neil nodded. "You'll owe me."

Relief loosened the knots in her shoulders. "Thank you."

She watched him leave, tapping into the stones of the Academy to track him, only taking a deep breath when he didn't double back to follow them.

It took ten minutes of hauling Ascher's ass up the stairs before she reached her destination.

Only to find the doors closed and warded.

Morgan knew she could hack the magic, but it would take time.

Time Ascher didn't have.

She slammed her fist against the door in frustration, and magic swarmed up from the wood like angry bees. It investigated her fist, the sensation like ants crawling over her skin. Then, much to her shock, the doors clicked open, the wards granting her access. Not willing to look a gift horse in the mouth, Morgan grabbed Ascher once more and shouldered her way into the barracks.

She guided him toward the closest empty room, right next to Atlas' room, and settled Ascher onto the bed. If anything, Ascher looked in worse shape, his face sweaty and pale, his eyes barely open, his wounds bleeding through the hastily-wrapped bandages he received at the coven.

She needed supplies.

After ransacking the main area and coming up empty, Morgan headed straight toward Kincade's room. He was too organized, too anal, not to have supplies. She found them in the army locker at the end of his bed, along with a slew of weapons.

As she straightened with her loot, a movement at the corner of her eye caught her attention. She whirled, dropping the box of supplies and grabbed her blades.

Only to confront a cloudy mirror.

But the longer she stared, the clearer the image became.

That's when she saw them…the guys. They were traveling through the trees at a run.

Hunting.

Drawn forward, Morgan touched the mirror, but a solid surface met her fingertips.

Not a portal.

"Son of a bitch!" Kincade's familiarity with her fighting style began to make sense.

He'd been spying on her.

Anger seared through her at his deceit.

At the lies.

It all made sense. The way he anticipated her moves when they fought, how he could mimic her exactly. Why he seemed so surprised when they first met…because he'd seen her before.

It all made horrible sense.

Not only did he know she could fight, but the bastard still gave her a hard time.

Made her feel inadequate.

It didn't explain his grumpiness toward her—or maybe it did.

He really didn't like her.

The longer she watched the mirror, the more exposed she felt, wondering what exactly he had seen while watching her.

The creep!

A thump and cursing drew her away from the mirror.

Ascher!

Quickly scooping up the supplies, she hurried two rooms down to find Ascher trying to pick himself up off the floor.

"What the hell do you think you're doing?" Morgan dropped the supplies on the desk, then grabbed his arm, helping him back onto the bed.

"You were gone."

Morgan rooted around in a medical kit the size of a piece of luggage, unable to connect this guy to the hellhound she knew. If she hadn't seen him change with her own eyes, she would never have believed it.

Knowing she couldn't avoid him any longer, she grabbed the swabs and began cleaning his wounds, concentrating on her tasks so she didn't have to look him in the eye. His skin was hot to the touch, the peroxide drying in seconds. A knot formed in her gut, and she wondered if he had a fever or if the heat was the result of him being a hellhound.

It felt odd to be close to him, touching him, and she was unable to stop recalling every word she ever told him, going over and over everything they'd shared.

Things she never would have told anyone else.

She had trusted him completely, and she wasn't sure where they stood now.

He knew everything about her, probably knew her better than she knew herself, while she knew nothing about him.

She didn't like it.

"Why didn't you tell me you could turn human?"

"I was going to, but you're prickly with others. I finally decided to get you used to me first. I couldn't risk losing you. It was more important to keep you safe."

He sucked in a harsh breath, and Morgan lightened her touch, realizing that in her annoyance she had been pressing on his wound harder than necessary to clean it. "Sorry." She paused, and swallowed hard. "I thought I lost you when you went through the portal. I never expected to see you again."

Morgan didn't know how to feel about him. To see him alive did something to her heart, but the lies left her emotions twisted into knots.

She wasn't sure how to react, so she decided to stick to a safer subject.

She owed him at least that.

"Thank you for protecting MacGregor. You saved his life." Morgan dropped another bloody cotton swab in a pile with all the others, then picked up the needle, carefully threading it.

"There are only two things you care for in this world, and he's one of them." His voice was rough, like he hadn't spoken for a long while, the tone a caress down her spine. "I had to try."

Morgan's head snapped up and met his startlingly familiar blue eyes. Disconcerted to find him staring at her, she looked down at the needle and thread. "Don't move. This is going to hurt."

He didn't make a sound while she stitched up the wounds along his ribs. Every time she pierced his flesh, her own skin flinched. The longer she touched him, the more her hands tingled. She needed a distraction before she completely lost her shit.

"If what they say is true, you're both powerful and rare. Why waste your time on me?"

"Not so rare." She felt his eyes on her face, studying her as if she was the most fascinating creature he'd ever seen. It was both heady and made her want to hide. She had to shake her head to clear her thoughts when he continued speaking. "It's just that we've learned to keep to ourselves. The others hunt us for our abilities, so we rarely venture out of our villages."

He winced when she tugged the needle through a particularly nasty gash on his side, barely pausing in his story. "The bloodlines are purer in some of us than others, making our beast stronger. We crave freedom, so we go for runs and hunt, doing whatever is needed to protect our village."

"You were captured." The fondness in his voice didn't allow for any other option. He would never have left his friends and family voluntarily.

He grunted, his voice smoothing out the more he spoke. "I was stupid. I wandered too far away from the village. I heard a woman scream and went to investigate. It turned out she didn't need rescuing. When I showed up to help her, she slipped a collar around my neck. She was a witch, and had heard rumors of a hellhound in the area, and wanted to cash in on the high black market price on our breed."

"No wonder you bit me the first time we met. You must have thought I set the trap." Biting off the end of the string, she grabbed a jar of salve and coated the wound.

"Sorry."

Morgan glanced up at his husky apology, charmed by the embarrassing blush on his face. "For what?"

"With the collar, we're locked in our beast form, which is why we take such care. If we're a hound too long, we'll remain stuck in that form forever. The only way free is to kill our master."

At his penetrating look, her stomach sank in dread.

She hadn't found him by chance that day in the woods.

He'd been hunting her.

"My cousin." She swallowed hard, unable to fathom what he had gone through because of her family. "He sent you after me, didn't he?"

Ascher clenched his hands into fists, his brows lowering, his jaw clenched tight.

It was answer enough.

"Does he still control you?" Morgan resisted the urge to back away from him.

She had to know.

She reached for the tape and bandages in the medical kit, unable to look at him while she waited for him to speak, knowing if he gave the wrong answer, he would break her heart.

"Not as much without the collar. His sway over me is fading, and the bindings are loosening, but if I don't keep up my guard, I can hear him in my head, slowly driving me insane with his demands." He shifted on the bed, breathing heavily through the pain, and closed his eyes. "Being around you quiets the voices."

The words were so soft, she wasn't sure she was supposed to hear what he'd said. As she taped the bandages to his chest and side, her hands shook. It hurt to know her cousin had enslaved him in such a way—probably for the sole purpose of finding her.

She felt responsible for Ascher's predicament, and she didn't know how to fix it.

If she pushed him away, she feared her cousin would gain control of him again, which was unacceptable.

Morgan stood and turned her back, struggling to contain her emotions. "I need your pants off to get at the wound on your leg. Did you want to remove them, or would you rather I cut them off?"

The bed shifted, and she tensed at having him so near her exposed back.

"I'm decent."

Swallowing hard, Morgan turned, trying to ignore the way the blanket barely covered his important bits, and focused on the nasty gouges in his leg, uncomfortably aware of his body so close to her own.

"Why stay if you're able to change to human form? Won't that break the bonds faster?" She grabbed the swabs and started cleaning his leg. The wounds were punctures, like a set of claws had been thrust into his thigh and twisted. Blood still bubbled sluggishly out of the worst of them.

"I'm only able to change when you're near. When you're too far away, I revert back to the hound."

She threw down the swab and grabbed a roll of bandages, then bent his leg up and began wrapping the strips around the thick pad of gauze tightly enough to stop the bleeding. "Then we'll need to kill him."

He jerked so hard Morgan had to grab his knee to steady him.

"Careful. You're going to undo all my work."

When he continued to stare at her oddly, she frowned. "What?"

"He's your cousin."

Morgan grimaced, concentrating on the bandages and not the way his nearness was making her head swim, or the fascinating rasp of his skin against hers. "Which makes it my responsibility."

He gave her a small smile, his eyes lightening even more, and she lowered her head, discomfited by his attention. Then she narrowed her eyes and swung back to pin him with a look. "Is that why he's not already dead? Were you worried about me?"

"No."

"Really?" Morgan wasn't convinced, and she began to shove the supplies back into the large box a little harder than necessary.

"Not completely," he finally confessed.

"Explain," she snapped at him, unable to keep the frustration out of her voice.

"If I go after him, you would be left vulnerable. It wasn't worth the risk."

Her brows shot up in disbelief at his simple reasoning. "Not worth your freedom?"

He was so earnest, she was both humbled and a little uncomfortable. It saddened her to know he would give up so much for her. "I'm not your responsibility."

Morgan wanted to say more, but noticed he could barely keep his eyes open. "You're tired. I'll let you rest. I'm protected now. We'll find a way to gain your freedom and send you home."

The thought of being separated from him permanently wrenched something deep in her chest, her heart cracking at the thought of never seeing him again.

His eyes shot open, panic darkening his eyes until he saw her. Faster than she could track, his hand shot out, and he dragged her closer.

"Can't go back." He mumbled the words, his eyes beginning to slide shut, exhaustion and a healing sleep finally taking over. "Your cousin is not the only one who bound me."

He lifted her hand and kissed her palm, placing it against his chest, then promptly fell unconscious after delivering that bomb.

Morgan jerked back in horror, but the instant she stopped touching him, his brows furrowed, and he began to shift in agitation, threatening to tear his stitches.

"Stop." She pressed a hand against his shoulder, and he seemed to calm at her touch.

Morgan racked her brain why he would say any such thing, and realized she must have accidentally bound them when they exchanged blood.

His fierce protection of her now made more sense.

It also explained why he craved her touch, and how she could counteract her cousin's control.

"I'll find a way to free you."

A way that didn't end in her death.

Ascher growled deep in his chest and yanked her toward him. He twisted, dragging her over his chest and wrapping her up in his arms. "No."

It was a command.

And she had a sudden suspicion she was speaking to the hound.

Morgan grabbed his arm to break his grip, but his hold didn't loosen. She froze when she smelled fresh blood, and knew he'd opened his wounds again. "Damn it. I need to re-stitch your ribs. Let me go."

"No."

Morgan knew she wasn't going to change his mind by asking. She had to play dirty. "You're bleeding all over me. If you lose much more blood, you won't be able to protect me."

He stilled, the muscles beneath her going rock hard. Then grudgingly, "I can heal faster in my other form."

Morgan patted his arm. "Good. Change."

His grip tightened more, pulling her even more snugly against him, before reluctantly releasing her. Morgan felt him pull away. When she stood to leave, he cleared his throat. "Will you stay?"

Morgan turned, surprised at his request, and found him sitting on the bed, his back against the stone wall, his eyes locked on the bedspread. His hands were clenched into fists, as if barely holding himself back from lunging for her.

She knew she should be afraid, but she trusted the hellhound completely. "Of course."

Morgan gingerly sat on the bed, and he cocked his head, peering up at her from under his brows, like she was a puzzle he couldn't figure out.

Wisps of charcoal smoke rose from his body, obscuring his form, his bones cracking and snapping as he shifted. The edges of the smoke drifted away to show a solid, familiar black shape. While he might be her Ascher again, she could no longer ignore the fact that he was much more. He lifted his big head, watching for her reaction, and she hesitantly reached out. It was funny. He was a big brute, a few years older than herself, but she sensed he needed comfort.

The hellhound heaved a sigh and leaned into her touch, carefully resting his head on her leg before closing his eyes.

Her heart flopped at his vulnerability. She highly doubted he'd ever shifted in front of someone who wasn't family. He was trusting her with his secrets, knowing that by telling her about his past, she could destroy his whole family.

The heat of him eased her sore muscles, and she haltingly ran her fingers over his head, marveling at the rough, velvety texture of his fur.

As she stroked his head, she noticed the filigree lines curling and looping over the back of her hand before crawling up her wrist. One line was a shiny obsidian, the other a strange, molten silver. The lines were ghostly, barely visible. They didn't hurt, easily moving and twisting with her movements, and felt like a part of her. Going through the portal, touching part of the primordial realm, must have somehow activated the runes in some way.

Not good.

Soon the torque wouldn't be able to stop the dark magic from escaping.

As she glanced around the room, Morgan realized she could never go back to the coven…possibly not even stay at the school.

Everything was spinning out of control, and she wasn't sure if she would land on her feet this time, or end up dragging the guys down with her.

Chapter Twenty

*A*fter twenty minutes of watching Ascher sleep, the adrenaline that kept Morgan going wore off, and her injuries ached like a bitch. While the worst of her wounds were on the mend, her body still felt battered and bruised and ready to crash.

But she couldn't sleep without knowing the guys were alive and okay.

She eased out from under Ascher's large paw, running her hand down his back when he whimpered in his sleep. She dashed out of the room, knowing she had only a few moments before he would wake because of her absence.

She skidded to a stop inside Kincade's room, then grabbed the mirror, hefting the heavy frame back to Ascher's room. Once she had the mirror positioned where she could see it from the bed, she crawled across the mattress and settled next to the big hound.

The hellhound stretched, then rested his head across her lap with a heavy sigh, effectively trapping her. She wouldn't be able to leave without waking him in the process.

The foggy mirror flickered, shadows moved, and she watched as the team's images took shape. They were at the rift, fighting the ghouls who were protecting the opening. Morgan reached out, wanting to join them, but cool glass met her fingertips. There was nothing she could do but watch them fight for their lives.

Catalina stood to the side, surrounded by her men, who were doing nothing but protecting her, while her guys risked their lives to kill the monstrosities. "The bitch!" She wanted to rip her apart. Ascher cracked open an eye when she was unable to keep still. After a few minutes, he heaved another sigh and shifted a safer distance away from her flying elbows and twitching legs as she mentally fought along with the guys.

It took twenty minutes, during which more and more ghouls poured through the rift, until Catalina finally managed to close it. It was another hour before the guys staggered to a halt, the last ghoul dead, but Morgan didn't consider them safe, not until they were back at the Academy.

She didn't have long to wait. As soon as they stepped through the portal, the mirror fogged over, and the image slowly faded.

She wasn't sure if the connection was lost, or if it didn't work inside the Academy, or if it only showed her what it wanted her to see.

She suspected all three.

Morgan gave Ascher an absent scratch, uncertain of her next move. Leaving wouldn't save more girls from being killed. Leaving wouldn't save Ascher or keep the other guys out of danger. They were the best fighters, but everyone was fighting with their hands tied behind their backs, trapped by lies.

It needed to stop.

Morgan eased out of bed, grabbed the mirror, then headed toward the main room and sat at the table. She didn't have long to wait for the guys to return.

"She has to be here somewhere. The wolves didn't see her leave. If we can't find her by magic, we'll search the place room by room." Kincade flung open the door, then froze when he saw her standing there waiting for him. A flash of pleasure and relief passed over him before he could mask it.

The rest of the guys piled into the room behind him, every one of them bruised and battered and bloody.

None of them seemed to be bothered that she broke into their room and took up residence.

Morgan crossed her arms and raised a brow at them. She picked up her feet, set them on the table, crossing her legs at the ankle to stop from going to them and inspecting them more closely.

"I thought the first rule after a mission was to check into the infirmary."

"We were too busy searching for you, since you vanished after going through the portal."

A muscle ticked in Kincade's jaw, but Morgan wasn't about to let him get the upper hand. She reached out and ripped off the sheet she placed over the mirror. "It seems we've both been keeping secrets. Would you like to tell me how long you've been spying on me?"

Instead of shame or embarrassment, the bastard only lifted his chin, his eyes flicking betrayingly toward the mirror.

"Dude. Bad move." Draven shook his head, walking farther into the room, and surprised her by taking a seat next to her.

"So that's how you did it." Atlas nodded as he studied the mirror. "It makes sense. You started fighting differently, and I couldn't figure out how you became so proficient so quickly. It was her." He calmly unbuckled his weapons, looking weary for the first time since she met him. Instead of sitting next to them, he dropped his weapons on the table with a thump, then stepped back and leaned against the wall to watch the show.

Ryder didn't do anything, didn't move, his muscles so tightly wound she wondered if he was about to snap. She dropped her feet to the floor, then walked into Ascher's room and grabbed the supplies, thumping the box on the table when she returned. "Sit down. All of you. I'm done with the secrets. Done with the lies. While we patch up everyone, we're going to talk. Your way isn't working, so we're going to try it my way now."

By the time she had all the supplies stacked up on the table, she found Ryder at her side. He touched her hair, and it crackled under his touch, the goop having dried it to a hard crunch. "You first."

His voice was barely human, more of a low grumble, and Morgan realized he wasn't giving her a choice. Either she washed or Ryder would lose control. He was barely holding himself together, his whisky-colored eyes glowing brightly, his teeth more pointed than usual, the tips of his fingers shaped into deadly claws.

"Come." Draven stood and held out a hand, watching Ryder the whole time. "I'll show you the bathroom."

She accepted his hand, then pointed at each of the guys. "I want everyone stripped, stitched and bandaged by the time I get back." Morgan ignored the hand pulling her from the room and continued to speak. "If it's not done to my satisfaction by the time I'm finished, I will do it for you."

It was a promise, and each of them nodded, understanding it as such.

Draven continued tugging on her hand, pulling her toward a narrow hall she hadn't noticed before. The bathroom split off in two directions. To the right, the room was utilitarian, no clutter, no glitz, and less than a handful of industrial-sized bottles lined up along a top of a three-quarter wall that marked off a shower. It had multiple showerheads and room for a half-dozen people. Four sinks were stretched out side by side opposite the shower, and a large mirror took up practically the whole wall. There was a soaker tub that looked like it had never been used, along with four separate doors. The left side of the room was dark, but appeared to be a mirror image.

"Strip." Draven propped her up against the sinks, then disappeared to turn on the shower, his jarring order at odds with his pleasant tone. He popped back out and walked toward one of the mystery doors, seemingly unconcerned with her standing there gaping at him. When he saw she hadn't moved, he smiled and opened the first door.

"Toilets." The room had four stalls. He popped open the next door, leaned against the doorjamb, crossed one foot over the other at the ankle, then pointed upwards. "Escape hatch. It opens up to the roof. Ah-ah-ah," he wiggled his finger when she leaned forward to peer up the ladder, quickly snapping the door shut. "Can't have you disappearing on us. The guys are worse than a bunch of girls when you're not around."

Morgan cracked a smile, appreciating his attempt to lighten her mood.

He pointed to the last door, and shook his head. "You'll have to leave us guys at least a little mystery." He went to the third door and pulled out a stack of towels, halting when she hadn't moved, all amusement gone. "If you don't want me, you'll have to choose one of them. Either way, none of us are ready to let you out of our sight yet."

Morgan hesitantly walked around the shower wall, and did as she was told. Her shirt had been lost long ago. She removed the last three weapons, placing two of them along the wall. The pants were past saving, so she used the last knife to cut them off, and dropped them at the edge of the shower with a sodden splotch. Wearing only her tank top and underwear, she watched dirt and blood spin down the drain. Most of her injuries were healed shut, leaving her body blotchy with an assortment of bruises. A quick glance over her shoulder confirmed her back was almost completely black, blue, and a nasty shade of putrid green from smacking into the trees one too many times. On the third scrub of her hair, Morgan sighed in frustration. She went to reach for a blade when she noticed they'd vanished.

"I need my knife."

There was a short, suspicious pause. "Why?"

"My hair is a knotted mess. I'm going to cut it off."

"No!" There was a heartbeat of silence, then he warned. "I'm coming around."

Morgan watched Draven walk toward her, a towel in his outstretched arms, his face averted. In seconds, she was wrapped in a big, fluffy towel. "It's safe."

She nearly snorted when a dull flush filled his face. For a siren rumored to have had his way with nearly every girl in school, she found his bashfulness around her charming. He'd washed his face and hair, which only highlighted the dark smudges under his eyes, and the bruises along his jaw.

"Come." He guided her toward the tub. "Step inside and lean back."

She did as she was told. Draven gathered her hair, pulling the snarled mess over the edge of the tub, then began to systematically brush out the strands. Morgan gradually relaxed, the coolness of the tub easing the knots in her tight muscles. "You've done this before."

There was a slight pause before he shrugged. "I had a little sister. She used to get into almost as much trouble as you do."

The sad fondness in his voice warned his story didn't end happily. "Did you want to tell me?"

He hit a particularly nasty spot, and yanked her hair for the first time. "Sorry."

Morgan shrugged it away. "I do worse brushing it on my own. The only reason I leave it long is so I can tie it back."

Seconds stretched to minutes, and she didn't expect him to speak again, so when he did, she jumped.

"My mother was a siren. My father was in love…obsessively in love. His whole world revolved around her. I was an accident. My mother wanted to leave, but promised my father she would stay until I was born." He switched to another section of her hair, concentrating fully on his task, as if he was merely telling a story. "Sirens don't need to actively seduce people. It's part of their natures, like breathing."

"I thought sirens lived in the ocean."

"The purer the blood, the more often they have to go back to the sea. It replenishes them. While giving birth to me, father locked her in chains, where she remained for years. He thought her compulsive need was all in her head, that she was sick. He was determined to fix her, stop her from wanting other men. He didn't understand he was starving her."

Morgan felt sick, wishing she'd never brought up the subject.

"It wasn't long before my little sister came along, but the delivery was rough. My mother wasn't strong enough, after years of starvation and being separated from the sea. She was nothing but skin and bones, despite the feeding tube he forced on her."

He parted her hair again, cleanly running the brush through the strands over and over. "I was four at the time. Our father blamed us for her death. I was left alone to raise Tamara, the one who made sure she was fed and clothed, while he drank himself into a stupor every night. I was ten when he began to notice we were different from other kids. Tamara was obsessed with water. She would remain underneath the surface for longer and longer each time."

Morgan grabbed his wrist, but when she tried to twist around to face him, he held her still. "Let me finish."

She nodded but didn't release him, needing him to know he wasn't alone.

"He decided he wasn't going to fail us like he did our mother."

Morgan twisted his arm up, displaying dozens of scars. "What happened? Belt buckle or whip?"

His head snapped toward hers, his eyes darkening when he realized she recognized the cause of his scars. "Both. I escaped. Tamara didn't."

She couldn't stand it anymore. She sat and turned, her chest a giant ache when she saw his red-rimmed eyes. The dead look he wore during battle, where he'd trapped his pain inside his soul and allowed it to fester, was raw and fresh. "Tell me you killed him."

He gave a watery, bitter laugh. "Sirens are mostly women. They're stronger. When I stepped between him and Tamara, he beat me unconscious. I wasn't there to protect her when she needed me. Even out cold, I heard her scream and scream. The power of her voice ruptured his ears, then his eyes. When I woke, he was lying in a pool of blood, gray matter oozing out of his ears. Despite being half my age, she was twice as strong.

"I searched everywhere for her, but Tamara was gone. I followed her bloody little footprints throughout the house and trailed her outside. She went into the water. I waited for days, dragged out the old man's rotting corpse and buried him, but she never returned. Months turned into years before someone from the Academy found me."

Morgan couldn't stand the aching loneliness and guilt anymore. She crawled out of the tub, settled into his lap and rested her head on his shoulder. "You didn't fail your mom, and you didn't fail your sister. Stop thinking of them as humans. If they are anything like me, they would've done what was necessary to protect you. They were stronger than you. They probably thought it was their job."

She ran her hand along his back, then reluctantly pulled away. "She's alive. You're alive. Hold onto that. She'll return when she's ready. It's more than what most people have."

He nodded, clearing his throat uncomfortably. "We better go, or the guys will come and investigate."

Morgan rose reluctantly, but when she stepped away, he grabbed her arm. "Stay here. I'll grab you some clothes."

He returned a moment later with one of his shirts and a pair of sweats, the bleak soullessness that lingered in his eyes having faded a fraction, the vivid blue reminding her of stormy seas. He politely left, and she dressed quickly, hurrying back into the main room. The guys were in different stages of undress, random bandages all over their bodies. Clearly exhausted, their movements became slower and not as careful. And every one of them was so physically fit, it was hard not to stare and drool.

Ryder had regained control of his voice. He held his shirt in front of him, and ducked his head, quickly finished dressing when he saw her watching, clearly self-conscious at being on display. He was the biggest of them, and the most buff. Each muscle was clearly defined, and she nearly groaned in disappointment when he tucked in his shirt. He must have shifted into his wolf again while she was getting cleaned up, since he had only minor scrapes and bruises compared to the others.

Atlas was dressed, raising a brow at her in challenge, daring her to strip him, but she saw a bandage peeking out from under his sleeve.

Kincade didn't carry any extra fat, his frame beautifully sculpted with muscles that were hypnotizing to watch when he moved. Though he wasn't bulky like a bodybuilder, he clearly knew how to stay fit.

They stood around the table, the ominous silence in the room stretching awkwardly as they watched her, tension holding them rigid, as if they expected her to start crying or something. "Tell me about the mirror."

Kincade tossed what remained of a roll of gauze on the table. "It shows you what you desire most."

Morgan frowned at him suspiciously when he refused to meet her gaze, wondering what he'd been thinking about when he stared at the mirror and saw her. He couldn't have targeted her—he didn't know anything about her.

So then...why her?

"I don't understand."

"The mirror allows me to monitor the school for any possible threats."

Nausea curled through her gut. "Why would the school summon me if I'm a threat?"

There was a thump under the table, and Kincade grunted as if he'd been kicked. His lips tightening, but not one of them spoke a word.

"It doesn't necessarily mean you're the threat. It can also mean danger surrounds you." It surprised her that Atlas would try to come to her rescue.

"You insisted on no more secrets. No more lies." Kincade's voice was silky smooth as he edged closer to her. "What are you not telling us?"

Her gaze flickered toward Draven, and he nodded. "I believe I was sent to the Academy not only to investigate the killings, but for protection."

Taking a deep breath, Morgan pulled her hair over her shoulder, turned, and lifted her shirt, feeling vulnerable being half naked in front of them.

The silence was deafening.

Kincade broke first and began swearing.

A finger gently traced the air above her skin, the hand hovering just short of touching her, and she shivered at the heat, a wave of pleasure spreading out from the near contact. When she turned her head to look, Kincade stood barely an inch away.

Ryder looked ready to jump out of his skin, but Atlas's reaction was more dramatic when he went deathly pale. "That's impossible."

"I believe my cousin is responsible. When he couldn't find me, he began to experiment on other girls, using them as substitutes. My cousin wouldn't hesitate to torture anyone, but he wouldn't make a secret of it. He also wouldn't leave their bodies to be discovered until he wanted them found. He must have an accomplice here at the school to do his dirty work while he's out searching for me."

Their faces became grimmer with each word.

"And now they found you." Kincade began to pace.

"You said you believe the stolen artifacts are connected to my case. Why?"

Draven was the one who spoke. "Primordial magic is a hundred times more potent than the magic witches use."

"You think someone is stealing the weapons to extract the magic from them." She glanced at each of them. "Why bother when it's too powerful for anyone to use?"

"The same reason they want you." Everyone stilled when Atlas spoke. "The magic in the blades—the same magic you carry in those runes—is powerful enough to rip open rifts anytime they want. If they catch you, they can harvest your magic to gain that power. Unfortunately, the process is very painful, and will ultimately kill you."

Morgan couldn't speak for a moment, her thoughts chaotic as she tried to understand what they were telling her. "That makes no sense. There are only two ways for a rift to be opened. Killing a witch and releasing a large burst of magic. Or..." Her mind went blank.

"A Pureblood. Only they can touch primordial magic, and even fewer can control it." Atlas was grim as he picked up his weapon and began flipping it in his hand, the only visible sign of his agitation.

"That's ridiculous." She couldn't be a pureblood. She reached up and grabbed the torque around her neck, needing the comfort. The chainmail guard twisted and spun down to a fine chain. Dangling from the tip was a tiny crown, the design so intricate, so dainty, she half expected her touch to crush it.

She jerked her hand away as if stung, while the guys stared at her in shock.

It was a coincidence.

It *had* to be a fluke.

"Where did you get that?" Atlas's voice was hushed, almost angry.

"I...I don't know." Morgan stuttered, curling her hands into fists to keep from touching it. "I was told it would protect me."

Now she wondered if it was a lie.

Atlas strode toward her, bent forward and inhaled deeply. She barely quelled the need to coldcock him. "It's a dampener, a precious metal mined by the dark elves to protect them from magic. It's damned near priceless." He straightened and eyed her suspiciously.

The need to smack him increased. "I didn't steal it, if that's what you're implying."

"It's not what he's saying." Kincade elbowed Atlas away, giving her room to breathe. "The light and dark elves are mortal enemies. He automatically turns into an idiot when he doesn't know the answer to something affecting them."

Atlas gave him the finger, not even remotely appeased, but he did back off.

"I'm not Tuatha Dé Danann, so what's the big deal?"

"While the torque might make you invisible to anyone hunting you, it also nulls every bit of magic you possess. It can only be removed by the person who placed it there." Atlas shook his head, his anger turning to concern. "You can't use magic while wearing the torque, which makes you extremely vulnerable."

Morgan was already shaking her head. "But I don't have any valuable magic. The witches did extensive testing."

She winced at the memories of the torture, still able to feel the five-inch needles piercing her flesh, the sound of power tools as they drilled into her bones, the pain as they forced magic into her body until it tried to rip her apart from the inside out, one cell at a time. She blew out a heavy breath, struggling against the need to hit something.

"Anyway, what you said isn't exactly true. I've been able to remove the torque for short periods of time. Unfortunately, since I started doing that, the runes have been leaking magic."

"During the rebellion ten years ago, half the royal court went missing and are presumed dead." The low, softly spoken words from Atlas raised the hair on the back of her neck.

"Morgan was found in the woods nine years ago with no memories of her past."

She glared at Draven for spilling the information. "Don't even go there."

"There is only one girl her age missing." Atlas stared at her, his hard green eyes glittering like emeralds. "The king's niece."

She snorted at the likelihood. "That's preposterous."

The guys' shared a look that made her want to smack them. "What?"

"If what he says is true, you might still have magic. The witches were simply searching for the *wrong kind* of magic." Draven's voice was gentle, but the impact nearly knocked her on her ass.

"No." She held up her hands to ward them off. "Just no."

Only purebloods could use primordial magic.

Royalty.

"It's possible." But Atlas sounded doubtful. He changed the subject and turned toward Kincade. "It's a rare gift to be able to transform metals. Has she been in contact with any of the void weapons?"

Kincade shook his head, then turned to the others. "She needs to be tested."

Morgan didn't care for the way the conversation was going. Based on her experience, testing was never simple or pain-free. "What are you thinking?"

"If you're a pureblood, the weapons will respond to your touch. They were created specifically to protect the royal family." Kincade and the others began to collect their weapons, heading toward their rooms to dress.

Things were moving much too fast for her. "Why does it even matter?"

Everyone paused, but it was Draven who spoke. "If you're the missing princess, you're the last pureblood of your kind."

Morgan was already shaking her head, but he continued to speak. "You're a direct descendent of the Titan bloodlines, the original primordial gods, and next in line for the crown."

She went lightheaded at the thought, grabbing the back of her chair to keep from keeling over.

Gods were larger than life and nearly unstoppable.

Maybe more frightening, they were eventually driven insane by their powers and had to be put down. The beginning of the end for them began over a millennium ago.

The gods split into two groups, those who wanted to save the humans, and those who wanted to preserve their own way of life. Neither could be accomplished while the human and primordial realm interacted, so they used their powers to build a barrier between worlds, keeping the humans on one side and the supernaturals on the other.

Whatever magic was trapped Earthside became diluted, mutating into the magic witches were able to wield today, while the ancient magic in the primordial realm thrived and kept the alternative dimension alive.

"You and the king are the last remaining direct descendants."

The world around her shifted, crumbling beneath her feet, and she couldn't find any solid ground.

She was just a plain old girl.

A hunter.

Nothing more.

But something niggled at the back of her mind, a suspicion that MacGregor knew more than he was telling her.

"Have any of you visited the MacGregor?"

"It's bad." Ryder's lips tightened. "His wounds are extensive."

Her heart sank at the idea of not having him around to order her about. He was an unstoppable force. Her brain couldn't process the thought of losing him. "Will he pull out of it?"

"He's a tough old coot. If anyone can, it will be him." Kincade stepped in front of her, the compassion on his face scaring her more than anything. "But he will never be able to fight again."

Her knees gave out, and she plopped to the floor before anyone could catch her.

It was every warrior's worst fear.

Warriors would rather go down in battle than be treated as an old invalid to be shuffled into a corner.

"I need to go…" she pulled herself to her feet and nearly fell flat on her face. There wasn't enough air in the room anymore.

Ryder trailed after her, his arms outstretched, ready to catch her if she faltered. She hesitated outside Ascher's room, and Draven sighed. "We won't touch him."

Morgan nodded and walked blindly out the door.

Her cousin's words came back to her, and she wondered what he was planning next.

He said he would make her pay.

The only way to do that would be to go after MacGregor again…or her men.

Chapter Twenty-one

$\mathcal{M}$organ couldn't go back to her room, too restless and overwhelmed with the knowledge that she might be a descendent of a god to be able to sit still.

Not surprisingly, she ended up outside the infirmary, feeling very young and wanting MacGregor to tell her it was all lies and everything would be all right.

A large wolf stood to attention outside the door, discouraging visitors.

She wasn't deterred. She nodded to the large brown and white beast, barely resisted the urge to fidget as he measured her with those big, brown eyes of his. To her surprise, she received a regal nod in return. He shifted over a few inches, silently granting her permission to enter.

The front office bustled with people, hunters being checked out, supply shelves being stocked and bloodied rags being tossed. No one seemed to notice her as she headed toward the separate room in the back.

"I'll wait here." Morgan jumped when Ryder spoke from behind her. She'd completely forgotten his presence. He gingerly lowered his large frame into a small chair by the door, tipped back his head, and closed his eyes.

Morgan watched him for a moment longer, appreciating his silent companionship, then blew out a heavy breath and opened the door. Only one of the twelve beds was occupied. She couldn't tear her eyes away from the still form tucked under the pristine blankets, shocked at his deterioration from virile leader to a broken old man.

"Stop hovering." He snapped, but ruined the effect when he wheezed. "Either enter or leave an old man to die in peace."

"You look awful." Morgan forced her feet to move, coming to a stop by his side.

He scanned her body up and down with the eye that wasn't swollen shut. "You don't look much better, missy."

Morgan fidgeted with her fingers, her anger at him fading. "I'm glad you survived."

"Too ornery to kill." He snorted, then winced, shifting slowly on the bed. "I see you didn't get yourself kidnapped."

She shrugged and wandered closer. "You trained me too well…plus, I'm too stubborn to allow myself to be taken."

His lips twitched with a hint of a smile, then he seemed to shrink as he leaned back into the bed.

"You knew they were after me."

MacGregor shook his head, wincing when his neck protested the movement. "I suspected. You were always special. I always considered it my job to keep you safe. Sending you to the Academy was the only way I could assure your safety anymore."

Morgan leaned her ass against the bed next to his, suddenly exhausted. "Do you know who I am?"

"Enough to know you're someone very, very important." He waved a hand as if to shoo away her questions. "You were a fast learner, always too smart for your own good. You were beyond skilled. Others sensed the difference in you and felt threatened. I gave you what I could. I tried to protect you by teaching you what you needed to survive."

Pride filled his face as he gazed at her. She stared at his tired, faded blue eyes, and couldn't be angry at him for keeping secrets. He was a rigid taskmaster, a slave driver who pushed her past her breaking point, then demanded more.

He was also a warrior who had never mated.

Nothing about him was soft.

And she realized he didn't know how to be anything but a hunter.

But he'd tried to be more for her.

He gave her everything he could, did what he thought was best for her. Though he didn't show it, she knew he would give his life for hers. She rubbed her right hand, trying to ease the sting of the growing marks, and he instantly noticed her furtive movement. His eyes narrowed, his attention shooting to her face, as if searching for something, then nodded to himself and released a deep sigh. "Stay close to those young men of yours. Dangerous times are still ahead. The ones who want you won't simply give up because they failed."

She scowled, wanting to protest that she could protect herself, but the worry in his eyes stopped her from voicing her thoughts. He would crawl out of bed to protect her if she didn't heed his warning. Instead, she stood and pulled his blanket up, smoothing away the wrinkles, surprised by how deep her affection for him went. Though he might not be the best father material, she loved him more for trying to raise an orphan girl for no other reason than she needed him. "Rest and get better. I still need you, old man."

He closed his eyes with a grunt, grumbling under his breath for her to go away, but the way his eyes crinkled at the corners told her he was pleased at her fussing.

When she slipped out of the room, she nearly ran over Mistress McKay. The teacher clutched a book to her chest, blushing slightly as she straightened her glasses. She'd done something to her hair...left it in a loose knot at the back of her head, softening her appearance. "Thank you for returning him to me...us." Her blush deepened, and she fiddled with the book she held. "I thought I would read to him."

"Good idea." Morgan stepped away from the door, biting her lip to keep from smiling at McKay's nervousness. "You clearly have the tougher job of getting him back on his feet again."

Determination flooded her face, and she lifted her chin. "Let me worry about that."

The tough, no-nonsense teacher she first met was back. Mistress McKay gave Morgan a brisk nod, then breezed past her, the door snapping shut smartly behind her, and Morgan had no doubt MacGregor would be on the mend in no time if McKay had anything to say in the matter.

A jarring bell blared overhead, and Morgan glanced around in confusion.

"Time for classes." Ryder spoke from her elbow. He moved so silently, she jumped.

"Class?" She groaned at the idea of getting her ass handed to her after a long night of no sleep.

Ryder gave her a sympathetic smile. "You best hurry, unless you want Kincade to single you out."

And the bastard would do it, too. She growled, then took off at a run. She quickly dropped by her room to change, then headed toward the gym. By the time she arrived, she was out of breath, and tried to slip into the back of the room without anyone noticing she was late.

Thankfully, when she scanned the front of the class, she didn't see Kincade.

Concern stirred in her gut for a split second, then Atlas stepped forward and took over the class. Through it all, Ryder remained at her side. While the other students were paired up, he raised a brow at her, and she heaved a sigh. "Let me guess…you're my partner?"

Ryder nodded. So not good. He was stronger and faster than most, his wolf giving him the edge.

"Where—"

"Kincade is meeting with the headmistress, preparing alternate plans of attack."

Morgan trailed after him as he led her to the corner of the room, unable to tear her eyes away from the way his broad shoulders stretched the black shirt he wore. She followed the sleek lines down his back, unable to keep her eyes from dropping and admiring the way his ass filled out his pants. When he stopped, she nearly slammed into him, quickly dancing around him, but not before his tempting wild, fresh green scent went straight to her head.

All playfulness vanished when she found the two weapons waiting for them. The blades were a dull black and wicked as hell. "The infamous void weapons?"

Ryder nodded, carefully straightening the blades in front of them. "Usually only third-year students are given the option to train with them. It takes years of practice and skill to wield the dual weapon and magic combination." He picked up the nearest knife, then closed his eyes. After a moment, sigils on the blade shimmered and glowed a pale blue. "Void weapons are deadlier than any other. They can kill anything. If you have enough training, if you can focus on the blade, it will alert you to danger and guide your hand."

He stepped back, gesturing for her to pick up the other weapon.

She clenched and unclenched her hands, staring at the innocuous blade, surprised she missed Kincade's overbearing, bullying presence. Whether she wanted to admit it or not, he pushed her for more, challenged her to do better. Without him there to steady her, her nerves began to fray.

"Why you?" She lifted her arm, allowing her hand to hover over the pommel. "Atlas lives in the primordial realm. Shouldn't he be training me?"

A muscle ticked in his jaw, and she winced when she realized how it sounded. "I'm so sorry. I didn't mean—"

"No. You're right. Kincade is the best. I'm a distant second. Most shifters don't have any skill with void weapons, but I had some training with them before my first shift." He frowned down at the blade he held. "The transformation only enhanced my natural talent."

He wasn't telling her everything. "But?"

"Just like when I step out of a rift, once I release the primordial magic, I crash hard." He shrugged away the fact that he would be violently ill and suffer for helping her.

Morgan didn't like it. "And Atlas?"

"Not his skillset." Ryder didn't say any more on the matter, gesturing for her to pick up the last blade. "Go ahead. I'm here. I won't let anything happen to you."

Though he would try, they both knew he might not have a choice. She needed to learn to fight her own battles. Taking a deep breath, she lowered her hand, and snatched up the weapon before she lost her nerve.

The expected pain never came.

Nor did the sigils glow.

"Maybe everyone was wrong." She wanted to cheer.

Ryder studied the blade, then shrugged. "Or the torque could be blocking you."

Her smile vanished at his more logical answer.

"Come." Ryder guided her toward the center of the mat and dropped into a fighting stance.

Two guys nearby laughed, and Morgan glanced over at them. One of them was the snide guy from the first day. "No fair training with a wolf. When you get cornered, all you have to do is smack him on the nose, and he'll back off."

His partner laughed nervously, but began to shuffle away when he caught the expression on her face.

"Excuse me?" Morgan unconsciously brought up her weapon and advanced on them.

Their eyes dropped toward the knife, then quickly flashed up to her face. They raised their hands in surrender, nervously clearing their throats.

"Leave them."

Morgan barely heard Ryder's command. "They need to be taught a lesson. A broken bone or two, a bruised spleen or kidneys should work."

He edged between her and her prey, gazing down at her curiously, and some of her aggression tapered off. "What?"

He shook his head, as if completely baffled by her. "Nothing you can say or do will change their opinion that shifters are an inferior species."

"That makes no sense." But she allowed him to draw her away after one last glare at the kids.

"Many shifters, upon their first change, never return to being fully human again, and some never return to their human form at all. To them, we're nothing more than beasts." He shrugged away the matter, and avoided looking directly at her. He did that a lot around her, as if trying not to intimidate her.

She found it...cute. Truth to tell, she liked his size, and enjoyed seeing all those muscles in motion. She eyed his wide shoulders, those amazing biceps, and shook off her thoughts. "You're beasts, and we're monsters. I don't see the difference."

Ryder raised a brow at her, motioning for her to drop into her fighting stance. "You're oversimplifying things, and you know it. They need no more proof than the wolves on duty outside these walls. They're pure wolf, barely human enough to understand orders and stand guard. I can tell the difference when I run with them. Nothing human remains in them."

Morgan instinctively countered Ryder's moves when he began circling her. "It's more than that. They listen to you."

"Most werewolves who can control their shifts are stronger, more dominant. The other wolves obey…mostly." He shrugged it off as no big deal. Though she didn't believe him, she dropped the subject.

"Tell me how to activate the weapon." She hefted her blade up, then spun sideways when he lashed out with his weapon. She kicked backwards in retaliation, but he was already gone. His foot shot out, knocking her leg to the side, both moving until they ended up facing each other.

When he lunged forward, she flung herself backwards, landing on her ass with a thump. She planted her feet in his gut, using his momentum to fling him over her head. He wasn't distracted in the least, bringing his blade down toward her neck midflight, and she barely brought up her own knife in time.

Sparks flew when the weapons met.

Ryder continued to sail over her head, landing on his shoulder, then rolled to his feet, crouched before her. To her shock, a deep violet mist lit up the sigils on her blade. Magic crawled through the metal and bit into her palm like a snakebite. Ice burned through her blood like venom. She tried to drop the knife, but she couldn't seem to make her fingers obey.

The runes along her spine shifted restlessly, then began to absorb the extra magic. As the pain faded, everything appeared sharper, the room brighter, the air fresher. Ryder stood over her, peering down at her with concern, and she was reminded again of how handsome he was.

A dusky blush colored his face, and she realized she must have been thinking out loud. She should be mortified, but she was too charmed by his reaction to care. "Why aren't you mated?"

"Are you okay?" His lips tightened as he tried to squash his smile. "I should've warned you the magic can have unusual side effects— like taking away your inhibitions and flooding your system with adrenaline."

Morgan leapt to her feet, waving away his concern. "Stop avoiding the question. You're older than the others. Why stay at the school?"

The sparkle in his eyes died, and he dropped his gaze. "We're not exactly human."

"None of us are." She barely waited for him to turn before she swung. "Isn't that a good thing?"

He easily dodged away, only to come back swinging. "Not when you're a shifter. Most don't consider me human enough."

"That's just stupid." Morgan leaned back to avoid having her throat slit.

"We're not like the other students. Vampires and shifters were purged from the primordial realm thousands of years ago. Lycanthropy and vampirism were viruses that spread throughout the realm. The rulers refused to condone mass genocide, so they lifted the ban between worlds, and expelled everyone who carried the virus."

Morgan ducked and dodged, barely keeping ahead of his swings while he spoke.

"The viruses were contained here, but they mutated. Now, lycanthropy and vampirism can only be passed through the bloodlines, or by those who were bitten and survived the transition, which is rare. Since we can no longer return to the primordial realm, we're considered second-class citizens."

"But you're a paranormal creature like them." She dashed forward and slashed out with the knife, and nearly lost her blade when he kicked at her exposed hand, missing it only by centimeters.

"Only to humans." Ryder gave her a cynical look. "They consider us diseased, or an accident of birth."

"All life is a mutation."

He stared at her like she was an oddity, then replied grudgingly. "Maybe to some. Others would fight you to the death for even suggesting it."

Then talking stopped as they began to fight in earnest. Every time he neared, she was already moving, almost able to read his intentions before they were formed. After twenty minutes, she noticed he was pulling his punches, slowing down for her, and she growled in frustration. He hadn't landed any blows harder than a light tap. "I won't learn anything if you're too afraid to hit me."

After a moment's hesitation, he nodded. Magic splashed into the room as his wolf rose to the surface. The smile he flashed showed sharp teeth, though his claws remained carefully hidden. Despite the longer hair, she could see his slightly pointed ears, and her fingers itched to touch them.

He didn't give any signals when he attacked this time. The fighting was dirty and brutal, and she landed on her back more than once with him leaning over her.

Every time he neared, he sniffed the air, and she wondered if her sweat offended his acute wolf senses. After the fifth time, she began to get a complex. She kicked him in the chest and confronted him on it. "Do I stink or something?"

His whole body tensed, a deep red climbing up his collar, and Morgan immediately felt like shit. She edged closer to him, and spoke softly so she wouldn't spook him. "Ryder?"

"Trying to figure out your heritage. Never smelled anything like you." His eyes were a combination of wolf and human when he peered at her, then he quickly dropped his gaze. "Smells good."

Morgan stiffened, not moving under his predatory gaze, uncertain how to react at having a hungry wolf tell you that you smelled good.

He flinched at her reaction as if she'd struck him.

Only then did she realize the hunger in his eyes was for something else entirely.

All expression disappeared from Ryder's face, and she knew she'd disappointed him, but decided not to correct his impression. She had too much to worry about right now, mainly keeping herself and the guys alive. She didn't have time for friends, much less a boyfriend.

The playfulness of his wolf vanished, as if he locked the best part of himself away from her. It stung, but she couldn't say she didn't deserve it. She was being an ass, and she knew it.

She glanced down at the blade in shame. While the primordial magic was active, the torque was keeping it contained in her body, and it was taking its toll, eating her from the inside out, wanting its freedom.

The longer she held the blade, the harder it was to concentrate and make her body obey.

Her moves were slowing.

Becoming clumsy.

Ryder frowned at her, the blade lowering to his side. "What's wrong?"

Draven smirked from the sidelines, rocking on his feet as he nodded toward the door. "Kincade just walked in."

"She wouldn't let him distract her." Ryder didn't take his eyes off her. "Drop the blade."

She shook her head, rubbing the back of her hand against her leg, but it did nothing to ease the burning heat. "Just sore. I can fight."

"Let me see." He didn't take no for an answer, grabbing her under her elbow, and lifted her arm, then froze.

The beautiful, almost dainty filigree marks had spread and darkened. Obsidian black and molten silver swirled from the tips of her fingers, twisting halfway up her right arm. "The blade is just reacting to the runes. I'm fine."

"These marks have nothing to do with your runes." Ryder's voice sounded strained. "These symbols have very specific meanings." He carefully pried the weapon from her grip, handing them both off to Draven.

She blinked up at him in confusion. "Then what is it?"

"Mating marks."

"Mating marks?" she replied stupidly. "As in plural?" Her voice rose to a squeak. "What the hell are you talking about?"

"Calm." Ryder lifted his hands. "Easy."

"Who?" She hadn't been aware she was advancing until he began to retreat. "Who would do this to me?"

Darkness rose, and the metal torque around her neck heated, trying to stop her from losing control.

"Christ. She's freaking out." Draven waved to someone across the room, and she snapped her head in his direction. "No one did this to you. It's natural selection. Females are paired with males, and they become your protectors."

"No." Morgan shook her head frantically. "No way. I would never bind anyone to me. It's archaic—worse than slavery."

Draven eyed her critically, his face softened when he realized she was serious, and he approached carefully. "These marks aren't a choice. They are an honor bestowed upon hunters by their chosen one. The markings can be formed by something as simple as a touch."

"What?" Morgan felt like she'd been punched in the gut. "Who?"

The guys exchanged a look, then each one rolled up his sleeves. Their arms were bare.

Ryder barely glanced at his bicep, clearly not expecting to be chosen, disappointment and acceptance shadowing in his eyes. Though Draven hid it, he was overjoyed not to have been selected. Atlas didn't even bother to hide his relief.

As one, they all looked across the gym to see Kincade scratching his arm.

"No." Morgan shook her head, backing away. "Not him."

"Shite. She's going to run." Ryder charged toward her, sweeping her off her feet and tossing her over his shoulder, heading toward the exit with long strides.

Atlas split off from them. "I'll head off Kincade."

Morgan bucked, nearly escaping from Ryder's hold. "Don't tell him."

All the men stopped and stared at her bug-eyed. "You would deny him this honor?"

Ryder snorted at the same time. "Do you think he wouldn't notice?"

Morgan felt trapped, the fight draining out of her, and she slumped in defeat. She didn't like the look the others were giving her...full of speculation and such damming hope that her chest ached. They were happy, even excited by the markings.

The fools.

She didn't protest as they carried her away, the strength draining away from her bones.

"Oh, Kincade's going to fucking freak out." Draven's voice was both grim and amused, and she barely bit back a groan.

Chapter Twenty-two

*E*veryone automatically headed toward the barracks. Draven and Ryder watched her pace back and forth with varying degrees of curiosity and concern. Morgan could feel the clock ticking down, and it was all she could do to keep her shit together.

The door slammed open with a bang and Kincade burst into the room, his hair wild, his chest heaving, his eyes savage. He located her immediately, unerringly, as if she was some damned beacon.

Pure possessiveness stared back at her, the cold reserve he hid behind when they first met was stripped away completely. The heat in his expression, his ferocity, frightened her more than any monster she'd ever faced.

Much to her shock, he tore off his shirt and advanced on her. She froze, distracted by his predatory grace and rippling muscles as he strode toward her, the sleek way he moved hijacking her sense of self-preservation, and she stood there like a dummy. To her surprise, his entire shoulder was covered in the same swirling pattern as her hand, the lines spilling down his arm to his elbow. Instead of dainty lines, the dips and swirls of molten silver were bolder, more masculine.

The more primitive side of her was pleased to see her stamp on him, but more than anything else, it scared her shitless.

He displayed his marks with pride, but the pleasure in his eyes faded as he drew closer, his gaze locked on the arm she'd tucked close to her body, instinctively trying to hide her markings. His brows lowered, and he grabbed her wrist, staring down at the markings accusingly, as if she'd somehow betrayed him.

"Who is the second person you've mated?" The demand was barely more than a snarl. He rubbed at the obsidian line as if he could wipe it away by will alone.

Morgan jerked away from him, flinging up her hands. "How the hell should I know? I didn't ask to be marked. This is a stupid, antiquated custom. You can't really take any of this seriously."

A snarl curled his lips, and her faint hope that he would back her up vanished.

"Whether you like it or not, you're mine, and I'll do whatever is necessary to protect you."

"Oh, dude, wrong thing to say." Draven dropped his head into his hands.

The life she'd envisioned vanished, her freedom evaporated before she even had a chance to be free. She narrowed her eyes on him and lifted her chin mulishly. "You can't force me."

"Watch me." He began stalking her across the room. "Who else marked you? Who else dared touch you?" Kincade glared at each member of his team, and each one shook his head. It only made Kincade scowl harder.

"I'm not a possession you can own." Morgan stood her ground, refusing to be treated as property. "You have no right to barge into my life or demand to know whom I touch. Butt out."

Draven shook his head and sighed. "Oh, sweeting. Wrong thing to say."

Any imaginary wall existing between them crumbled to dust, and he barged into her personal space. The hot stone scent she associated with him nearly had her rocking forward to seek more. She didn't know why it smelled so good; her mouth was actually watering.

"Who?"

Thankfully, the sharp demand snapped her back to her senses. She leaned forward, speaking through clenched teeth. "I will say it more slowly so it will penetrate that thick skull of yours. I. Don't. Know. It's not like I asked for this shit! I don't date. I don't hang around guys. I kept my distance from everyone for a reason—to avoid any chance of this happening. Coming here was a mistake."

She spun away, gripping her hair, feeling like she was bashing her head against a stone wall trying to get through to him.

Kincade pushed her forward until he had her pinned to the wall. She struggled to throw an elbow, twisting to get away, but he held her too firmly, every inch of him covering her back. His lips brushed the side of her neck. A second later, the press of his fangs against the crook of her neck froze her to the spot.

Instead of fear, instead of fighting, she reacted to his nearness on the most primitive level. Her body softened, her breathing picked up, and she desperately longed to get closer. She barely bit back a groan, the urge to push against him nearly overwhelming, and she cursed her body's betrayal. "Get off me!"

"Calm." His rough voice whispered in her ear, sending shivers down her spine, and she was terrified to move lest she did something stupid…like curl around him the way her body craved.

Ryder leaned against the wall next to her, and hunkered down to capture her attention, ignoring the way Kincade growled at him to keep his distance. Her stupid body heated, perversely loving Kincade's possessiveness. "You fear he will be turned into a slave, forced to obey you."

She frantically searched Ryder's eyes, looking for any spark of reason in this insanity.

"Does he feel like a slave to you?"

Kincade retracted his fangs, then began to gently lick at the wound, the rasp of his tongue weakening her knees.

"No."

"The bindings can be what you make them." Sadness darkened Ryder's eyes, and she felt him pulling away. "You've seen how the bond can be perverted, but that is actually pretty rare. The markings can also be a lifeline, and often are the best thing to happen to us. Bonding happens infrequently, especially for those as young as you two. It usually takes decades of searching. I suspect it happened because you two are so very powerful, or maybe it was triggered since your life is in danger. You don't see pairs often, because they are assigned their own territories to protect, but seeing a true mated couple fight is a sight to behold."

Some of the fight went out of her. "Why two?"

"The stronger the female, the more male protectors she attracts." He gave a shrug. "I honestly expect you to have more. You just haven't found them yet."

"And the mating?" Her voice was barely a whisper, her face burning. She could already tell touching Kincade was different. He stood silent, practically vibrating with so much primitive emotion she wondered if he was beyond speaking…or maybe he was heroically resisting the urge to strangle her. She wouldn't put either past him. She might have been curious about him before the mating marks, now she actively hungered for his touch.

She hated it.

Didn't she?

Ryder swallowed hard, his eyes caressing her face. "Your body will automatically seek your mates for comfort. You will find their touch pleasurable, but no matter what happens, you will always have your own free will. They will not force you or rush you. It's ultimately your choice who you chose to love."

When she saw the determined look in his eyes, she suspected he would make sure of it.

To her surprise, his promise of protection eased her misgivings.

Then he went and ruined it by talking again. "It's usually not an issue anyway. The mating bond will make you crave each other. You'll seek each other out for something as simple as taking comfort by being in the same room with each other."

Morgan thumped her forehead against the wall. When she lifted her head to do it again, Kincade loosened his grip and slipped his hand between the wall and her forehead, already trying to protect and coddle her. He would never let her fight now. Unable to think with him so close, she wiggled free. While he allowed her to step away from him, he didn't let her go far.

It didn't matter.

The feel of his body was imprinted on her mind down to her soul, and she feared she would never be able to forget it.

"We need to find your other mate and begin making plans." His voice was gentler, but his eyes were no less intense as he gazed at her.

Morgan felt overwhelmed by the enormity of the coming changes.

What did it mean exactly to own a mate, much less two?

She wasn't sure she was strong enough to survive one, let alone two people barging into her solitary life.

"You're connected to us on a basic level." Kincade kept his distance from her, hardly less than a foot, but she noticed the clenched hands at his sides, as if to keep himself from reaching for her. "If you concentrate on the connection, you should be able to sense him."

Morgan narrowed her eyes on him. "Great. So you're saying we're basically lo-jacked with these marks?"

His lips twitched, but he ignored her question. "Close your eyes and concentrate."

She eyed him suspiciously for a moment longer, then did as he suggested, feeling vulnerable with them watching her fumble around.

She focused on the marks on her arm and jolted when a combination of fierce joy and total terror swept over her.

It was Kincade, and his turbulent emotions threatened to swallow her whole.

She hastily pulled back, cutting off the connection, and Kincade grunted as if she'd kicked him in the balls.

Her eyes popped open, her breath ragged, fighting the instinctive urge to run away from him, as far and as fast as she could.

Kincade recovered first. "Try again."

She licked her lips and closed her eyes.

The smell of fire and charcoal wrapped around her in a warm hug. Ascher. In hellhound form. His complete devotion came through the link, his pleasure at the connection so bright and shiny it brought tears to her eyes. The sweet taste of his relief at finding her well swamped him, and he gave a victorious howl that echoed throughout the school.

"That son of a bitch." Kincade grabbed her shoulders, practically picking her up and setting her aside, jerking her away from the connection.

Ascher chose that moment to pad out of his room on silent feet. He eyed the others, his growl ceasing the moment his blue eyes settled on her. He came to her side as if the others didn't exist, and leaned against her leg. She could see the shimmering lines of the mating mark covering his shoulder, the black lines highlighted by a dusky red that resembled live coals.

Morgan couldn't help herself, and brushed the back of her hand against him in welcome. He'd been a part of her life for so long, it felt natural to have him at her side.

Kincade glared murderously at the hellhound, his eyes flickering to her hand as if jealous, which was ridiculous. He didn't even like her, made it clear from day one. Mating didn't change that…right?

She stepped away from Ascher and faced Kincade. "Refuse the markings."

It was a demand.

"No." He didn't even bother to think about it, the bastard.

"You two don't even like each other." She pointed a finger between Kincade and Ascher. "You can't want this any more than I do."

The two males glanced at each other and shrugged. "Our feelings no longer matter. Keeping you safe is our priority now. We'll work out our differences later."

He sounded so reasonable she wanted to scream.

Kincade relented slightly. "It's an honor to be chosen. Men never refuse their markings. It's what we've worked toward since our birth. It's a privilege, a once-in-a-lifetime opportunity that will give us the one thing we want most, and the one thing no one can ever take away from us—you. You're our future, our greatest hope, and the only thing that will ever make us feel complete."

He made it sound…beautiful.

An unbreakable bond.

Unwavering support.

The yearning to belong nearly swayed her, but she knew firsthand that what Kincade described wasn't always what happened. Her memories flashed back to the witches at the coven, how they would sleep with different men every night, then pit them against each other the next day for fun. The behavior taught the protectors to be competitive jerks.

Obsessive and controlling.

It would be a prison.

Her stomach churned at the thought of having her every choice, her every action judged and criticized and monitored.

"Is there any way to break the connection once it forms?" She would not have them risk their lives for her. Trouble was coming. If Ethan found out about them, he would use them to destroy her.

The hellhound pressed so hard against her leg, he nearly knocked her off her feet, giving her a combination of a whine and growl from the back of his throat she easily translated to *over my dead body*. Kincade's face darkened, a muscle jumping in his jaw, apparently too angry to speak. If Ascher wasn't between them, she didn't doubt he would have lunged for her.

In less than a day, the idea of breaking the connection devastated her.

She imagined the feeling would become worse over time.

Her pulse pounded in panic, the feeling of being trapped tightening her lungs.

The room fell ominously silent, and she glanced beseechingly at Draven. "I can't be responsible for others. I can't." Only he would understand firsthand what an overwhelming and impossible task it was to protect someone else. Neither of them wanted to risk getting close to others, only to lose them.

It hurt too much.

Her throat tightened at the sympathy in Draven's eyes.

Kincade finally managed to unclench his jaw enough to grit out one word. "No."

Sorrow burrowed deeper in her chest when she realized she'd hurt him.

It hadn't even been an hour, and she already sucked at this mating thing.

"I want her moved into the barracks with us." Kincade turned toward his team, ignoring her completely, not even bothering to ask her first. "She's a security risk and needs protection. They're not going to stop coming after her unless we make them."

"Agreed." Ryder grunted, and Draven nodded as well.

Kincade's shoulders relaxed at their easy capitulation.

"Don't I get a say?"

"No." All the guys spoke at once, even Ascher giving a bark of denial.

"I'll speak with the headmistress and ask to be removed from the hunting roster. We can't risk being lured out and ambushed." No one even bothered to argue with him. "And I want one of us to be with her at all times."

Morgan scowled. She could understand them feeling helpless in the face of the threat hanging over her head. She felt the same way, and voiced her worry. "Don't you think you're going a bit far?"

"No." Kincade didn't even bother to look at her. "The headmistress called an assembly for later today, and will announce whether they will be sending the students home or if it will be safer to keep them here and fortify the Academy. If we hurry, we can have you settled before we're called to attend."

In a matter of minutes, he'd taken over her life completely, her opinion mattering not at all.

Morgan felt like she just fell down the rabbit hole and landed in Hell.

Chapter Twenty-three

$\mathcal{M}$organ was in her newly appointed room, situated between Ascher's and Kincade's, staring blankly at her meager possessions, not quite sure how things had gone so wrong.

"Where's the rest?" Draven leaned against the door with a frown, and she turned back to stare in confusion at the duffel bag on the bed.

"This is it." She closed the bag, deciding not to unpack. Why bother? As soon as this mission was over, she would either be dead or gone.

"Girls like a lot of shite." His frown darkened, and he crossed his arms, rubbing his thumb over his bottom lip. "What happened to yours?"

She glanced at her possessions and shrugged. "I had to leave some of my weapons back in Maine."

His brows slammed down, as if troubled by her comment, then gave her a charming smile. "We're going to be heading down to the assembly in a few minutes."

"Fine." Morgan stifled a huff over her pampered prison. While the room was bigger, and much nicer than the last, she had absolutely no privacy. She could hear them talking, laughing, but wasn't deceived. They were all watching her room, waiting for her to attempt an escape, suspicious of her easy capitulation.

She was tempted, but in the end, her relocation simplified things.

She could keep an eye on them as well.

She expected to feel crowded with them right outside her door, but she liked hearing the rumble of their voices, their abrupt laughter as they joked. It was…comforting. One by one, they left the main room to get ready for the assembly. Draven and Ryder took a shower, and she couldn't help but smile over their primping.

Morgan set out her weapons, then began tucking them away on her person. As she slid the last two daggers in their sheaths at her waist, she turned to go…only to find the guys crowding her door, watching her in various degrees of fascination. The only one missing was Kincade.

Draven noticed her distraction. "Since Kincade is head of security, he is with the headmistress. All teachers are required to attend."

Morgan didn't like that he left without letting her know. He must have slipped out while she was being escorted to her room to collect her belongings. When she walked into the common area, her gaze landed on Ascher. "Can you change to your human form? Can you change to your human form? I'm not sure it's wise to bring a hellhound into a group of assassins in training."

He padded toward the bathroom, then paused to glance at her over his shoulder.

"I promise we won't leave without you."

As he disappeared, Morgan wondered if his connection to her conniving cousin was finally broken by their mating bond. She focused on the three remaining guys, eyeing them up and down. As one, they all stepped back a pace.

"Draven." He gulped when she said his name. "Do you have any spare clothes Ascher might be able to wear?"

"Of course." He released a heavy breath of relief and hurried off to do as bidden.

Ten minutes later, Ascher exited the bathroom, his wet hair tousled. There was a wildness around him that drew attention, a pure predator staring back. His shirt was a little too tight, revealing every line of his chest, his pants a little too large, hanging mouthwateringly low on his hips. He prowled toward her, and her stupid stomach dipped in anticipation.

He came to a stop at her side like he belonged there. "Ready?"

She licked her lips and had to turn away, struggling to remember how to speak. "Uhmm...yeah."

Afraid he would touch her and reduce her to a puddle of lust, she darted for the door, practically racing toward the auditorium to escape her troubling emotions.

The auditorium was half full. Ryder saw her confusion, and answered her unspoken question. "School doesn't actually begin for another few days for most of the students."

Then there was no more speaking as they began to climb the bleachers. She and Ascher followed Ryder's lead, heading toward an empty bench off to the side of the large room, conscious of people staring. She tugged at her black T-shirt, acutely aware she didn't really fit the group of hot eye candy.

Only a few minutes had passed when the teachers strode toward the center of the auditorium. Her eyes were instantly drawn to Kincade, and her mouth went dry. He actually dressed up, his button-down shirt molding to his form to perfection. He looked almost unassuming until she spotted the weapons strapped to his body, changing him from sexy professor to deadly assassin. He reminded her of a warrior from the ancient legends she'd read about in one of MacGregor's many books, and she couldn't tear her gaze away.

Before the teachers could take their seats, the runes on her back flared to life, stealing the air from her lungs. Pain rippled down her spine, sending shards of agony into her every nerve ending, threatening to drop her to her knees when she doubled over. The guys were shouting, but their words were nothing more than a low mumble that didn't penetrate the buzzing in her ears.

Ascher knelt in front of her, carefully lifting her face. His warm touch centered her, dragging her away from the crippling pain threatening to consume her. "What is it?"

Her lips were numb as she forced the words out past her clenched jaw. "Something's coming."

He scanned her face once, then nodded. "Someone is using a lot of primordial magic. We have to go." He shot to his feet, hauling her upright with him. He tucked her next to him and headed for the nearest exit. Before they took two steps, the air in front of them rippled, and a rift tore open not ten feet away.

Screams erupted around them, and Morgan spun to see two more rifts. When she heard thumping from behind her, she turned to see dozens of small rocks tumbling from the portal. They uncurled and straightened, opened their large mouths and roared.

Rock trolls.

They were about as tall as her knees, a porous, dusty brown, with heavy beer bellies. Their faces were squished, making their bulbous noses seem even larger, their large tusks giving them an underbite. They had small, flat ears, and pure black eyes that reminded her of the beady eyes of a spider. They usually lived in tunnels under mountains, their bodies like rocks, and often ate unwary travelers. They almost always kept to themselves, and Morgan couldn't imagine what could have enticed them to attack.

Ascher yanked on her arm, dragging her out of the path of a nasty spiked cudgel. Morgan grabbed the railing leading up to the auditorium, ripped it from its moorings, and swung. The impromptu bat cracked into the troll, the impact reverberating up her arms like she'd hit solid stone, but served to launch the little bastard back through the rift.

Ascher lifted a brow at her, then mimicked her by tearing off his own railing. Ryder didn't bother with anything so small. He peeled up the nearest bench and used it like a bulldozer to scrape the lot of them back into the rift, the muscles of his arms and legs straining under the weight. She followed a step behind, swinging at the ones who tried to jump over and bite him.

Draven and Atlas had pulled their blades, whirling and spinning as they hacked away at a slew of warty red imps stampeding for their unprotected backs, deftly dodging the wickedly sharp, twisted horns that sprouted out of the imps foreheads, and leaping over the lash of their speared tails.

Beyond them, the whole auditorium was in chaos.

At the far end of the room, a horde of bloodthirsty gnomes threatened to devour anyone foolish enough to get too close. They resembled innocent lawn statues until they turned and you saw their blood-drenched teeth and vicious, bulging black eyes. Sores covered their faces and hands until they resembled tiny little zombies, the end result of waking a gnome while it was still daylight.

Another group battled a decaying crowd of ghouls, while another struggled to escape what appeared to be a large yeti at least seven and a half feet tall, broad as a small car, and probably weighing as much as one.

More than half the students had taken up arms, and anarchy reigned.

Kincade leapt off the stage, cutting a wide swath through the creatures as he made his way toward her, his eyes hard and determined. Even the teachers picked up arms and descended into the crowd.

Her team surrounded her in a protective circle, but there were too many attacks from all fronts. "The portals need to be closed. We need to get to the witches."

Werewolves snarled in the distance, and Morgan snapped around to see a small knot of students surrounded by a swarm of imps. "There."

Even as she watched, the werewolves were torn apart. Not waiting for approval, Morgan headed in their direction, letting the wildness inside her free, using her speed and flexibility to shove through the crowd.

Harper was at the center of the group, doing her best to blast whatever came too close, but the circle around her was shrinking alarmingly fast. Morgan caught one nasty creature on her blade like a freakish shish kebob. It screamed in pain, took a swipe at her, then slumped forward, his dying breath stinking of the rotten gore stuck between his teeth.

She broke through the circle, took stock of the witches versus fighters, and knew they didn't stand a chance without help. "Harper, gather all the witches and close those rifts."

Harper's pale blue eyes met hers, fear bleaching her face of color. When she didn't respond, Morgan cracked her palm over her cheek.

A snarl curled Harper's lips, the spark of life flowing back into her eyes. "You're going to pay for that."

Morgan snorted. "Fine, but later. Those who can't help close the portal, use your power to keep the creatures at a bay."

Harper glared at her for another second, then began orchestrating the witches. One witch used the power of air to catapult a small group of creatures across the auditorium. Another was using her ability to control animals to freeze a few of the closest creatures while Atlas and Draven slashed them to bits.

Ryder remained at her side, fangs bared, claws at the ends of his fingers, nothing human remaining as he guarded her. "Ascher? Kincade?" Morgan whirled, searching for them in the mosh pit that had taken over the auditorium's main floor.

To her surprise, the two men fought back-to-back, the sight awe-inspiring as they demolished everything within their reach. Kincade's moves were systematic and controlled, while Ascher's were wilder and more daring—both men were stunning to watch.

But while they were the best, there were just too many attackers.

"Stay here and get those portals closed." Without waiting for the witches to respond, Morgan shoved her way back into the fight, ignoring Ryder's shout of outrage. One student had a gnome clinging to his back, his teeth latched tight to the kid's shoulder. She hesitated for a split second at the sight of blood, terrified touching him would bind them together, then she shoved away her fear, pried the little beastie away from the kid and smashed the creature against the floor until he was still.

The guy gave her a nod of gratitude, then spun away to rejoin the fray.

She didn't make it two steps before an imp latched onto her leg and began to scale her like a frickin' tree, its claws puncturing her thigh, then slicing into her hips and back as it climbed. Morgan hissed in pain, then threw herself backwards, squashing the little shit like a bloated tick. Blood and ichor drenched her back and oozed down her legs when she stood, the stench so strong it felt like she was inhaling sulfuric acid. Her eyes watered, and her throat burned until her lungs felt like they were on fire.

She stumbled, and came face-to-face with a ghoul. He bared its jagged teeth when it locked eyes on her, reaching for her with meaty fists. She flung herself sideways and twisted.

A second too slow.

Nails scored her hip and raked down the outside of her leg. Seeing her injured and under attack, a small rock troll grinned at her in triumph and leapt toward her. She snatched him out of the air, then spun and bashed the ghoul over the head with him over and over. Shards of rock and brain matter splattered her until they both fell dead.

By the time she reached her team, she felt like she'd run the gauntlet. Her leg was on fire, her back aching, and blood was trickling down the side of her face where chips from a rock troll she'd demolished had sliced her brow.

"What the hell do you think you're doing?" Kincade cursed when he saw her, while Ascher looked furious.

Morgan drew back her blade and sent it spinning through the air, watching it plow into the eye of the ghoul leaning down to take a bite out of Kincade. "Saving your ass."

They managed to hold the rift, but they were being crowded on all sides, the number of hunters slowly dwindling as they were overwhelmed and dragged through the rift.

That's when she noticed it. "They're not trying to kill the students, they're trying to capture them!"

Kincade cast a sharp glance throughout the auditorium, then cursed when he noticed she was right. "If we don't get our asses in gear, we'll be next."

A large roar reverberated through the room, and Morgan spun to see the giant yeti bearing down on her. Ascher returned the challenging roar with one of his own and launched himself through the air, transforming midflight.

The hellhound and yeti collided, their bodies slamming together with a thud she could feel in her chest. Ascher sank his teeth into the yeti's shoulder, his claws raking through the dense fur, instantly staining it red.

The big creature howled in pain and rage, then clamped arms bigger than Morgan's entire body around Ascher and began to squeeze. Ascher yelped, and she watched them stagger toward the rift.

"No!" Taking advantage of her smaller size, she darted between the fighters, slashing at anything that got in her way.

She was two feet away from Ascher when arms grabbed her from behind and wrenched her backwards. She instantly recognized

Kincade's hold, his hot stone scent enveloping her. "No! No! No! Lemme go." She kicked and punched, but the bastard refused to release his hold. "Please."

No matter how hard she struggled, his grip remained unbreakable, his arms like granite. Ascher must have heard her yelling and increased his attack, using his claws to shred anything he could reach. The yeti bashed his fists against the hellhound's ribs, and even with Ascher's protective hide, Morgan heard bones break.

The yeti strained to keep his hold, then flung himself and Ascher through the rift with a roar of triumph.

"No!" Morgan watched in horror as Ascher disappeared, and knew with a certainty that this time he wouldn't be returning.

The portal rippled, and the rift began to shrink. The creatures gave a screech of warning and stampeded toward the portals, knowing if they were caught on this side of the rift, they would be hunted down and exterminated.

Less than a minute later, the rifts slammed shut.

Morgan stood frozen, devastation shattering her soul, until she felt gutted. "Get your hands off me."

His touch made her skin crawl. "Morgan—"

"Now!" His betrayal cut so deep, she had a hard time catching her breath. When his arms dropped away, her legs shook so hard she was barely able to remain upright and not curl up into a ball and scream. "I could've saved him."

"They would've taken you, too." He reached for her, and Morgan flinched, hastily backing away.

She couldn't believe she fell for that fairy tale crap he told her about being a family, cursing herself for being so gullible.

The rest of the guys gathered around her, but she didn't pay any attention to them.

"You bastard." She shoved Kincade away, unable to stand having him anywhere near her, and he stumbled back in shock. "You go on and on about your elite team, promising we would never be alone, but at the first opportunity, you turned your back on him. How dare you! You're just like those at the coven where I was raised. At the very least, Ascher was in the school, which means he was your responsibility to protect."

She lifted her hand, twisting her arm until the intertwined marks were clearly visible. "These mean nothing if you pick and choose when you honor them."

Kincade's face hardened with every word, then he advanced on her. "What do you think would've happened to him if they managed to take you?"

"You—"

"No. It's your turn to listen." He grabbed her arm when she tried to back away. "Our first duty is to protect *you*. Your hellhound understood that. He wouldn't want you to risk your life for him, and you know it. The people they took are only alive right now because they *didn't* capture you. Once your cousin gets his hands on you, their lives are forfeit. Are you really so selfish that you would risk all their lives to save your precious hellhound?"

His words began to punch holes in her rage, and she bit back a curse.

He was right, she was being selfish.

She would have gambled and risked everything to save Ascher.

And though Kincade didn't know it, she would have done the same for him or any of the other men on their team.

"He's still alive." Kincade's voice dropped, and he eased closer like she was a skittish animal. "Feel through the connection." He traced a finger lightly over the marks. "Close your eyes and concentrate."

Her heart pounded frantically, the fragile hope in her chest a dangerous thing. If Kincade was wrong, if anything happened to Ascher, she wasn't sure she would be able to forgive herself...or him.

Morgan closed her eyes, and after a second, the obsidian and silver lines flared to life. Pain seared along her nerve endings, so sharp it stole her breath.

Only it wasn't her pain.

Some of it came from Kincade, her angry words having wounded him deeply...the rest came from Ascher. It lasted only a split second before he blocked her, but it told her enough.

He was alive.

Kincade pulled her closer, and she allowed herself the luxury of leaning against him, needing his strength when her legs abruptly went weak. "We'll get him back," he promised.

Morgan believed him, feeling his determination through the markings.

He would do it...because it mattered to her.

She marveled at the novelty of having her opinions and feelings matter.

Having someone care.

"We need to go." The headmistress paused next to Kincade, bloodied and ruffled, but relatively uninjured. "We need to organize everyone, evacuate the remaining students, and get the injured to the infirmary."

Kincade stiffened, his grip tightening like he didn't want to let her go—or out of fear she would be torn from him—and she knew he was going to object.

"Go. I'll wait with the guys in the barracks."

He eyed her suspiciously, then glanced over her head at the guys. When they nodded at his silent question, he grudgingly loosened his hold, and was immediately swarmed by people needing his attention.

Chapter Twenty-four

"**M**organ!" Her head snapped up to see Neil weaving his way through the crowd. He was bruised and banged up, but didn't appear injured. "You all right?"

She ignored his question, her mind on one thing. "We're heading upstairs to strategize a rescue mission."

"Mind if I tag along?" He was jittery, and Morgan felt bad for leaving him stranded without a roommate. He didn't have many friends, and after the attack, she didn't blame him for not wanting to be alone.

"Sure." She gave him a forced smile. "Welcome to the party."

He straightened his ever-crooked glasses, flashed her a relieved smile, and something in her chest loosened at seeing he managed to survive the massacre.

Everyone was silent as they entered the barracks, and she surveyed each of them. "Are any of you seriously injured?"

While Atlas and Draven were bloodied and covered with black goo, they appeared relatively sound, with nothing more than minor scratches and bruises. Ryder seemed to have taken the brunt of the injuries, his shirt so shredded it was practically falling off him. He was still on edge, his eyes a little wild yet, his teeth still sharp, his ears a little longer and more pointed than normal.

Morgan nodded to him. "Do you need the infirmary, or can you change?"

Ryder paused from scraping blood off the bottom of his shoe, his broad shoulders stiffening as he glanced at her warily from the corner of his eye, clearly uncomfortable with the discussion.

"Change. You?" The word emerged as more of a growl, his teeth and jaw still not back to normal, and she knew it took a concentrated effort for him to speak in his current state.

She must look bad if he was willing to try to communicate with her. "I'll be fine after I have a shower. You all have ten minutes before I commandeer the bathroom, so you best hurry."

She didn't wait for anyone to agree, but immediately went to her room and gathered her last set of clothing. She removed and cleaned her weapons, her body stiffening now the fight was over, a few of the nastier cuts still bleeding sluggishly. She gave the men an extra five minutes, then hobbled out of her room to get cleaned up. To her surprise, the bathroom was empty.

She carefully locked the door, needing to be alone for a few minutes to process what happened. It was the one place where she was guaranteed they wouldn't follow. The warm water felt so wonderful, she groaned. Blood and black sludge disappeared down the drain, and she stood under the spray until the water ran clean, and her muscles gradually unlocked.

After twenty minutes, the silence was beginning to get on her nerves, her mind kept seeing Ascher disappear into the rift over and over again. She punched the wall to banish the image. The tile cracked, the skin across her knuckles split, but the pain did little to distract her, the cuts healing under a minute.

She needed to *do* something.

The injuries from the fight had scabbed over, leaving lines and punctures marks scattered all over her body, until she resembled Frankenstein's monster…or maybe his kid sister. In a few more hours, the trauma under her skin would knit together, and the scars on her body would fade as if they never existed.

Morgan toweled off and hastily dressed, then wiped the steam from the mirror. Her image shimmered before being replaced with that of her cousin. "I tried to warn you what would happen."

"Warn me?" Her hands curled into fists, and she cursed herself for foolishly leaving all her weapons in her room. It was all she could do not to lunge through the mirror and strangle him. "You killed dozens of innocent people and kidnapped twice that many."

"Whoa!" He held up his hands, shaking his head, his eyes concerned. "It wasn't me. The primordial realm is on the brink of war. I was trying to protect you, but the other faction must have discovered your location. They're the ones who attacked. They know you're the one who will decide which side wins the war."

Morgan narrowed her eyes, uncertain if he was telling the truth or lying.

She knew only one thing...she didn't trust him.

When she didn't respond, Ethan gave a gentle smile. "You really don't remember your past."

Morgan decided to bide her time and see if she could trip him up somehow. "No."

"You were born for one purpose...to save the two realms. Our world has split into two factions—one wants to remain here, while the other wants to invade Earth." He heaved a sigh and shook his head. "Even when you were little, you knew your duty. You were the strongest of all of us, and volunteered to have the ritual marks placed on your back. You were going to seal the portals completely, but before the ritual could be completed, you were kidnapped and your memories wiped."

He peered off to the side, his face whitening, and he fidgeted nervously. "They're coming. You need to come home and finish the ritual before it's too late. I can open a portal, but it will last only a few seconds. You'll have to hurry."

The truth and lies were so intermixed, she couldn't sort them out.

When she didn't immediately jump at his offer, he scowled and changed tactics completely. He dropped the charade, going from meek and scared to hard and cruel. "You are as stubborn as always. If common decency doesn't work, maybe this will help you decide."

The image whirled as he turned the mirror, and she sucked in a startled breath to see Ascher bound in chains in some dungeon.

"Morgan? You okay?" She heard the guys knocking on the door behind her, but she couldn't tear her gaze away from the image of a beaten and bloodied Ascher. His face was bruised almost beyond recognition, both of his eyes nearly swollen shut, his lips were split, and so was his brow. Knowing he could heal almost as quickly as she could told her how badly he was wounded.

"You can get him back. All you need to do is turn yourself over to me."

Her back stiffened at his demand. "All you do is lie. How am I supposed to believe anything you say?"

Humor lightened his face. "Not all lies. War *is* coming. If you weren't so damned hard to locate, none of this would've happened. It took me years to find where you disappeared. I've tried to spare you, tried to find substitutes, but none of the other girls were strong enough." His eyes turned hard. "They just weren't you."

"Or maybe you found an incompetent cohort." She noted his sneer and cocked her head, her own smile turning hard, more a baring of teeth. "Why don't you come here and finish the ritual yourself? I'll even wait right here for you."

The polite knocking on the door became pounding.

"If you don't open this door in the next minute, I'm going to break it down," Ryder's voice thundered into the room, echoing off the tiles.

She didn't have much time.

"Coward," she taunted. "Don't you have enough balls to do it yourself? Or maybe what they say is true, and you don't have enough power to open even a simple portal."

A snarl curled Ethan's lips, his eyes darkening to murderous. "I wasn't lying to you. The Primordial World is on the verge of war. With the power in your blood, I will be able to permanently open a portal between worlds. While the others conquer your world, I will be left in charge to rule the primordial realm. By turning yourself over to me, you would be saving a life. Mine. They're growing impatient. If I don't keep my end of the deal soon, they will hunt me down and try the ritual using me as the sacrifice."

A shoulder hit the door.

The wood shuddered but held.

"Sounds like a fitting end." Morgan smirked, knowing it would piss him off.

A muscle ticked in his jaw. "You don't get it, do you? I'm trying to help. With me gone, do you really think they will stop hunting you? At least I can make it nearly painless. They will tear you apart to gain control of your magic."

Another thud sounded behind her, and the door cracked ominously. Hands wiggled into a small opening, prying the door apart, removing large chunks of the wood paneling at a time.

"I will take the third option, where I kill you, then them, and I live. I spent the past ten years of my life training to kill, and I'm very, very good." Something he saw on her face made him blanch. "I'll take those odds."

She spied Neil wiggling his small frame through the hole in the door and dragging himself into the bathroom. While she was distracted, primordial magic flickered to life. The runes along her spine sank deep, warmth spreading through her and wrapping around her until she couldn't separate herself from it anymore.

"Morgan, look out!" Neil shot to his feet, then ran toward her.

Morgan whirled to see Ethan was chanting. A trickle of blood ran down his upper lip, his eyes turned milky, and the mirror began to ripple as a portal ripped open.

The force of the blows against the door escalated and shards of wood peppered the room.

She was being dragged toward the rift when Neil knocked into her. Instead of being sucked into the portal, her feet slipped out from under her, and her back slammed against the floor, knocking the breath out of her. She watched in horror as Neil was yanked forward in her place and inexplicably pulled toward the mirror. He twisted and reached for her, terror blanching his face white.

Morgan heard the door splinter, but knew they wouldn't get there in time. Ignoring the pain, she lunged for him, the tips of his fingers barely brushing against hers, when Ryder and Draven tackled her from the side and they all went skidding across the tile.

"No!" Despite her shout of denial, Neil was sucked into the primordial realm. As the portal began to close, she struggled against the guys' hold, but the bastards were too strong. She slammed an elbow into Draven's face, twisting and wiggling, using her feet and knees to land blows to Ryder.

Neither of them gave more than an inch.

"Someone get Kincade."

"Fuck, you have the luck of a leprechaun, you troublesome

bitch." Ethan looked pissed, his deathly pale complexion taking the starch out of his words. "You have twenty-four hours to turn yourself over to me, or your friends will die a very painful death in your place. If I can't have you, their sacrifices might give me enough power to get me what I want."

Morgan struggled harder, accidently cracking her head against the tile floor as she tried to flip Draven off her, but they were like octopuses, and she was unable to escape their arms and legs no matter what she did. She watched the mirror slowly cloud over with silver.

"What the hell is going on here?" Kincade's roar thundered into the room. He didn't hesitate to grab Ryder and drag him away by his feet, then fling him away.

The wolf rolled and came to a stop, crouched on his hands and feet. "Stop. Don't let her go."

But Kincade didn't seem to hear him. He plucked Draven off her and tossed him across the room, where he crashed into the wall.

Draven pushed his palm against his right temple and blood immediately trickled through his fingers. "She was going to trade herself for the others. She was almost taken. If not for Neil, she would be gone."

Kincade stood frozen, his chest heaving as he stared down at her like a soldier deciding what to do with his stolen plunder. He crouched, then grabbed her foot, and began to pull her toward him. She kicked out with her free leg, but he easily captured it, not deterred in the least. "I felt your fear and rage through the connection."

He spoke hoarsely, easily subduing her struggles by pinning her legs between his. He leaned forward until he was crouched over her, and she stilled when she spotted his deadly pale green eyes.

He was a second away from snapping.

"You were going to do it." He sounded devastated.

Shattered.

"You would've left me behind with no way to get to you." He cupped her face, his hands gentle but firm. "You would've abandoned me."

He gathered her to his chest, and she finally noticed he was shaking. She hesitantly touched him, felt him shudder, and shot a concerned glance at Ryder.

"When a witch dies, her protectors usually die within a year. They generally throw themselves into one battle after another until they're killed, eventually driven insane by the loss."

Morgan's breath halted in horror, the world narrowing to a pinpoint. "I didn't know."

A lame excuse.

She wanted to protest that she had no intention of dying, but she honestly hadn't considered the risks, her thoughts consumed with killing her cousin and saving Ascher and Neil.

Ryder limped out of the bathroom, Draven staggering behind him, leaving her alone with Kincade. She wanted to call them back, but bit her lip against the urge.

She did this.

Meaning it was her job to fix it.

"You were leaving."

"But I didn't." She tried to pull away, but his hold was set in stone. "I'm here."

It was like he couldn't hear her, his mind locked away in his own private hell. Morgan hitched her leg over his thigh, then used her hips to flip him until she was on top. It allowed a precious few inches to separate them. His hands flexed and clamped down on her hips, preventing her from escaping.

His eyes made it impossible to breathe.

Anguish and longing were scored into his face, and she knew if she made the wrong move, he would shut himself away from her forever, reverting to the unfeeling assassin she'd first met. If she destroyed this bond between them, she would be no better than Catalina.

"Kade…"

At the shortened version of his name, his eyes took on a deep glow, his gaze dropping to her mouth in complete fascination, and he gave a tortured groan. "Please."

Unexpected heat flared between them, and her lips tingled with need, her nerves fluttering like small furies had taken up residence in her stomach.

She'd never voluntarily kissed anyone before, except once...him.

He had been her first.

And right then, she wanted nothing more than to kiss him again.

She hesitantly leaned forward, lightly brushing her lips against his. His guttural groan sparked a deep yearning for more, setting her heart to thumping against her ribs.

This time when her lips touched his, he jackknifed into a sitting position, wrapped his arms tightly around her waist and ran his hands up her back, taking complete control of the kiss. His lips were hot and demanding and so damned good, she wrapped herself around him, unable to get enough.

He tasted intoxicating, each drag of his lips pulling her deeper under his spell, until she wanted more. She ran her hands across his shoulders, his skin as smooth as polished marble, but so very hot to the touch.

She marveled at the flex of muscles under her fingertips, wanting to explore him further, and cursed when her fingers tangled in the clothes that separated them. When she scraped her nails down his back in frustration, he growled deep in his chest, pulling her harder against him, and she gasped in shocked pleasure, the wild, wicked emotions wonderful and hypnotizing...and so consuming they scared the crap out of her.

It was too much, too soon.

How could she fall for someone she'd just met, who acted like he hated her half the time?

If she allowed herself to care any deeper for him, it would devastate her if things between them fell apart.

As if sensing her conflicted emotions, Kincade eased back with one last nip, then pressed his forehead against hers, as if unable to put more distance between them. "You're going to kill me."

Her heart spasmed, and she covered his mouth with a shaky hand, stricken at his husky comment. "Don't ever say that again."

The words hit too close to home.

When she pushed away, he released her... reluctantly. When he helped her to her feet, he stayed within touching distance, hovering close enough to snatch her away from danger. The few minutes of no worries, no fears, evaporated, and everything came rushing back.

"We're going to get them." Kincade hesitantly touched her lower back, the confident man suddenly uncertain of his welcome.

The hair on the back of her neck rose at the hard note in his voice, and she whirled on him. "You are not going to leave me behind."

"They're hunting for you." His voice was hard and implacable. "You're too important—"

"Bullshit!" She thumped his chest with her fists, but he didn't even have the grace to stumble back. "That is not how this group is going to work. None of you are expendable. Understand?"

She began to pace, Kincade watching her with frustrated, calculating eyes, and she knew he was going to try to slip away without her. "Who is to say you leaving isn't part of their plan? As soon as you enter their realm, they'll know I'm not with you—that you left me behind...alone...vulnerable."

A scowl hardened his face. "Why do I get the feeling you would make sure of it?"

She gave him a sharp smile. "I have no idea what you mean."

His shoulder's slumped in defeat, and she almost felt bad.

"Is there anything I can say to make you stay?"

Morgan was already shaking her head and snorted. "Not on your life. You're the one who wanted to be a team, so from now on we work as one."

Chapter Twenty-five

"We have twenty-four hours to rescue the students who've been taken."

Morgan avoided looking at Kincade as she spoke to the guys in the main area of their barracks. She wasn't ready to face him yet after the explosive kiss they shared. One look, and everyone would know what happened, and she wasn't ready to deal with anything but the mission.

Draven narrowed his eyes on her, sensing what she wasn't saying. "What happens after twenty-four hours?"

Morgan lifted her chin, swallowing back the turmoil churning in her gut. "I either turn myself over to my cousin, or he will kill all of them in my place."

She would do what she must to save Ascher, Neil, and the rest of the students.

This was her fault.

If not for her cousin, none of this would have happened.

"Fuck." Draven stood abruptly, his chair clattering to the floor as he began pacing. "I take it you have a plan? Because I'm not turning you over to that bastard."

Morgan recognized the determination in their eyes.

The team would never allow her to surrender herself.

She needed to think of something brilliant, and soon, or the students' deaths would be on her head.

"There is only one plan." Morgan wouldn't accept anything less.

"We get back our people."

Something kept pestering her about the attack, and she frowned as she tried to pin down what was bothering her. "Which brings up the question of how they managed to open three rifts in such a confined space."

Kincade's silence spoke volumes.

"You know something."

"When we were clearing the auditorium, we found three witches with their throats slit. They weren't even aware of anyone sneaking up behind them until it was too late. A sigil was carved into each of their foreheads."

Morgan felt sick to her stomach. "Someone in the school is helping Ethan. Why?"

"Power." Atlas gave her a cynical look, his expression softening a little when he spotted her confusion. "Why does your cousin want you so badly?"

Morgan didn't want to tell them. She could handle being hunted wherever she went, looked at with either suspicion or avarice, but it would destroy her to have them look at her the same way.

"You have to tell them." Kincade's eyes were uncompromising.

Her throat ached, and she hated that he was right. She couldn't ask them to risk their lives without telling them the truth. "He needs me to perform a ritual that will allow him to harvest my magic and open a rift between realms…a permanent bridge for an army to pass through.

"And he's running out of time. He made promises, and if he doesn't keep his end of the deal, the other supernaturals will take their anger out on him. If he can't have me, he will kill everyone he captured in a last-ditch effort to open that bridge."

"An invasion would mean outright war." Even Atlas looked startled, maybe even a little impressed at Ethan's ambition. "What does he hope to gain?"

"He's been promised control of the primordial realm if he holds up his end of the bargain."

Atlas nodded, as if it all made sense, while Ryder looked grim. Draven stared at her with dead eyes, a hardened warrior who knew they might not all survive. To her surprise, Kincade seemed unconcerned, determination burning in his eyes. To him, there was no acceptable outcome but winning the battle.

She envied him his confidence.

"If we're going to attempt a rescue, we need to be prepared." Kincade leaned against the wall, his arms crossed, staring down at his feet.

The starch wilted out of her spine, the weight threatening to crush her vanished, and she ducked her head when tears crowded her eyes.

He was going to help her.

They didn't blame her for this mess.

They didn't look at her like she was a threat.

Her throat tightened painfully, hardly daring to believe it, and she cleared her throat twice before she could speak. "What do you suggest?"

Kincade lifted his head, his gaze landing on each man. "I can't order you to accompany us—"

"Shove it." Draven picked up his chair, gripping the back of it. "Just tell us what you need."

Kincade relaxed marginally, a pleased smile brightening his normally stoic expression. "We need to balance the scales."

"You want to raid the armory." Ryder rose to his feet, tying back his hair, drawing her gaze to the stunningly sculptured angles of his face. "I can get us the void weapons."

They were talking about breaking into the armory and stealing them.

She was really starting to like these guys.

Everyone trooped toward the door.

"While you guys do that, I'll talk to Harper."

Morgan very nearly tripped over her own feet as she whirled to face Kincade. "What? Why?"

Possessiveness shattered every other thought in her head, and everything inside her protested the idea of Kincade going anywhere near that bitch. Black, ugly emotions consumed her, and the urge to rip the other girl's throat out was nearly overwhelming.

He's MINE.

She breathed heavily, trying to control her primitive instincts, and the oh, so tempting compulsion to kill.

"There are only a handful of witches at the school with the ability to open a portal, and the teachers are more apt to lock us up than help." Kincade strode toward her, and every muscle in her body tightened with each word he spoke. "We need her help if you want Ascher back."

It was all she could do not to growl at him. Her lungs felt tight, and she spoke past stiff lips. "I can open a portal."

Kincade stopped in front of her, studying her face as if memorizing it. "I know you don't want to ask for help, but it would take too long to train you. We need someone who knows how to control a rift, or we run the risk of becoming lost in the void. Are you willing to take the chance?"

No, she wasn't.

Her magic was unpredictable at the best of times. She couldn't risk anything happening to them over something as stupid as jealousy. "Fine, go to her."

Before she could turn away, he grabbed her arm. "Guys, why don't you head down for the weapons? Atlas, stay and guard the door. No one but us gets in or out."

The men's eyes ping-ponged back and forth between them, before they beat a hasty retreat. Morgan pulled away, crossing her arms protectively in front of her, still able to feel his touch, and wishing she didn't want more. "What do you want?"

"How badly are you hurt?" His eyes were locked on the matted blood seeping through her pant leg and down the side of her shirt.

His eyes easily stripped her of clothing, and if she lied to him, she had no doubt he would put his thoughts into action, and she'd end up naked, so he could judge for himself. "I'm healing. Wrestling with the guys broke open some of the wounds."

A muscle ticked in his jaw, his hands fisted at his side, as if resisting the urge to touch her. "I don't think it's a good idea for you to enter the Primordial World while you're bleeding. You'll draw attention to us the second they catch the scent of your blood."

Morgan dropped her arms to her sides and took a threatening step toward him. "No way in hell are you leaving me behind."

Kincade wasn't the least bit intimidated. Running a frustrated hand over his head, he studied her, his intelligent green eyes missing nothing. "You heal fast. Faster than anyone else. Why?"

Morgan stopped a foot away from him, halted by his question. "You think my magic can heal me?"

"Maybe. I don't know." His attention came to rest on her throat. When she brought up her hand, it landed on the torque.

"What would happen if you take the necklace off?"

The idea of removing it scared the shit out of her. She hadn't been without it since she woke up in the forest nearly ten years ago. "I don't know. Every time I remove it, my magic rises, but I've never kept it off for more than a minute or two at a time."

Kincade reached out, then hesitated. "May I?"

Her stomach somersaulted, and she wasn't sure if it was at the thought of removing the torque or in anticipation of his touch. She swallowed hard, hastily twisting her hair into a messy knot at the nape of her neck, then took a deep breath and nodded.

The brush of his fingertips against her throat sent her pulse skyrocketing, and her body tingled with anticipation of what he would do next. She gazed up at him to find his eyes dilated, his breathing accelerated, telling signs for a warrior trained to hide any revealing reactions. Then his brows lowered. "I can't find the latch."

Morgan blushed, having completely forgotten the purpose of his touch. "Uh...there isn't one."

She reached up and, much to her surprise, the metal came away in her hands, but when Kincade went to touch the limp metal strip, it curled its way around her wrist like a snake, the coils hardening around her arm in a spiral. The metal was surprisingly heavy, and her neck felt naked without the familiar weight.

"That's amazing, not to mention a powerful tool." He brushed his thumb over the silver bracelet, but it was only metal once more. "Where'd you get it?"

"No clue. I've had it for as long as I can remember." The runes etched along her back warmed, and her heart sank at the familiar sensations. Knowing she would probably need her magic when they entered the portal, Morgan clamped her mouth shut. She would work through the pain of her magic manifesting, but she refused to have Kincade watch. "You need to go. The others will return soon, and we need to have the portal ready."

He narrowed his eyes at her sudden change of heart. "Look, I've already stopped bleeding."

Indeed, power flooded her bloodstream, the excruciating pain feeling like she was being turned inside out. It was all she could do to hold back a whimper. After another minute of studying her, he reluctantly nodded and left. As soon as the door thumped shut behind him, Morgan dropped to her knees, sweat breaking out on her forehead and trickling down her back as she struggled to keep the magic contained in her body.

After she spent five minutes curled up into a tight ball to stave off the torture, the agony finally leveled off. Knowing she needed to clean up before the men returned, she staggered to her feet, cursing when the room spun, and limped into the bathroom. She tugged her shirt over her head to wash out the blood, admiring the rainbow of bruises marching down her left side.

As she bent to her task, her gaze snagged on the edge of the runes. She turned and studied her back. While the etched runes were still there, the magic they normally contained was gone.

They appeared lifeless and dull.

That can't be good.

She quickly stripped out of her pants and rinsed off the worst of the blood. The claw marks down her hip and thigh were still nasty, but the bleeding had stopped.

Kincade was right.

If she went, she would be a liability.

But instinct warned her if she didn't go, no one would return.

Morgan limped to one of the closets and pulled out a medical kit, determined to sew herself back together. She'd be damned if she would let the guys risk their lives for her while she sat back and did nothing.

Her palm began to sting like she was being stabbed with needles, the pain growing until the muscles of her hand began to cramp. It felt like someone was trying to pull out her nails with a pair of pliers. She dropped the medical kit, cursing the noise as it clattered to the floor. She bent double, biting back a whimper when the pain burrowed up her arm, like fire ants were eating her from the inside out.

"Give the girl some privacy. I'm sure she can manage to go to the bathroom without help." Harper's snarky voice grew louder as she neared the bathroom.

The door swung open, then clicked shut. "Or not."

Harper's shoes clicked across the floor as she approached. "You're pulling too much magic. You need to dial it back or it will eat you alive."

"No shit." Morgan hissed in a deep breath. "How?"

"Control it. Don't let it control you." Harper had a scowl on her face, clearly not happy to be helping. "You're holding onto the magic. You need to release it. What were you thinking about when you called it?"

"I didn't call it." Not intentionally at least. But she had been thinking about her leg.

Very hesitantly, Morgan uncurled her hand and pressed it against her thigh.

The instant her palm touched her skin, the burning sensation spilled into her damaged hip and thigh, and the wounds began to knit themselves back together, the muscles twitching and pulling as she fought off the worst charley horse ever.

Once the wound healed, the magic faded, and she was able to breathe without panting. "Is it normally so painful?"

"No." Harper was staring down at her intently, her blue eyes alive with curiosity. "But I've never seen magic as strong as yours, either. Wounds that severe should have taken days to heal, and would still scar."

She didn't seem pleased about the revelation, either.

Morgan struggled to get to her feet, her muscles rubbery as she pulled herself upright, noting Harper didn't offer her hand. "You're going to open the portal."

"I want revenge. If there is a chance of getting our people back, I'm not above using you to do it." Harper turned away and headed toward the door, but not before Morgan saw the pain. Not only had Harper's friends been kidnapped, but two of her guard dogs were torn apart before her very eyes while trying to protect her.

A tough pill to swallow for anyone.

Before Harper left the bathroom, she paused. "You owe me. When you get back, I want you to teach me to fight the way you do."

Morgan couldn't have been more flabbergasted if she'd offered to be besties.

Harper took her silence as agreement and left.

After another minute, Morgan almost felt normal, her body better than ever, and she hurriedly dressed. By the time she pushed open the bathroom door, everyone was waiting for her in the main area with a slew of weapons spread out over the table.

"The creatures living in the primordial realm are stronger than those we normally face. They will be harder to kill. Void weapons are the only thing guaranteed to kill whatever we come up against." Kincade began to divide up the weapons, avoiding looking at her, and Morgan was chilled by the unexpected coolness between them when she was just getting used to the heat in his eyes.

When she touched the marks on her arm, concentrating on their connection, it was like running into a brick wall.

The sudden loss was devastating.

She tried to believe it was so he wouldn't be distracted, but it didn't ring true.

No, it was as if he was putting distance between them because...he didn't expect to return.

The idea curdled her stomach, and she was suddenly terrified he would take too many risks. When she opened her mouth to call him out on it, Ryder cleared his throat, subtly shaking his head, and Morgan swallowed hard. He grabbed two of the blades from the table, never removing his gaze from hers, silently promising to keep watch on Kincade.

It would have to do.

Between the two of them, they would keep him safe.

Everyone gathered around the table, collecting their assigned weapons. As soon as she touched the twelve-inch tactical knife, the sigils on the blade sparkled a smoky purple.

The tip of the black knife melted, lines of liquid metal wrapping around her fist, then ran up her left arm. It felt like ice sliding under her skin. The black liquid webbed together in a shape she didn't recognize, solidifying into a four-inch-wide black cuff. When she opened her palm, the blade was gone. It happened in a matter of seconds. "What?!"

"That's not possible." Harper sounded furious.

All sounds, all movement stopped. Harper and the guys stood in shock, staring at her like she'd pulled a rabbit out of her ass. "Does anyone care to explain?"

"The royal court often wore jewelry whispered to protect them. It was said they were able to pull weapons out of thin air." Atlas became unglued first. He didn't seem surprised. "Make a fist."

It wasn't the answer she wanted.

She wanted nothing to do with his royal bloodline foolishness, but she was curious enough to do as directed.

Nothing happened.

She raised her brow in silent demand, breathing a silent sigh of relief.

"Another answer is you're a metallurgist with the ability to shape metal." Kincade sheathed his weapons. "Without the torque blocking your magic, your powers are going to develop faster than normal."

Which also meant a sharper learning curve.

Great!

Atlas was still staring at her hands, clearly not giving up on his harebrained idea of her being royalty. "Try again, but concentrate on forming a blade."

Morgan tried again, but received the same response.

Jack shit.

"Enough. Figure it out later. We don't have time to play games." Harper began casting. Without a spelled mirror, it took raw talent to open a portal.

The temperature gradually dropped until Morgan's breath frosted the air. The hair on her body rose, the static crackling around her, turning almost painful. It took ten minutes for the air to ripple as the portal between worlds tore open. The process took so much power, Harper wilted, as if it had actually sucked the life out of her.

"Give me the signal when you need the portal open again."

Morgan glanced at the guys. "What's the signal?"

Atlas didn't wait, jumping through the rift, his weapons at the ready. Draven wiggled his eyebrows and shot her a wicked grin, his eyes devoid of anything but the thirst for violence as he jumped through next.

"Find a mirror. Harper will monitor them like a radio station. When she catches the signal—our location—she'll open the portal." Ryder grabbed her arm, nudging her toward the rift. "You're next."

Without hesitation, Morgan ran toward the shimmering disturbance and leapt into nothingness.

Chapter Twenty-six

*T*he absolute silence in the void sounded loud to Morgan's ears, but oddly comforting after her hectic thoughts. The magic residing under her skin settled into her bones with a comforting sigh. Cold burned along the runes on her back, the markings now completely drained of magic.

The darkness of the void was more shades of gray as the shadows shifted in the dark fog, the shapes almost human-like...possibly other people crossing or those who were trapped between worlds. Little specks of light shone in the distance, and she realized they were other portals.

The torque warmed, tightening around her wrist when the shadows drew too close, acting like a shield. The black cuff along her other arm shimmered in a deep purple mist, and her hand instinctively curled into a fist. She could almost feel the blade in her palm, but resisted the urge to call for the weapon. The last thing she needed was to lose the blade in the void.

A bright light streaked directly toward her. She lifted her arm to protect her face when she slammed into it...and found herself spit out into a whole new world.

She stumbled to keep her balance. When she straightened, she saw all four guys were present and waiting for her. Atlas simply nodded and appeared ready to go. Draven picked himself up off the floor, checked over his weapons, studiously avoiding her gaze, but she could tell he'd been concerned. Ryder remained seated, and she suspected he was fighting the motion sickness of traveling through the void. She would have gone to him, but didn't think he would appreciate her concern.

A muscle jumped in Kincade's jaw. After a few seconds, he shook his head and let his anger go. "I don't like how long it takes you to cross."

Morgan kept her mouth shut. She doubted she could actually get lost in the darkness, but didn't think he would be comforted by what she saw in the void. She couldn't risk him refusing her access to portals in the future.

She glanced around the small room, then stilled when she recognized it, a sense of déjà vu making her feel like she was standing in two places at once. "Are we still in the school?"

Draven shook his head. "The Academy is a mirror image of the castle. Look." He pulled open a curtain, and Morgan peered out into an alien world. The view was definitely not of Earth.

Instead of mountaintops, the sky had two moons and a larger planet that dominated the horizon. It was so close, she could see the beautiful swirl of clouds and landscape, similar to the images of Earth astronauts took from space. It looked like…Earth. She tore her attention away from the glittering sky, and saw silvery moonlight spilling over the area for as far as her eye could see, the landscape a combination of wilderness and cosmopolitan living side by side.

It was both beautiful and exotic…or it could have been if the gray mist hovering so ominously on the horizon didn't appear to be consuming all the light. Even from the distance, she sensed a wrongness to it that sent a shiver of dread down her spine. Though it was disturbing to look at it, she was even more afraid to blink, petrified it would move closer if she took her eyes off it even for a second. "What is that?"

Draven's mouth tightened. "It's kind of like magical residue. This realm was created and held together by magic, but people are slowly syphoning the magic off for their own purposes. Without magic, the world is dying."

"No, not dying. They're killing it." Morgan was horrified at how far people would go for power.

To destroy something so beautiful was criminal.

"Can't they bind the people from using magic?"

Draven gave her a cynical smile. "The people who need to be banned are the very ones who are in charge of the decision. No way would they give up their power for something so tiresome as saving their planet."

Her gut churned as bile climbed the back of her throat. "That's why they need me, why they want to build a bridge to Earth. They want to plunder our world, and are willing to kill our realm to save their own."

"Not going to happen." Kincade interrupted, then glanced over her head. "Ryder has recovered. Time to head out."

Morgan turned, but Ryder didn't seem any better, and she said so.

"His species are not from this world, or rather, they've been gone from it for too long. The magic in the atmosphere is slowly poisoning him. His wolf will help him adapt, and his body should regulate after a bit." Draven sounded grim. "Others aren't so lucky."

Morgan stared at him in sickening disbelief. "You. The guys. The students."

"We'll be fine for awhile. We've traveled through the void often enough that it acts like an inoculation, but most of the students don't have our immunity or Ryder's beast to filter the magic. Some have been Earthside too long. If we don't get them out of here soon, they will die whether your cousin kills them or not." He cast a critical eye over her, then smiled. "You appear fine."

"I—" Morgan shrugged and confessed the truth. "It feels like home." If anything, she felt better, stronger than she had in a long time. The magic in her bones was a pleasant buzz, no longer fighting her, the markings on her back silent for once. The eerie feeling of something foreign living under her skin, the wild urges to hunt, the sense of not being normal, vanished.

"We need to move." Atlas slipped into the room, keeping his attention on the hallway. "If they don't know we're here already, they will soon."

Morgan exhaled, then closed her eyes and focused on the obsidian filigree that twirled up her arm, doing her best not to fall too deeply into the connection and alert Ascher to her presence—he wouldn't react well to knowing she'd followed him.

"Find."

The mark grew heavy, giving her a distinct tug that was slightly disturbing to feel under her skin, but she didn't hesitate to follow. She dashed down the hall, her senses hyperaware, searching for any sign of life. She ducked in and out of rooms and passageways, easily avoiding people, the layout of the palace disturbingly familiar.

They traveled down two levels, the guys a silent comfort at her back. When she rounded the last corner, Morgan skidded to a stop in front of a large, lifelike portrait of an exquisitely beautiful, dark-haired woman. "Mom?"

She wore an elegant gown that clung to her slim form, everything about her bearing too impossibly regal and graceful to be remotely human. That's when Morgan noticed the familiar torque around the woman's neck.

The guys surrounded her, some urging her to continue, a few of them glancing between her and the painting, but she heard none of it.

Flashes of memories struck her hard, a stabbing pain threatening to crack her skull open, and she clutched her head as she fell to her knees.

Images of her mother, wounded and covered with blood, filled her mind. Her mother was kneeling before her, placing the torque around her neck with a wobbly smile.

Time skipped, and Morgan was being dragged down a hall by her mother, tripping over familiar bodies, people she knew, friends, their blood soaking into her clothes. Shouting erupted, and guards flooded the hallway, surrounding them. Fear tasted metallic in her mouth, and she clutched a small blade in her hand, standing next to her mother, preparing to defend her.

"*Run*, baby. Get to the portal." Her mother didn't wait, but charged toward the guards, her battle yell echoing in Morgan's head, even after all these years.

Morgan did as she was told only when a spell grabbed hold of her, one she couldn't break.

And she ran.

Like a coward, she ran.

She skidded to a stop in front of the portal, waiting for her mother. Only she never returned. Agonizing minutes later, the spell finally broke apart, and Morgan sneaked back through the halls. She froze in shock when she found her mother lying in a pool of blood, a man standing over her, wiping the gore on his blade against his pants.

A scream built up in her throat. The man turned toward her and smiled. Morgan didn't hesitate. She threw her knife, pleased when it sank deep in his thigh. Without waiting for retaliation, she turned and leapt through the portal.

"Morgan!"

The world spun as arms swept her off the hard ground, and she blinked to see Kincade's intense green eyes peering down at her. "He killed my mother."

It hurt to speak.

Kincade's expression was grim as he clutched her to him. "Ethan?"

Morgan nodded dumbly, tucking herself closer to him, unable to get warm. Grief thickened her voice. "She died protecting me."

Atlas threw open a door, quickly clearing the room, then waved at them to enter. "I've heard stories about the night of the attack. It was a bloodbath. Alayna was an amazing fighter. Reports said she killed at least a dozen guards before they took her life."

Kincade sat, and she huddled on his lap, traumatized by the images still flashing in her head. "Seeing her portrait must have triggered your missing memories."

Atlas knelt in front of her, and Kincade's hold tightened protectively. "I can tell you about your mother...I met her a few times...but now is not the time. You need to lock away your emotions and focus on the mission."

"Bloody hell, man. Give her a couple of minutes." Draven glared at Atlas, murder darkening his eyes.

"No." Morgan pushed away from Kincade's warmth, nausea churning in her gut. "He's right. Now is not the time for me to lose my shit."

Kincade stepped in front of her, blocking her view of the rest of the room, and gently wiped her cheeks. Mortified by the tears, Morgan ducked her head and scrubbed her face, feeling like she'd been gutted.

"Hey," Kincade slipped his hand over the back of her neck, his grip strong and sure. "Take a deep breath. You're not alone anymore."

She hated they saw her fall apart, and his comforting words only served to rock her already unstable emotions when she needed to be clearheaded.

She shoved away from him, ignoring his promise, tucking it away to take apart and study later. "The longer we stay, the more dangerous it is for us."

He scowled down at her. "You can take a fucking minute to grieve."

But Morgan didn't want to grieve.

She didn't want to think or feel, and she certainly didn't want to drown in the helplessness swamping her. Only two things mattered. Getting everyone else out alive—and making her cousin pay. "Let's go."

Rage burned in her chest, filling the gaping hole where her heart once beat. She clenched her fist, surprised to feel warmth pool down her hand, and the press of warm metal in her palm. She ran into the hall, vengeance sizzling through her veins, warming her muscles for battle.

The passageway was dimly lit, dirt crunching under her boots with every step, the air stale from long disuse. The gray stone walls showed surprisingly little wear after centuries of use, the building steeped in enough magic to keep it maintained. The dual combination of old and new made the tight confines all the creepier, and the walls began closing in on her, the urge to run and escape the claustrophobia became nearly overwhelming.

She didn't know if it was the sense of time growing short or a spell of some sort urging her to hurry, but she didn't care. Dread began to build in her gut, tightening with every breath. They had to go now or it would be too late.

Ten minutes later, Kincade dragged her to a stop in the lower levels of the castle, and she whirled on him. "What the hell?! They're right ahead of us."

She shrugged out of his hold, but the other guys had her cornered, Ryder's big body blocking the narrow, dungeon-like hall. "Don't you find it suspicious that we haven't run into any guards?"

"It's a trap." Morgan shrugged, trying to slip around him, but the big bastard refused to let her pass. "We always knew it was a trap."

Ryder hunched down, until he was right in her face. "That doesn't mean we have to make it easy for them…got me, little one?"

She didn't like having him so close, his nearness twisting things up inside her when she didn't want to feel anything.

She dropped her eyes, quickly stepping away, her chest tightening. She could scarcely stand still. She was beginning to unravel, her magic swelling with her emotions, and she feared what would happen when she finally let go. "We're running out of time."

In more ways than one, she feared.

A wet, hacking cough echoed down the hall, and she recognized the sound from late at night in the dorm room next to hers. "Neil!"

Morgan barely resisted lashing out when Kincade grabbed her arm. She opened her mouth to ream him out when he pushed his way in front of her. "Stay behind me."

The last thing she expected was his capitulation.

She was behaving rashly, every instinct warning her there was nothing but trouble ahead, but she couldn't seem to stop.

Ryder and Draven took the lead, Kincade remained stubbornly at her side, prowling one step ahead of her, while Atlas took up the rear. The darkness of the tunnel began to lighten, and everyone slowed. She tightened her grip on her weapon, creeping forward along with everyone else.

The first thing they saw beyond the tunnel seemed innocent enough.

The circular room was at least twenty feet across, but the domed ceiling made it appear larger…and seemingly empty. The stones were a funky, rusty brown that for some reason sent a chill chasing over her skin. More alarming, scored into the floor in a perfect circle around an altar were the same markings carved into her back.

On the altar rested a body beaten so bloody, it was hard to tell anything about the person except that it was male. She couldn't take her eyes away from the figure. There was something startlingly familiar about the blood-streaked blond hair, something about the muscular shape of his arms and shoulders that sent her heart ricocheting against her ribs.

"Ascher?" Morgan couldn't move, couldn't breathe.

"Here!"

Morgan spun and stared dumbly to see Neil and a number of other students waving their hands to gain their attention. Large holes pocketed the perimeter of the room, almost like a big worm had burrowed through the walls at random, leaving behind an intricate cave system. Thick bars covered the entrances, turning the tunnels into cages.

Kincade cupped her face, waiting until she focused on him. "Go, I've got them."

The ice inside her snapped at his command, freeing her from the paralysis holding her in place ever since she spotted Ascher strapped to the table. Pleased by his understanding, Morgan didn't bother to control her wild impulse, and bounced up on her toes to kiss him, her lips lingering for a few seconds despite the urgency of the situation. "Thank you."

Without waiting for him to respond, she slipped out of his hold and rushed toward the center of the room. The knife melted, the liquid metal running up her arm to form a now-familiar cuff, leaving both of her hands free to help Ascher. As soon as she crossed the circle, she knew she'd made a mistake.

Magic sprang in the air, drenching the room like she ran into a sudden downpour.

A single clap echoed around the room over and over, and she whirled to see Ethan applauding while dozens of armed guards flooded the room behind him. Magic was firmly wrapped around each soldier, draping Ethan's minions in human form, so they could impersonate the guards and enter the castle undetected.

With none of the cell doors open, the five of them didn't stand a chance against so many.

"Brava, cousin." Ethan smirked at her, a malicious gleam in his eyes. "I knew you wouldn't leave your people to die, but I really didn't think you would be stupid enough to accompany your team."

Morgan's heart sank until her chest ached.

Because of her recklessness, she'd doomed them all.

"Drop your weapons." Ethan's cockiness seeped away when no one moved, and he glared at her. "Now! You know I have no compunction about killing your little friends."

Her throat tightened painfully, and she reluctantly dropped the three weapons she had stashed on her body, studiously avoiding her two bracelets.

She turned to her team. "Do it."

Draven cursed, but followed suit. Atlas and Ryder complied after a slight hesitation. Kincade narrowed his gaze on Ethan, clearly calculating the odds. His eyes slipped betrayingly to her. For two heartbeats, she feared he was going to defy her, she could feel his need to protect her swell through their bond, and she gave him a subtle shake of her head, silently begging him for more time.

A muscle ticked in his jaw, his expression like she'd asked him to castrate himself. Almost in slow motion, his fingers loosened from around his weapons and the blades clanked to the floor.

He trusted her...she only hoped she could live up to his high expectations.

"Gather the whelps up and kennel them with the rest." Ethan ignored everyone else and sauntered toward her with a smugness that made her want to break the fucker's nose.

The soldiers weren't taking chances, wisely keeping their distance, using the tips of their swords to prod the guys toward the yawning opening of the cage door.

Morgan flinched when the cell clanked shut behind them with an ominous thud. Kincade kept his back toward her, his head bowed, fighting against the need to throw himself at the bars—to do something—anything.

They were the same emotions she was struggling to contain.

With every passing second, she could feel the noose tightening around her neck.

"What about Ascher?"

Ethan gave a moue of distaste, and she knew what he was going to say before he opened his mouth, so she beat him to it. "If you try to kill him, I'll fight you every step of the way. If you think you're going to get out of this unscathed, think again."

"I have you exactly where I want you. What could you possibly do to me?" He laughed at her threat like she was a bothersome gnat, but when he reached for her arm, the torque shimmered to life and flung him back ten feet to slam into the floor.

When she went to follow and snap his scrawny neck, the symbols on the floor glowed a deep crimson, the light stretched to the ceiling and surrounded the altar like a curtain. As soon as she reached the barrier, it was like she slammed into a wall. She pressed her hands against the shield, running her fingers along the reddish sheen in search for even the smallest gap. Her palms prickled painfully the longer she persisted, as if a corrosive acid was gnawing at her flesh.

"I can assure you, my dear, you will not escape me this time."

Now that the symbols on the floor were activated, she felt them trying to siphon off the primordial magic in her veins, the sensation like she'd rolled in a pile of itchweed. The nagging itch under her skin was unrelenting, and she knew it was only a matter of time before it drove her insane. Morgan reluctantly dropped her hands and stepped away, lifting her chin defiantly. "Then it looks like we're at a standstill."

He cocked an eyebrow at her, his smarmy attitude pissing her off. "Not quite. I have dozens of hostages. If I start killing them, you'll fold."

Morgan forced her jaw to unlock and act like bile wasn't crowding the back of her throat. "You're going to kill them anyway."

Lying was one of the hardest things she'd ever done. She was counting on Ethan's callousness and selfishness to help her. He would never give up his life to save others, so he wouldn't be able to conceive of others doing anything so stupid. She prayed he wouldn't call her bluff.

"If you can't harvest my magic, you'll still need them. They're your backup plan. I'm older now, not a little child. I will fight you every step of the way. Without my help, you have less than a fifty percent chance of this ritual working, and you know it. I'll probably die either way, but I'll have the satisfaction of not giving you what you want." She gave him a nasty smile. "Believe me, it will be worth it."

Morgan crossed her arms and lifted her brow at him, knowing she'd planted a seed of doubt when he turned to gaze at the students contemplatively.

It was now or never, and she drove home her point. "Your

choice."

By leaving the decision up to him, she knew she had him, almost like it had been his idea all along. He scowled at her before finally relenting. "Fine. Unleash your mutt, but leave the collar on him." He lifted a little remote from around his neck and pressed the button. Ascher grunted in pain, and Morgan whirled to see Ascher arching off the altar, his body spasming as electricity coursed through his every nerve ending.

Only when he collapsed back to the altar, panting for breath, did Ethan speak again. "You try anything, and I will hold my finger on this button until his brain is fried."

Morgan gritted her teeth, not doubting him for a second.

She turned, unlatching the thick metal cuffs from Ascher's ankles first, then unstrapping the chains around his waist, before moving to his head, getting her first look at his face. The damage was so extensive, his eyes so swollen, he could barely even blink. The white of one eye was filled completely with blood, and she knew he had a severe concussion, if not a fractured skull. Dried blood was caked around his nose and one ear, while his lips were so bruised, they had split.

He scanned her face, his eyes tortured, his only concern was for her.

Foolish man.

The total defeat on his face broke her heart.

Tears stung her eyes, and she closed them for a second, knowing she would be haunted by the image of his battered face for the rest of her life.

Because of her.

She gently brushed his hair back from his face, lightly running her fingertips down his jaw. When he flinched, she jerked her hand back, afraid she'd hurt him more, but he only leaned into her touch. "Why?"

The word was garbled, barely audible, his jaw clearly broken.

She flashed him a lopsided smile. "I'm rescuing you."

When he flinched and closed his eyes in defeat, she clucked her tongue. "You can't believe I would leave you here." She struggled to unhook the shackle from his arm with shaky fingers. As soon as he was free, he latched on to her wrist.

"You would never have abandoned me. How could I do any less?" Morgan gave him a gentle smile, then her eyes widened as she saw the black cuff melt away from her arm to twine around his own forearm. "Don't count me out yet."

She reached over and unlatched the last cuff, then helped prop him up. He clutched his ribs, and she wasn't even sure he was breathing. He had so many broken bones, she could practically hear them crunch when he moved.

"Hurry it up or the deal is off."

Morgan glared at Ethan, wanting to leap the distance between him and rip his head off. Magic tingled along her arm, as if willing to aid her.

Ethan's eyes widened, then glimmered with greed, and he wiggled the damned remote in his fingers. "Uh-uh. Careful."

Using the utmost care, Morgan practically dragged Ascher's abused body off the altar, shouldering most of his weight as she helped him toward the barrier. The warm heat of him seeped into her body, a deep possessiveness waking, and she struggled against the urge to shove him behind her and tell Ethan to go fuck himself.

As if reading her thoughts, Ascher lurched out of her hold and stumbled across the barrier. She lunged forward to grab him, only to receive a nasty shock for her trouble when she hit the barrier. The magic slammed into her hard enough to knock her on her ass. A persistent scratching began at the back of her mind, like a colony of mice had taken up residence, and were frantically searching for a way out. She pushed back, until a slight ache began to build behind her eyes, and the feeling of being invaded faded a fraction.

"So stupid." Ethan lifted the remote and pressed the button, knocking Ascher to his knees, only letting up when two guards approached and began dragging him toward the cages. "Did you really think you were going to simply waltz in here and just rescue them?"

Morgan's gaze automatically slid to the guys who were coming to mean so much to her. Sadness welled up in her at the thought of their time together being cut short. She didn't even get a chance to know them, and everything in her rebelled at the idea of losing them.

It couldn't end like this.

She wouldn't let it.

A beginning of a plan started taking shape. If Ethan really wanted the primordial magic from the void, she would give him the void. If it was the last thing she did, she would drag him to hell with her.

"No," she answered Ethan, then resolutely turned away from the guys as they prowled their cage.

She would not be distracted.

The dreaded bang of the bars clanging shut jolted through her, and she slowly began pulling magic from her bones, her skin tingling as it began to course through her veins.

"What about me?" Neil shoved his way toward the bars of the cage, his thin frame emaciated after only a few hours in this realm, his skin pale and pasty, sweat darkening his hair. "I did my part. I got her here. Release me, and give me what you promised."

Chapter Twenty-seven

"**W**hat?" Morgan could only stare at Neil, feeling crushed after everything they risked to get him back. "Why?"

"Release him." Ethan chuckled, taking pleasure in her pain. "He's been a somewhat shoddy partner, but he did ultimately help me achieve my goal—locating you."

Neil couldn't look her in the eye as he was hauled none-too-gently out of the cage.

"Enter the circle and strap her down."

"But you promised—"

Ethan spun and backhanded Neil so hard, his head whipped violently to the side, and nearly sent the kid to his knees. "Strap her down."

Neil shuffled forward, blood trickling from the corner of his mouth, and she struggled not to feel sorry for him. Morgan could overpower him in a second, but it would solve nothing. Neil crossed the barrier and the wards wobbled, but held. When he stopped in front of her, he couldn't lift his gaze from his feet.

"Please." His voice was a hoarse croak.

Everything inside her rebelled at the idea of being strapped down, but she was conscious of the guys still being held behind bars. If she fought, they would be the first to die.

No, she had to wait and bide her time.

It hurt to docilely lie on the altar.

Draven was yelling at her to fight, while Atlas watched

impassively, his dark green eyes stormy with the emotions he so hated to show. Ryder was struggling to remain human, but Ascher and Kincade worried her the most. They stood side by side at the cage door, their faces carefully blank as they were forced to watch while she was slowly tortured to death.

It was beyond cruel.

Their rage and helplessness rippled through the bonds, and she did her best to sever her ties with them. If she couldn't break free, she wanted to spare them at least that.

She was hurting them by not fighting, but she couldn't bring herself to trade their lives for hers. Wouldn't.

Something inside her would shatter if anything happened to them if she could've prevented it.

She ruthlessly kept gathering magic, until it practically crackled in the air around her. The barriers were doing their best to crush her control, but she refused to relent, waiting for the perfect moment to strike.

Cold shackles clamped down on her ankles first, the chains surprisingly heavy. Neil circled the altar, his throat bobbing painfully as he picked up a metal cuff. He moved jerkily, his chest heaving. "I'm sorry. I never wanted this."

"Then why?"

"I'm dying." For the first time, he looked up and dared to meet her gaze. His soft brown eyes were dark and tortured. "The void weapons were keeping me stabilized for a while. They staved off death, but didn't stop the progression. My powers were consuming me from the inside out faster every day. I needed more. He promised me a cure, something only the primordial realm could provide."

"Why didn't you tell me? I would've tried to help." He secured the cuff on her wrist, studiously avoiding her eyes.

"You are helping me." He scurried around to the opposite side of the altar, and clumsily snatched up the last cuff, hastily snapping it around her wrist before backing away. "You're saving my life."

"Weeeelllll, not exactly." Ethan smiled from outside the circle, spinning a black dagger between his fingers. "I mean, if you asked her, she probably would have been able to save your life by filtering and purifying the magic—she has an affinity with the void like none

I've ever seen—but seeing as she's busy and all tied up with other things at the moment, she just doesn't have the time."

"What?" Neil barely croaked out the question as he slowly straightened. "You promised."

"And you took too long," Ethan snapped, his patience at an end. "You're too far gone. Your body interprets the magic you so love as poison, and it's trying to rid you of it. We all know removing magic from a witch will kill them, you most of all—especially after all those girls you experimented on at the Academy. It would take too much valuable magic to reverse the effects of magical poisoning, and you're not worth the effort, even if I was inclined to try."

Neil slowly turned toward her, defeat slumping his shoulders, his spirit completely broken.

"I've been waiting years to finish this ritual, years waiting for just this moment." Ethan entered the circle, practically crowing his victory.

The muscles of her back flinched as memories of the runes being seared into her flesh flashed in her mind. She tugged on the cuffs, surprised to feel a slight give, the metal thinning even as she watched.

"This bridge will create a vast new world of possibilities."

Morgan tore her gaze away and focused on Ethan, not wanting to draw attention to the cuffs. "Too bad I won't be around to witness it."

Ethan nodded, completely missing her sarcasm. "Yes, it is unfortunate that the process has the nasty side effect of killing you, but the portal can only have one master—me."

Before she knew what he intended, he lashed out with the knife, slicing a deep line down the length of her arm. The instant the blade came into contact with her blood, it glowed a deep red. Because it was a void weapon, it was sharper than most, and would take longer for her body to heal. Blood splashed to the floor in a steady drip, but instead of collecting in a puddle, small droplets began to roll toward the symbols etched in the circle.

When her blood struck the first symbol, it blazed a dark purple, and it felt like someone had punched a hole into her chest and squeezed her heart in their meaty fist. Her back arched off the altar, her vision dimmed, and she struggled to stay conscious.

She now knew what it felt like to have her soul ripped from her body—every hint of emotion, every second of joy in her life was being taken from her.

The rusty color of the stones now made sense—they were stained with blood after decades of sacrifices.

She barely felt the cuts on her legs.

"It's working!" Ethan sounded giddy, and she had to struggle to focus on him. She turned her head, her neck so stiff it felt like it was made of stone and creaked as she moved. "More than half the symbols are done. No one else has ever survived this far."

He beamed at her like a proud father. "I knew you could do it."

And he was right. Magic thickened the air, reminding her of what it felt like to travel in the void. The wonder and awe. The sense of coming home.

It was beautiful.

And it was slowly killing her.

A nasty cut on her arm yanked her back to the present, and her eyes snapped open. The magic around her wavered, reacting to her emotions. It didn't like that she was in pain. The more she fought, the clearer her head became, but it also made the torture more painful. Pressure pounded in her skull like a pickaxe, the insistent thudding shredding her concentration.

Very slowly, the magic began to perforate her mental barriers, and blood leaked out of her pores like she was being wrung dry.

Neil shuffled slowly closer, watching Ethan like a mouse caught in a hawk's gaze. "I'm sorry."

Morgan tried to nod, but her head felt too heavy. "Me too."

She couldn't blame him, not really.

If one of the guys was dying, she wouldn't even hesitate to kill if she thought it would save them.

"You were my only friend, and I…" His throat bobbed painfully as he swallowed, then a hard look settled on his face, and his gaze sharpened on Ethan. She could feel his magic, an almost alien thing compared to hers, gathering in the air. "I made a mistake. I hope someday you can forgive me."

Despite knowing his magic would kill him, he didn't stop. She tried to grab for him, stop him, but he remained out of reach. "You will never kill him, not within the circle. If you want to help, get the others out."

Neil hesitated a moment, peering down at her for the last time, his glasses askew and smiling at her like he did when they'd first met. "As you wish."

He brought his hands together, and a clap of thunder rocked the room when his magic exploded out of him. The screech of metal as the cage bars were wrenched open was like music to her ears. Neil dropped to his knees, completely spent and dying, blood dribbled down his face from his eyes and nose, staining his lips red as it bubbled out of his mouth.

The guys came out of the cave system swinging, tearing into the guards. Body parts, hell—whole people went flying across the room. The students were outnumbered nearly two to one, but it didn't matter. Their rage fueled them, and blood quickly spilled on both sides.

Kincade and Ascher fought back to back. Ascher used her black blade to hack away at anything that got too close, while Kincade destroyed his opponents with one blow, his inhuman strength giving him the edge. Draven and Atlas were unstoppable, anticipating each other's needs as they destroyed one soldier after another in a whirlwind of motion. Ryder fought alone, systematically working his way closer to her, his size and brute strength clearing a path.

Ethan spun in a circle, watching the chaos in disbelief.

"No! No! No!" Ethan stormed toward her, lifting his blade high, ready to plunge it into her chest, when Neil lurched to his feet and threw himself between them.

He gave a startled gasp as the blade sank into his back, staring into her eyes as life slowly drained out of him, his weight settling over her.

Morgan was stunned that he would sacrifice himself to save her, and she gave him the only thing she could "I forgive you."

He gave her one last, sweet smile, tears glistening in his eyes, before they slid closed for a final time.

She began to suffocate from much more than his weight as grief welled up in her, tightening her throat and stinging her eyes. When Ethan reached to pull his body off her, Morgan allowed her need for vengeance to break free. She pulled on her arm and the metal stretched, then shattered like glass.

She lifted her hand in time to catch Ethan's arm as the blade descended, blocking the blow meant to slice her throat. A vicious roar of absolute fury thundered through the room as Ryder launched himself through the barrier, plowing his bigger body into Ethan's much smaller frame.

Both men flew back, crashing to the floor in a bone-jarring thud, and she winced in sympathy. Morgan used the distraction to break the shackles binding her ankles, the metal twisting away at her command.

She twisted and sat upright in time to see Ethan and Ryder circling each other. Ethan was battered and bruised, but he managed to land a few good blows with his knife, the cuts on Ryder's chest and arm bleeding freely.

Instead of being scared, Ethan appeared unconcerned as he calmly twisted his arm up and activated a sigil tattooed near his wrist. A bright red mist floated in the air around Ryder like little gnats attacking. Ryder stepped back, swinging his hand to dispel them, but with every breath, he inhaled more and more of the spores.

She watched in horror as Ryder slowed, then stopped completely.

"A nifty little safety measure I had installed. It freezes my enemies for ten seconds." He gave her a malicious smile. "It was very effective on your mother, too, when that bitch had the audacity to whisk you away before I could follow through on my plans. She suffered for defying me." Ethan smirked at her and lifted his blade toward Ryder. "I'm going to enjoy this."

Morgan rolled across the top of the altar, only to lurch to a stop when the last chain on her wrist pulled taut, nearly jerking her arm out of its socket. She watched in horror as Ethan walked up to Ryder and calmly gutted him while he remained frozen.

In slow motion, she watched the big wolf drop to the ground.

Devastation eviscerated her, and she watched as blood pooled under Ryder's too-still form.

Something inside her snapped.

She ripped her arm free of the last chain, barely feeling pain when the rough metal edges tore into her wrist. Rage and loss twisted inside her like an unstoppable force, an untamable wildness that rekindled her magic like a spark to tinder, and the shimmering runes on the floor faded when the power was sucked back toward her like a giant, unstoppable wave.

The red barrier wilted until a light sheen of purple rose, preventing Ethan from escaping her wrath, and stopping anyone else who wanted to keep her from doing what needed to be done. "This ends now."

"Agreed. I've come too far to be thwarted again." His face settled into hard lines, his eyes darkening a little in desperation when he noticed the change in her, his grip tightening on the knife as he began circling her.

From the corner of her eye, she saw Ryder hold his gut closed as he dragged himself across the floor toward her. When Ethan lunged for her, Ryder dropped to his side and stretched his arm out as far as he could reach, catching Ethan's ankle.

Her cousin shouted in surprise as he began to fall. Morgan didn't hesitate and swung her leg, kicking the blade out his hand. She grabbed the torque around her wrist, and it easily uncoiled into a thin strip of metal. Before Ethan could push himself off the floor, she wrapped the garrote around his throat, knelt on his back, and heaved back with all her strength.

He bucked and twisted, but Morgan refused to relent, not really feeling the blows, nor his nails as he desperately clawed at her forearms like a frantic little rat trying to break free.

Blood trickled down his back, coating her hands and the knee she had pressed against his spine. Only when he stopped moving, when his arms dropped uselessly to his side, did she finally loosen her hold and watch dispassionately as his lifeless body thumped to the ground.

It was over.

Or it should have been.

Yet the fighting around her continued unabated. Her men were surrounded, bloody and battered, and losing ground. Morgan staggered to her feet, her torque dropping to the ground as she grabbed every ounce of magic around her. The shield bowed under her demand, then began to stream toward her. She ignored the way the magic burned through her body like a fever, short-circuiting her brain. The only thing that mattered was protecting her men. The rest of the world fell away.

The air rippled when a rift tore open at the entrance to the room, revealing a dark pit of nothingness. A wicked, ice-cold wind whipped through the room, the howl deafening. The instant it touched one of the soldiers, an inky blackness gathered behind him like a giant fist and yanked him through the portal.

One after another, the soldiers disappeared.

When the others noticed the disturbance, a few tried to run, but it did no good. The students and her men hurriedly put their backs to the wall. The wind ruffled their clothes, tangled their hair, but ultimately left them alone. As the last man was sucked into the portal, the rift snapped shut with a loud crack and vanished in a puff of smoke.

Her strength deserted her, and she fell to her knees.

Beneath her, the floor was wet, and her brain had a hard time processing what she saw.

She lifted her hand from the sticky mess, staring blankly at the blood, when memories rushed back so fast her head spun.

Ryder!

"No." The denial was torn from deep in her soul. Knowing she was too late, Morgan frantically searched the room, then scuttled across the floor on her hands and knees when she finally spotted his still body.

Careful not to hurt him, she cradled his head in her lap, her tears splashing his face. When his brows wrinkled in annoyance, her sob caught in her throat.

He was alive.

Her senses returned in a rush, time returned to normal, and the world came back into focus.

But even as she listened, she heard his erratic heartbeat slow, his lungs rattling as he struggled for air.

Morgan ran her fingers through his hair, gently brushing it away from his face. "I know you can hear me. I need you to fight. I need you to change into your wolf. You told me he can heal anything. Will you do that for me?"

Those glorious brown eyes of his opened, but they were dulled with pain, his wolf nowhere to be found. Panic speared her chest when his heart skipped a beat.

It took forever before she heard the next thump, and she knew they were running out of time.

Only a foot away rested the knife that had almost killed them both, still glowing feverishly from her blood. A reckless, dangerous idea came to her, so stupid it might actually have a small chance of working. Conscious of the men heading toward her, she knew she had only a small window of opportunity.

Snatching up the knife before they could reach her, she lifted her arm, and slashed the blade deep. She didn't even feel the metal bite into her flesh until seconds later, when it began to hurt like a bitch, throbbing in time with her heart. Kincade and Ascher both swore, and she snarled at them when they tried to pull her away. She held her bleeding arm over the wound in Ryder's gut, watching the bright splash of her blood dribble down into his wounds.

The blade in her hand warmed, and she instinctively brought it over his chest. The tip of the metal beaded up, and a blob of liquid metal dropped next to the gaping wound in his abdomen. Two more drops fell in rapid succession, and she watched them break apart and sprout legs until they resembled little black spiders. In an instant, they scrambled into the wound and disappeared.

The metal began to drip faster, and more spiders burrowed under his skin.

Ryder gave a terrible scream, his agony sending her stomach pitching wildly, and her hands shook. She nearly lost her nerve and jerked what remained of the blade away, until she saw the little spiders were weaving his injuries together, both on the surface and underneath.

Seconds began to stretch, her body drooping with exhaustion, her shoulders slumping, and she realized she was slowly being drained of magic as surely as her blood continued to escape her veins.

But she didn't stop, didn't relent.

She refused to give up on him.

Ryder's eyes began to glow, his wolf rising, and she knew if she could hold out a little bit longer, he would survive.

Her head swam, and she distantly noted her many cuts weren't healing. As she stared into Ryder's wound, she sensed the metal shaping organs, threading together his injuries.

He needed just a few more seconds.

Her heartbeat thundered in her head, and she realized the beats were gradually slowing.

Morgan heard the guys yelling, but couldn't make out what they were saying. Hands were pulling her away from Ryder. Someone cradled her gently, and she struggled to stay conscious, knowing the longer she held out, the better chance Ryder would have to survive, but she couldn't seem to make her body obey.

"You did it. Ryder will live. He's resting. You have to let go." Kincade's voice reached her from far away, darkness was beginning to crowd the edges of her vision, and the world gradually dimmed.

She didn't need to be told she was dying, it was written in their devastated faces.

Kincade's arms tightened around her as if to stop her from leaving him.

Fear came through their bonds, Kincade's and Ascher's emotions a living, breathing presence that threatened to consume her.

"What the hell is wrong with her? Why is she not healing?" Kincade's question was a demand.

"For humans, magic can be lethal. The opposite is true for those who hold magic. Our magic is tied to our life force. The little fool drained herself to save us." Atlas's voice was as grim as she'd ever heard it. He almost sounded like he cared what happened to her.

"She couldn't have known." Draven tapped the edge of his bloodied knife against his leg in agitation.

"Of course she knew." Kincade gently threaded his hands into her hair. "She did it anyway to save us. What are our options?"

Ascher was the one who spoke this time. "She needs more magic. Gather every void weapon you can find. Get her torque."

Cold metal wrapped around her throat, the weight comforting. More metal curled around her wrist and twined around her fingers. The magic hummed against her skin, a lick of energy that eased her pain a fraction, but did little else.

"It's not enough." Draven swore viciously. "What else?"

"In the Primordial World, only one place is guaranteed to have magic." Ascher didn't lift his gaze from where he was wrapping a nasty wound on her arm.

Atlas turned his grim stare on the hellhound. "You can't be thinking of sending her into the void."

"The void might make some sick, but not her. She's drawn to the rifts because of the primordial magic." He ripped another piece of his shirt off, then wrapped the wound on her leg, his complete attention focused on his task, as if it was the only thing that mattered. "She's a pureblood. The void will protect her. In fact, it might be her only chance." Ascher tied off the bandage, then stared blindly at his bloodied hands, his lips flattened in a thin line. "She will die if we do nothing."

"He's right." Kincade brushed a strand of hair away from her face. "When I step through a portal, I feel a bite of freezing air, a second of darkness, then I'm out. Every time she goes through one, it takes her longer and longer. She lingers in the void. Haven't any of you noticed how much more relaxed she is when she steps out. Her eyes shine, not to mention her injuries heal in record time. The pure primordial magic acts like a dose of medicine. I don't like this better than any of you, but I don't think we have a choice."

Silence followed that comment.

"Anyone else have any ideas?" Draven gripped his weapons, as if looking for something he could physically fight.

No one spoke.

The vote was unanimous.

Kincade didn't lift his gaze from hers. "Someone find me a mirror and some rope."

Chapter Twenty-eight

$\mathcal{M}$organ swam in and out of consciousness, her mind struggling to piece together what happened. When everything came rushing back, concern for the guys dispelled the last bit of fog from her mind. Unfortunately, the moment she turned her head, her stomach rebelled. She rolled and puked over the side of what appeared to be a bed.

She sensed movement, then a pair of hands clumsily drew back her hair, careful not to tug at the strands. *Ascher.* He brushed his warm fingers over the nape of her neck, trying to offer comfort. Agony unlike anything she'd ever known riddled her body, and her brain felt like it would ooze out of her skull at any moment. When she managed to open her eyes, she saw Kincade holding a trashcan for her, his white face tight with concern.

When her stomach had nothing else to give, she flopped back onto the bed, completely exhausted, her muscles protesting the abuse.

A cool, wet cloth covered her forehead, and her eyes flickered open to see everyone staring down at her.

They were all alive.

Her heart fluttered wildly as she looked from one to the next, greedily scanning every inch of them, noting every bruise, scuff and bandage.

Even battered, they were a breathtaking sight, bringing tears to her eyes.

"Give the girl some room to breathe." Morgan recognized that gruff voice. MacGregor pushed his wheelchair closer to her, forcing the guys to step back or risk being run over. Despite the harshness in his tone, she detected the thread of anxiety in his voice. "They haven't left your side since they carried your sorry self through those doors three days ago. You cut it pretty close this time, girlie."

He patted her leg, clearing his throat roughly, and rolled his chair back. "I would stay longer, but I'm late for my appointment. I'm told I have you to thank for siccing Mistress McKay on me."

Morgan ran her hand over her blanket, studiously avoiding his gaze. "Maybe."

MacGregor chuckled. "Then I'll feel no remorse for leaving you in the care of these fine men. I'm sure they have a thing or two to say to you."

Morgan watched him leave, increasingly uncomfortable in the oppressive silence following his exit.

Ryder gingerly settled on the bed next to hers, while Ascher and Kincade resumed their seats on opposite sides of her bed, slouching in their chairs. Draven stretched out in the bed across from her, his legs crossed, arms behind his head, gazing contemplatively at the ceiling. Atlas stood guarding the door, watching them instead of the hall.

Not ready to face the guys yet, she absently noted the familiar black cuff was back on her arm, but the black rings encircling her fingers were new, the webbed design making them appear to be a matched set.

"How are you feeling?" Kincade kept his voice carefully neutral, a dangerous sign.

Morgan noticed wicked scars on her arms, a result of the cuts Ethan had inflicted with the void weapon. Although the injuries were healed, the path the blade cut still ached deep under her skin, hard knots of scar tissue burning every time she moved. "Sore. Tired."

She stopped dead when she saw a dew-covered metallic spiderweb spread across her lower palm and up the wrist of her left hand. It was stunningly beautiful. She ran her thumb gently over the almost-embossed-metal web, and the strands thrummed under her touch. Seconds later, she felt a sharp pinch at the side of her palm.

When she turned her hand, she saw a dainty spider perched on the edge of the web next to a tiny pawprint, its sharp little legs rooting into her skin, as if refusing to leave.

To her surprise, instead of sensing a spider, pure wolf hummed under her touch, the beast crouched in submission, almost like he didn't want to draw her attention.

Ryder.

Though the marks were different, she had no doubt they meant the same as the other two.

They were mated.

"I'm sorry." Her gaze immediately flew to him, remorse making her throat thick. "I never meant to drag you into this mess of my life."

The big man lifted his head, and gave her a direct stare. "Do you regret saving me?"

"What?" Morgan was horrified he would ever think such a thing. "No! Why would you even think that?"

"Then stop feeling bad." He shrugged, a warm blush spilling into his cheeks. "I'm glad it happened. I would do it again if it meant saving you. I'm where I need to be."

Morgan opened her mouth, then closed it, unable to scrounge up a response. She would fight tooth and nail against anyone who tried to claim her, control her, but they seemed content, even happy, to be tied to her. It was baffling…but she couldn't deny she craved the sense of belonging they shared, the knowledge that they would have her back no matter what life threw at them.

"What do you remember?"

She turned to face Kincade, wincing at his haggard appearance. His hair looked like he'd been trying to pull it out. He was pale, making the dark shadows under his eyes look like bruises, and she hated knowing he hadn't been taking care of himself. "Nothing much after trying to heal Ryder. Why?" She eyed him suspiciously. "What happened?"

"You were dying." Ascher spoke bluntly, his blue eyes shattered. He reached out, then rubbed his fingers back and forth against her arm, as if to reassure himself she was alive. "Kincade carried you through the void, hoping it would heal you. You were gone for three hours. We thought we'd lost both of you."

Her head snapped around, and she studied Kincade in confusion. "I don't understand. I thought pure magic was like poison to those not born to that world."

Draven sat up on his bed, swung his feet over the edge and stared down at them darkly. "He was the only one strong enough to hold you safe while you healed, and still be able to drag you back out when he knew you would live."

A spark of anger burned in her chest, born of raw fear, and she wished she was strong enough to punch him. No wonder he looked so wrecked. He said he was fine, but she could see the toll traveling through the void had taken on him. "Why would you stupidly risk everything for me?"

Kincade jolted out of his chair, his face darkening as he stepped toward her. He leaned over until his forehead rested against hers, then dragged in a deep breath to capture her scent. He smelled of hot stone and warm earth, and she wanted to bask in his warmth.

His light green eyes were tortured as he gazed at her face. "You are everything to me. Did you really expect me to let death take you so easily? That I wouldn't fight for you?"

She gasped, and her heart did a silly little dance at his ragged confession. Through their connection, she felt terror chipping away at him, only her nearness seeming to ease the volatile emotion. Very gently, she cupped his face, marveling when he closed his eyes with a sigh and leaned into her. Then she reached out and smacked him on the back of the head. "Don't you ever risk yourself like that again. Do you understand me?"

Kincade jerked back and straightened in surprise, and Draven snorted.

"You are not invincible."

Draven snorted again, and she leaned over to glare at him. "Do you have something to say?"

"Ah…" He nervously cleared his throat, rubbing his fingers over his chin. "No, ma'am."

She narrowed her eyes, then gave Kincade a suspicious look. "Explain."

Kincade seemed to find the cheap tile floor suddenly fascinating.

"I…" he tugged at his shirt, as if it no longer fit. "I'm a gargoyle."

His confession was so awkward, so nervous, she half expected him to say he was coming out of the closet. Her mind flashed back to the fearsome gargoyle in the garden, but instinctively knew the statue wasn't him, and couldn't help wonder how he would look in his other form.

She thought of the small clues about his identity she'd dismissed as unimportant— the only thing she cared about was learning how to beat him in a fight. What species he was didn't matter to her then or now. Sure, gargoyles were rare, nearly an indestructible force, and highly prized, but to her, he was just…Kade. "Okay."

His head snapped up, and he studied her face intently. When he didn't see what he expected, he relaxed, his confidence pouring back. "I picked you up, locked you in my arms, and stepped through the portal. I turned my skin to stone the instant we entered the void…it protected me. I half expected us to end up at the Academy, but it was like stepping into another world. Millions of bright stars were everywhere. It felt like we were floating in space. The magic was a living thing, wrapping you in this intense heat. It tried to pull you away, take you from me, and only relented when I refused to relinquish my hold. It soaked into your skin, and I watched it heal you."

He sounded awed and disturbed at the same time. "That's why it takes so long for you to pass through the portals."

Morgan shrugged. "Those stars are other portals. I think if I wanted, I could step through them. Did anything happen to you while you were there? Did you see anything else?"

"Like what?" Kincade tensed, and she wished she'd kept her mouth shut.

"Oh, I don't know." She fiddled with the rings on her fingers. "Like the soldiers I sent through the rift?"

Silence filled the room.

After a minute, she crossed her arms defensively and glared at them, refusing to feel bad for killing the soldiers. "They were trying to kill you."

Atlas straightened, then took a hesitant step toward her. "Do you mean you can see not only other portals, but people as well when you're in the void?"

Morgan gave a hesitant nod. "I can feel them. Each time I pass, they become clearer. I think they can sense my presence."

Atlas practically collapsed against the wall behind him. "We've always assumed the people lost in the void had died. That no one can reach them."

He was so distressed, Morgan wanted to ease him. "I get the sense that the magic in the void is keeping them alive."

Atlas shoved away from the wall again, taking a determined step toward her. "No one can ever know what you can do until you've learned how to control your powers and protect yourself. You're safe for now, but if anyone discovers your heritage—"

"If I'm discovered, this will happen again. I can never return to my old life in the primordial realm." She could never go home. Morgan expected pain, not the nearly overwhelming relief that she wouldn't have to choose between her old life and her new one. "I understand."

Atlas looked at her intently. "You will be giving up your birthright."

"Yes."

"Your right to rule."

Morgan shrugged, barely holding back a shudder at the thought of being in charge of thousands, even millions of people. "Yes."

"If you return, you can change things, heal the primordial realm." He spoke softly, almost to himself.

A chill slipped over her skin at the tiny spark of hope in his dark green eyes, the burden of saving a whole world nearly crushing her under its weight. "Or it could all go horribly wrong if others discovered my real identity."

"You're both right." Kincade's mouth tightened in annoyance. "It's too dangerous for this information to get out. We need to keep it a secret for now, until you've had a chance to be fully trained. We'll double your training regimen and speak to the headmistress about special classes, so you can learn how to cast magic."

Her breath halted painfully in her chest.

They weren't going to send her away.

She watched in wonder while they argued back and forth about what needed to be done first. While they talked, they each watched her like a hawk, ensuring that she hadn't moved, that she was safe, and she knew she had a long road ahead of her to earn back their trust.

While they might think her life was more important than their own, they were wrong.

She wouldn't change what had happened, but she had to be more careful in the future. She had more to live for now. She needed to learn how to fight smarter, fight harder, and make sure they never came so close to losing anyone on their team again.

A brisk knock sounded on the door.

Without waiting for a response, it swung open and the guys jumped into action, grabbing their weapons, arranging themselves protectively between her and the door. The headmistress took them in at a glance, then nodded, her shoes clicking on the floor as she came near. "This came for you while you were away."

She reached over and handed Morgan a familiar, gilded envelope of heavy vellum.

Across the front, the word champion was printed in beautiful, gold-leaf calligraphy.

"We would be honored to have you remain with us. This school used to teach and train all the champions. It will be good to go back to the old ways again." Her dark eyes were appraising as she surveyed Morgan from head to foot. "You will need to be prepared for the future. The void needs to be put into balance, and you're one of the few champions remaining. Your affinity for primordial magic will be invaluable."

Morgan could only blink in surprise, a spurt of panic tightening her chest. "I don't understand."

"Too many rifts are tearing through the barriers between the worlds. Only someone who can handle that type of magic, someone with your skills, can uncover the cause and help fix it. Your abilities would be wasted on normal rift duty."

The men were all grim, their bodies tense. "Headmistress—"

She waved Kincade away. "Save your breath. You and the others will remain as her personal guards. Only a few of us know her true identity, and we plan to keep it that way. The Academy has made us aware of the situation so we may help you train her properly for her new role."

Morgan felt like she'd just been dropped into the deep end of the pool with a kraken dragging her under.

"I'll leave you to rest." The headmistress gave the guys a pointed look, then turned on her heel without another word.

Morgan should be afraid, but only one thing mattered to her— they wouldn't be separated.

She wasn't being sent away.

She could live through anything with the guys at her side.

They seemed to come to the same conclusion, slowly beginning to relax for the first time since she woke, and she was startled to realize they were willing to give up everything in order to stay with her.

Warmth filled her soul as she studied them, one at a time.

They were her friends.

Her family.

And if she wasn't careful, they would keep her permanently cocooned in bubble wrap. They needed to learn she wasn't going to let them get away with simply protecting her. They were going to be a team, whether they liked it or not.

"I'm starving. I don't suppose I could talk you into stealing me something from the kitchen?"

Kincade promptly straightened at the chance to do something. "Of course."

As the door closed behind him, she immediately turned toward the others. "Now what do I have to do to get out of here?"

She hated hospitals.

The only hunters who ever visited them were the dead or dying.

It reminded her how close she came to losing everything.

At her question, all conversation stopped, and the men froze as if caught by a predator.

Draven looked troubled, rubbing the back of his neck. "Kincade wouldn't like it."

Morgan lifted her arm and pointed to the markings. "He'll be able to find me. We might as well begin as we mean to go on."

She raised an eyebrow at him in a silent dare, and Draven burst out laughing and shrugged. "Rooftop?"

Morgan beamed at him, unable to remember when she'd ever been so happy. "Perfect."

She peered up at Ascher, blinking up at him innocently. "Will you be my chariot?"

He leaned over, smiling indulgently, easily plucking her out of the bed before she even finished asking. He planted his face in her hair and inhaled, his arms pulling her tight against him, but she didn't mind, snuggling against him when she remembered how close she came to losing them all.

She was done with pushing them away.

It hadn't worked anyway.

They still managed to find a way into her heart.

Bonus Material

*R*yder studied the small group on the rooftop in silent amusement as battle-hardened, ruthless assassins were turned into a bunch of bumbling idiots over a girl.

Not that he could blame them.

The instant Morgan set her dainty foot in the Academy, their lives had been irrevocably changed.

Kincade had been watching her from afar for years, and she'd slipped under his guard. No matter how hard he tried, the too serious, surly soldier couldn't shake his infatuation with her.

Even now, Kincade fussed over Morgan, covering her with another blanket, which to Ryder's count was number five.

She didn't complain, dutifully snuggling under the covers, then smiling brilliantly up at the gargoyle in thanks. Kincade was so dazzled by that smile, he practically tripped over the chair behind him.

She had no idea of her effect on him…on any of them, really.

Ascher and Draven sat on the ground, playing cards on a coffee table. Draven hid behind his devil-may-care attitude, but he was hounded relentlessly by demons from his past. Morgan was like a bright light piercing his darkness, leaving the siren both amused and baffled, since he'd never run across anyone immune to his charms. It seemed to strip Draven of all his confidence. The siren didn't try to work his magic on her—Morgan mattered, and Draven knew it. He didn't want to risk fucking anything up.

Ascher leaned lightly against her leg, every so often touching her foot or inhaling her scent. He'd been around her the longest, knew her the best, but his subterfuge whilst in his hellhound form put a certain awkward distance between them, leaving the hellhound uncertain of where he stood, which Ryder understood all too well.

Though Ryder didn't trust the mutt completely, he admitted the hellhound was a good choice for a protector. Even better, he was completely devoted to their girl.

Atlas cleaned his weapons some distance away, and Ryder was slightly disturbed to see the elf discreetly studying Morgan with a confused, unsatisfied expression. Ryder didn't trust the damned elf. His kind cared only for duty and honor and their homeland.

Since they'd confirmed Morgan carried royal blood in her veins, Atlas's fascination with her only grew. Ryder didn't like it. To Atlas, Morgan was a way to regain everything he'd lost, a way to restore the tarnished honor he wore around him like a cloak, a way to free himself from the self-impose exile he took in penance for his sins.

But, against his will, Ryder admitted the bastard honestly cared for their girl, willing to go to hell—or the primordial realm as it were—for her.

When Morgan caught Atlas staring, she gave him a small smile.

Atlas scowled and went back to his work, but Ryder saw the way the elf's eyes lingered on her when he thought no one was looking. It was easy to recognize that longing, the need to belong—Ryder felt it himself every time he saw their ferocious little Morgan strut around the school.

She didn't seem to notice their faults, and none of the guys knew how to react when she turned those striking blue eyes of hers on them.

To his amusement, each of the guys kept unconsciously sneaking peeks at her, inspecting her injuries, and generally making sure she was comfortable.

They were worried, and so was he.

She'd come a long way since she first arrived. She no longer flinched when one of them approached, even allowing them to fuss over her—not because she needed it, but because she knew it made them feel better.

A lot of pressure rested on her small shoulders. With their help, she would be able to withstand anything...but not without a lot of training.

She was reckless, without an ounce of self-preservation, and it terrified him shitless.

He would have to watch her more closely, and protect her from herself.

He absently touched the black, metallic webbing that stretched up along his stomach, marveling that she had claimed him.

He never thought his lowly self, a bitten wolf, would ever be worthy of being claimed, much less by someone like her. Whenever she was near, his wolf wanted to burst free from his skin and beg for her touch.

His beast was braver than Ryder—the wolf didn't worry about rejection, didn't understand the consequences of his actions. Ryder couldn't help but be envious of the freedom.

He was two hundred pounds of solid muscle. If that wasn't intimidating enough, he could turn into a vicious animal at a drop of a hat when riled—not a stellar combination when making friends, much less even talking to a girl.

But Morgan didn't seem to care.

Ryder didn't give a shit about the mating marks. He'd been hers the instant she smiled at him with such joy as she ran next to him while he was in his wolf form. The marks only gave others visible proof of her claim on him.

He traced the obsidian metal webbing running up his chest and along his shoulder, where an inch-long spider sat perched, a graphic display of ownership he wore with pride. It was similar to the dainty spiderweb marking the inside of her small hand, and wicked pleasure tore through him when he saw them etched on her body. Even his wolf seemed smug when he spotted his own pawprint stamped on her flesh like a tag of possession.

Warmth hummed along the connection, and he glanced up to find Morgan watching him.

Ryder froze, unable to drop his gaze as heat raced through him.

It felt like she'd reached across the room and run her hand along the markings on his chest.

He instantly hardened, her phantom touch leaving him panting for more.

Then Kincade asked her a question, drawing her attention, and the spell broke.

Just one small look from her, and his heart slammed against his ribs, his wolf clawing to get out. But along with the pleasure was a darker emotion—how close she came to nearly dying to save his worthless hide. She risked everything for him, and he was determined to do whatever it took to make sure she never regretted her decision.

Whether she admitted it or not, nearly losing them affected her as well, and he wasn't sure that was a good thing.

Though she proved she would do anything for them, it also left her in grave danger if anyone discovered her weakness for them.

After what happened, they could no longer put her magic back in the bottle. The torque would help her with control, but she still had a long road ahead of her. While the creatures of the primordial realm would leave her alone for now, they wouldn't forget—or forgive—what happened.

In a burst of pain, claws snicked out of his fingertips at the thought of anyone taking her away from them, and he quickly curled his hands into fists to hide the change, ducking his head so no one would notice the way his teeth lengthened.

While Morgan deserved better than lowly assassins, no one would protect her better or care for her more—even with their rough edges and broken pasts. It was up to them, as her protectors, to ensure she was prepared for what was to come, and he would do whatever it took to keep her safe.

To him, being chosen as her mate was worth any price.

~ Tethered to the World ~

ONE TOUCH CAN SAVE YOU FROM CERTAIN DEATH…OR SENTENCE YOU TO AN ETERNITY IN HELL.

Born with the ability to defy death, Annora has been warned to keep her gift secret, but her greedy uncle can't resist exploiting her by any means necessary. Starvation, beatings, broken bones—she's survived them all and emerged stronger. But it's not enough for him. It will never be enough. When she discovers her uncle plans to sell her to the highest bidder, she risks everything to escape the prison that has become her life.

The last thing she expected was to land at a university for supernaturals…or be paired with a pack of men as broken as her. As students go missing, Annora can't get over the suspicion that she's being hunted. To protect her, the guys must set aside their personal troubles and begin working as a team. But as her past collides with her present, she must make the ultimate sacrifice and expose her secrets to save the guys who've become more than family to her…and hope she's strong enough to live with the consequences.

A Phantom Touched Novel: Book 1
Meet the Pack: Annora, Camden, Xander, Mason, Logan and Edgar.

~ Daemon Grudge ~

WHEN THE GODS VANISHED, DAEMONS TOOK OVER PROTECTING HUMANS FROM THE THINGS THAT GO BUMP IN THE NIGHT...UNTIL DAEMONS DECIDE THEY DESERVE MORE.

Orphaned young and raised by the military, Octavia only knows the world of duty and honor. When she discovers they're sacrificing people to create the ultimate super soldier, men engineered specifically to rid the world of what they consider the supernatural plague, she rebels and vows to do everything in her power to stop them.

The last thing Octavia expects to find is daemons willing to help her survive. Or that she may be one of them. To make things worse, an ancient power has awakened inside her.

Sworn to protect her, the daemons decide to teach her how to use her new abilities. They never expected to fall in love with their infuriatingly vexing charge, who maddeningly risks everything to get justice for past wrongs. If they can't find a way to remove the magic before the demigods discover the truth, Octavia will die when they rip it out of her, and the world will crumble into chaos.

A Clash of the Demigods Novel: Book 1
Meet the elites: Octavia, Warrick, Keegan, Nikos, and Atticus.

~ *Electric Storm* ~

A WOMAN WITH TOO MANY SECRETS DARES TO RISK
EVERYTHING TO CLAIM THE PACK DESTINED TO BER
HERS.

Everything changed when Raven, a natural born conduit, accidentally
walks in on a slave auction. She only wants a night out with her
friends before her next case as a paranormal liaison with the police.
Instead, she ends up in possession of a shifter and his guardian.
When your touch can kill, living with two touchy-feely shifters is a
disaster waiting to happen.

POWER ALWAYS COMES WITH A PRICE...

To make matters worse, a vicious killer is on the loose. As mutilated
bodies turn up, she can't help fear that her new acquisitions are
keeping secrets from her. The strain of keeping everyone alive, not to
mention catching the killer, pushes her tenuous control of her gift
and her emotions to their limits. If they hope to survive, they must
work together as a pack or risk becoming hunted themselves.

A Raven Investigations Novel : Book 1

~ Coveted ~

Discover what happens when a woman stumbles across a Scottish werewolf imprisoned in a thousand-year old dungeon. Magic and mayhem, not to mention a lot of kick-ass action and some sexy hijinks, of course.

Pack alpha Aiden vows to do whatever necessary to protect his people. When he discovers a plot to harvest blood from his wolves to create the ultimate drug, he's determined to stop them at any cost. And quickly finds himself taken captive. After months in prison, Aiden barely manages to hang onto his sanity. The last thing he expects is a shapely little human to come to his rescue and bring out all his protective instincts.

Shayla is being stalked because of her abilities as a seeker. When offered a job in Scotland, she leaps at the chance to escape. With danger pursuing her at every turn, she must decide if she could give up her magic in order to live a safe, ordinary life. Never in her wildest fantasies did she expect to find a feral-looking man imprisoned in a thousand-year-old dungeon...or be so wildly attracted to him. She didn't need more trouble, but when fate presents the means to help him escape, she doesn't hesitate.

Now they are both being hunted, and Aiden is determined to do everything in his power to protect Shayla...and seduce her into becoming his mate. As the danger intensifies, Aiden begins to suspect that Shayla might be the key to saving not only his people but also the future of his race...if he could keep her alive long enough.

~ BloodSworn ~

Ten years after they bound her powers and banished her, Trina Weyebridge had successfully carved out a new existence in the human world. She put her life as a witch behind her. But, her magic would not be denied, the bindings holding them in check are weakening. Vampires who crave a taste of the powers stored in her blood are hunting her with deadly force and have kidnapped her sister to lure her out. In a desperate bid to free her sister and gain her own freedom, Trina bargains with the all-too-tempting lion shifter who calls out the long forgotten wild side in her...she would be his concubine in return for pack protection. She'd be safe...until they found out the truth.

UNDENIABLE DESIRE. FORBIDDEN LOVE. INESCAPABLE DESTINY.

When Merrick spots a female intruder living on his property, he's intrigued by her daring. Curious to find out more, he follows her and comes to her aid when she falls prey to an attack. After weeks of unnatural silence, his beast awakens at her touch, and he suspects that she might be the only one able to save his race from a disease killing his kind. Not willing to take the chance of losing her, he binds her to him the only way he knows how...by claiming her as his own. All he has to do to save her is uncover the secrets of her past, stop a pack revolt, convince her that she's desperately in love with him in return, and prevent a war.

~ The Demon Within ~

As a punishment for failing his duty as an angel, Ruman finds himself encased in stone in the form of a guardian statue. Every few decades he is given a chance to repent. And fails. Until the totally unsuitable Caly Sawyer accidentally brings him back to life. Nothing is going to prevent him from gaining his freedom, especially some willfully stubborn human determined to kill him.

Caly doesn't trust the mysterious stranger who came out of nowhere and risked his life for hers. As a demon hunter, she knows there is something not quite human about the sexy bastard. Her ability to detect demons is infallible. She should know. She used to be one.

War is brewing between demons and humans. The demon infection that Caly had always considered a curse might just be the key to their survival…if Ruman can keep her alive long enough. Despite the volatile attraction between her and her sexy protector, Caly's determined to do whatever it takes to keep everyone alive. The more Ruman learns about his beautiful charge, the more he questions his duty and loyalty…and dreads the call to return home. If they can't learn to trust each other in time, one of them will die.

~ Druid Surrender ~

A DARK, ENCHANTING TALE OF LOVE AND MAGIC IN VICTORIAN ENGLAND.

Brighid Legend has been on the run for over a year, hunted by the people who murdered her mother. Born a Druid with the power to control the elements, Brighid knows her pursuers will never stop until she is under their control. To escape detection, she struggles to hide her powers and finds safety in a small, out-of-the-way village. But after a series of mysterious accidents, she fears something sinister has invaded her new home. While she searches for the source of the trouble, suspicion falls on her, and Brighid flees, only steps ahead of the villagers seeking vengeance.

Wyatt Graystone, Earl of Castelline, retires when the life-and-death clandestine investigations he did for the Crown becomes more tedious than adventurous. Something vital is missing from his life. The last place he expects to find the missing spark is in a woman he literally leaps through fire to rescue from being burned at the stake. But the danger is far from over. To his frustration, the infernal woman adamantly refuses his assistance, pushing him away at every turn, when his only desire is to claim her for his own.

But someone has targeted Brighid for a reason. As the threats to her life intensify, Wyatt is determined to uncover her secrets and do whatever it takes to ensure she survives. When their pasts come back to haunt them, they must overcome their worst fears or risk losing everything. Saving her life is the biggest battle he's ever faced...and the only one that has ever mattered.

WILL THEIR LOVE BE STRONGE ENOUGH TO SAVE THEM . . .

A Druid Quest Novel: Book 1

ABOUT THE AUTHOR

Stacey Brutger lives in a small town in Minnesota with her husband and an assortment of animals. When she's not reading, she enjoys creating stories about exotic worlds and grand adventures...then shoving in her characters to see how they'd survive. She enjoys writing anything paranormal from contemporary to historical.

Other books by this author:
BloodSworn
Coveted

A Druid Quest Novel
Druid Surrender (Book 1)
Druid Temptation (Book 2)

An Academy of Assassins Novel
Academy of Assassins (Book 1)
Heart of the Assassins (Book 2)
Claimed by the Assassins (Book 3)
Queen of the Assassins (Book 4)

A Raven Investigations Novel
Electric Storm (Book 1)
Electric Moon (Book 2)
Electric Heat (Book 3)
Electric Legend (Book 4)
Electric Night (Book 5)
Electric Curse (Book 6)

A Phantom Touched Novel
Tethered to the World (Book 1)
Shackled to the World (Book 2)
Ransomed to the World (Book 3)

Clash of the Demigods
Daemon Grudge (Book 1)

A PeaceKeeper Novel
The Demon Within (Book 1)

Coming Soon:
Daemon Scourge (Clash of the Demigods – Book 2)

Visit Stacey online to find out more at www.StaceyBrutger.com
And www.facebook.com/StaceyBrutgerAuthor/